THE OUTREACH COMMITTEE

Because Marriage Can Be Murder

by C.L. Woodhams

C.L. Woodhams
www.clwoodhams.com
clw@clwoodhams.com

Author: C.L. Woodhams
Editor: Jennifer Thomas, Beyond Words Editing
Designer: Jennifer Thomas, Beyond Words Editing
Design and Layout Assistant: Alessia Vittone

ISBN: 978-0-9908924-0-3, Paperback
ISBN: 978-0-9908924-1-0, ePub
LCCN: 2014918629

First Edition
Published in the United States of America
Printed in the United States of America

The Outreach Committee
*is dedicated to my maternal grandmother,
the original C.L. Woodhams.*

*It is published in memory of Mary Vandever,
Sig Porter, and Orin Parker.*

Acknowledgments

My deepest thanks go out the following people:

Jennifer Thomas of Beyond Words Editing,
without whom this book would not have survived.

**My fellow writers in the North County Writers Bloc
and the Novelettes critique groups,**
who helped me fine-tune my prose and tighten my plot.

Dr. Nancy Shuler, Ph.D.,
who helped me round out my characters.

**My first readers from Atlanta, GA,
and from the Encinitas, CA, YMCA Mystery Book Club,**
who spurred me on.

The many victims of spousal abuse,
who inspired me to continue writing
until the manuscript was completed.

Ann Malsbary, Bud Malsbary, and Mavis Porter,
for their support and encouragement.

THE OUTREACH COMMITTEE

PART I

The Outreach Committee

Chapter 1

Mora

"WE SHOULD GO IN." Mora Rey skied up to her husband at the bottom of the lift. "The snow report in the lodge said 'Blizzard conditions approaching.'"

Mora huddled in her down parka and watched Sherman closely. She had had enough of the wet cold. Mammoth Mountain was Sherman's favorite—not hers. She rubbed her sore butt. At least her many falls had landed her on her soft spot.

Sherman shot her a black look. "You're a gutless female, Mora. That's why you were fetching coffee for a junior manager until I married you." Sherman Rey knocked the powder off his skis and checked his bindings. His self-satisfied smirk morphed into a snarl of disgust.

Mora pulled her wool cap down over her ears. *Not again.* She must have heard this ten thousand times.

She tried to tune out Sherman's tirade, but he shouted in her ear. "If I hadn't had the wherewithal to set you up in your own bookkeeping business, you'd still be content working for someone else. You have to take risks to move ahead in this world." Sherman shook his head, his smile taunting her.

Risks? I face them every day. I could die from your beatings if I don't leave you.

Mora stooped to adjust her boots. Sherman prodded her in the back with the tip of his ski pole. She sprang back up to face him.

"You're a pathetic little rabbit," he went on. "For the life of me, I don't know why I thought you'd grow up under my tutelage."

With that, Sherman pushed off in the direction of the ski lift. He didn't look back, but Mora knew he expected her to follow.

Mora hesitated—she *could* go back to the lodge. She shook her head. *If I don't join him at the top, my night will be pure hell. I'll follow him for one final run.* Mora couldn't remember the last time her husband had flattered her or whispered loving words in her ear. *He's expert at hurting me. His words create more pain than his punches.*

Mora trailed behind Sherman, wincing at the pain he had delivered that morning. She'd suggested they stay in their condo—go back to bed and watch a movie instead of hitting the slopes. She should have known better than to challenge his decision to ski on a stormy day. Should have expected him to translate her request into an attack on his skiing ability—or his masculinity.

Mora stopped to adjust her goggles. She gripped her ski pole and sliced an angry arc through the snow with its tip. It was time to take action on her own behalf. She vowed to start divorce prep as soon as she got home. First, she'd get her finances in order, hire a lawyer. She'd copy all the documents she needed: bank and investment records, titles to their home and cars, etc. No matter the fifteen-thousand-square-foot home she'd be giving up—complete with stables and a tennis court. And all the other luxuries she enjoyed? They simply weren't worth it. But before she took the big D-step, she'd at least make sure she had a place to stay and enough money to live off until she could forge a new life.

As the two rode up the chairlift, Sherman continued his tiresome lecture about his wife's deficiencies. Mora massaged her sore arm and considered her plan to break free from him. She'd do *whatever* it took. Even if it meant leaving town. But she had to be careful. She knew what Sherman was capable of. Had no doubt that he might try to kill her if she filed for divorce.

At the top of the climb, Mora shoved off the chair into a blizzard. She pulled to a stop when she was clear of the other skiers and looked around for Sherman. He'd shot off the chair when it paused. Where had he gone? She couldn't see more than five feet in front of her ski tips.

A patrolman approached Mora in the worsening storm. "Ma'am, you have to ski down now! We're closing the hill."

Mora continued to peer through the blowing snow. "But…"

He pointed back toward the now-obscured chairlift. "If you're not an advanced skier, we can put you on the lift going down. But you'll have to hurry over there." He looked around. "Is anyone up here with you?"

"Ye— No." Mora caught herself. After Sherman's latest tirade, she'd have to endure even more pain if she dared direct the ski patrol to him. She looked down at her feet.

"My husband was way ahead of me," she said, regaining her composure. "I'm sure he's at the bottom by now." She could picture Sherman down there, fuming at not being permitted to come back up yet again.

After riding the chair back to the base of the hill—that had been a relief—Mora searched for Sherman. He was not anywhere outside or inside the lodge.

She unlocked her skis from the crowded rack and trudged with them over her shoulder to the parking lot. The SUV was still there, but Sherman was not in it. Mora snapped her skis into the empty roof rack and plodded back to the lodge. She approached the patrolman who had directed the shutdown operation. Sherman would be mad, but he had the car keys. She had to find him.

"I thought my husband would be here, but I don't see him."

"We're sweeping the slopes now, ma'am. Give me both your names and his description. Then go wait in the dining area. We'll send him to you."

As the minutes ticked away, Mora's apprehension increased. She paced past the windows that overlooked the slopes, struggling to see through the white storm. Her fear of Sherman's anger intensified. He had probably tramped off in a tantrum, embarrassed at having to come down with the ski patrol. That would have sent him over the edge.

Mora stopped to watch a young couple who'd just found one another. Not waiting to brush the snow from his ski suit, the man rushed up and hugged the woman, kissed her long and lovingly, and helped her put on her jacket. Then he pulled her hat down over her ears and nuzzled her neck. Holding hands, they checked out with the ski patrol and headed to the parking lot.

The young couple could have been Sherman and Mora when they first married. He'd applauded everything she did, complimented her choice of clothing, and made her feel like a queen when they made love.

But soon after their honeymoon days, she had recognized that her agreeing to let Sherman plan and control their lives had been a mistake. It did not give her the feeling of security that she thought it would.

What forces had changed their relationship to the abusive one he'd shown her today? For the millionth time she wondered if she had done something to deserve his abuse. He told her it was her fault, but now she rejected that. Had he grown tired of her? The reason didn't really matter at this point. The decision she'd made while she was on the lift held firm. When she got home, she'd start preparing to divorce Sherman: gather papers and information, pack, and hire a lawyer who was not one of his friends.

Families around Mora continued to reunite and depart. Finally, she was the only one left.

"Ma'am, er, Mrs. Rey, come with me please."

"Did you find him?"

The patrolman led her into the infirmary where a doctor approached her, his face somber. "I'm sorry, ma'am, but we have some bad news. Your husband took a tumble off the edge of the face, and—"

Mora caught sight of Sherman covered by a space blanket on a gurney behind the doctor. She rushed to his side.

"Sherman! Are you hurt?" Dried blood laced his face. She brushed the ice from his hair. Then she reached out to pat his cheek—and recoiled from its deathly chill.

A hand touched Mora's shoulder. "I'm so sorry, but he can't hear you. He didn't survive the fall."

Didn't survive…

The doctor took her arm and led her to a table across the room.

Mora slumped into a chair. Sherman—dead? She covered her face with her hands and her body shook with sobs. What lay ahead? How would she support herself, handle her daily life? Mora had depended on Sherman for everything. She was *alone* now.

As suddenly as the shock had struck her, a tidal wave of relief flooded over Mora. With Sherman gone, there would be no more angry words, no more beatings, no more forced sex. No acrimonious divorce. Mora continued to grieve the loss of the man she thought she had married: ambitious, intelligent, powerful, and generous to his community. The man who loved and cared for her. But she couldn't mourn the man on the table: the tyrannical, sexually insecure, abusive man she had come to know in the fifteen years of their marriage.

Mora wiped her tears and reached for the hot chocolate the patrolman had set before her. She sipped the welcome warm liquid, gazing upon her husband's body and contemplating her future. She bit her lip to hold back the smile that threatened.

Finally, she stood up.

One by one, Mora gathered her belongings. She zipped up her jacket, straightened her shoulders, and reached into Sherman's pocket for the car keys.

Twelve years later

Mora took a final pass around the ballroom of the Beverly Hills Hotel. She smiled with satisfaction that everything seemed perfectly in place for tonight's fundraiser. As always, she felt both excited and sobered by the festivities ahead.

Mora stopped at one of the round ten-person banquet tables and fingered the black-framed triangular tabletop poster card. The memorial promo pictured the famous actress Helen Neil in a stunning pose from her final movie. Mora sighed.

Mora and Helen had been friends since childhood. They'd grown up amidst families aspiring to do great things in the movie industry; surrounded by a world of pretense and pretend, a world of social climbing, bed-hopping, and headline divorces. Neither had learned the art of delving into the real person behind the façade. Both had married men who needed public adulation to feel worthy. Men who were insecure about who and what they were away from the fawning and worship. Men who took out their frustrations and failures on their families.

With Sherman's death, Mora had been lucky. Helen had not. Mora's thoughts turned to the last time she'd seen Helen.

"Please tell me she's not going to die," Mora whispered to the doctor.

The dreadful silence of the hospital room was broken only by beeps from the machines keeping Helen alive and the scratching of the doctor's pen on his clipboard.

Of course Helen won't die, *Mora assured herself.* She's young and vibrant. Besides, I won't let her. *Mora tiptoed over to the bed, not wanting to disturb its occupant. She took in the tubes connecting Helen to life and shuddered.*

The doctor shook his head. "We've tried to prevent that. But barring a miracle…"

"Why? What's wrong with her?"

"Blunt force trauma; fractured skull, brain swelling, broken pelvis. I'm sorry, but the tests indicate her brain is not functioning." He paused. "She won't regain consciousness."

Mora sucked in her breath. She heard the doctor's words but could not believe them. Would not believe them. Clutching her purse with one hand, Mora rummaged for a tissue with the other. Her tears blocked her view of the room, but she could still make out her talented friend, lying white and motionless on the bed.

Mora refused to accept an end to this companion she loved so much, an end to all the good times they had shared. The laughing over coffee, the detailed analysis—at the actress' insistence—of each of Helen's performances. The only time she'd seen the light leave Helen's eyes was when she'd shared confidences about her fights with Deacon, her spouse of eleven years. Mora reached for Helen's foot under the covers and squeezed it, willing her to wake up.

The intern closed the cover on Helen's chart. He looked up at the clock. "Her husband has approved the termination of life support. That's scheduled for three o'clock." Apparently this student had not yet learned, in his bedside-manner class, to look a patient's loved ones in the eyes while delivering bad news.

Mora grabbed the young man's arm. "Her husband? Where is he?"

"I'm not sure, ma'am." The intern adjusted the saline drip on its hook. "His attorney brought in the release a few minutes ago." He shifted his shoulders inside his lab coat. "I understand her husband, Mr. Southern, is out of the country."

"That figures. The bastard!" Mora ground her teeth so hard her jaw ached. "He did this. He's twice her size, with fists as big as boxing gloves." She waved her own fists in protest.

Mora had never liked Deacon—his eyes that wouldn't quite meet hers, his insistence on being right. Even his pomaded hair, unreasonable as she knew that was.

But Helen loved him. He should be here with her, talking to her—in case she could hear him. Mora knew Helen longed to hear loving words

9

from her husband. Instead, the clicking and whirring of machinery were her beautiful friend's only company. Accompanied by the stench of nose-tingling antiseptics—and death. Mora took Helen's hand in both of hers and rubbed it to drive away the cold, wanting life to flow back into it.

The young doctor finally looked at Mora directly. "I wouldn't accuse him of causing this in too many places if I were you." His fingers fussed with his tie. "Deacon Southern is famous. He'll send his lawyers after you."

Mora's mouth flew open—and then closed. This man was a doctor. He was obligated by law to report abuse. Was he cowed by Deacon's celebrity? Had he been threatened by Deacon's attorney?

"You said she was beaten?" she pressed.

"Wellll...she has severe head trauma and multiple fractures. It appears some of the injuries are old. I don't think their cause has been determined by the police."

Old? *Mora shook her head in disgust.* Doesn't that give you a clue she's been abused?

Mora put a hand over her churning stomach, imagining the physical and emotional torment Helen had suffered. "I took her to the women's shelter last week. She left home in the middle of the day, wearing a curly redhead wig and a maid's uniform. Her husband was at work. The paparazzi didn't even know she'd gone. I'm sure she wasn't injured at the shelter."

"The EMT told the admitting nurse that her husband called 911, said she had fallen on the stairs."

Mora scowled at the young man's words. It had taken three days to convince Helen to leave her home, to break free from her abusive marriage. What had made her go back?

"According to the housekeeper," the intern continued, "her husband found her at the shelter and made such a scene that Helen volunteered to leave with him."

Mora put her head in her hands. Deacon had found Helen at the shelter? How? Probably a private investigator. Or maybe he'd called his sailing buddy, the police chief, to learn the shelter location. Damn it! She should have thought of that.

Mora, of all people, knew about the network maintained by influential men in the Palos Verdes community—and the information available to them. She'd been married to a successful builder. There was no limit to the favors they sought from each other. Her own Sherman had gotten many a speeding ticket dismissed—even a DUI. He'd contributed large sums to the "public servants' retirement fund."

Mora's tears dropped onto Helen's cheek as she bent down to kiss her friend goodbye.

"Helen, love, I let you down. I should have hidden you out of town. I'll never forgive myself." She swallowed another sob. "But I _will_ make up for it," she vowed. "I don't know how, but I will—some way, some day."

Mora replaced the poster card and stepped away from the banquet table. No more mourning the past. Today, she _was_ making up for Helen's death—and in ways she could never have imagined ten years ago.

Chapter 2

Taylor

IN THE GRAND BALLROOM, the crowd hushed as a willowy woman in a form-fitting black gown took her place on the dais. She tucked a few stray hairs into her loose up-do and donned her horn-rimmed reading glasses.

"L-L-Ladies and gentlemen," she began, glancing at her notes. "Tonight, with your d-donations, you have saved the lives of many abused women." She clasped one shaking hand in the other and surveyed the room. "Good evening. I'm Taylor Whitmore, owner of Wilderness Outfitters, one of your sponsors, and F-F-Finance Chair for the Battered Women's Escape F-Foundation."

Oh God. Is she going to make it through the speech? Mora felt her shoulders stiffen. *Those shaking hands are not like her, and her stuttering gets worse when she's anxious. She must be worried about Erin.*

Taylor cleared her throat and pulled her notes closer. "Welcome to our annual fundraising event. The battered and handicapped women of our community thank you." She held up a giant check in victory. "I'm proud to announce that tonight we have added two hundred fifty thousand dollars to the Helen Neil Fund."

As the black-tie crowd in the Beverly Hills Hotel applauded, Mora and her table companion shared an aggrieved look. Mora again picked up the poster card of Helen.

"*That* performance gave her brutal husband his first foreign film trophy!" Carol Ewald whispered fiercely, rolling her wheelchair away from the table.

"Well, at least he couldn't leave the continent to accept it." Mora grimaced.

"For those of you not well-acquainted with us," Taylor continued her welcome, "I'd like to take a f-few minutes to tell you who we are." She pushed another stray hair from her face. "The Battered Women's Escape Foundation is twenty years old and currently operates four s-secure emergency shelters for battered women. We can house up to n-ninety women and children at a time. In addition, with the help of Erin Craig's Azalea Construction, we retrofit the homes of handicapped women to accommodate wheelchairs and other aids." She nodded to the empty chair at Mora's table. "Unfortunately, Erin was unable to attend tonight, as she's away on important f-f-foundation business." Taylor's notes rattled in her hand as she turned her head back to the audience.

Mora frowned. Taylor, like Erin and other career women she'd encountered in her practice, was a strong, capable, and successful business woman. Running her own store while raising two great kids. But at home she'd been physically abused and belittled by a brutal husband from whom she was powerless to escape. Fortunately, she'd asked for the Outreach Committee's help before it was too late.

Mora had never seen Taylor so shaken. It may have been a mistake to let her lead this event—today of all days While Erin was away.

"Our financial c-counseling and job training help these women launch new lives," Taylor continued. "Tonight's proceeds for the Helen Neil Fund will go specifically to support our Outreach Committee, headed by Mora Rey."

Mora straightened her shoulders with pride. While her psychiatric practice gave her the opportunity to help many abused women, running the Outreach Committee—"the OC"—with Carol was her *true* passion. Catching Carol's eye, the pair shared a secret smile. Goose bumps freckled Mora's arms. Sadly, she would never be able to share the committee's *full* accomplishments with others, but she didn't need to. Its success spoke for them.

"B-B-But enough about us." Taylor's brow furrowed as she struggled to steady her voice. "Let me tell you about the wonderful man next to me. We are indeed privileged to have as Chief Advisor to our Finance Committee, our keynote speaker, Quentin Pryor." Taylor's stiff shoulders relaxed as she turned to smile at the man seated to her right. "Those of you in business know him as the CEO of Western States Bank. We who volunteer in the community see his name on the boards of directors of the Boy Scouts, the Arts Council, and the Architectural Advisory Board." Taylor consulted her notes. "In his personal life, Quentin is an avid golfer, swimmer, and sailor. His lovely wife, Leigh, formerly a prima ballerina with the London Ballet, accompanies him tonight." Taylor removed her glasses. "Please join me in welcoming Quentin Pryor." She led the audience in a round of applause.

Mora sagged in relief. Taylor had made it through. Still, a small pit of worry settled into the base of Mora's stomach. Taylor had seemed like such a perfect fit for the Outreach Committee; she had agreed readily to join. And Mora had felt confident in Taylor's endorsement of Erin's mission.

Mora exhaled deeply to release her tension. If Taylor's jitters didn't settle down, they'd all be done for.

Chapter 3

Leigh

THE KEYNOTE SPEAKER removed his arm from the back of his wife's chair. Leigh smiled up at him as Quentin smoothed his hair and rose. His presence commanded the attention of the entire room. Mora had been surprised—and quite pleased—that the bank had sent one of their most prominent executives to help the BWEF, and by extension, the OC.

"Battered women and children are a scar on our society," Pryor began. "Thank you for your contributions this evening. Your gifts are a benefit to your community and to its citizens who are victims of abuse."

Mora joined in the enthusiastic ovation. She couldn't agree more.

Quentin continued, "Society often asks why men harm their women—what, or who, brings violence into the home." He looked around the audience. "I can think of few causes more important than yours. I am humbled when I see the amount of money you've raised and the way you direct its use—supporting four shelters *and* the special Helen Neil Fund for the ambitious outreach to women with special needs." He leaned forward. "I myself started life with an abusive father. I know about the fear, the tiptoeing around to avoid attention, the inability to express what you really think and feel."

Mora started in surprise. The odds of the man sent to help them having grown up in an abusive home must be slim. *Actually,* she chided herself, *the odds must be pretty great. In California alone, a little over one percent of children are abused.*

Mora knew that men who physically abused their wives often grew up in violent households. Through her training, she'd come to understand that these men saw only two roles in a marriage: the bully and the victim—and of course, they want to be the one with the upper hand. Still, the trend disturbed her. Why shouldn't the abuse make them abhor brutality instead of perpetuating it? Surely they were aware of the effect the beatings had on their mothers.

Mora shook her head, thankful that not *all* children who were tormented at home grew up to be abusers.

The chamber music wafted over the crystal-and-silver-appointed tables, a background to the polite after-dinner murmur of cultured voices in the chandelier-lighted ballroom.

Mora observed the honored guests at the head table. Were they enjoying the roast quail? At least they were eating.

Leigh Pryor put a hand on her husband's arm and whispered in his ear. He shook his head, glanced at the crowd in front of them, and stood to pull out her chair. She rose stiffly from her seat, tugged at her long-sleeved gown, and turned toward the steps. She stumbled and grabbed the chair back. Then—as though remembering she had an audience—she extended her body to its full regal height before leaving the podium.

Mora observed the interaction between the Pryors with interest. They seemed tense. Had they had a tiff? Was that why they were late for the social hour? She caught Carol's eye and inclined her head toward the speaker's wife who was making her way across the crowded ballroom. "Shall we introduce ourselves?" Mora asked.

Carol nodded.

Rising from the table, Mora smoothed the skirt of her cerise silk dinner gown. She liked the way the color complemented her fair skin and her raven hair, swept back tonight with an amethyst clip.

Carol pivoted her high-tech titanium wheelchair towards the ballroom's gold entrance doors. A black crepe evening suit set off her wavy blond curls and gave her an air of tasteful elegance while concealing her too-thin legs. The two women followed Leigh from a distance. Mora wanted their meeting to seem casual.

"I'm so excited by how well our gala has turned out," Mora said.

"Yeah," Carol replied, grinning. "Operation Cash Cow sure is a winner."

Mora groaned aloud. It was Carol's personal game to come up with an "Operation" name for each of their committee's projects—always with the initials OC.

"And now you sound like a dying cow!" Carol laughed. "Good thing you didn't do *that* at the table—no one would have touched the quail."

The ornate women's lounge was empty when Mora and Carol entered, save for Leigh in one of the stalls. Mora sat on the red plush settee to check her makeup. "Did you notice the diamond necklace at the next table? Maybe I'll buy myself one for my birthday." Her fingers danced around her neck, mimicking the stones' sparkle.

"Your neck isn't long enough." Carol's grin spread. "But I like the idea of your buying yourself a birthday present. I'd go for a cruise instead of jewelry though."

Leigh Pryor emerged from a stall, looking a bit shaky. Had the dinner made her ill?

Mora waited for her to wash her hands and regain some composure before greeting her.

"Well, hello. You're Mrs. Quentin Pryor. Leigh, isn't it?" Mora donned a broad smile and extended her hand. "I'm Mora Rey. I serve on the board of the BWEF with Quentin." She gestured toward her seated friend. "This is Carol Ewald, my co-founder of the Outreach Committee."

Leigh tugged at her sleeves and then offered her hand to Mora. Mora felt warmth in the handshake but was taken aback when Leigh withdrew her arm quickly, as though it were pulled by a marionette's string.

"I deeply regret our tardiness to the cocktail reception," Leigh said with a lilting British accent. "I simply couldn't decide on an appropriate outfit—you understand, I reckon?" As Leigh bowed her head, the light reflected off her auburn hair, tied up in a perfect dancer's bun.

Mora glanced at the Dior gown. "I can see why you chose this one. The blue is becoming on you." She rested a hand on the heavily beaded long sleeve.

Leigh jumped. "Oh, forgive me. I'm rather a bit nervous tonight. This benefit is so important to my husband." She smiled and headed toward a brightly lit makeup mirror. "Plus, I do have a bit of arthritis from all my years of dancing." She lowered herself gingerly to the red velvet bench.

"I'd love to see you perform," said Carol. "Are you appearing locally any time soon?"

Leigh's smile turned wistful. She shook her head. "Regretfully, I no longer dance. My husband— Er...my husband and *I* decided I'd not dance once we wed. It takes undue time and energy away from our family life."

Carol tilted her head. "Do you have children?"

"No, it's just the two of us."

Mora and Carol watched Leigh pat powder on her face. Mora wished she could apply makeup with the same expertise. But then, she hadn't been on the stage.

"We are so pumped that your husband is taking the time to work with us," Carol said.

Mora nodded. "Yes. When we asked the bank for help with our finances, we had no *idea* they'd send their CEO." She fished in her silk evening bag. "Here, take my card. Let's talk soon about your serving on our Shelter Committee. You'd be a welcome addition."

Leigh hesitated, and then accepted the proffered card. "Oh, I don't know." Leigh's languid body bent to face Mora. "I'm a dancer; I'm not schooled in financial matters like Quentin." Leigh dropped her lipstick and the card into her purse. "Besides, I'm not sure how he'd react to my getting involved in *his* business activities."

"Surely you understand the needs of abused women," Mora continued her campaign.

Leigh's mouth dropped open. "Oh, my no. I have no experience…"

"I'm sorry," Mora backtracked. "I only meant that the news is so full of stories of abuse, that I tend to assume all women must hurt for the poor women who need our help."

Leigh looked abashed. "Oh. Of course. Sometimes American speech is so direct, I misunderstand."

Whoops. Mora berated herself. *Am I projecting? I don't want to alienate Quentin's wife. But why did she react so strongly?*

"We can convince Quentin." Carol swiveled her chair to face Leigh. "Not only would your membership provide an assist for his work with the BWEF," she said, "but you'd be doing something for the community. Playing in the game instead of cheering from the bench." Carol paused. "With your husband's experience, I'm sure he'd support you one hundred percent."

Leigh's mouth opened in a half-smile. "His experience?" A frown flitted across her face. "Oh. You mean his childhood." She paused. "Of course, you're right. I don't know what I was thinking. That sounds simply lovely."

On the way back across the ballroom, Mora studied Quentin. He stood tall, his tuxedo fitting perfectly over his athletic frame. The right amount of cuff tipped his sleeve and a shock of gray showed at his temples. He looked every bit his role of CEO of the largest financial institution in the region, and now the biggest fundraiser for the BWEF. He was deep in conversation with a distinguished-looking man, whom Mora recognized as the bank's chairman of the board.

Reaching the pair, Leigh put out her hand. "Mr. Coughlin, how generous of you to attend." She introduced Mora and Carol.

"Thank you for loaning us Mr. Pryor," Mora said, extending her hand as well. "We're excited about all he brings to us." She turned to Quentin. "And, we'd like to enlist your wife to work with us too. I hope you'll agree."

Leigh turned to her husband, her eyes downcast. "I told them I'd ask you."

Quentin pressed his lips together and frowned at Leigh. Glancing around the group, he said, "I'm not—"

"Grand idea, Ms. Rey." Coughlin patted Leigh's arm. "She'll be a great asset."

Quentin's mouth lifted in a half-hearted smile. "Of *course* she would. You'll do it, won't you, darling?"

At Leigh's nod, Mora and Carol shared a satisfied glance.

Chapter 4

Carol

MORA LOOKED AROUND the now-empty ballroom, exhausted but elated. By all accounts, the evening had been a smashing success. Carol rolled up beside her, also basking in the satisfaction of all they had accomplished.

Mora and Helen had met Carol in the rehab hospital after Carol's accident. Helen was entertaining the patients and had asked Mora to go with her. Helen had so admired Carol's determination to live a full life despite her partial paralysis. The three of them had formed a friendship that had endured. Carol and Mora remained close after Helen's death.

Now, especially, Mora cherished Carol's strong presence in her life. After failing the actress so tragically, Mora counted this ex-Olympian skier as her first success. Mora *knew* how hard it was for an abused woman to change, to become strong; she'd struggled to do it herself. After establishing her own practice as a psychologist, Mora had helped Carol conquer the "I'm Worthless, the Beatings Are My Fault" Syndrome. She was gratified her friend had gone on with her life so positively. Carol now coordinated meets for the Special Olympics.

Mora smiled down at her friend, marveling yet again at how far this remarkable woman had come.

Eight years earlier

"Mora…can I talk to you?" Mora looked up from the garden catalog she'd been immersed in. Carol sat in her wheelchair inside the gate, her sweater drooped on slumped shoulders, eyes red and face puffy. Mora rushed to her friend's side.

"What happened?" Mora wheeled Carol under the awning to the white wrought-iron table. "Hang on—don't say anything 'til I get you a cup of chamomile tea. It won't take a minute."

Waiting for the tea to steep, Mora watched from the kitchen window as her friend swiped her wet face with the hem of her T-shirt. Carol was normally so upbeat. An optimist. Concern filled Mora.

As she returned with the tea, a short-haired Burmese cat sauntered over to Carol, stared up at her with knowing eyes, and jumped gently into her lap.

"Hello, there, lovely fellow. Where'd you come from?" Carol stroked the gray fur. A purr erupted under her touch.

"That's Clyde," said Mora, setting the tray on the table. "He belongs to a woman in the Lawndale shelter. I'm fostering him until she gets a place of her own."

"Wow, I never thought about abuse victims' pets," said Carol. She smoothed the contented cat's thick fur. "I guess they can't accept them at the shelters."

Mora pursed her lips and nodded. "Only a few have facilities for them." She reached out and rubbed Clyde's head. "And he was abused, too. Weren't you, poor fellow?" She gave the grateful animal another pat and reached for the teapot. She filled Carol's cup only halfway, in consideration of her friend's unsteady hands.

Mora pulled up a chair to the table. "Talk."

"I can't take it anymore, Mora. If this goes on, I won't be able to hold my head up." Carol combed her short curly blond hair with her fingers. "I must look a mess."

Mora patted the arm of Carol's chair. This wasn't the first time Carol had dumped frustration about her condition onto her friend. Mora had worked with many handicapped clients in her private practice as a psychiatrist, and she knew they all suffered down periods.

It was natural, considering the obstacles they encountered to get through even a normal day.

"Hey, gal, you've lived with your wheelie here for twelve years now. What's changed?"

"Nothing." Carol looked down at her lap. "Except Reggie. I don't know how to say this. I…"

"What about Reggie? Is he sick?" Mora's concern deepened. What was this about?

"No, it's nothing like that. It's…I…" Carol shifted uncomfortably. "It's that I can't take his abuse anymore."

"Reginald hits you?" Mora's words exploded in the quiet of the country garden. Carol nodded, her eyes still focused downward.

"That *bastard.*" Mora had liked Reggie at first, but as time went on, she didn't like the way her friend acted around him—withdrawn and submissive. Why hadn't she recognized the signs? She pointed to the cut on Carol's face. "Did he do that?" Mora could feel her own face heating up.

Carol nodded almost imperceptibly as she warmed her hands on her cup and inhaled the tea's weedy scent. "It started with calling me a cripple, complaining about my weight, laughing at my attempts to walk. All the while, he was basking in my fame, going through my savings with bad investments. Now he refuses to pay for physical therapy that 'his' insurance doesn't cover."

"Carol, why didn't you tell me?" Mora rubbed her best friend's shoulder gently as she poured more tea.

"How many of your friends did you tell about Sherman? You must know how dumb I feel: a smart woman who made a stupid mistake. Besides, since it's my fault, I figured I needed to handle it myself." She snorted. "Imagine, me—a paraplegic—thinking I could find a decent man to marry. I guess while I was training for the Olympics, I skipped Relationships 101."

Clyde snuggled closer, concerned eyes fixed on Carol's face.

"It's not *you*." Mora's voice spat anger. As Mora leapt to her feet, a startled Clyde jumped from Carol's lap and hid under the azalea bush. "Any man would be lucky to have you as a wife."

"When we met, Reg was attentive and sexy. I couldn't go anywhere or do anything without his wanting to be with me, doing what I was doing, loving me."

"Attentive, or controlling?" Mora asked the question with as much restraint as she could muster. Her experience and training told her it was surely the latter. The fledgling sprouts of the now well-developed abusive relationship.

"What's the difference? When I met him, I was mourning my ruined skiing career, scared about earning a living, and—frankly—a has-been when it came to attracting men. Someone in my life who would support me, make decisions for me, was heaven-sent."

Mora didn't respond right away. When she spoke, she couldn't control the force of her words. "If you—for a minute—think you're responsible for Reginald's abuse, stop it. Right now."

"But it was my weakness that made me choose a domineering man. You have to admit that much."

Mora stroked her chin. "Possibly. But more likely, your vulnerability is what drew this man to you."

What Mora didn't say aloud was: *He's probably so damned insecure, his ideal woman is one he can isolate and control absolutely. A woman other men wouldn't want.*

"I used to wish I knew who the real Reginald was; he always seemed to be playing a role."

"Have you found the real one now?"

"Yes, yesterday—when he threw my gold medal at me." Carol touched the bandage on her cheek.

"Shit." It wasn't a professional response. But it was heartfelt.

Mora took both of Carol's hands in hers and forced her to make eye contact. "I want you to tell me *exactly* what happened."

"But I *am* making progress. If I quit now, I'll lose all the mobility I've gained." In the family room of the Ewalds' Rolling Hills home, Carol sank into her wheelchair as Reggie's anger rolled over her. She lowered her head and gripped the chair arms.

Carol wished that she weren't so dependent on Reggie. She'd been Miss Self-Reliant before her accident. Now, she felt more helpless because of him than because of her wheels. Damn, she wanted to go back to controlling her own life.

"I'm sick and tired of this," raged Reggie. "No thanks to you, we have a comfortable living. My endorsements of skiing gear are still paying our bills. But that doesn't mean I'm willing to pay for useless physical therapy, simply so you can feed your little psyche into believing you'll walk again."

Despite her husband's dismissive attitude, Carol knew they could well afford the treatment she was asking for. She'd already gone from being bedridden to walking short distances supported by the railings on the treadmill. She could even stand by herself for a few minutes.

As Carol reached to turn her chair away, Reggie grabbed the Olympic gold medal that hung above the fireplace, next to his silver and bronze ones.

"Prove you've made progress." He stood two feet in front of her, his smile grotesque, as he swung her most cherished possession on its blue ribbon. "Walk over and take your precious medal from me." He took two steps backward. "Come on. Prove it."

Carol pushed herself up and stood facing him, then collapsed into the chair. "You know I can't walk unaided yet. And I won't ever, without intensive— and consistent—PT."

Carol put her hand over her mouth and bit her lip. She recognized from Reggie's snarl that she had challenged him too hard. Reggie hurled the medal at her. The gold disk hit her on the cheek and opened a bright red gash.

"This is the last time I want to hear about treatment that's not covered by our medical insurance. A medical plan, I might add, that I earn, not you."

As Reggie stormed out of the room, salty tears slipped down Carol's cheeks and stung the gash in her cheek. When would she learn to stop pushing him? You'd think she'd know his flashpoints by now.

"If only Reggie would let me take a job!" Carol fumed. "There's no reason I can't coach. I could earn my own health benefits—and money to pay for the additional therapy." She looked down at her lap. "I thought he was so romantic at first, wanting to keep me to himself, not wanting to entertain my friends. I found things to do without him only when he was gone." Creases covered Carol's face; tears shadowed her blue eyes. "Now he wants me to stop seeing you, and quit working with the Special Olympics—even while he's at work. He expects to reach me at home at all hours of the day and night." Carol swallowed hard. "And he says we can't visit my sis during the holidays. She's the only relative I have left."

Mora bit her tongue. She ached to tell her friend that she'd just recited all the signs of an escalating and dangerously abusive relationship. But this was not the time. She needed to listen closely now. She remained silent, making space for Carol to continue.

"He threatened to throw away all my skiing trophies—even the Olympic medal—if I told anyone. Those trophies mean a lot to me and he knows it. They remind me of what I've accomplished. Show me I can do anything I set my mind to. Even learn to walk again." Carol sighed. "If Reg permitted me extra physical therapy, that is."

Mora shook her head in disgust. "Reg *has* to deny your capability; it's your vulnerability that attracted him to you." Mora tried to keep her voice calm, but it was difficult to contain her frustration and rage. "At your wedding reception, he told me your paralysis was not an obstacle—he'd take care of you." She drummed her fingers on the table. "He didn't realize how strong you are. When you show independence, he feels threatened. Becomes more controlling."

"Early on, he might have believed he could control me," said Carol. "Then his career waned; the endorsements dwindled. He started on steroids to enhance his downhill slalom speed and stamina. That's when his personality became even more mean and unpredictable." Carol drained her cup and held it out for a refill.

Mora was pleased to see color returning to her friend's cheeks. She poured the tea and then grasped Carol's hand in both of hers. "Let's get practical. Where is Reg now?"

"He went hiking with his college fraternity buddies this morning. He'll be back tomorrow."

"Good. That gives us time to locate a shelter and get you moved in." Mora reached for her day planner and its list of phone numbers.

"I can't do that, Mora." Carol shook her head sadly, looking down at her useless legs.

"You have no choice. You have to get away. Our facilities are equipped for the handicapped." Mora hesitated and then offered, "You could stay with me—or in my mountain cabin."

Carol shook her head again. She stroked Clyde, who'd returned to her lap. He nestled closer.

"That's too dangerous for you. His anger's a volcano. When he's in one of his rages, I don't even recognize him." Carol wrapped her arms around herself, as if closing out the world. "As for the shelter... Reggie has ins with all kinds of influential people, people who could give him the address of every shelter in the city. He'd find me; I know he would." She looked up at Mora imploringly. "Just like Deacon found Helen—so he could kill her."

Mora shuddered. Carol was right. Mora couldn't make the same mistake again; she'd never be able to live with herself. But what now? She had to do something.

Carol reached out her hand and gripped Mora's arm. "I have something to ask you." She removed her hand and pushed her chair away from the table. "But I want you to promise you'll think hard before saying either yes or no."

"Carol, you know I'd do anything to help you. *Anything.*" Mora had vowed to set Helen's death right; maybe successfully helping Carol was the answer. She tried to read her friend's face, praying for a solution.

Carol's mouth set in a firm line.

Mora broke the silence. "Tell me. What is it?"

"Well...I keep thinking how you said you were so relieved when Sherman died in the accident."

"Yes..." Mora replied.

Carol swallowed. "I can't hope for a blizzard. I need your help."

Chapter 5

Erin

"TAYLOR'S RIGHT. You are a shithead." Erin Craig adjusted her binoculars to track Marshall Whitmore as he drifted down the Colorado River towards her camping spot. She could see his greedy eyes sweep up and down her bikini-clad body. He licked his lips.

It was a hot day in the Grand Canyon, but Erin shivered watching her friend's husband of twenty-plus years remove his wedding ring and zipper it into his shirt pocket. She bit her lip to prevent herself from cursing at him.

Today's adventure was not Erin's first mission for the OC, but it was her first solo one. She'd volunteered, determined to give Taylor the freedom she herself had been blessed with when her own husband had fallen from a Colorado cliff.

With some help, that is.

Erin prepared for her mission as she did for her many construction jobs: by thinking through each step. First, a tourist helicopter trip to choose her camp location; next, her examination of the river to find just the perfect spot for her needs.

Erin moved so that the sun wouldn't reflect off her binocular lenses. She watched her prey scratch some dirt from the bottom of his shoe and rub it over the white line on his ring finger. *I take that back. You're a double—no, triple—shithead.* He steered his rubber raft toward the shore.

Feeling his lecherous eyes burning on her, Erin thought again about Taylor. Although the two women had worked together at the BWEF, Erin had never met Marshall. Taylor seldom talked about him and his abuse, only said she enjoyed the time alone when he was away guiding tours on the river.

Erin was prepared when Marshall beached his raft. As she pretended to struggle putting up her tent, in her peripheral vision, she saw tanned legs topped by faded khaki shorts slink toward her. The man moved like a hungry coyote.

"Hello there. Let me show you how to do that." He sounded amused. "Women always get it wrong."

Erin looked up from her fake attempt to wrap a rope around the tent stake. "Aren't *you* the lifesaver!" *Here we go, Taylor.* "I remembered too late that this damn thing's too awkward to put up by myself." Erin stood to welcome him. "Should be a snap with *your* help, though." She thrust her breasts in his direction.

Marshall pointed to her binoculars. "Seen anything interesting?"

Erin laughed. She gazed up at him with flirty eyes. "What if I said I was looking for you?"

"I'd say you're lying." He stepped a breath closer. "But I like the idea."

Marshall scanned her camp. "Out here all by your lonesome?"

"Yes…" She looked him up and down. "But I'm open to making friends."

Under her scrutiny, Marshall squared his shoulders and sucked in his trim gut. Erin hoped the falseness of her smile wouldn't register with him.

"You got a name, Miss Lonely Camper?" He paused and held up his hand. "No. Let me guess. It must be Sunshine. You shimmer."

What an amateur.

"My name's Er— Uh, call me Eve. What's yours?"

"Well, Eve, you can call me Adam, then. Adam Marsh." Marshall pulled on the rope to raise the nylon tent over its supports.

Just like a spider weaving a web.

Marshall crawled in to inspect the dome from the inside.

Whatcha looking in there for, Big Boy? Ha! No mystery what you're thinking. I'm glad I have my knife. Poor Taylor, having to put up with you— a cheater as well as a beater.

Marshall emerged and looked around the camp. "How'd you get here? I don't see a raft."

"Don't own one; I hiked down from the rim. I'm only going to stay a few days. I can fish, so I didn't have to carry much." She gestured to a small backpack leaning against a boulder, its pockets pouched with provisions. "Wish I had a boat, now, though. I'd give up a month of my nonfat lattes to try those rapids. Riding them has to be a fuckin' high."

"Well, now…" Marshall put his hands in his back pockets and stuck out his chest. "I can arrange that, you know." He pointed in the direction of the roar that lent background music to the camping spot. "We'll steer around the waterfall up ahead and then shoot the rapids below. I'll tie the boat downstream, and we can walk back on the shore path."

Got him.

"Sounds perfect!" Erin bounced and she felt her boobs jiggle. *Yes, perfect.*

After Marshall had left on his guide trip, Taylor had shown Erin the detailed map of the river he had mounted on his den wall. Erin had studied it carefully, memorizing it. She'd tackled rough water before, but she would *never* venture near the class six rapids closest to the campsite. Not usually, anyway.

Marshall hung his water bottle over a tent post. "Let's finish setting up the campsite first," he said. "I have a waterproof flashlight in case the sun goes down on the hike back, but setting up camp in the dark isn't fun." His smarmy eyes narrowed as he shot Erin an alluring smile.

Marshall transferred a waterproof packet to a zippered pocket in his cargo shorts and removed his fisherman's vest. He looked up to see Erin watching him, her head tilted.

"Tips from my guide jobs." He grinned, a mischievous kid. Then added, "And some Las Vegas money my wife doesn't know about."

I bet it's money you took from Taylor's store. After you beat her and forced her to sign it over to you.

"You're married?" *As if I need to ask. I've seen Taylor's bruises.*

"Not out here." Marshall looked down at his empty ring finger. "We have a free marriage."

You double, triple, triple shithead. I bet you bite the apple every chance you get.

Marshall must have sensed her disdain. "I work hard for my money. This last trip, acting the genial host was painful. Thank God it's over. I've earned some play time." He took off his shirt, tossed it into the tent, and flexed his muscles.

Suppressing her urge to gag, Erin turned her attention to Marshall's boat.

"Adam,"—she smiled back up at him—"if you would gather up some wood, we can have a cozy fire when we get back."

"Sure thing, Sunshine." Marshall loped eagerly toward the foliage.

As soon as he was gone, Erin donned her shorts and shirt and ran through her mental checklist. She slid her knife into her right-hand sealed pocket and her waterproof binoculars into the left side. Then she trotted down to the beach and climbed into the rubber boat. She'd examined a similar one in Taylor's store, but checking out the real thing was crucial.

As she finished her walk-around, Marshall dropped an armload of wood near the fire ring and trotted towards the beach.

"Everything look all right?"

Erin started, experiencing a mixture of fear and something else. Guilt? *No.* Anticipation. Erin turned on her sunshine smile again. No time to waste. Taylor deserved to be free.

Marshall's smile turned to a scowl when Erin climbed out and launched the boat into the shallows.

"Hey, babe. Wait up! I'm the captain. You take orders from *me*." He jogged to the water's edge and commandeered the tow rope. "Get in. I'll launch her and join you." Erin did as instructed.

After leaping into the raft, Marshall donned his life vest and motioned Erin to grab one from the bottom of the boat as well.

As the two settled in for their float downriver, Marshall seemed to relax, his anger gone. "It's nice to have some new company." He corrected their drift with his paddle. "Almost threw my last clients into the river. Damn fake naturalists."

"Oh? Fake how?"

"These idiots paid me a hefty fee to guide them through the grandeur of this canyon and then had the nerve to complain about the 'bleak nothingness.'" Marshall swept his hand toward the cliff walls. "Not one appreciated the subtle colors and the variegated tones that stratify the eons it took for the canyon to form."

Erin was taken aback. Apparently Marshall did have some depth to him—when it came to nature, at least.

"I guess that's one of the risks of your business?" Erin asked, somewhat genuinely.

"Definitely. And on top of that, not a single woman graced the group. Except the cow who was married to the youngest guy."

Ah, there's the Marshall we love to hate.

"I mean, it's not *natural* for a man to go without a woman for so long." Dimples popped in Marshall's cheeks as lust filled his eyes.

"Listen to those rapids!" Erin interrupted his monologue. Flirting with Shithead was important, but the sooner it was over with, the better. She leaned toward him. "How long before we hit white water?"

"At least a half-mile. When we get close, I'll motion you up front to paddle."

"The hell with that!" she said. She faced him and loosened the ties on his grubby orange life vest. "I'm staying right here—next to you." She reached her hand in and caressed his nipples.

Marshall sucked in his breath. "Hey, Eve. Let's work first and play later."

Erin pouted. "Aww…don't worry. We'll have even more fun later. Besides, Adam," she said, reaching for his shorts zipper, "it's too late— I've already tasted the forbidden fruit."

Marshall swallowed hard as Erin's hand slid into his shorts. He grabbed for her shirt buttons, which she'd already undone. He caressed her bra-less breasts, then leaned down to kiss them.

"Let's get these off you, Adam," Erin panted, yanking at his shorts. "I mean, if you go by that name, you *have* to be naked…"

Marshall pushed her away. Hard. "What the hell are you doing? Pushing me around."

Uh-oh. Erin put her hand on his arm to placate him, but Marshall was having none of it. He yanked her off him.

"Now, get away, cunt. Can't you hear the rapids?"

I can, Shithead. Just where I planned.

"Damn it. Dumb broad! How could you be so careless? I told you we need to avoid the right fork. There's a dangerous drop-off there."

Erin imagined this wasn't the first time Marshall had approached danger on the river—nor the first time his dick had gotten him into trouble. He shouted instructions over the water's deafening roar. "Go to the bow! Throw me a helmet!" He reached for his oar with one hand and waved her forward with the other and then motioned frantically for Erin to pull left.

His jaw dropped when, instead, she casually fastened her blouse and braced her feet on the bottom of the craft. Erin raised her eyebrows at him slightly before launching herself backwards over the side—both life vests trailing behind her.

"Hey, cunt, what the fuck are you doing?" she heard him shout. "Swimming the rapids?"

Erin dove and bobbed to the surface on the opposite side of the raft.

"Where the hell are you? All I need is to have you drown on me."

"Here I am." Erin brought her knees up to her chest, propped her feet on the side of the rubber raft, and shoved off. The boat careened even further toward the river's right fork.

Erin saw Marshall's mouth gape as she rotated her arms in an Olympic-strength backstroke toward the river bank.

"Forget you, you stupid bitch." Marshall turned his full attention to steering the eight-person rubber boat back to the left fork—without success.

Adrenaline pumping, Erin reached the shore and unfolded her binoculars. She saw the panic on Marshall's face as he realized the raft was not responding. He pressed on the rubber beside him; his thumb and then his whole hand sank in.

Erin raised her fist. *Hot damn!* The raft must be leaking like a sieve through the dozen holes she'd slashed in its belly. But would he jump ship? She guessed not. He wouldn't abandon his craft and all his gear. He applied more pressure to his oar. Still no response.

As Marshall approached the waterfall, he flailed the paddle and then dragged it in a futile attempt to guide his raft away from the falls.

"Help. Help. Heluuuup."

Erin clutched her binoculars with white-knuckled fists. She remained engrossed as the force of the water rushing over the rapids tossed first Marshall and then his ragged raft high into the air and over the waterfall. Not even an experienced rafter could survive the protracted drop to giant boulders below.

Erin lowered the glasses and brushed her hands together.

Operation complete.

PART II

Operation Compassion

Chapter 6

A S THE DODGER THIRD BASEMAN hit a home run, Rick Maris rose and grabbed the back of the couch to steady himself. What a great way to spend a Sunday: watching the game with his neighbor and gambling buddy, Dan—especially since the favored Dodgers were well on their way to covering the three-point spread. The fifty bucks he'd win from Dan would easily fund a weekend trip to the Hustler.

Rick squeezed an empty can in his fat fist and tossed it onto the pile rising from the coffee table. Wiping the sweat from his face with the sleeve of his T-shirt, he vaguely wondered if he'd broken his record of ten Buds per game; but he didn't stop to count the empties. Instead, he fished through the icy water and felt along the bottom of the tub.

"Shit. There's no more beer. My dumb wife must have left the rest in the fridge."

How many times had he told her he needed lots of beer chilled for game days? What was wrong with her? She never listened when he tried to tell her things. Didn't she realize he had much more experience than she did?

Rick scratched his scraggly beard. It felt good not having to shave all weekend. He stumbled towards the kitchen and shouted over the noise of the game, "Bitch, bring in the rest of the beer."

His eyes on the game, he didn't see his wife tiptoe into the room.

"Rick, I put it all in the tub," Trudy whispered. "Did you check the bottom?"

"You slut!" he sneered, pushing her back into the kitchen. "I *told* you to buy enough for all afternoon." Why couldn't that woman do what he told her? Always making her own decisions about what to buy, how much to spend.

Rick's slap echoed in the small kitchen. He knew his buddy could probably hear them, but he didn't care; men stuck together on things like this. A man was meant to be boss in his house—and what either of them did with his own wife was none of the other's business.

If only the snoopy lady in the apartment on the other side would keep *her* nose out of his life, too. Calling the cops on him like that. What did that old maid know about a man and a woman? Good thing Trudy at least had the sense to keep sending the pigs away.

As Trudy pulled away from him, Rick yanked open the refrigerator door so hard it slammed against the wall. "You dumb bitch. You don't even know how much beer to buy for a game. Now I have to go get more."

"I spent all the money you gave me. If you'll give me more, I'll go to the liquor store." She reached out a shaking hand.

Rick grabbed her fingers and pushed them back until they cracked. Trudy moaned and bit her lip.

"Shut up! Stop that noise!" Everything she did annoyed him. After all this time married, he shouldn't have to hit her to get her attention. "I'll teach you to embarrass me in front of company!" He punctuated his remarks with a blow to her stomach and a pair of backhands to her face.

Rick's tirade was interrupted by a weight thrown against him and a tugging on his arm. "Dad—please don't hit my mom! *Please!*" Rick looked down, surprised to see his son—his pride and joy—looking up at him pleadingly. In his anger, Rick had forgotten it was the weekend; the kid didn't have school today. He released his wife's arm.

"Hey Rick, man! I'll see you tomorrow," Dan called out, obviously not wanting to be a part of this. Rick heard the front door shut.

That damn bitch! Now she's ruined my whole afternoon. He'd have to keep a lid on his temper until his son was out, though.

"It's okay, baby," Trudy was saying. "Why don't you go to your room and I'll bring you some orange juice." She patted her son on his head. "Cookies, too." Rick watched silently as Trudy ushered the boy to his bedroom. At least the bitch knew how to keep their son in check—now that she'd gone and upset him.

When Trudy returned to the kitchen, Rick grabbed her arm. "Don't think for a minute, bitch," he muttered, "that I've finished with you."

Rick shoved her out of his way and staggered out of the apartment.

Cruising southbound down Pacific Coast Highway alongside her partner Harry Adler, Sharon Collins squinted at the cloud-muted sunset as the pair started their afternoon shift in the black-and-white. They served Los Angeles County as deputy sheriffs. As Harry turned east towards Lomita, she flipped through their duty roster.

"*This* call is priority: Domestic dispute. Unincorporated Torrance, on Carson east of Normandie. The perp is out of the apartment, according to the deputy. Neighbor who called said it's happened before, and she's afraid the beatings are escalating. Units have been out there in the past and left a brochure on our VINE program, but the vic's refused to make a charge. We need to get a handle on this."

Harry looked over at Sharon. She knew what he was thinking— and he was right. Sharon remembered all too well what it was like to be the punching bag in a domestic dispute. And she couldn't bear to see it happening to anyone else.

"Any kids?" Harry pulled a left turn and headed north on Normandie.

"Neighbor said one little boy, eight."

"Geez. Even at *that* age, he's learning the wrong way to treat a wife." Harry pulled to the curb in front of a faded blue stucco three-story apartment building. "Let's get an action figure from the trunk before we go in."

Sharon nodded, smiling inwardly. At the station everyone teased Harry about his trunk full of toys, but she knew they all thought it was great.

So did she.

At Sharon's knock, Trudy Maris opened the door, the chain still in the latch. Her blotchy face appeared at the crack. "Yes?"

At least she's still conscious.

"Mrs. Maris, Trudy Maris?" At Trudy's nod, Sharon continued, "Ma'am, we're from the Los Angeles County Sheriff's Department. Your neighbor called, said your husband hurt you." Sharon showed her identification to the young woman. "May we come in?"

Fear crossed Trudy's face. "I…I don't know. He could come back any minute." The woman clasped her hands together. "He sees your car, he'll be so mad! Please just go!"

In the dim light, Sharon could see a swelling eye and ugly bruises forming on Trudy's left cheek. "We're here to protect you from him. We need to come in."

Trudy closed the door and removed the chain. The officers entered a living room that reeked of stale beer and unwashed bodies. Sharon sucked in her breath.

A young boy appeared from behind Trudy. "Are you going to arrest my dad?" The sturdy copper-haired boy stood tall, with his hands on his hips, but his quivering lips belied his brave stance. He reminded Sharon of her own son at that age.

"This is my son, Ricky." Trudy smiled crookedly at the spike-haired, grimy-kneed boy.

"No, sir," Harry reassured him. "We're here to help your mom and you; make sure you're both safe." Harry Adler held out the Batman doll he'd been holding behind his back. "How 'bout you and I go to the kitchen and get something to drink? I'll show you all the tricks you can make Batman do."

Ricky looked at his mom, who nodded. "Go ahead, hon. I'll be okay with the sheriffs here." Trudy laid a hand on her son's shoulder. "You've done such a good job protecting me. Get you and the policeman some pretzels, too." Trudy's face was filled with such love and sadness, it was hard for Sharon to watch.

As Harry and the boy disappeared through the kitchen door, Trudy murmured to Sharon, "Thanks for coming. I don't know what to do. He's gotten drunk a lot before, but this is the worst he's ever been." She shook her head as if to clear it, and then winced and pressed a hand against her neck.

"Ma'am, before you tell me what happened," said Sharon, "I want you to know that I'm an abuse survivor myself." Sharon inhaled deeply, ignoring the stench. "I know what it's like to be hurt by someone I loved. I can pretty much imagine what you're going through, physically *and* emotionally." Remembered pain brought a muscle spasm to Sharon's back. She rotated her shoulders to relieve it. Her own ordeal was over. It was her turn to help someone else.

Sharon cradled Trudy's arm as she helped her into a straight-backed chair. *Gad!* She saw so much of this. Why?

"He's always so sorry, so loving, when he sobers up. For weeks, he treats me like a princess: Flowers, dinners out, movies." Trudy wiped her face with the hem of her T-shirt. "I kn...know he loves me."

"What went on?" Sharon spoke softly, not daring to take out her notebook. She'd depend on her memory rather than risk agitating the distraught victim.

"It was *my* fault. I didn't buy enough beer for him and his friend to watch the Dodger game. Rick left to go buy more; said I embarrassed him in front of his buddy." Trudy shivered, though the apartment was unbearably hot to Sharon.

"How long has he been gone?"

"Since yesterday afternoon." She looked over her shoulder. "My neighbor wanted to call you then, but I wouldn't let her. She did it anyway this morning when she saw my face." Trudy put a hand to her swollen cheek. "He usually don't come back 'til he's sober."

"Where does he go to sober up?"

"I don't know. Maybe the jobsite; he works in construction." Sharon leaned forward to catch the mumbled words. "Could be minutes, or it could be hours or days before he comes back."

"We need to get you out of here, ma'am, before he does." Trudy shook her head. Sharon held Trudy's gaze. "He'll only get worse." Trudy sniffled but didn't respond. "The Battered Women's Escape Foundation has a shelter in Torrance," Sharon continued. "It's secluded, secure. Even the neighbors around it don't know what it is."

"But what about Ricky?" Trudy asked. "Do they have room for him there, too?"

"Of course—and other kids in the same situation that he can play with."

For the first time, Sharon saw a light in Trudy's eyes. She helped Trudy to stand.

"Now, I'll help you pack."

"I don't have a suitcase. Rick don't like to travel and don't let me go anywhere without him."

"Do you have large plastic trash bags?" Trudy nodded. "Good." Sharon headed toward the kitchen. "They're quicker than suitcases, and hold more."

Chapter 7

"UNDER OLD BUSINESS, we have to finalize plans for this weekend's Operation Chase—a.k.a. the marathon." Mora smiled indulgently at Carol as she drew papers from her briefcase. "We've confirmed the park venue. Erin and I met with the rangers last week and walked the race route."

Mora clasped her hands and looked around the group—all the OC members, except of course Erin, who for security's sake was not due back until next weekend. Saturday night's gala had been a lot of work, but there was no time to rest. It was Monday morning and time to move forward with their next mission.

Quentin Pryor smiled. "I'm happy to see you ladies support the general health of our community by staging a marathon. But I do have some questions about it. Is this a good time to raise them?"

Mora nodded. She was happy to see the CEO taking an interest in the organization's projects. His preliminary analysis of their budgets and spending plans had already given her confidence that the charity would continue for years to come.

"What about the funds for renting the venue?" Quentin began.

Carol looked up from her note-taking. "We're home free on that. We've used money from the advance registrations—seven hundred so far—for the down payment. And we'll pay the remainder from the take on race day." She pulled her sweater around her, watching Quentin as she spoke. "We charge the last-minute entries ten dollars more."

Mora shifted so she could face Quentin. "That includes entry fees for both the 5K and 10K—which are substantial."

Quentin cleared his throat. "That's all well and good, ladies. But will you bring in enough to *actually* cover the venue?"

Mora bridled a little at Quentin's probing. But of course, that *was* what the BWEF wanted him for.

"Oh, you can bet on it!" Carol exclaimed, unfazed. "Plus," she added, winking at Mora, "over and above that to support our organization."

Mora nodded her agreement. She *knew* they'd meet expectations— even if she and Carol had to contribute some of their own money. They'd already discussed it.

"Let's hope you do. I'd hate to see our general fund depleted any more. You—*we*—need it for shelter maintenance. We can't have anything drag down our most important mission."

Mora patted Quentin's hand. You'd think he ran the charity with his own funds, he was so careful with their money. "We love your concern for us, Quentin. But let me assure you that the marathon is one of our biggest fundraisers. Many graduates of the shelters participate."

Carol laughed. "All of Erin's workers love it! She gives them the day off with pay if they run."

Mora turned to Carol. "Is the order for the T-shirts ready? Our lead time's getting short."

"Yes." Carol held up a white T with the green outline of a runner on the front. "This is the artwork we've chosen. Single-color printing keeps the cost down. They offer a daffodil-yellow shirt, but that costs three dollars more. I vote for white shirts with green lettering."

"Just a minute, ladies." Quentin rose and took the sample from Carol. "This is a high-quality shirt; your graphics are a special design." With sad eyes he turned to each one at the table. "Excuse me for saying it, but isn't it irresponsible to spend so much money on shirts? That part of the entrance fees could help at least three abused families."

Mora's back stiffened. *He really is interested in the shelter families,* she lectured herself. Was she so sensitive to his motives because of her experience with Sherman?

Mora vowed to relax until she knew Quentin better. After all, they'd hired him to help direct their funds to the right accounts. But he seemed intent upon questioning every single decision they made.

She understood that it was part of his job, but not at the expense of their enthusiasm. Looking around the table, she saw her feelings reflected in the slumped bodies of the other women there. Leigh hung her head and twirled her wedding ring around her finger. Mora wondered fleetingly what Quentin was like at home.

Breaking the silence, Carol said, "We paid for the graphics two marathons ago. That's why we chose it."

"True," Taylor Whitmore finally spoke up, "but he's r-right about the expense of the shirts t-t-taking money from the shelters." She thought for a moment. "*I'll* buy the shirts, if you agree to put the Wilderness Outfitters' logo on the sleeve." She turned to Pryor. "That's my wilderness supply store in Hermosa Beach." Turning back to the table, she added, "We…We'll both benefit: the BWEF and my shop. And, I can write off the cost as ad-advertising, or a charitable donation."

Warmth tingled Mora's face. Taylor was a good negotiator and a staunch supporter of the BWEF—financially savvy, too. And assuming Erin's mission had gone well, Taylor was now free to help them out as much as she wanted, with no one to answer to.

Carol sat up straight in her chair. "Quentin, it's true that our shirts are an expense, but they are *not* unnecessary. They're a part of our community liaison." She looked around the room. "Sixty percent of the women in our shelters are referred to us by someone who heard about us informally. I wear my marathon Ts all the time, especially when I help out with the Special Olympics. They never fail to receive comments."

"Okay, I give up!" Pryor raised his hands in surrender. His grin looked genuine. "You ladies want the Ts, we'll have Ts. But I accept Taylor's offer." He bowed to Wilderness Outfitters' owner. "Thank you."

Quentin's wife let out her breath with a whoosh. Mora turned and smiled at her.

"We'll need to move fast on this, Taylor." Carol took charge. "How soon can you get me the logo?"

Quentin rose from his chair. "Come, darling." He turned to his wife. "While these ladies work out the details, let's get you home so I can get to the bank and earn the money they pay me." He helped Leigh on with her coat and the pair exited, Quentin's arm still draped over Leigh's shoulders.

Mora wandered around the conference room, pushing the chairs into the table, closing the draperies, and shutting down her laptop. Something about the just-completed meeting troubled her; something in the interaction between the people in the room. It was her job to understand these things, but she couldn't quite get a handle on the strange undercurrent. She fished in her purse for her keys.

Mora had a good life. She'd invested wisely over the years and didn't need to work to maintain her lifestyle. She basked in the freedom to keep her own schedule and to associate with whomever she pleased.

However, there had been a time in Mora's life when she'd felt so desperate, so down, so trapped, that she'd imagined herself on a cliff, tumbling down a steep slope to the ocean below, with no trees or other barrier to stop her slide. That was one reason she had gone back to school for her psychology degree and had joined the BWEF: to counter lingering memories of those days. But, first and foremost, to aid women who no longer had hope.

The Outreach Committee existed because of her willingness to take risks to help others who could not help themselves.

Eight years earlier

The sports announcer's voice lost its usual exuberance and became somber.

"I have some sad news to report." He glanced down at the paper in his hand. "Reginald Ewald, prominent slalom competitor in the last decade and spouse of Carol Leher Ewald, former Olympic downhill champion, has died. He met an accidental death during a practice run on one of the world's fastest and most treacherous courses. His ski flew off as he turned sharply to aim at a mid-course gate. Authorities investigating his death say it appears Ewald's ski binding did not operate correctly. The malfunction could have been caused by a too-loose setting or by something jamming the release mechanism so it didn't close properly. When the binding malfunctioned, the force of Ewald's downhill momentum threw him against a tree."

The picture on the screen moved from a video of Ewald's snowball tumble to his portrait.

The announcer continued, "Reggie Ewald's wife—also the victim of a tragic skiing accident—has prepared a statement."

The camera cut to live feed of Carol in her wheelchair, surrounded by reporters in front of the hospital.

"Thank you for your concern and expressions of sympathy." Dressed in black, Carol sat erect in her wheelchair, holding a framed snapshot of Reg skiing. She swiped at a tear with her hand. "Reginald died doing what he loved most in the whole world. I will remember only that." She dropped her head and wheeled her chair from the microphone.

Chapter 8

Seven years earlier

"Mora, I can't believe how excited I am!" Carol pumped her arms. She had come straight over from physical therapy where she'd walked on the special treadmill that gave her extra support. Her legs had moved. Sure, barely, but she'd seen and felt it. Carol laughed. "I hugged the therapist so hard, she yelped!" Carol sobered. "I would never have come this far if Reggie were around."

Mora squeezed Carol's shoulders. "I love this change in you."

"Thanks to our 'Operation,' I no longer jump when I hear a car drive up to the house. I know it can't be Reginald. His moods don't direct my life anymore." Carol stretched. "It's almost like he was never even a part of it."

Carol blinked several times. "When he died, the news stories brought back memories of how sweet he was when we first met." She paused. "I've tried to focus only on those positive remembrances. But now, I worry that I'll forget what Reg was like leading up to his accident." Her laugh was hollow and subdued. "And I can't let myself forget that. If I do, I'll choose another loser like him—and hate myself all over again."

Mora shook her head. "You've come so far with your self-confidence, in defining what you want, you won't go back to that. I promise."

"I couldn't have escaped without you, Mora."

Mora looked down at her hands. "I'm really glad I was able to help."

Carol hesitated. How should she put this? "What happened today gave me an idea." She leaned forward. "What if we could help others too?"

"You're already helping them." Mora waved her hand. "The marathon never ran so smoothly, or made so much money for us, until you took it over."

Carol shook her head. Sure, the marathons were successful, but the help they gave wasn't immediate. "I need to do something more concrete. Giveback—payback—whatever you want to call it. Does that make sense?"

"Payback?"

"Direct help for women like Helen. With husbands powerful enough in the community that shelters aren't an option." She looked Mora in the eyes. "Help like you gave me."

Mora looked at Carol askance. "Are you saying what I think you're saying?"

"I'm saying we could arrange accidents." It felt strange to voice it aloud. Carol exhaled.

"Fatal accidents?"

Carol nodded, still holding her friend's gaze.

Mora shook her head. "I don't think that's something we should make a habit of." She grimaced. "Well...one or two, maybe."

Carol squeezed her friend's arm. "We'd be helping desperate women and taking rabid animals off the streets for good."

Mora frowned and shook her head. "Aside from the obvious moral dilemma, we don't have the expertise."

"We could enlist others from the BWEF, others who have—or had—husbands like ours." Carol's eyes misted.

Mora shifted uncomfortably, but Carol could see she'd grabbed her attention—that she was actually considering the proposal.

"We'd be acting like God," Mora said slowly. "Doesn't that bother you?"

"God is too busy; we'd be doing Him a favor. Our being so happy ourselves has to mean something!" Carol's words came out in a rush as her excitement grew. "And we'd exhaust all the other options first. Plus, we'd make sure the man really deserved an accident before we staged one."

Carol watched in silence as Mora rose from her chair and paced to and from the window, methodically clenching and unclenching her fists.

"Think about Helen," Carol finally whispered. "Think how much we could have helped her."

Mora sank to her chair and sat straight as a pillar. Finally, she turned to Carol and gave a quick nod.

"Agreed," she murmured.

Chapter 9

ERIN ENTERED the handicapped toilet stall at a dirty rest stop. She unsheathed a camping knife from her backpack and laid it carefully on the sink. She yanked off the oversized fisherman's vest she was wearing and sliced it into unrecognizable lumps. Next, she removed Marshall's life vest and faded shirt from her knapsack and gave them the same treatment.

After mixing all the shreds into a pile, she stuffed the mess she'd created into a plastic bag with the garbage from her campsite. For good measure, she used a piece of the jacket to grab trash from the feminine protection bin in the stall—*that* should deter anyone from investigating!

Finally, she pulled Marshall's driver's license from her pocket and cut the plastic rectangle into fine bits. The flushing toilet carried the pieces away.

Chapter 10

MONDAY MORNING, instead of her khaki uniform, Sharon donned a pair of shell-pink sweats. She gave her children a hug, checked that they had their homework, and left them at school. She was glad she didn't have to make this trip after-hours and leave them at the YMCA, like she usually did. The kids had been saying they were old enough to be left by themselves, but she couldn't bring herself to do it. She trusted *them*, but she didn't trust others in the community she served. She'd seen too much.

As Sharon drove her aging Honda Civic up the Harbor Freeway, she worried about the wisdom of enrolling her kids in summer school. She'd *like* to give them a carefree summer. But what would they do with their time? It was difficult making all the parenting decisions by herself. There was really no one else to seek advice from. Certainly not their father—in prison.

Sharon parked in a quiet neighborhood in Torrance, its sidewalks lined with decades-old ficus trees. Children skateboarding in the street shouted and laughed. A mission-style house stood in the center of the block, partially obscured by an eight-foot-high crimson bougainvillea. Practically speaking, the thorny plant served to discourage anyone inclined to climb over the cinder-block wall it covered. To Sharon, the colorful adornment represented the bright dreams of the residents.

A black wrought-iron gate protected the path from the street to the front door. Sharon spoke into the intercom. "Hi! It's Sharon Collins." A closed-circuit camera silently revolved, verifying her identity. The gate latch buzzed.

Sharon felt cocooned whenever she entered a BWEF facility. This was not the one she herself had lived in for four months, but they all shared a safe-world feeling. *This* period home had once housed a physician and his family. He had seen patients in the front area, while normal family life continued in the hidden rooms beyond. With its ten-foot ceiling, deep baseboards, and bay window, the front room looked every bit the Victorian parlor. But today, desks, computer consoles, and file cabinets had replaced the marble-topped tables and plush chairs of that era.

Sharon stepped into the family room, relishing its warmth. Her kids had made new friends in a home like this. Friends who understood the misery of abusive fathers—and the confusion of suddenly single–parent homes. She didn't know what she would have done without that refuge. Thank heaven for the rich women who had time to run the foundation. She'd heard that none of them were paid for their work.

"I've come to talk to Trudy Maris," Sharon addressed the staffer.

"Have you found her husband?"

The intensity behind the woman's question told Sharon she was talking to an abuse survivor. She shook her head. "No, ma'am."

"I saw Trudy carrying a towel toward the pool a few minutes ago," interjected a pretty Asian woman who had yellowing bruises on her face but a twinkle in her eye.

Sharon approached the patio where a half-dozen women were basking in the sun. Several greeted her by name.

"Hello, Trudy. Soaking up some rays?"

"Oh!" Trudy started, then smiled sheepishly. "Hi, Deputy. I didn't recognize you at first." She smiled through swollen lips. "They should let you pick your uniform color; that pink looks so good on you!"

"I can't go wrong with pink. It jazzes me." Sharon set down her tote bag. "I always come here in civilian clothes. We make sure no one sees a law enforcement connection to the home; it's part of our security protocol." The deputy pulled up a lounge chair. "And, ma'am, just call me Sharon—no title."

"Well," said Trudy, "I'll agree to call you Sharon if you'll call me Trudy. 'Ma'am' makes me feel like a schoolteacher."

Sharon smiled and nodded her assent. "So, how do you like it here?" She looked around. "Are you getting settled in?"

"It's so quiet, except for the kids playing." Trudy pointed to the ballgame in the rear of the deep backyard. "And safe," she added in a whisper, as if afraid to chase away the silence. "Until it stops," she continued, "you don't realize how draining constant harping can be. And fear."

Sharon grimaced. "I know."

Sharon took in Trudy's battered face and puffy eyes, feeling remembered pain with each blemish. Second only to death, facing abuse was the most dreaded part of Sharon's job—in fact, sometimes it was worse. "How are you feeling? Has the doctor seen you yet?"

"She came early this morning. Said she didn't think I had any broken bones, but she ordered me to take it easy." Trudy gulped her Diet Coke. "She said the physical pain'll probably be gone in two weeks…I guess it's the emotional that takes longer, huh?" Trudy attempted a smile.

Sharon nodded. It was good Trudy understood that.

"Deputy, uh, Sharon." Trudy squirmed in her lounge chair. "How am I going to pay for all of this? I don't have a job and my secretary skills are rusted shut!"

Sharon tilted her head. "Trudy, you aren't going to pay for your care here. You probably don't remember us telling you yesterday, but the BWEF covers everything. You and Ricky can stay here for up to three months—or longer, if we feel your husband is still a threat. There's a search warrant out for him now."

Pressing on the chair arms, Trudy pulled herself upright and groaned with the pain the movement caused. "You can't arrest him!" She bit her lip as she eased back down. "Ricky needs a father."

Sharon spoke quietly but with authority. "We have to, Trudy. He could have given you a concussion—even killed you." Sharon held her gaze. "And you don't want Ricky to learn that hitting a woman is okay."

Trudy nodded. She pressed her hands against her tearing eyes. "I loved him so!"

Sharon raised her eyebrows. "*Loved?* Not *love?*" She was gratified by such early progress.

Trudy shrugged. "I don't know…The talk with the psychologist last night made me think maybe I loved what I wanted him to be, not what he is." She raised her chin. "She also told me that I need to cherish myself more. That the beatings weren't my fault and that I didn't cause them by not doing what Rick wanted." Trudy looked down at her lap. "I want to believe that, but it's so hard."

Sharon rubbed Trudy's hand. "Don't worry—you'll get there. I learned that, too, in a shelter like this." Sharon had come to the shelter feeling numb—physically and emotionally. It had taken several visits with the psychologist to bring her out of her funk. The kids had stayed glued to her. They'd told her later that they'd thought she was dying, she was so still. Sharon's head ached thinking about it.

"I also learned that the staff will help you get your life together," Sharon continued. "Move on. That's why Harry and I brought you here."

Trudy forced a smile.

"I'm sure the BWEF would welcome your volunteer time, though. They always need someone to entertain the kids, do office filing." Sharon smiled and patted Trudy's knee. "And don't worry about earning money. When it's time for you to try your wings, the BWEF helps with that, too. They'll get you some training, probably in computers since you've worked in an office, and help you find a job—or get a scholarship if you want to continue school. Employers tell the BWEF that their candidates make reliable workers; they want more of them."

"Wow." Trudy's eyes twinkled. "For the first time in years, I can… hope. Thank you so much for all of this."

"Don't thank me," Sharon said. "Thank the BWEF supporters. They're the ones who make all of this possible."

Sharon was stung by a pang of guilt. It had been years since the BWEF had saved *her*, given her the support and space to turn her life around. It was past time to give back. She vowed then and there to sign up for this weekend's marathon. She'd give up take-out coffee for the next two weeks to make up for the entry fee. Once she was able to leave the kids home alone, she'd volunteer at the shelters, too.

"*Now*,"—Sharon returned her attention to Trudy—"we need to talk about your husband." She leaned over and withdrew her notepad from her bag. "So we can find that man and get him off the streets. Get *him* some help, too." Sharon's left hand gripped Trudy's, her right one poised over her pad. "Now, tell me Rick's habits, from the time he gets up in the morning, to the end of the day when he drops into bed."

Chapter 11

Taylor leaned against the doorjamb of the treatment room, tense and hurting.

"Come in, Mrs. Whitmore! How are you this morning?" Chang, the acupuncturist, checked the room's temperature. "Anything special you want to work on?"

Thursday was usually the day Taylor set aside to catch up on the store's paperwork, but today she'd taken an early lunch break for an emergency treatment. Thank God she could trust her son, Rob, to manage the store.

Taylor held out her arms. "Actually, I'm having quite a bit of h-hand pain. I can barely hold a p-pen or type." She winced as she flexed her fingers. "The computer's the lifeline of my shop; I enter everything in it."

"Could you have carpal tunnel syndrome?" The acupuncturist smoothed the cover on the treatment table and motioned Taylor to lie down.

Taylor pulled her robe around her, sat on the table, and lifted her legs. She relaxed as Chang fluffed a pillow and placed it under her knees. "No, Chang, I don't have carpal t-t-tunnel; my hand was injured at home. In an ac...accident."

Though Taylor admired and trusted Chang, she couldn't bring herself to tell him what had really happened. That her husband had twisted it. Marshall's physicality terrified her, and this certainly hadn't been the first time she'd gotten injured. But if Chang had figured it out by now, he was always polite enough not to say anything.

Chang's eyes softened. "I am so sorry to hear that," he said, gently moving her bruised hand so it was accessible to him. "We'll work on the nerves." He inserted a needle and twirled it in his expert fingers.

Eyes closed, listening to the soothing music, Taylor barely felt Chang's ministrations. But try as she might, Taylor could not push away the horror that had begun two weeks ago.

"What do you mean, you won't deliver the equipment for my Grand Canyon trip?" A fist to Taylor's right shoulder punctuated Marshall's words. Her shoulder was one of his favorite targets. He knew she'd injured it previously, when he'd whipped her horse on the PV riding trails, causing her to fall, shoulder first, to the rocky ground.

Taylor needed to be strong—to stand up, for once, to the supercharged man she lived with. When it came to the success of her store—a store she had lovingly built from the ground up—she simply couldn't allow herself to be bullied. Or bankrupted.

"First, I don't work for you," Taylor said through trembling lips. "Second, I will not release the equipment to you or any of your employees until you pay for it."

"Pay for it? Why do I have to pay for equipment from my own store?" Marshall twisted Taylor's wrist, causing her to cry out in pain.

Tears streaming, Taylor somehow found the courage to reply. "I don't need to remind you, Marshall, that we agreed to keep our businesses separate when we married. If I went on one of your wilderness trips, you would expect <u>me</u> to pay for it."

Marshall slapped the back of Taylor's head. "What a joke! You couldn't endure my rigorous trips. I don't know how you make even a short scuba dive, with the condition your body's in." He pointed to his wife's lower limbs. "And those piano legs of yours would drag you to the bottom if you fell into the rapids."

Marshall grabbed his cell phone from the counter and charged out to the Porsche parked in the driveway.

On the treatment table, Taylor jumped.

"Ms. Taylor, you are not relaxing today. Should I schedule you for a massage after this?" Chang's voice reflected his concern.

"Oh, yes, please. I desperately need one. I've been thinking too much about my business lately."

"Marshall, you're hurting me! Let go." Struggling against his strength, Taylor felt her arm pull out of its socket and snap back.

"Well, at last! I've gotten your attention. Maybe now you'll act like a wife instead of a feminist dyke."

Taylor cradled her left arm in her right. She tried to dodge his angry punches but another landed on her breast. She gasped and bit her lip. She'd already gone too far, but she might as well let it all out.

"What's the matter with you?" she cried. "We agreed that when it came to business, we'd treat each other like customers."

"A stranger would treat me better. And I've been married to you for thirty years! After all that time, you don't trust me." Marshall's face was corpse sallow. His eyes black beads.

Taylor leaned forward, only to have him grip her right wrist and wrench it up behind her back.

"Stop. You'll break my arm!"

She reached behind her with her throbbing left arm, and tried to pry his fingers from her right wrist. He thrust her arm up harder. She shrieked in pain.

This wasn't worth it, Taylor decided. She'd give him the equipment and make up the cost some other way. Because aside from this physical torture, she couldn't take the emotional pain: the thought that her husband saw nothing wrong with hurting her this way and the realization that he could ruin her business—and her—on his whim alone.

Taylor went limp. The steaming man let her fall to the floor. She doubled into a fetal position. "Okay, what do you want me to do, Marshall?"

"Sign this release so I can pick up my supplies from your distributor." Marshall clicked a ballpoint pen and wrapped her fingers around it. He dropped a stapled document to the floor, the pages creased back to the signature page.

Taylor flipped the document to look at the front. Marshall slapped the back of her head and rearranged the papers. "Sign where I showed you, Ms. Business Woman!"

Squinting to see through her tears, Taylor picked up the pen and scribbled her name on the bottom line. Marshall snatched the papers, slapped the back of her head again, and slammed the door behind him.

Taylor flexed her hands as she undressed for her massage. Chang had worked his miracles—the pain had lessened. Still, she struggled with the knot in her sash; her hands worked like boards. She crawled under the warm blanket and waited for Heidi.

"Taylor, how nice to see you. How are you feeling today?" Heidi dimmed the lights and turned up the speaker volume. Soothing wave sounds with a flute accompaniment engulfed the room. Lavender scent floated from the votive candles on the credenza, adding to the otherworld atmosphere.

"To be honest, not very good. My whole body is tense."

"Well, we'll have to work on all of you then." Heidi spread warm lavender-scented oil on Taylor's back.

Taylor felt her muscles respond one by one to the woman's expert hands. But her mind returned to Marshall. *Damn him!* She had come here to escape. But her thoughts continued to torment her.

"Taylor, this is Dave Johnson. Do you have a minute?"

Taylor transferred Dave's voice from the phone receiver to speaker, then checked that the door between her office and the store was still closed. She was hiding her bruises from her customers.

"You're back from the Canyon! Did you see the turquoise falls?"

"Yep. We got in last night and we did indeed see the falls. The whole family enjoyed it, even the jaded teenager twins." Dave laughed. "In spite of themselves, they actually smiled and laughed!"

"Beauty has its own way of getting to folks." If only Taylor could find more of it in her own life. She'd smile more too.

"Reason I called: There's something I'm curious about, like to discuss with you." Dave's voice turned serious. *"After our tour, we gave Marshall a ride to the park ranger's office so he could meet his next group. On the way, he kinda implied he was taking over the store, since you weren't capable of running it anymore. Is everything okay with you?"*

Taylor's throat went so dry, she was not sure she could speak. She choked down a sip of water.

"N-No, Dave," she squeaked. *"E-E-Everything's fine. You must have misunderstood."*

"Are you sure, Taylor?" Dave's voice expressed deep concern. *"You know I'm an attorney. And Marshall sounded pretty clear when he talked about a conservatorship and transfer of ownership documents."*

Taylor's whole body quivered. She took a deep breath to steady herself. She couldn't collapse now, for her children's sake if nothing else.

"D-Dave, I understand so li-little about legal documents and Marshall even l-l-less." Her attempt at laughter came out as a snort. *"I a...appreciate your concern, but the store is fine."*

Dave hesitated. "You know, my wife and I think the world of you and your kids. Really respect your abilities in running your business." His praise sounded genuine. *"Anything I can do to help, you'll let me know?"*

Taylor swallowed hard. "Th-Thank you s-s-so much. But really, everything's f-f-f-fine." Taylor felt like she was going to throw up. "I'm sorry, Dave—I gotta go. I appreciate your checking in."

Taylor dropped the phone and doubled over as reality hit: That document! She'd signed the store over to Marshall.

Taylor lay stone-still on the massage table, Marshall's betrayal still burning in the pit of her stomach. How dare he use physical violence to steal what she had worked so hard to build?

Marshall's treachery had turned Taylor into a whimpering child— at first. But then it had finally compelled her to take action. The OC was the only answer.

Buzzing bees swarmed in Taylor's stomach as she inserted her key into Wilderness Outfitters' bolted front door. The key stuck as she tried to turn it, causing fear to slice through her. Could Marshall have called someone in his absence to have the locks changed? She jiggled the key again and heard a loud click. Thank God. Calling a locksmith wasn't a bad idea, though. She'd do that tomorrow. After all, tonight marked the trailhead of her hike toward freedom. Shedding herself of Marshall's abuse and trickery. She pulled open the door.

At the sight of Erin getting out of her car, the bees in Taylor's stomach morphed into seagulls that dove straight into her gut. Her pulse increased to its mountain-climbing pace.

Erin's hug did little to quiet her demons. The contractor jogged in place as Taylor led the way inside and relocked the bolt. Had she ever seen Erin stand still?

Taylor moved ahead of her friend, flipping light switches, straightening clothing racks. Erin touched her friend's back with a gentle hand. Taylor jumped.

"What's wrong?" Erin's face softened. "Nervous?"

"Y…Yes." Taylor looked away and shuffled toward the back of the store. "A…About why I called you." Finally, Taylor stopped and steadied herself on a rack of trail books. She raised her head and her eyes locked with Erin's. "I want this to be the last time I have to worry about Marshall."

Erin's eyes widened. "Taylor, are you sure?" Erin reached to smooth her friend's tousled hair. "You've backed out before, after our pre-event counseling. I don't want any regrets."

Taylor looked around her shop, taking in the brilliant colors of the rain jackets, the racks of tank suits and bikinis, and the display of mountain bikes, helmets, and boots. She licked her lips. "Marshall forced me to sign the st-store over to him." She hiccupped. "If he comes back, he…he'll expect me to work here as always, but with him as my b-b-boss." She hiccupped again, even more loudly.

"That shit!" Erin punched her fist into her palm. "Wilderness Outfitters is your baby! You've nourished it for thirty-five years. How could he do that to you?"

Taylor lifted her shirt and showed Erin a still-angry six-inch bruise over her ribs. "The same way he could do th-this."

Erin gently lowered Taylor's shirt and nodded. "In that case, we have no time to lose. Operation Cascade is already in place—when do I leave?"

Chapter 12

CAROL PULLED HER VAN up to the park entrance and pointed to the "Sponsor" sign propped on her windshield. The guard that she and Mora had positioned there at sundown yesterday motioned them through the gate. As Carol pulled into the handicapped parking spot, the sun crested the hills east of the park.

Mora checked the dashboard clock. "Five forty-five a.m.; one hour to get set up for the marathon. Should be plenty of time."

"Operation Chase, here we come." Carol tapped the horn. "I hope we best the take for last year. Our outreach activities need a boost." She breathed in the perfume of newly mowed grass.

Mora nodded. "*And* Erin reminds us that two of the shelter residences need a coat of paint—one of them, both inside and out."

As Mora spoke, an athletic-looking woman in flowered pink leggings and a rose T-shirt approached the driver's side of the van.

"Hi, I'm Sharon Collins. Anything I can do to help?" The woman glanced at her watch and then looked back up at Mora and Carol. "I looked at the clock wrong and got up early. Got the poor kids up, too."

"Hi, Sharon. I'm Carol and this is Mora." Carol looked around. "Where'd you park the young ones?"

"They're playing games in the car."

Carol pointed to a picnic table at the opposite edge of the parking lot. "I could use a team over there to man the sign-in sheets and hand out the number shells. Are they old enough for that?"

"Sure, they're eleven and sixteen. Responsible, too." The young mother turned towards the old Honda at the far end of the lot. "I'll go get them."

While Mora unloaded the van, Sharon and her kids set up tables and Carol stacked the T-shirts.

Pushing a dolly loaded with water bottles, Mora approached Sharon. "I didn't get a chance to welcome you properly." Mora parked the hand truck and hefted a carton onto the table. She wiped her grimy hand on her white shorts and extended it toward the early arrival. "Thanks for coming. How did you hear about us?"

Sharon shook Mora's hand firmly. "I was fortunate enough to find one of your shelters six or so years ago when I *really* needed it. I've wanted to help ever since. So here I am!" The corner of her mouth dimpled. "I decided that since I jog every day to keep in shape for my job, the least I could do is enter the half-marathon. Make money for the shelters." She consulted a list she withdrew from her waist pouch. "In just one week's time, I got twenty people at work to pledge money for my run." She replaced the list and smiled. "What else can I do to help?"

"Here, take these to the next watering station," said Mora, handing her a carton of water bottles.

Carol had finished stacking shirts and rolled up to join them. Mora gave her a case of water as well, setting it on her lap.

"So, Sharon," said Carol, "what kind of work do you do?"

"I'm a deputy sheriff."

Mora swiped the sweat that popped out on her upper lip. She put her hands on her hips.

"Wow," said Carol, swigging from the almost empty water bottle she kept in the holder on her chair. "See many abuse cases?"

"Yes, ma'am. Every day! That's another reason I'm here: to help get the word out about your organization. We usually get called in too late."

Mora patted Sharon's arm. "Well, we appreciate your support." Sharon hefted the carton of water to her shoulder.

As she jogged off toward the next table, Carol let out a big sigh. "Whew! A policewoman in our midst. We'll have to be on our best behavior."

"A new member for the Outreach Committee?" Mora giggled as her friend threw her empty bottle at her.

Chapter 13

As the marathon was about to start, Carol gathered together her water volunteers. "Like a surgeon's assistant, you have to make sure you hit their hand." She smiled at the group: Sharon's kids and several women from the shelters. "There are at least a thousand runners here, and they'll be thirsty by the time they reach you." She rolled to a group of women waiting for the racers to pass by.

"Can we cheer the runners on? Margot from my shelter is running."

"Of course! The more cheering the better."

"Carol," a soft voice spoke from behind the others. "Are you sure we're safe from our men here?" Trudy Maris—whom Sharon had pointed out to Carol—closed her arm around her son's shoulder. "And what can I do with Ricky if I run?"

"Those are two very good questions." Carol swallowed hard. "As you go about your day, you always run the risk of your abuser finding you, if he's still at large. But know that we have taken every precaution to keep you safe here in the park."

"Is that why the patrol dogs were at the entrance?"

"Yes. And the reason you had to show a ticket to get in."

"But couldn't they sneak in the back way pretending to be a musician or something?"

"*Everybody*—including all the timekeepers, musicians, and other entertainers—had to be vetted and ticketed. We work with the police, sheriff, and a private investigator to ensure all of that."

Carol smiled at Ricky. "And *you* can help us out as a volunteer! That is, if your mom's going to run?" She raised an eyebrow at Trudy.

"Yeah." Trudy's lips parted in a half-smile; her eyes brightened. "As long as Ricky will be safe."

Carol reached for Ricky's hand. "Come on. I'll introduce you to Sharon's son and daughter. You can help them out while your mother races. In fact,"—she patted her knee—"I'll give you a ride there on my wheelie!"

Taylor glanced at her watch—again. Not really out of concern for the runners; more out of nervous habit.

Was Erin in the Canyon yet? Had she done the deed? Taylor couldn't remember the schedule they'd worked out. Fear threatened to freeze her brain.

And what if Erin *had* completed her mission? Could Taylor handle it? Being free—and responsible for Marshall's death? Did he really deserve it? She should have divorced him instead. Taylor pressed her fist against her abdomen, suddenly nauseous. She hadn't expected this guilt.

Taylor *already* lived a good third of her marriage without Marshall—when he was on his adventure trips. She managed her finances, the store, their home, without him. But she'd miss the telling of his trip when he returned. The animals he whittled while in the wilderness, his snapshots of rapids and multihued rock formations.

When Taylor was younger, she would have missed the glad-to-be-home sex, too. But the forced sex of later years had been a punishment, not passion. She was better off without it.

No, she shouldn't worry. She'd get by admirably.

But what about the effect of Marshall's absence on their children? They were grown now, but they still needed their father. Didn't they? If she'd divorced him, they could have stayed in contact.

"No!" Taylor's outburst startled even herself. She jumped, almost toppling the T-shirt table she was manning—or "womanning," as Erin liked to call it.

Marshall had told Taylor so many times—the last scornful shot less than a month ago—that he'd kill her before he'd let her divorce him. Taylor couldn't understand why staying married to her was so important to him, but for some reason it was. He'd never let go of her without a severe beating. She might not survive it.

Still…shouldn't she have been willing to risk her life for her children's sake?

Taylor put her thoughts on hold as the first batch of runners crossed the half-marathon finish line. She walked over to congratulate them and handed each an OC Race Finisher T-shirt with her store's logo on it.

This is what I should be doing, she thought. *Helping abused women—not worrying about Marshall. He deserves what he gets.*

Chapter 14

MORA WAITED PATIENTLY at the full marathon's finish line.
"According to my calculations, we have about half an hour until the lead runners come around the bend." She turned to Sharon, who had joined her after completing the half-marathon. "How did *you* do?"

Sharon shook her head. "I was in the second pod." She rolled up on her toes and back. "Still, my time was better than I expected."

As the women talked, a small pack of newspaper reporters gathered in the parking lot behind them, joking amongst themselves and assessing angles for a standout photo.

"I wish I'd signed up to run the whole thing," said Sharon. "I procrastinated when the flyer came in, and then used the entrance fee as an excuse." She sighed. "A small sign that my 'fear of success' shadows me. The shelter really helped me grow out of that, but it still rears its ugly head sometimes."

"Which shelter were you in, Sharon? I don't remember counseling you."

"The northern one in Torrance. My counselor there said she was a fill-in."

"We have to rely on outsiders when the load is heavy, like around the holidays." Mora glanced down the racecourse. "Was she helpful?"

"She's the reason I'm here. She challenged me to overcome my poor self-image and do something to help other women." Sharon swiped her eyes. "Back then, I never would have dreamed I'd become a sheriff."

There was something in this woman Mora found attractive. Must be her openness about her feelings. "How long did you stay in the shelter?"

"Six months. Afterwards, I went back to junior college to study criminology. It was hard doing all that—working and being a single mom." Sharon nodded toward her kids. "They kept me going. I could see them relax after their dad went to jail."

"Good for you! Have you run marathons before?" Mora admired the runners she met at these meets, but she had no desire to race with them. She preferred the elliptical machine at the gym. It kept her trim for her frequent trips to the mountains, and that was enough.

"Only this same OC one, when I was in the shelter. Matron insisted we all do something athletic; said the endorphins would help erase our bad moods." She looked down at her shoes and smiled. "I didn't do well, but I wore that T-shirt until it was in shreds. It was the first time I'd ever done something like that."

Mora pointed to Sharon's children. Mike and Cailin sat on the curb, disposable camera at the ready. "Your kids have been a great help this morning. Who's that little boy with them?"

"That's Trudy Maris' son. I took him and his mom to the South Torrance shelter last week. We're still looking for her husband."

Mora nodded sympathetically. "How are *your* kids doing with Dad gone?"

"Most days, okay." Sharon glanced at her children taking pictures of each other and Ricky. "I know, from what they say occasionally, that they miss their dad. But they seem to accept that he shouldn't be living with us—should stay in prison."

"Do they go see him there?"

Sharon nodded. "About once a year, when their grandparents, his mother and stepfather, come to town. The kids are very quiet and moody for a day or so afterwards, so I don't know how they really feel about him. Knowing him, I'm sure he charms them."

"Other than the abuse—obviously—was he a good dad?"

"Yes…*when* he was sober."

Mora's heart went out to this woman. She was the poster model of success for their organization. The BWEF would benefit greatly from her presence. But was that too risky? She'd have to direct Sharon's activities away from the OC.

"Sharon, I'd like you to become an active supporter of the BWEF," Mora said firmly.

Sharon's eyes lit up, then her smile turned to a worried frown. "I'm not sure I have much to contribute." She laughed. "Certainly not money."

Mora gestured toward the runners. "We have other means to support our work." She took Sharon's hand. "We want to help you make contacts in the community. You're out there where abused women most need to hear about us." *Besides,* thought Mora, *you need to be kept out of the boardroom.* She patted the deputy's hand. "Please consider joining us."

After the last half-marathoner checked in, Taylor dazedly made her way to the full-race finish line.

"Glad you made it in time." Mora gave Taylor a hug and then turned to her companion. "Taylor, meet Sharon Collins. She's a deputy sheriff who deals with domestic violence cases."

"Hi! Can I help you give those out?" asked Sharon.

Taylor started. She turned away from the deputy to hand a T-shirt to a finisher. Could the sheriff see her hands shaking? Taylor took three deep breaths before turning back around and shaking hands with Sharon.

"W-w-welcome. We a...appreciate your help." Lips trembling, Taylor smiled at Mora. "W-w-wasn't the turnout great?"

Carol approached, her face flushed and eyes sparkling. "Twenty percent over last year!" she answered Taylor's question. She raised her hand for a high five. "Did you meet Sharon, Taylor?" Carol's eyebrow raised. Taylor nodded and swallowed hard.

"Mora asked me to help the BWEF with community liaison," said Sharon. "Isn't that great?"

Biting her lips, Taylor nodded. She saw Carol's eyes widen.

"I don't know about you all," said Carol, recovering, "but I'm bushed. I think it's time to leave. The cleanup team can wait for the stragglers and clear the route at the same time."

Mora put her arms around Taylor and Sharon. "Tea time."

"I'm sorry, but I can't stay," said Sharon. "I have to take the kids home and get ready for work."

Taylor's sigh whooshed out like a wind gust. Mora tightened her hug.

"Erin would have really enjoyed today," said Carol as the OC members made their way to the van.

Taylor dodged a young mother receiving hugs from two blond teens—girls about the age of her own granddaughters—and her stomach took a nosedive. Marshall's death would affect not only her own kids, she realized, but her precious twin granddaughters. Wouldn't they suffer by their grandfather's not being around to teach them about the wilderness? He always brought them a treasure when he came home: a uniquely patterned rock, an Indian craft, or one of his carvings. What had she done—depriving them of his attention?

In fact, Marshall spent more time with his granddaughters than he had his own children. *Up until recently,* Taylor realized. Come to think of it, her own visits with her granddaughters had declined dramatically too. She'd have to remedy that.

Chapter 15

"MOM! WHAT ARE YOU DOING HERE? Is the marathon over already?" Taylor hugged her daughter tightly. "I *n-needed* to see you." She gratefully accepted the glass of lemon ice water her daughter fixed for her.

"What's up, Mom?" Ruth's face filled with concern.

"I'd like to t-take the girls to the beach on Sunday. Gi-Give you a break."

Ruth squirmed, clearly uncomfortable. "Mom, I'll check our family calendar and get back to you. Okay?"

Taylor frowned. So, it wasn't her imagination. Why was her daughter so hesitant about letting her take the kids these days? Had she done something counter to her daughter's modern mothering techniques? Or were the teens resisting spending time with the old folks?

"I gu…guess it's okay." Taylor sank onto the large stool at the kitchen counter. "No!" The strength of her conviction startled even her. "It's *not* okay." She held her daughter's gaze. "What's going on, Ruthie? Why am I seeing so little of the girls lately?"

"Mom, I…I…" Poor Ruthie sounded so stressed. Taylor's mom radar went into full alert.

"Out with it."

Ruthie cleared her throat twice, and then once again. "I…It's that I want to be sure Dad will be gone." She looked down at her hands.

Taylor tried to calm her rising hysteria. *Oh, yes, he'll definitely be gone,* she wanted to say.

Taylor brushed her daughter's hair out of her face. "Wh…why? Do his gruff ways scare them?" Taylor had tried *so* hard to protect both her children and her grandchildren from the worst of Marshall's tirades. Apparently she hadn't done as good a job as she thought.

"Yes, there's that…" Ruthie looked uncomfortable again. "But…"

"But?"

Ruthie's words came out in a rush. "I don't want to give him the chance to hit on the twins' friends, like he did *my* friends when I was their age." Taylor's heart broke at Ruthie's sob. What was Ruthie saying? What had Taylor allowed to happen? "What if he starts in on them?" Ruthie continued. "Or abuses them?"

"Hit on? You mean, s-s-sexually?"

Ruthie's nod was wooden. "Mom, I didn't want to tell you. Didn't want to hurt you."

Taylor shook her head numbly. What kind of a mother was she? Why hadn't she seen something was wrong?

She had to ask: "Di…did he ever…I mean, did you ever…" Taylor couldn't finish the sentence.

Ruth shook her head. "Thankfully, no. It was directed only at my friends. And he didn't force any unwilling participants."

Taylor felt sick. Had Marshall hit on her own friends, too? She'd sensed he had affairs while on his trips. But fearful of physical and emotional pain, she'd never challenged him about it; though she'd made sure to check her own body regularly for STDs. Still, she'd never dreamed he would try for underage girls.

"Honey, are you saying that Dad was seducing your friends and you didn't tell me?" Taylor swiped at the tears slipping down her cheeks.

"He said he'd kill you if I told," Ruth whispered.

Taylor doubled over, clutching her stomach. Her beautiful daughter having to watch her own father— And then being threatened by him? Taylor couldn't bear to think about it. Though she could at least take solace in the certainty that she had finally done the right thing.

"Ruthie, I n…need to hug you. I am so sorry." She squeezed her daughter tight, holding her until Ruthie finally squirmed and pulled away. "Honey, I had n-n-no idea! You *have* to believe me. I would n-never, *ever* have l...let you go through that."

Ruth nodded. "I believe you, Mom." She wiped her own tears. "Now, let's have something stronger than water while I look at our schedules. I know the twins miss seeing you."

Chapter 16

"Taylor, it's Erin. Meet me at Starbucks. The twenty-four-hour one."

Taylor looked at her alarm radio. It was four in the morning. She was wide awake.

"Now?"

"As soon as you can. I've been up all night. Once I hit the bed, I'll stay there for the rest of the day."

"T-ten minutes."

Taylor struggled into a sweatshirt and pulled on her jeans. Combing her hair with her right hand, she grabbed her car keys from the hook with her left. She was numb with lack of sleep; she could use that coffee. Her hand shook as she started the car. Maybe she should get decaf.

She might not be safe to drive. Should she call a cab? No, the streets were empty—she could make it. No one to bump into. Or to notice she was driving erratically.

Taylor parked her car in the small lot next to the nearly deserted coffee shop. Her body was paralyzed; she couldn't get out.

What would Erin tell her? Was it possible Marshall was really gone? Was Taylor now free from the demeaning words, the pain, the bruises to hide from the kids and her friends? Was Ruthie free from fear, too? Were Taylor's granddaughters and their friends now safe?

Taylor pulled the key from the ignition. In slow motion, she picked up her purse and slid out of the seat. Somehow she compelled her legs to move her to the coffee shop door.

Erin's hug was so tight it smothered. Taylor's heart pounded as she felt her friend tremble.

"I needed to see you right away." Erin pulled away breathlessly. "It was awful and awesome at the same time."

"I'm g-g-glad you're safe."

Taylor looked over Erin's shoulder at the one other customer in the shop: an L.A. County deputy. Taylor's eyes fixed on his gun. Had he followed Erin? Taylor braced herself against the counter, then relaxed as he took a tray of coffee out to the black-and-white at the curb. Would she be afraid of the law forever now?

"Let's take our coffee down to the beach to watch the sunrise," Erin said.

The two were silent on the walk downhill to the Strand. Taylor waited until they reached the wet sand and the voice-covering surf's roar before she spoke. "Tell me everything. I need to know exactly what happened. To make su-sure. To bring me closure—p...peace." The two walked slowly, their feet leaving shallow prints in the sand.

"Peace you shall have." Erin gripped her friend's hand. "You're a free woman, Taylor. Your ordeal is *over*."

A tidal wave of emotion swept over Taylor: elation, fear, relief, guilt. She squeezed Erin's hand and gazed at the surf as a beach security control vehicle rolled by.

"Are you su-sure?" she finally whispered. "Did he g-go over the f...f...falls?"

"Yes." Erin nodded repeatedly. "I made sure of it. I couldn't see around the river bend, but I heard it all. Sound really carries in the Canyon."

Taylor shook her head to will away the mental images. Even though she needed to know every detail, she didn't want to imagine Marshall's actual fall, his moment of impact, his—

Erin bowed her head. "It was much harder than I thought it would be. Much harder." She gulped her coffee. "Making sure he believed I was interested in him, putting him on, that was the easy part—but then, we *knew* that would work." Erin's accompanying smirk lacked its usual edge. "The second part—leaping overboard and sabotaging the raft— that took all my strength, both physical and mental."

Both women fell silent.

"Didn't it b…bother you?" Taylor finally spoke. "To actually d-d-do something like that? Especially for someone else?"

Erin stretched her back. "Shit. It bothered me a lot. I listened to the Anonymous Four's chants all the way back to Las Vegas to help calm me. And every time my mind returned to Marshall's screams—his guttural cry when he went over the falls—I thought about the bruised ribs you showed me. I focused on the lives I'd helped save from further destruction. That turned the screams to gentle music."

Taylor's stomach grumbled and she bent over gagging, her body repulsed by the information. Marshall had been horrible to Taylor and had inflicted so much pain. Still, the thought of him—

Erin rubbed Taylor's back as she continued to heave for several minutes.

Taylor finally lowered herself to the sand, feeling limp. Empty. Erin offered her some coffee, which she took with a shaky hand to help soothe her ragged throat.

Taylor looked at her friend—usually so strong and unruffled—with new sympathy. "I'm forever ever *ever* in your debt." She meant it.

Erin shrugged. "I know. *I* owe everything to all the OC gals who helped *me*." She rubbed a scar on her forehead, her permanent memento of abuse. Holding her coffee in both hands, she took a long sip. "Anyway, he's gone; that's the important thing. He either died from the fall or drowned." Erin paused and clasped Taylor's hand. "Oh, I'm sorry to be so insensitive. You look so sad."

Taylor *was* overcome with sadness. Marshall could have been such a neat, caring man, husband, father. Why had he chosen to be a tyrant? A monster? Was it something genetic—and should she worry about her kids getting it? Was he *really* gone?

"What about other people—could they have heard him? Called someone?"

"No one else was in the Canyon at that spot. I hiked the trail before and after. Besides, it's already been a week, and no news has been reported. I've been holed up in Vegas just in case. I tried to get something out of the Building Products trade show there, but I couldn't get interested in anything. Not even the giveaway stuff." Erin raised up her coffee cup. "So enough of sadness and worry. Let's forget the past and drink to your future."

Taylor lifted her own cup in a reluctant toast.

Chapter 17

SHARON COLLINS STOPPED chopping onions when she heard whispering behind her. It had already been a tedious oh-so-Monday-ish Monday...what now?

She turned to look at her kids. "What?"

Her son, Mike, looked up at her. "Mom...are you and Dad going to get back together?"

Now, where did that come from?

Mike's sister, Cailin, looked up from her homework at the kitchen table. Two sets of intense blue-gray eyes focused on Sharon; one set fearful, the other, defiant.

Sharon closed her eyes in silent prayer. She wanted to be a good parent, but having her ex-husband—a husband who'd abused her—in prison complicated things. She couldn't seem to close this issue.

"No, we're not. I've explained this to you both before." She turned from the stove. "Why are you asking, Mike?"

"There's a Little League father-son banquet this Friday; I want to go." Mike looked down at his grimy fingers, shoulders drooping forward. "We have to turn in our list of names tomorrow after school."

Mike had always felt the breakup of the marriage more keenly than Cailin. Probably because of things like this—he needed more male influence. God knows Sharon tried, but she was his mother, not his dad.

Sharon put down her knife and walked to where her son was sitting. She cupped his chin in her hand and pushed sun-bleached hair from his eyes. "Honey, if it were possible, I'd let you call your dad and ask him to go with you. You know that, don't you?"

"Yeah, but..."

"But what?"

"You're too young to remember what Dad was like, Mike," Cailin broke in. "He even hit *you* once when you were crying."

Sharon remained silent. She was saddened, despite everything, by Cailin's hurtful memories of her father.

Mike ignored his sister. He started to get up, but his mother's firm pressure on his shoulder prevented it.

"Mom, Dad was drunk!" Mike wrenched himself free. "He didn't know what he was doing."

Sharon tried to envelope him in a hug, but he continued to resist her embrace. He jumped up and faced her, arms crossed.

"I mean it, Mom. He didn't know what he was doing." Earnest eyes pleaded with her. "Why didn't you—*don't* you—give him a second chance?"

Sharon approached her son slowly, and this time he let her put her arms around him.

"I gave him a hundred second chances," she said quietly.

"Remember what they taught us in Al-Anon?" Cailin interrupted. "Excusing behavior because someone is drunk doesn't help the poor person who should never drink again."

Sharon smiled at her daughter. Cailin would be an adult soon. Sharon was proud of her independent spirit.

"Besides, it wouldn't be the same if he came back to live with us, Bikey Mikey." Cailin sat up straight and flipped her ponytail. "*I* feel like I don't know him anymore, like I wouldn't know what to talk to him about." She shot a dare at her brother: "You wouldn't either. You'd probably get all tongue-tied like you did when you had to make a speech in geography." She slapped her brother's shoulder.

Sharon returned to the stove and dumped the chopped onions into a skillet.

"But Mom, at church, they teach us to forgive." Mike came up behind his mother. "Don't you believe that?"

Sharon turned to face him. "Yes, I do; and I've tried very hard to forgive your father." Sharon patted her son's cheek.

Mike rubbed his eyes with his sleeve surreptitiously, obviously not wanting his mom to mention his tears. She didn't.

"I remember that time he came to get his clothes," said Cailin. "He did say he was sorry." Cailin looked guilty for defending her brother.

Sharon walked over to her daughter and enclosed Cailin's hands in her own. "He *was* sincerely sorry, each time he sobered up after hurting me. I believe that with all my heart. But that didn't prevent him from repeating the same pattern again and again and again." Sharon's voice trailed off into remembered horror.

Sharon returned to Mike and took his chin in her hand so he faced her squarely. "I'd give *anything* to be able to give you guys a real family, with a mom and dad at home. But your father and I had some big problems, and it's better if we're apart."

Dropping her hand to her side, Sharon sighed. She had forgiven her ex many things in order that she could go on with her life. But what she could not forgive—or allow—was making a six-year-old boy and a thirteen-year-old girl face the reality of living with an abusive alcoholic.

Sharon engaged Cailin and then Mike with her eyes. "You *both* need to remember that you could have inherited a tendency to become an alcoholic, like Dad, Granddad, and several others in his family," she said. "You can't prevent the tendency, but you can surely do something about not drinking."

She waited for each child to nod before continuing.

"I left your father for several reasons, one of which was his hurting me. Another was that I didn't want you two to grow up thinking that abuse, verbal *or* physical, man against woman or woman against man, is a normal part of marriage."

Sharon dropped her spoon and faced her son again. "If I never teach you anything else, Mike, I want you to know that you never, *ever* have the right to hit a woman or a child."

"And honey,"—she sat down across from her daughter—"I hope you never have to experience what I went through." She stroked Cailin's hair gently. "There's something I learned in the shelter—something that you, and all of your girlfriends, need to remember: No woman should stay with a man who hits her. Whether you're his wife, daughter, girlfriend, sister, or a stranger. Men who do that need help, certainly; but because of the difference in physical strength, women best stay away from them in the meantime, no matter how much they think they love them."

"But Mom, he's our dad!" Mike blurted.

"That's true, Mom," said Cailin hesitantly.

Sharon breathed deeply. "And he loves you, as you love him. I know that and welcome it. But love shouldn't be blind. You can accept and love him *with* his flaws—not as an idol on a pedestal. Okay?"

Mike and Cailin looked at each other and nodded, apparently accepting her words.

Sharon gave each of her children a bear hug.

"Mike, I bet if you ask Harry to go to the banquet, he'd say yes." At her son's relieved smile, Sharon continued, "Enough of this serious talk. It's time for dinner and then homework. Mike, go wash up and set the table. Cailin, you pour the milk."

Chapter 18

"Y<small>OU HAVE A LOVELY HOME</small>, Ms. Whitmore." Quentin Pryor smiled charmingly at Taylor. "But may I ask why we're having a meeting here instead of the charity's offices? I don't like to be a stick in the mud, but this *is* a business meeting." Quentin handed his briefcase to Leigh who'd followed him in; Mora and Carol trailed them, with Erin bringing up the rear.

"G…Good morning, Quentin." Taylor smiled with tight lips. "Th-Th-Thank you for the compliment; I wish this were my home!" What an exhausting week she'd had! It'd been five sleepless days since Erin had delivered the news about Marshall. She was still trying to deal with her guilt and fear. She'd thought about canceling this meeting, but this was her pet project and they needed Quentin's approval to proceed. Besides, it gave her something to think about other than how she should act when she received official notice of Marshall's death. If she didn't think about his death, she'd act more surprised when they told her, wouldn't she?

Taylor motioned the group. "Follow me, please. We'll start the tour of this project in the kitchen. I have c-coffee and goodies ready for you."

"Oh, look! A circular countertop and *two* stoves!" Mora crossed the large expanse of kitchen and opened an oven door to look inside.

"Better yet: two freezers!" said Carol, pointing to the side-by-side refrigerators. "I could store a month's worth of butter pecan ice cream in there! Of course,"—she patted her stomach—"it would just end up *here.*"

"Well, you can have those," said Erin. "I'll take the two dishwashers—and maids to go with them." She looked at her calloused palms. "My hands take enough beating on the job. Subjecting them to damned dishwater is torture."

Leigh walked to the archway opposite the door they'd entered. "And look at this! I know I'm jumping ahead a little,"—she glanced sideways at Taylor—"but the great room could seat at least thirty for family gatherings—or a charity meeting."

Taylor returned Leigh's smile, gaining confidence from the enthusiasm in the room. Quentin's presence still made her nervous, but despite his apparent confusion, he seemed to be in good spirits.

Once everyone had poured coffee and taken a seat at the breakfast counter, Taylor tapped a spoon against her cup. "With this house, we can raise one hundred percent of next year's operating funds." She smiled at each of them in turn. "*If* you agree to this project, that is."

"Exactly what are you ladies up to now?" Quentin's smile was teasing. "I haven't received a briefing on any new money-raising proposal."

"It's Taylor's Operation Chance," said Carol. "Our charity house raffle!"

Taylor grinned. "But don't feel left out, Quentin. No one got a briefing. While we tour the house, I'll detail the project plan. I thought it would be best if everyone heard the information at the same time."

Quentin looked at the others' eager faces and then back to Taylor. "Okay, you win—*this* one. But don't expect me to cast a vote until I have reviewed *written* information thoroughly." He pointed to Taylor's laptop, propped open on the counter. "You've made copies of your presentation for us?"

"Yes—but to hand out at the *end* of the tour." Taylor gave Quentin her best smile. "It's an old trick. I want your full attention while I talk."

"Touché," said Quentin, raising an eyebrow.

Taylor breathed a sigh of relief. She wanted to do a good job and really wanted this man's approval of her idea. She felt strongly that it would benefit the BWEF in a big way.

Taylor forced herself to stay calm. "We can raise the operating funds I mentioned by buying this home and raffling it off," said Taylor. "We can sell twenty thousand raffle tickets for two hundred and fifty dollars each."

The room was silent as all eyes turned to Quentin. Taylor held her breath.

"You're proposing that the Battered Women's Escape Foundation support a *gambling* scheme?" Quentin's tone was incredulous.

Taylor slumped. Not exactly the reaction she was hoping for.

"Oh, Quentin dear!" Leigh laughed loudly and laid a hand on her husband's arm. "You *do* have a way with words!" She turned to the group. "Don't let his hard-nosed attitude get you down, ladies! I'm sure you'll win him over with the rest of your proposal."

Taylor shot Leigh a grateful look. Then she straightened her back. The bank had recommended Quentin for his expertise with small businesses; but *she* was an expert too. Hadn't she created Wilderness Outfitters from nothing? Besides, Quentin was merely doing his job: asking her questions because he wanted the BWEF to win. Win big! So she needed to do her job, too—and answer them.

"This type of fundraiser has already proven its viability," said Taylor, leading the group into the foyer as she spoke. Then she faced Quentin directly. "It worked for our own PV Art Center, and art centers in Tucson and Santa Barbara as well."

Quentin met her gaze. "Are you sure that those raffle sales weren't simply disguised ways of supporting the arts? Something beautiful?" He looked around at each of them. "*Your* organization supports something ugly, something people don't like to think about."

Taylor gasped, accompanied by every other woman in the room, including Leigh.

Quentin raised his hands in surrender. "I'm just trying to be realistic, ladies. Sorry if I wasn't politically correct."

Taylor smiled a little at his discomfort. He was learning about them at the same time they were trying to understand him.

"I agree," said Mora loudly. Taylor looked at her in shock. "We should *all* try to be realistic," she continued. Mora turned to Quentin. "And *realistically* speaking, we do recognize that you have much more business experience than we do. And believe me, we're honored to have you here. But the other reality is that we owe it to Taylor to listen to her complete presentation with open minds before passing judgment. She's put a lot of thought and effort into this."

Taylor looked at the ground, both pleased and intimidated by Mora's words. She prayed she wouldn't embarrass them all.

"I'd like to hear it," said a timid voice from the corner of the room.

Quentin's head jerked around at his wife's comment. But he recovered quickly and turned back to the group.

"Of course, ladies." He cleared his throat. "Ms. Whitmore, please proceed. I will follow you around and listen, until you ask for questions. However," he said, looking pointedly at his watch, "my time is unfortunately limited." He looked back at Taylor. "You have thirty minutes to convince me."

At the top of the stairs, the ladies waited for Carol. "The elevator alone sells me," said Carol as she rolled onto the upstairs landing. "Where do I buy a ticket?"

Taylor smiled at her. Gosh, she loved these women.

"You can tell from all the a-amenities that this is a l-l-l...luxury home." Taylor struggled to keep her mind clear and focus on her presentation. "But I made sure our inspector went over it thoroughly." She looked around the room for support as Quentin thumbed through the sales brochure Erin had distributed.

"Quentin." Erin paused until the banker looked up. "I want you to know that we used the same inspector that we use when we purchase a shelter. He's licensed, and very thorough." She pointed to the ceiling. "We made sure the roof is sound, and the entire house is newly painted—in and out." She waved her hand towards the double-sized master bath. "The baths and kitchen are modern, all with high-quality copper plumbing." Erin's periwinkle eyes twinkled up at Quentin. "No fixer-upper for us!"

Quentin nodded in acknowledgment, but his poker face told Taylor nothing. This man was so frustrating!

Taylor led the group toward the dressing rooms.

"This walk-in closet is the size of my kitchen!" said Carol.

"And that's for the *man* of the house!" Leigh's voice sparkled. "Look at the *woman's* dressing room: a makeup mirror and sink, shoe racks to the ceiling, and lots of hanging space. They've thought of everything!"

The women oohed and ahhed their collective pleasure.

Taylor moved to the door. "Shall we continue?"

Pryor gestured at Taylor. "This is your show."

Taylor took another fortifying breath. "We have only a few more rooms to view up here. After you look at the backyard, outdoor kitchen, and four-car garage, my tour will be over." She smiled through stiff lips at Quentin. "And this nice man can get back to his real job."

As they strode onto the back patio, Quentin asked, "Where did the funds come from for the inspector you talked about?" He barely looked at the expanse of lawn, the pool, the ocean view, or the rose arbor that led to a quiet area. Boy, this man really was all business!

"Quentin, you'll see when we g-go over our b...books with you, that we have contingency funds specifically for home purchase expenses." Taylor decided to skip the yard for now and steered Quentin toward the garage. The others followed.

"I'm familiar with your accounts, Ms. Whitmore," Quentin said smoothly, motioning Leigh to precede him through the garage door. "And according to my understanding, that fund is for the abused-women shelters."

"We'll pay the contingency fund back from the raffle income," Taylor replied quickly.

Quentin's eyes narrowed, but he said nothing.

"I'll show you the paper later, Quentin." Erin shouldered Taylor aside. "But suffice it to say, the money's use for this purpose is consistent with our bylaws."

Taylor's shoulders relaxed. Thank God for Erin! She always knew how to deal with tough people.

"The owners are anxious to sell," Taylor continued, glad to be back on solid footing. "They're transferring to the East Coast. Their furniture will be leaving in about three weeks." She glanced at her notes. "What else? Here it is: the school system is the Peninsula. There's also a well-known private school nearby."

Taylor folded her notes and faced Quentin.

"Am I free to ask questions now?" he teased her. Taylor laughed and nodded.

"Okay, then. Let's forget the realtor's pitch and get to the bottom line. How much?"

I bet he's this way with all his clients, Taylor thought. *I probably shouldn't take it personally.* But it was hard not to.

Taylor braced herself. "The listing price is 3.1 million. Our realtor feels we can get it for 2.6, or maybe even 2.5."

Quentin nodded, apparently unfazed by the sum. "Forgive my saying so," he replied, "but all that money *could* be put directly to the stated objective of your organization."

Erin smiled sweetly. "But this project will generate over three-quarters of a million dollars towards operating expenses—and *cut* our other fundraising costs."

"I'm still not convinced that you can get twenty-thousand people to spend two hundred and fifty dollars on your scheme."

Taylor sighed. Did he have to keep calling it a "scheme"? She led the group back to the kitchen and poured a cup of coffee for Quentin. She lifted an empty mug toward Leigh, who shook her head.

"We have secondary prizes that will attract purchasers as well," said Taylor. "From five hundred to a thousand dollars. Participants could double or quadruple their money on those alone."

Quentin cocked his head, appearing to consider this. "I'll need to see a comprehensive financial analysis," he said sternly.

"Oh you will, Quentin," said Erin, reaching for a chocolate croissant.

Quentin sat back in his chair and interlocked his fingers. "What if the winner doesn't want the house? Or can't come up with the required taxes?"

"We put the house back on the market and give them the guaranteed amount," Taylor said, gaining confidence. "In fact, the art center resold their house last year for a ten percent profit over their purchase price—in addition to the raffle proceeds."

"Madam, we are in a soft housing market at this time," said Quentin. "There *is* downside potential." He looked at his Rolex.

Taylor bit her trembling lip. "Of c...course. But we'd still have the proceeds from the ticket sales—enough to meet and exceed our six-month budget!"

Quentin glanced at his watch again. "Ms. Whitmore, I'm sorry to say I've run out of time. However, I'll look forward to reviewing your written proposal."

Taylor nodded. "I'll send it right over to the bank," she promised. At least she'd survived Phase One!

Erin reached for her datebook. "Quentin, I'd be happy to meet with you in your office to discuss the financial analysis and any other questions you have about the idea." She waited for Taylor's nod before opening her calendar. "Is next Monday agreeable?"

"You'll have to check with Kyle, my assistant. He keeps my schedule."

With that, Pryor nodded to each of the women, motioned to his wife, and left the room.

Leigh smiled at the women on her way out. "Thank you so much for your patience with my husband's questions. I hope you know how much he cares. As do I. In fact, we appreciate *all* you do."

What a nice woman, thought Taylor, watching Leigh hurry to Quentin's waiting car.

A sudden overwhelming sorrow shook Taylor as she gazed at the expansive flower garden.

Her reverie was interrupted by Erin's approach. "Damn, you did a great job today, you free spirit!" Erin opened her arms to her friend.

"Thank you." Taylor accepted the hug and stood back, looking at her feet. "You helped me out so much."

"It was no problem," said Erin. "With a man like Quentin, sometimes you have to take the bull by the horns."

"No—I mean, thank you for that too!" Taylor laughed softly. "But what I meant was…" She looked up and met Erin's gaze. "What I meant was that, thanks to you, I really *am* free." Taylor's words came out in a whisper as she absorbed the aftermath of her sorrow.

But why hadn't she been notified? Surely Marshall's body had been found by now. She didn't want to say anything to Erin, afraid her friend might think she was ungrateful. But these thoughts kept rising, in spite of her effort to ban them.

Allowing her body and mind to finally relax, Taylor realized that the tension and stress of today's presentation *was* nothing compared to her relief in knowing she wouldn't have to sneak around or face Marshall's wrath for participating.

"How can I ever th…thank you for what you've given me?" She looked at Erin earnestly.

"That's easy." Erin shrugged. "Do what I did. Help someone the same way I helped you. Shit—it isn't that difficult if you do your homework."

Taylor hugged Erin, her emotions frazzled. Although she welcomed her relief from domestic violence, Taylor doubted she could do what Erin had done.

PART III

Operation Commander

Chapter 19

QUENTIN CLUTCHED THE STEERING WHEEL, his knuckles white. Those do-gooder women were going to be the death of him. Why had they accepted his appointment if they were going to waste his time and experience with these endless amateurish and weak money-making projects? They might as well hold a car wash at the corner gas station.

He had no idea how that Taylor What's-Her-Name stayed in business, with all the crazy ploys *she* came up with. Erin Craig wasn't much better; from the look of her hands, she had to dig and hammer with the manual laborers to maintain her contracting business. And then there was that shrink, Mora Rey—always watching and analyzing him. Like he needed *that*. She was the worst of the entire bunch.

"You can let me out at the next corner, Quentin. I'd fancy a walk home to get some exercise." Leigh reached for the door handle.

Quentin slammed on his brakes, skidding to a stop on the isolated street. He grabbed his wife's arm. "You think you're getting off that easy?" he asked, twisting her to face him. He pulled the car over to the curb and shoved the lever into park.

"First of all, you are never *ever* to contradict me in a meeting. Do you understand?"

"I didn't—" Leigh bit her lip.

"*You* said you wanted to see that horrible Cinderella house after *I* said I wanted to see a briefing paper first." He punched her in the side and she cried out. "Those women are a bunch of losers. If you were in commerce, you'd see right through them. Instead, you embarrass me by acting like one of them. '*I'd like to see it.*'" He mocked her words in a high-pitched sneer.

"And furthermore, you are *never* to apologize for me. When I ask questions, I do it for a business purpose that I wouldn't expect you or those do-gooder women to understand." His fist hammered her shoulder. "And saying *we* thank those women for all they do—what a phony you are! You couldn't possibly know what they do after attending *three* board meetings. And you certainly don't know whether *I* thank them or not."

Leigh looked at her lap. "I'm sorry, Quentin. I'll not say anything in the meetings unless you ask me to."

Yeah, fat chance! Quentin looked at his watch. He didn't have any more time to drive the point home right now. He'd have to remind her again later.

"It's not only the meetings. You are never to speak for me under *any* circumstances. Understand?" He emphasized his demand with a twist of her arm. Leigh grunted and nodded.

"Well, what are you waiting for?" God, the woman was a simpering idiot! "Get going!"

As Leigh fumbled with her seat belt, Quentin reached across her and opened the passenger door. As soon as Leigh freed herself, Quentin pushed her onto the curb, pulled the door shut, and drove off.

Chapter 20

ERIN BOLTED AWAKE. She couldn't see through the darkness. *Where am I? What's happened? Why is my heart beating so fast?*

Oh. She steadied her breathing. *Another dream.* She'd been back in the Canyon.

Erin pulled off her sweat-soaked nightgown and headed for the shower. She needed to wash the smell of fear from her skin. Showers calmed her. She'd used them often in the years before Benning died, when he'd been so abusive.

Erin looked at the clock. It was five past three. *Might as well stay up—finish the assignments for today's weekend crew.*

As she dressed in her jeans and pink T, Erin thought about the home they were renovating today. She liked remodeling better than building new houses; it offered more challenges. And doing pro-bono work for the handicapped was best of all, even though she made no money on it. She wished she could do more. Helping someone start a new life—when they'd lost hope—gave her joy. Like she'd done for Taylor in the Canyon.

Chapter 21

"Trudy? Hi. I'm Erin Craig. Are you ready to wield a hammer?" Erin pushed open the passenger door of the pink truck's cab and beckoned Trudy inside.

"Oh, Erin, I *am*. Excited, too. And grateful. I worked as a clerk long ago for a builder." She frowned. "That's where I met Rick."

Trudy climbed into the passenger seat, pushing aside a tool belt to find room for her feet. "But working outdoors always sounded a lot more fun." Trudy's face clouded. "Are you sure I can learn to be a carpenter?"

Trudy's stooped posture and unsure smile could have been Erin's own, six years ago. It would be a while until the new shelter resident felt safe, and proud of her independence. Erin would be teaching her a trade that would help.

"I'm very sure. And after today, you will be too." Erin laughed as she turned the truck around. "You'll be marathon-tired, covered with sawdust, and absolutely *positive* you can hammer nails."

Erin pointed at Trudy's feet. "That's your gear for today. You'll be working as a rough carpenter."

"I don't want to make mistakes."

"Well, you will." Erin smiled. "But that's all part of the learning process. Are you interested in long-term work?"

"Oh yes, Erin. I mean, of course I need a job." Trudy hesitated. "But more than anything, I want to build Ricky and me a home. Doesn't have to be big. I was reading about Habitat for Humanity yesterday and the homes they help people put together." She turned towards Erin. "Do you think it's possible they would help me get a home?"

"Yes—if you help them build it." Erin patted Trudy's knee. "If you're serious, we can start you this Monday on one of our regular jobs as a traveler."

"What's a traveler?"

"We put you on as an extra hand with whoever needs help. That way you learn lots of skills."

Trudy's face flushed with excitement. "Oh, Erin—thank you so much! And of course I'll work for free while I'm learning—at least while I'm still at the shelter."

Erin shook her head vigorously. "No. Not Monday—or ever." It was important that these women learn immediately to stop devaluing themselves. "I pay all my workers the going wage for the work they do for me." She smiled. "Except today—this is different. We're *all* volunteering our time."

Despite her own strict payment policy, truth be told, if Erin could afford it, most of *her* work would be free to the needy. She'd been in Trudy's position once, and she knew how much housing and support were needed by women who were starting over and had no resources to call on.

"So where do the supplies come from? Do you have to buy those?"

"They're donated by the lumber yard or the big home centers," explained Erin.

Erin smiled to herself. Trudy was asking all the right questions.

"How many workers will be there today?"

"Five others besides us. It's a smaller job, mostly carpentry and painting work." Erin parked in front of a one-story home. "How are you at painting?"

"My husband said I was messy."

"Are you?"

"No, not really."

"That a girl! Keep believing in yourself."

Trudy blushed at the encouragement.

Erin pulled into the Azalea Construction lot, pleased to find her five volunteers assembled and raring to go.

Climbing out of the cab, Erin activated her cell phone. "All right, Carol, we're locked and loaded for Operation Castle. We got our tools, we got our lumber, and we got our crew. Any last-minute instructions?" She listened intently to Carol's description of a wheelchair-bound woman's mobility problems. "Thank you so much. I sure appreciate your insight into what Jessie needs done."

She walked to the back of the truck where her team awaited the morning's tailboard session. Trudy followed.

"Mr. Hampton just called." Erin removed her cell phone earbud. "He's at the hospital picking up his wife. You angels are really going to be appreciated!" She smiled at the group's eager faces.

"Here's the address." She passed each woman a sheet with directions and a map. "It's in North Torrance, near the 405. Let's roll!"

The morning fog was burning off at Harbor Hospital as Jessie Hampton, a newly discharged bone cancer amputee was wheeled to her car by her husband and a hospital volunteer. She inhaled deeply, imagining she could taste the ocean.

"It feels so good to be outdoors!" she said as her husband, Mark, lifted her into the front seat.

"We'll spend the afternoon in the backyard while the contractor lady fixes up the house," he said. "I'd hoped to have it done before you got out, but you're such a fighter, they couldn't keep you down long enough!" He smiled lovingly at his wife. "Besides," he added, "I know how you feel about the house—I figured you'd want to have some input about the changes."

Jessie's lips trembled. Why was everything so hard? "What are the lady contractors going to *do* to our house? Will it look terrible?" The doctors had promised her an artificial leg in six months or so. Was it necessary to tear up the house she'd so lovingly decorated?

"Sweetheart, I know how important appearances are to you, but I'm more interested in making the house so you can move around in the wheelchair, get inside and outside, and sit down in the shower."

Jessie sighed. The dear man was coping the best way he knew how—by taking action; trying to fix things. She'd get through this. For him.

Jessie patted Mark's thigh. "Thank you for thinking of me."

He smiled softly. "You *are* the most important wife I have."

The couple pulled into their drive. "There's the contractor." Mark pointed to the rose-pink crew-cab truck with *Azalea Construction* emblazoned on the doors and tailgate. "I told them to start on the outside with the wheelchair ramp—we didn't need to be here for that."

Over the next twelve hours, Erin's crew removed doors, widened doorways, re-plastered, and re-painted. Grab bars were installed in the bathroom and next to the bed—everywhere Jessie would need assistance. In the kitchen, they built a ramp to an elevated platform alongside the counters so that Jessie could work while sitting in her wheelchair.

Erin kept an eye on Trudy, who listened carefully and then followed the directions of the forewoman on building the platform. Trudy was timid but capable. It wouldn't be long before she was as good as the rest of her crew. Maybe Trudy really *could* become a permanent member of an Azalea team.

Erin went out to inspect the work on the front porch. A sheriff's car pulled up to the curb, and a female deputy emerged from the passenger side. Erin's heart fluttered but then calmed. She knew she was being silly—there's no way anyone could have traced her to Marshall.

The builder approached the car. "Can I help you?"

"I'm Sharon Collins." The deputy nodded at Erin. "I understand from the shelter that Trudy Maris is working here today." She looked around.

Erin's stomach tightened. "Uh, yes, she's inside. Give me a minute to go get her."

Erin walked toward the house. *A shelter-related call.* Was Trudy in danger? Had she been found by her husband?

When Erin and Trudy returned to the squad car, Trudy stopped short. "Sharon. You're in uniform today. This must be an official visit."

Erin raised her head, alert. If Trudy already knew Sharon, maybe she really *was* in a lot of danger. Erin steeled herself; she would do *whatever* was needed to protect her newest worker.

Sharon turned to Erin. "I'd like a private word with Mrs. Maris."

Erin looked questioningly at Trudy, her stance protective.

"Please let her stay," said Trudy.

Sharon shrugged. "Mrs. Maris, your husband was arrested in Arizona for vehicular manslaughter."

A stunned Trudy stared at Sharon in silence, her hands shaking. Erin held Trudy's arm to steady her, noticing her own sense of... *what?* Was it relief?

"So what happens now?" Trudy asked. "Do I have to testify against him in court?"

Sharon shook her head. "Not yet. *Our* case against him will be delayed unless he agrees to be extradited to this state." She waved her hands. "And *that* won't happen until he's tried on the manslaughter charge."

Trudy bit her trembling lip. "Ricky will be crushed."

Chapter 22

"IT'S BEAUTIFUL! And functional, too." Jessie gripped the hands of each worker as her husband rolled her around their newly renovated home. She turned to Erin. "Thank you, thank you, thank you." She smiled sheepishly. "I feel like I'll *never* be able to thank you enough. I thought I'd be stuck in the living room while my husband was at work! Especially since my wheelchair wouldn't fit through the hall doors and I'm not strong enough for crutches yet." She spread her arms. "Now I can use my *whole* house!"

Erin squeezed Jessie's hand. "You're more than welcome, Jessie. Your joy is all the thanks we require." She looked around. "But there *is* one last accessory the house needs." Erin nodded to Trudy, who headed out to the van.

Trudy returned carrying a ceramic pot; in it grew an azalea plant covered with ice-pink blossoms. Trudy centered it carefully on the coffee table.

After the last tool was stowed and the crew had left, Erin finally dropped off Trudy at the shelter.

Poor Trudy, she thought as she drove away. *What a bastard that Rick is!*

Of course, Erin *should* feel relief that Rick was behind bars; Trudy was safe. But why didn't she feel satisfied with that?

Erin thought about the two facets of her personality: feminine and soft; masculine and hard. From the soft side, she designed and built homes for many satisfied customers and needy people. From the hard side, she worked for the Outreach Committee, accepting no compromise when it came to dealing with cruel husbands.

105

It was the *second* job, she realized, that really fulfilled her: bringing freedom to trapped women, releasing them to lead productive lives. But did she overly relish—even *need*—to dispatch men who abused? Had she been *too* eager to help Trudy in this way—to the point of feeling disappointed that Trudy's husband was captured?

The high from Marshall's kill still invigorated her. Had she enjoyed it *too* much?

Chapter 23

SHARON DROPPED INTO the passenger seat of the black-and-white. "Well, Trudy seemed relieved, though sad, when I told her Rick had been apprehended." She reached for her seat belt. "And on another topic—'fore I forget—thanks for taking Mike to the father-son banquet last night. He had a wonderful time!"

Harry sat straighter in his seat. "You don't have to thank me; Mike did that last night by introducing me around as his friend. He seemed genuinely proud to have me there."

"He was. Wore Cailin and me out at breakfast telling us all about the dinner and how envious his friends were that he brought you."

"I coached him on the way home to say nice things to you about me."

Sharon snapped her fingers. "A-ha! Now *that* sounds more like you!" As Harry turned the corner, Sharon blew out her breath. "Whew! Now, I can relax—and treat you like yourself and not a saint." Her expression turned serious. "I *do* have one bone to pick with you, though."

"What'd I do now?"

"You bought Mike a new catcher's mitt. Your giving up your evening and going with him was enough." Sharon didn't make enough money to give her kids all the stuff they wanted, and others doing it made her feel like she wasn't a good enough mother-slash-father.

"Aw, Sharon, don't spoil my fun. You know me and toys. I went to Target to stock up our car trunk and the mitt was on clearance. I *had* to buy it. Besides, when he called to ask me to the dinner, we chatted about what position he played. I knew he'd like it."

Sharon nodded. "Okay. *This* time." She socked her partner's arm.

"And just wait 'til you see the action figure I found!" Harry's voice proclaimed his enthusiasm for anything smacking of toys. "It's bright green and morphs from a dinosaur bird to a modern bird, and even flies a few inches off the ground." His hand traced the trajectory of his latest find.

"Harry, I don't know how you ever grew up enough to graduate the Sheriff's Academy. You're always buying the latest kid stuff!" And he wasn't alone: The whole department kept on the lookout for special items to donate to Harry's toy drive, headquartered in the trunk of their black-and-white. "I hate to tell you this, pal, but we all know what you're up to: you acquire toys so you can play with them when the rest of us aren't looking."

Harry slapped his hand to his chest. "Hey! That was uncalled for!"

Sharon put a consoling hand on Harry's arm. "Don't pout. I'll let you demonstrate the green bird as soon as we stop for coffee!"

For the rest of the day, Sharon continued to ponder Harry's influence on Mike. Her partner had offered to help whenever he could, so she'd felt comfortable suggesting Mike invite him to the father-son banquet. Of course, she'd never dreamed Harry would give him that expensive glove. Harry had two grown daughters; buying that mitt for Mike must be a guy thing.

Lying in bed, Sharon sighed as her mind flipped to a word-for-word rerun of her conversation with the kids earlier in the week. She knew her children may have been too young to comprehend the full force of their father's cruelty. And even if they *had,* they may have blocked it out.

Sharon hated it when divorced parents criticized each other to their kids. Still, every time Mike and Cailin mentioned their father, she felt compelled to make a point—as she had the other night. She tossed the blanket off. Sure, she missed Sean: the fun trips; the sex—when it was mutual desire—but she would *never* let him back in her life.

When she'd interviewed for her job with the Sheriff's Department, Sharon had assured the staff psychologists that she had put the abuse behind her. But it came back with a vengeance tonight as sleep eluded her.

"What the hell do you think you're doing?" A pull on her arm launched Sharon from the couch where she'd plopped moments earlier to absorb the pain of another debilitating blow to the stomach. "Get up and get me a sandwich!"

Sharon stumbled in the direction of the kitchen and fell as an empty beer bottle hit her in the back of the head.

"And a beer."

Sharon pulled herself to her knees, only to be kicked flat. "Never mind, worm; I'll get it myself." He walked on her calves instead of stepping over her.

Groggy after a night of rape and further beatings, Sharon watched through swollen eyelids as Sean stalked to the street and jumped into his dirty Dodge truck and drove off. Whimpering, she struggled to lift the phone to call 911. After taking the minimum of information, the deputy who responded referred her to the BWEF shelter. And then sent a team looking for Sean Collins.

Rousing herself from the horrifying memory of her last night with Sean, Sharon vowed to get even more involved in her kids' extracurricular activities and to forge a new life for herself as well. The past had controlled her for too long.

Chapter 24

"WELCOME TO YOUR POST-PASSING COUNSELING, ladies." Mora sat on the leather couch in her home office, facing Erin Craig and Taylor Whitmore. "It's now been a week since the operation, and I admit I regret not holding this session a bit sooner." Mora pointed to a stack of files on her desk. "I've seen new clients every day this week in addition to the already loaded schedule." *Plus*—she added mentally—she'd hoped they could meet *after* Taylor had officially been notified of Marshall's death, so as not to sway her emotions leading up to that ordeal.

Erin shook her head. "I needed to sort some things out in my head, so it's good we waited."

Taylor dropped her head in her hands. "I haven't been sleeping, so I don't even know what a good time would be."

Mora pulled a notebook from the corner of the coffee table and picked up a pencil. "First we'll chat together as a group, then I'll counsel each of you individually. Afterwards, you two will talk without me, to resolve any issues between you." Mora turned to each woman and held her gaze. "Be assured you can call me to mediate if you reach an impasse."

Mora had arranged the office carefully. This was to be a working session, not a meeting between friends. Even though the operation had been successful, these women had been through major trauma, both of them.

With trained eyes, she observed the two facing her. Taylor was worrying a hangnail; Erin rubbed her neck. Overall, they seemed calm, considering what they'd accomplished.

"Why all the down talk?" Erin shifted in her chair and finger-combed her blond locks. "We talked this out before—in our Pre-Expiration Counseling—didn't we?" She looked at Taylor who nodded in agreement.

"You did, and *that* was to make sure you wanted to go through with your plans. In those meetings, we also made sure that you, Taylor, truly *were* being abused by your husband, *needed* to obliterate him, and were not only after his insurance." Mora leaned forward and set her coffee cup on the desk. "Now it's time to deal with your feelings after the fact."

Taylor and Erin looked at each other and nodded.

"We'll also start grooming you both as facilitators and trainers."

Taylor's head jerked up. "Trainers, like t...teachers?" She reached for a tissue and blotted her sweating palms.

"You'll remember, Taylor, that when you agreed to become the beneficiary of the Outreach Committee, you also agreed to help the next beneficiary in her quest for freedom. That commitment includes priming a pre-widow about what to expect and about how to act afterwards. And of course taking a part in the operation itself."

Taylor tore her Kleenex into miniature marshmallow puffs.

"I don't know if I could k-kill someone."

Mora took in Taylor's shaking hands and slumped posture. She was clearly still in mourning. Not unusual so soon after the loss of a husband of twenty-five years, no matter what the problems in the marriage—*or* the cause of death. Mora crossed the room and patted Taylor on the shoulder.

"It will be *my* job to test your mettle," Mora assured her, "and assess when you're capable of being the primary in an operation."

Taylor shuddered. "What if I never am?"

Erin straightened in her chair. "Believe me, Taylor, once you get used to living liberated from Marshall's abuse, you'll *demand* to return the favor—to give someone else that freedom." Erin gestured widely with her arms. "There is no feeling so grand."

Concern tickled Mora's thoughts. Did Erin actually *enjoy* killing? She'd have to see about that.

In the meantime, Taylor would have to finish grieving before she could help someone else. Unfortunately, she hadn't even had a funeral for Marshall yet. Where *was* that man's body, anyway?

Chapter 25

"WELL, GOOD MORNING!" A man in a white coat walked into the small room. "Glad to see you're finally awake. I'm Dr. George Appleton."

Groggy, the patient followed the stranger's movements through blurred eyes as the doctor lifted his arm and pressed his forefingers to his wrist.

"Your pulse is strong. How are you feeling?"

The patient stretched his legs and touched the footboard. His hand reached gingerly toward his face.

Where was he? And why did his face hurt so damn much?

He looked up at the doctor. Was the doctor looking at him strangely? Was he in some sort of trouble?

He spotted a pad and pencil by the bed, obviously left there for him to communicate with. Given the bandages on his face, he doubted he could speak, let alone make himself understood.

What happened? He wrote.

"You were found about a week ago near the Colorado River by a couple out hiking. They called the ranger and he had you medevaced here; we're at a relatively small hospital outside Flagstaff, Arizona."

He remembered a woman hiker. Was that the one the doctor was talking about? The leggy blonde with those blue-jean-colored eyes?

He grunted.

The doctor slipped his stethoscope in his ears and held a hand up for silence. The scope felt cold on the patient's chest. But it didn't bother him. It seemed he was used to braving the elements.

"Your face was badly injured," said the doctor, folding the instrument back in his coat pocket. "Broken nose, smashed cheek bones, concussion." He grimaced. "We've been keeping you sedated to give you time to heal." The doctor ran a hand down the side of the patient's head. "You'll need extensive plastic surgery to get your nasal passages functioning. It looks like your eyes are okay, though."

The patient inhaled deeply. *Ouch!* He started. This only intensified the pain. *Son of a bitch!*

"Be careful," said the doctor, easing him back on the pillow. "Your ribs and clavicle are cracked, too."

Appleton pulled back the bed sheet to expose the patient's body. "Your legs and arms are badly bruised, but our X-rays show no broken bones there." The patient could only gaze blankly at his unfamiliar limbs.

The doctor re-covered the patient and sat down in the side chair. "Doesn't mean you won't hurt, though." He paused. "Want to tell me what happened?"

The patient picked up his pad and pencil but then held them away from him in a gesture of ignorance. Somehow, he felt that whatever he'd been doing, he shouldn't have been doing it. He definitely shouldn't admit to knowing anything until he remembered.

"You have a name?"

I don't know. His hand shook as he wrote this.

The patient shivered. He was telling the truth, he realized. Fear gripped his stomach. God, was he going to cry like a puking baby?

All I remember is waking up here. He waved his hand to take in the bed and room.

"Well, I'll call you Mr. Lucky, then—lucky to be alive, that is! We think you may have been in a rafting or camping accident on the river; your shorts—what was left of them—were damp when they found you."

Pain meds? The note ended in a squiggle as Lucky—guess he'd have to go with that name for now—scooted up in the bed.

"Sure, but we need to discuss your care here before I do. I want you lucid when we make decisions."

How will I pay for care? Lucky blotted spittle from his mouth with his hand.

"That's one of the things we need to talk about. We looked for your wallet or some ID. There wasn't any." Lucky started to write, but the doctor held up his hand. "But—we did find a waterproof packet zipped in your shorts pocket. And fifty thousand dollars in it."

Fifty thousand dollars?! Lucky kept this reaction to himself. *Holy crap.* Where had he gotten that much money? Had he robbed a bank? And the doc said the bills were in a waterproof pouch—he must have known he was taking it in the water.

A smile lit the doctor's face. "Let's assume you didn't steal it, shall we?"

Lucky grunted again. *Hold onto that thought!* Thank God the doctor couldn't read his expression.

The doctor pulled a prescription tablet from his pocket and turned it over. "Here's what I plan to do with your face. Unfortunately, since we don't know what you used to look like—not even via a poor DMV picture—I'll be doing the best I can with what you have left." He sketched the facial repair he would make. "I'll take a digital photo of your face and try to reconstruct it with a computer-aided design program."

Guess no choice. Lucky threw the notepad down on the bed.

"Not unless you can tell me who you are and we can get a recent photo from your family."

Damn these tears. They weren't normal for him; he knew that much.

Chapter 26

"KYLE, WHAT'S MY NEXT APPOINTMENT?" Monday morning, Quentin Pryor looked up from his desk at his nattily dressed personal assistant. Some days he wished he were still that young and naïve.

Kyle Norbest consulted Pryor's daily calendar. "It's Ms. Erin Craig, from that charity you're involved with."

Quentin grimaced. That's all he needed to start the week: having to deal with the do-gooders again. Why, oh why, hadn't he challenged the bank's assigning him to the group? And, worse, they were involving Leigh now. He'd have to change that. He knew how women were: they got together and talked and thought they were doing good when all they were doing was wasting time. He certainly didn't want Leigh involved in *that*.

"Is she here yet?" Maybe he could knock out a few putts in the corner of his office before talking with her. That should relax him.

"Yes, sir. Security just called from the entrance. I told them to send her up."

Quentin sighed.

"Did you research her background as I asked?" Surely he could make short shrift of their conversation and the ladies' gambling project. What nonsense!

"I did. Seems she owns her own contracting business. She hires only women."

Quentin rolled his eyes. That's all he needed. Another fucking feminist! "Is she successful? Is she gay?"

"I don't know about the last, but she's quite successful. Not on the scale of the contractors you usually work with, but she's solvent. Builds new homes on spec; remodeled twelve homes last year, as well.

They ran an article on her in the local paper: she does pro bono work retrofitting homes for newly handicapped women. Like that policewoman who got shot. Actually, boss, if her company were a little bigger, I'd bet you'd already be working with her."

Quentin shot Kyle a look that would have unnerved a less hearty assistant. He admired Norbest's fortitude but wished he weren't *quite* so cocky and sure of himself.

"Surely you found *something* bad about her! No one is goody-goody all the time."

"The only negative is that her husband was killed in a climbing accident. Fell down a cliff. Erin wasn't on the trip; she'd stayed here to build a house."

"Well, I'm still not impressed with her business acumen if she supports this house lottery stuff." Quentin reached for his putter. "Keep her waiting half an hour then send her in."

"Mr. Pryor," Kyle's head appeared in the office as Quentin sank his eleventh putt in row. "It's time to see Ms. Craig." *Damn, already?* He'd been on a roll! Kyle ushered Erin into the room and pulled out a chair at the conference table.

Quentin picked up a folder from his desk and joined her. "I hope you have some information for me. This PowerPoint presentation has no depth to it." He pulled in his stomach. *She sure is good-looking, even if she is a builder with rough hands. I didn't notice those unusual blue eyes in our other meetings.*

"I have the best, Quentin." Erin smiled sweetly. "As I mentioned during the house tour, *your* mortgage department reviewed it for me. I wanted to make sure you had all the information you needed for a quick agreement to buy the house we've chosen to raffle."

"Well, I'm not about to make a flash decision without weighing all the factors. So you can forget your 'quick agreement.'" Quentin flashed his gotcha smile. *If she knows what she's talking about, maybe there's a brain inside that pretty head.*

"We're proposing to buy the house you toured with us. We eliminated two others before the tour." Erin pulled the broker's sales brochure from her folder. "Shall we start with the neighborhood comps to evaluate the validity of the asking price?"

Talks like she's a realtor. More likely one of those empty-headed salesladies.

"Here's our cash flow analysis; the return on investment analysis; the itemized costs to set up the lottery; and the award schedule with our projected interest income on the ticket sales."

Quentin cocked his head. Well, he wouldn't be able to fault her for preparedness. Might as well focus on the merits of the numbers—or lack of them.

"I note here that you have a contingency for maintenance and any 'minor' repairs you encounter." Pryor steepled his hands. "Tell me why *your* company can't do the work pro bono? You'd show me more confidence in the project if you did."

Quentin realized he was grasping at straws—he'd never believed in unpaid work, so why was he suggesting it?

"Quentin, I'd love to be able to. But you'd be the first to criticize me if I did, with my small margin. The pro bono work I do for handicapped women also involves *volunteer* help from my employees—which you'd know if you were more familiar with Azalea Construction." She paused, shooting him a triumphant look. "You'd also be the first to criticize when I had to call them off the job to complete another paying one. Besides, our projects involve tough remodeling, not the touch-up jobs any handyperson could do." Erin folded her hands on the table in front of her.

Quentin shook his head slowly. The figures looked okay so far—and this was one tough cookie. He'd have to come up with a good reason to turn these ladies down on their hair-brained scheme. Why, oh why, had the bank appointed him to this damn job?

"Well, Miss Craig, let's put it this way: There are a lot of risks involved in this project—among them, the volatile real estate market and the assumption that people will actually lay down what you project, in order to have a *chance* to win this house."

"I—we *all*—understand the risks. I came here today to address any hard financial objections you have as our Finance Director, and barring that, to obtain your approval." She paused. "Assuming I've answered all your questions, do you approve the project?"

Quentin had to admit one thing: The woman knew how to close a deal. He couldn't really think of another way to get rid of her, so he made a decision.

"Let's just say that I won't stand in your way. But rest assured, if this 'project' fails, I will *not* take the blame for it. Is that clear?"

"Yes, sir. And am I correct in assuming you won't assist us in any other way in this home raffle project?"

"You are, Ms. Craig. Now, if you'll excuse me, I must get to my critical work." Quentin Pryor pushed back his chair. "Kyle will show you out."

Kyle watched the becoming Ms. Craig exit Quentin's office wearing a look of victory. Now *that* was a rare sight. Most visitors left with their heads hung low, tail between their legs. Kyle gazed upon her with renewed respect.

Hmm…Ms. Craig's background check had shown she was single, and she *was* quite—

"Kyle, get in here!" Quentin's angry voice reverberating over the intercom interrupted Kyle's thought. Kyle should have known that for the rare "yin," he'd have to face Pryor's "yang." He sighed and entered Pryor's opulent office.

"I specifically told you I wanted this Manhattan Beach tract contract in a binder so it's easy to hold and read!" Pryor pitched the bound three-inch document at him.

"Yes, sir." Kyle turned his back to his boss and stuck out his tongue. He knew Pryor had told him no such thing. In fact the executive's exact words had been: "Get a binding on this thing and bring it back. I don't want to take the chance of losing pages."

Why am I putting up with this SOB and the crap he throws at me? Kyle asked himself for the millionth time. He hadn't gotten an MBA to spend his career as a tyrannized flunky. *I put up with him because I get to meet a lot of important executives,* he reminded himself. *The ones whose loans are big enough for them to deal directly with Pryor. Executives who might offer me future jobs.* Networking was how the best positions were obtained.

Kyle sent the document from his computer to a high-speed printer. *But is it worth it?* Pryor always charmed the brass but seemed to take out all his aggression on Kyle—his lowly assistant. Kyle was even having trouble sleeping at night.

When Kyle returned with the three-ring-bound document, Pryor tossed it into the trash. "I'm finished with it. I'm going to turn down Dimitri's request for the loan extension on that tract."

"If there's nothing further you need, I'm ready to leave for the day." Kyle stood rigidly in front of Pryor. His eyes twitched as he tried to hide the scorn for Quentin that surely must be reflected there.

Pryor glanced at the clock on the wall. "It's only five-thirty. Can't you... Oh, never mind. Be sure you get here early tomorrow. I have an appointment with Dimitri to turn him down in person. I want you here in case he gets violent." He laughed. "Man must think we make a practice of approving loans to financial fools or something."

"Sir, when he called, Mr. Dimitri explained that the El Niño storms put him two months behind schedule, and he'll already have one month made up by the time the loan expires."

"You believe that, Kyle baby, and I'll sell you a plot of land in the Hawaiian lava fields, sight unseen."

"With all due respect, sir, Dimitri homes are known for being high-class and well-designed."

"Norbest, since when did you become a real estate expert? You should partner up with that Craig lady." Pryor waived his hand dismissively. "Go on. We have a long day tomorrow."

Kyle made his way down to the parking garage, still fuming. *Maybe I should start hammering nails with Ms. Craig! It would be a hell of a lot better than dealing with this bastard. Geez, Pryor's heart is so hard they'll use it as his tombstone when he dies!*

Kyle suddenly smiled. *Hmm…what a cheerful thought: a dead Quentin Pryor!*

Chapter 27

"THAT A BOY, MIKE!" Sharon shouted from the bleachers, cheering her son's Little League team on its quest for a championship. She scooted over as a team father squeezed in beside her.

"Hello. I'm Ernest Hazelton, Joe's dad."

"Hi. I'm Sharon Collins, Mike's mother."

"So nice to finally meet you!" The man, slender, square-faced, in jeans and a sport shirt, grinned a casual but warm smile. "He and Mike hang out together, so I've heard a lot about you."

"Oh?" Sharon pulled her jacket close. Her lip lifted into a lopsided smile. "That sounds ominous."

"I met Mike's friend, Harry, at the father-son banquet. But I haven't seen you here before."

Sharon crossed her arms. "I feel bad about that. My work schedule conflicts with a lot of stuff I want to do." It was strange talking to a man outside of work. She felt suddenly shy.

"Mike said you're a deputy sheriff."

"Yeah. Harry's my partner. His wife loaned him to us for the banquet." Why did she feel a need to explain Harry?

"Mike's really proud of you."

"Thanks." Sharon returned her attention to the game. "Way to go, guys! Keep it up."

"Joe suggested I ask you and Mike to join us for pizza after the game. How about it?"

Sharon's head turned toward Ernest with a robotic jerk. "I…I guess that would be okay—if your wife doesn't mind, that is." *Oh my God, is he asking me for a date? I don't know how to act.*

"We lost Sue to breast cancer two years ago."

Warmth, and she knew a bright red flush, rose from Sharon's neck to her forehead. "I'm sorry. I should have remembered that. Mike did tell me about how hard Joe took it."

"Will you come?" Ernest's eyes probed hers.

"Yeah. Sounds like fun."

Sharon waited while Mike fastened his seat belt.

"Fun time! Huh?"

She put the car into drive and pulled out of Italia's Pizza's small parking lot onto the busy street.

"Yeah." Mike scooted down in his seat and looked out the side window, his mouth turned down, his brow creased.

Oh, oh. Looks like a teen storm coming.

"What is it, Mikey? Why the glum face? You seemed like you were having fun with Joe and his dad. And the pizza had your favorite sausage on it."

"Why do I have to tell you everything?" Mike crossed his arms. "Can't I feel bad without you sticking your nose in?"

Sharon was silent for the rest of the short ride home, taking time to collect her thoughts. As she pulled into their parking slot under their apartment building, she stole a glance at her son. No change. Sharon turned off the ignition but made no move to go inside.

"Mikey, you have the right to feel anything you want. It's just that—in our family—I thought we agreed that it's not fair to the other people if you aren't honest about your feelings." She looked at him and tilted her head.

Mike unfolded his arms and looked back at her defiantly. "Fine. I don't want you dating Joe's dad."

Sharon took a long slow breath and let it out.

"Well, thank you for sharing that. I respect your honesty." Sharon unfastened her seat belt. "Well, for one thing, he hasn't asked me on a real date. But I admit that if he does, I'll probably go." Sharon removed the key from the ignition and gestured with it toward Mike.

"Help me understand, Mike: Joe's your best friend and Ernest's his father. What's the problem?"

Mike looked down at his lap. Sharon grasped his arm. "C'mon, Mike. I can't work this out with you if I don't know what the problem is. Let's hear it."

"If you date Ernest, you're cheating on Dad." Mike wrenched his arm away and opened the car door. "What if Dad wants to get back with you when he gets out of prison?"

It twisted Sharon's heart to see her son's anguish, but she had to pop his balloon before this got so big it engulfed them both. She got out of the car and shut the door. She felt like slamming it, but it might fall off if she did that. Sharon caught up to Mike on the stairs.

"Hon, your dad and I will never remarry. That's certain."

"But…"

"But?"

"I miss him."

"Of course you do. I'm happy you love him that much." Sharon opened the apartment door and guided her son inside. "I promise when your dad's released, he'll still be part of our lives. But he and I will not marry."

"What if you're married to Ernest?"

Sharon laughed, releasing her tension. "Don't jump the gun. We all went out for pizza; that doesn't mean marriage is anywhere in the future. Okay?"

"Okay, but…"

"If I were ever to marry again, I'd make it clear to my future husband that you and Cailin are the most important people in the world to me and that your dad is part of the package, too. They can accept that or leave."

"Promise?"

"I promise."

Mike gave a half-smile. "Wow. Thanks, Mom. Can I have some leftover pizza?"

Chapter 28

LUCKY PROBED THE FRESH BANDAGES on his face with a feather touch. He tried to speak and realized his jaw had been wired shut and then wrapped with bandages. *Shit.* Pain dominated his whole body. Even moving his eyes hurt, though bandages didn't cover them.

He felt around the bed for the nurse's bell, gripped it, and pressed hard. *Damn, where were they?*

The blond nurse—he couldn't remember her name—came into the room smiling broadly. "My favorite patient woke up!" She moved closer and frowned. "Feeling pain?"

He wanted to snarl but couldn't. He nodded instead. Did she think he'd pressed that bell just so they could chat?

"How severe is your pain? Hold up your fingers. One is low and ten is high."

Shit, she wanted to play games. He held up ten fingers, then fisted his hands and held up ten again.

She gripped his waving hand. "Ooh. Really hurts, huh?" She grabbed his index finger and guided it to a button on the IV tube hanging by his side. "This is your morphine pump. Now that you're awake, you can work it yourself." She put her hand over his and pushed the control.

He relaxed as the narcotic flowed into his veins. He made a writing motion.

The lovely nurse smoothed his hair and handed him a notepad and pencil.

What's going on?

The nurse cocked her head and studied him. "You just had your reconstructive surgery." She smiled. "You're gonna be a *real* lady-killer now!"

Somehow that sounded right to Lucky. He nodded slightly and then surrendered to the morphine.

Chapter 29

"I CAN'T STAND THE SILENCE!" Taylor checked her makeup as she waited for Erin inside the BWEF ladies room. She had already ensured that they were alone.

"You mean not having Marshall ranting and raving all the time?" Erin opened the stall door and caught Taylor's eye in the mirror. She headed to the sink.

"No! Why haven't I been notified that Marshall is d-d-dead? It's been two weeks and I haven't h-heard *anything*." Taylor washed and dried her hands. Instead of feeling free, all she felt was trapped in worries she couldn't prove or disprove. "I keep looking over my sh-shoulder, afraid someone is following me to see if I'm guilty."

"Well, friend, if they were following anyone, it would be me. And I'm free as a bird."

Taylor reapplied her lipstick with a shaking hand. "Then why haven't I *heard*?"

Erin dried her hands and hugged her friend "I'm so sorry— I didn't even think to tell you: Marshall left his vest at the campsite, with his driver's license in the pocket. I disposed of the vest and destroyed the license. Perhaps they found him and have no way to identify him." Erin thought for a moment. "Maybe if he was reported missing, they could match him with a photograph."

"Should I?"

"Should you what?"

"Report him missing."

"Let's think about that, talk to Mora and Carol." Erin paused. "What have you told the kids?"

"Nothing—yet." Taylor returned her stash of makeup to her purse. "Marshall's actually not due home for another week; they have no reason to suspect anything is wrong—oh my gosh!" Taylor waved her purse in the air. "I just thought of something."

"What?"

"Marshall's clothing had Wilderness Outfitters tags. They c-c-could come in a…asking about it! What do I s-say?" Erin grabbed Taylor's purse and used it to steer Taylor toward the door. "You don't have to say anything," she replied calmly. "You could tell them that hundreds wear your gear. Right?" Taylor nodded. "If they show you a picture of a dead Marshall, you just cower from the picture." She paused. "A statement like 'How gross!' might be appropriate."

Carol cringed at the tension in the air as she rolled into the BWEF boardroom. Before she could apologize for being late, Quentin Pryor launched into current business, as though refusing to be kept waiting even a moment longer.

"What's this about a new project, Carol?" he asked.

Carol sat tall and pulled on her sweater. The BWEF Board was meeting on a foggy gray May morning. Refusing to be hurried, Carol took time to smile at the women gathered around the table, noting that Taylor's expression was especially somber. She'd have to confer with Mora about that situation.

"You'll remember we've been helping newly handicapped people," Carol said as brightly as possible. "Mostly paraplegics—adapting their homes to their new limitations." She gestured towards her still legs and wiggled in her chair. "I'd like to expand that to Operation Caring: sprucing up homes for widows living on Social Security only. They want to stay in their homes but can't afford repairs."

Quentin laid his portfolio on the table. "Ladies, I know you mean well." He sighed. "But you can't accommodate *every* hard-luck case in the city." To punctuate his remark, he tapped his pen against the table so hard it flew out of his hand. It bounced off Carol's arm and dropped to the floor. Leigh leaned over to pick it up and handed it back to him without comment.

"If I'm to be responsible for the finances of this organization," Quentin continued as though his display of temper had not happened, "things are going to have to change."

Carol steeled herself for his objections. Didn't he realize this project could be self-supporting with donations from suppliers?

"Who's doing the construction?" Mora asked—already knowing Carol's plan. Carol rolled her shoulders. She welcomed her friend's directing of the conversation.

"More importantly," Quentin interrupted, "where are the funds coming from to pay for it? These construction guys go for a premium in this town!" Quentin circled scrolls on his tablet.

Carol smiled at Erin. "Well, Erin graciously volunteered her own money to *pay* Azalea Construction crews to perform the work on slow days." Carol combed her fingers through her blond curls as she spoke.

Quentin nodded. "I am aware that Ms. Craig's firm does do pro bono work. That's why I suggested she do repairs on the raffle house." He grimaced. "She turned me down, saying she couldn't *afford* more pro bono work." He waved his hands. "But that's no longer my concern; you ladies are on your own on that."

Carol sighed inwardly. They'd better prove him wrong on the raffle or they'd never hear the end of it. She glanced again at Taylor, who stared down at her notes.

"We have a paraplegic's retrofit lined up for next weekend," chimed in Erin. "You could come help, Quentin, if you like. Get a feel for what we do—and why we do it."

Carol caught Mora's eye and winked; Carol enjoyed Erin's expert handling of the banker's objections. But why was Quentin so negative about their community projects? Carol was impressed with his supposed financial savvy, but what had he actually *done* for them except object to every project they proposed? Just like Reggie had objected to every suggestion she'd made during their marriage, she thought ruefully. Thankfully she was free of that.

Pryor looked down at his hands and said nothing.

Leigh spoke up. "*I'd* like to help"—she looked sideways at her husband—"if our schedule permits, of course."

"What would *you* do, dear?" Quentin asked, poker-faced. "Dance for them?"

Leigh laughed as though Quentin had just made a very funny joke. Carol didn't find it funny at all.

Mora pushed back from the table. "Carol, how will we find the people who need the services?"

"We can talk to the people at the senior centers, find out who needs help. Many of those centers provide free meals, so we could find some people to help among the women that come." Carol clasped her hands in front of her on the table. "We'd keep in touch with the homeowners afterwards, too. Sort of a support group."

Quentin cleared his throat. "Ladies, this is all well and good—and very touching." He looked around the table. "But can you explain to me what this has to do with battered women?"

Carol paused for a moment. "We're an organization that supports *troubled* women, which includes preventing problems before they start." She looked down at her lap, self-conscious. "Also—" Carol's eyes pooled. "When our paraplegic beneficiaries heard about the BWEF shelter work, two of them offered to provide emergency housing to battered women, even in the middle of the night."

"It's a win-win situation," said Erin.

Pryor looked over his reading glasses at Erin. "Your crews really *are* all women?"

Erin beamed. "Yes, I'm proud to say. One hundred percent." She looked at Quentin squarely. "So, what other concerns do you have about our project?"

Quentin threw up his hands. "Look, I know you ladies like to think you can change the world." He looked around at the now-smiling group. "But let me caution you, you are spreading yourselves too thin." He shook his head as though he knew he was yelling into the Pacific Ocean for all the effect his words had on the enthusiasm in the room. "You may want to think about that."

Quentin turned to Leigh. "Well, it looks like we're done here, darling." He rose and reached for Leigh's hand.

"Quentin, dear, I'd like to stay until the meeting is over." She looked at him hopefully. "Perhaps Carol can drive me home?" She caught Carol's eye and Carol nodded.

"Certainly not. I'll drop you home on the way, so you and Cook can plan this weekend's dinner for the councilman."

Leigh's body sagged, but she straightened up immediately and smiled broadly at the women at the table. "Oops! I'm constantly forgetting my 'first lady' duties. Of course you're right, dear. I shall see you at our next engagement, ladies!"

Leigh grabbed her purse and rushed to catch up with Quentin, who was already out the door.

The room was silent until the outer door to the office closed behind Quentin and Leigh. Mora locked eyes in turn with Taylor, Carol, and Erin. "Is it just me, or is Quentin being overly difficult?"

"Today he acted like he did when I called on him about the house raffle!" said Erin. "First, he kept me waiting half an hour, and then he objected to everything I said."

"To give him the b-benefit of the doubt, he may just be playing d-d-devil's advocate—to ch-challenge us," said Taylor. "But what about the investment and contract advice we expected? I sometimes wonder if he th...thinks his only mission with us is to say no."

"His behavior's also a controlling technique," said Mora. "I'm becoming concerned about Leigh's demeanor with him."

"Gee, *that* would be ironic, wouldn't it?" joked Erin. "If the BWEF Finance Chair were a damned abuser?" Her eyes stopped laughing.

Taylor shook her head rapidly. "Erin, no! It c-c-*can't* be."

"But look how Leigh acts around him," said Erin. "Always being falsely bright. Agreeing with everything he says—even when that shit insults her!" She balled her hands into fists. "His crack about dancing made me want to…"

Carol nudged Erin. "Do you think it's *possible* your imagination is running wild? You've admitted openly that you don't trust men."

"Besides, we just *c-couldn't've* hired an abuser as our financial advisor!" Taylor looked around the room. "We're all *far* too aware of an abusive man's b…behavior." She paused. "Although Marshall *could* be charming—when he wanted something."

"But what would Quentin want from *us*?" asked Carol.

Mora turned to Erin. "You said he acted this way in his office." Erin nodded. "I suspect what Erin saw," said Mora, "and what we saw this morning, is Quentin's normal business demeanor. In the hierarchy of the banking community, it may bring him desired results." She sighed. "Maybe we should be *happy* he's finally treating us like businesswomen instead of empty-headed do-gooders."

Chapter 30

"DEPUTY ADLER TO DEPUTY COLLINS." Harry leaned over and waved his hand in front of Sharon's face. "Come in. Over."

Sharon turned her head towards her partner and blinked. "Sorry." She straightened the papers on her desk. "What is it?"

"I should ask *you* that. You've been in a fog all day. Is something bothering you?"

"No. Not really." Sharon shook her head to clear it. "Just feeling strange, that's all."

"You sick?"

"No. It's just that…well, I had a date—well, not a real one—this weekend." Sharon looked down, examining her fingernails. "Mike's friend's father asked me and Mike to join him and his son, Joe, for pizza after the game."

Harry knuckled her shoulder. "Does this father have a name? Or did you forget to ask?"

"It's Ernest, and he lost his wife to cancer two years ago."

Harry bent over to look her in the face. "Well?"

"Well, what?"

"Did you enjoy your date?"

"It wasn't really…Yeah, I did."

Harry clapped his hands together. "Hallelujah! *Now* maybe I can convince you that some men are okay." He grinned. "Me included."

Chapter 31

PAIN PULSING THROUGH HER BODY, Leigh Pryor sat crouched on the edge of the tub. She bit her lip to keep from crying out as she cradled her arm under her breasts in a futile attempt to stop the rib pain. Her other hand covered her mouth so that her body-wrenching sobs would not be heard in the bedroom next door.

Leigh looked in the mirror to see bruises forming on her arm where Quentin had gripped her with one hand while he punched her midsection with a hard fist.

Why don't I learn? I know better than to think he'd discuss his next week's schedule with me—even though it was just so I could plan his meals.

Leigh rose slowly, holding to the wall for support. Her thoughts drifted in a brain muddled by pain and despair. *If only I could know what he wanted without having to ask.* A sigh escaped from her core.

How did a successful, independent woman get herself into this bondage? Why couldn't she summon the courage to divorce Quentin? He'd taken control of her money when they'd married; said he was most knowledgeable about investing. *Idiot me, why did I let him?* She sighed again. *I was in love with what he told me he was—that's why. Now, if I leave, I won't have a cent.*

Leigh stood up. She'd better get ready to go. At least, if he acted like other times, the worst was over for today. He'd feel sorry like he always did and treat her like a queen for a while. Maybe a whole month.

But I wish he wouldn't slap me so hard. And I wish I could demand he not punch me. But she knew that would make him hit harder.

"Hurry up and get ready. If you make me late for our meeting with the mayor, you'll make me *really* angry." Her husband jerked open the bathroom door and looked around the room, his face still too-red from his raging tantrum twenty minutes earlier. He took in Leigh's spreading bruises but said nothing more.

"Yes, dear. I'll have to change the dress I planned to wear—to cover my arms. I'll wear the pink with the long-sleeved jacket, the one you picked out." Her voice wavered as she cowered into herself, bracing for another tirade.

Instead, Quentin lowered his eyes and nodded, before leaving the room.

"Be downstairs in ten minutes!"

Mora looked at her watch for the third time. "Leigh is late; that's not like her. She seemed excited about working with us on the raffle house interior."

Mora had asked Carol and Leigh to lunch. She'd chosen the East End Grill, an upscale restaurant on the Peninsula, for its widely spaced tables, positioned to preserve confidential conversations. Now seated, Mora wished she'd chosen the chair facing the door so she could watch for Leigh.

"I'd like a sherry; how about you?" Carol signaled the waiter.

"Sounds good," agreed Mora.

"Hello, ladies," a quiet voice spoke behind them. They turned to see Leigh, a timid smile pulling at her lips.

"Hello, yourself!" Mora jumped up to hug her. "I'm happy you could join us." She felt Leigh recoil before going through the motions of hugging her back.

"You look a bit sore again today," said Carol.

"Oh!" Leigh shrugged. "I guess you're referring to the benefit dinner. Yes, I was stiff and sore that night. I think I repressed my fantasies of becoming a botanist when I decided on ballet. I'd been working in the garden all day."

"I remember you saying you had arthritis from all your dancing." Mora smiled at her, ignoring Carol's raised eyebrows. "I didn't realize you had been gardening, too. Do you have any unusual plants in your yard?"

"I said that?" Leigh busied herself with spreading the napkin in her lap. "Oh yes, I have lots of flowers to cut. I always have fresh flowers in my rooms. It gives our big, cold house a homey feeling."

Mora couldn't help but think it would take more than flowers to make the Pryor home warm. "Let's order you a drink and then have a talk about the BWEF."

Leigh nodded to the waiter offering sherry. "I skipped breakfast; Quentin and I had a meeting this morning with our councilman about the upcoming election. I'm starved." Leigh smiled crookedly. "So, what's good here?"

Mora smoothed her napkin in her lap. "Actually, if you can wait a few minutes, I'd like to take a moment before we order and talk about *you*, Leigh. Get to know you better. Hear about your dance classes for the kids."

At the mention of dance, Leigh's entire demeanor shifted. Her eyes twinkled as she told them about the classes she'd set up at the Boys and Girls Club.

Mora wondered why someone with such passion had left the stage. Leigh's whole body became fluid when she talked about dancing. Was that a wistful expression? Mora thought about Leigh's hesitant hug and her stiff walk the night of the benefit dinner. Was her arthritis so bad it precluded continuing a rigid dance schedule?

Mora's thoughts were interrupted by the waiter's arrival. After they'd given their orders, she and Carol continued their informal interrogation of Leigh.

"So how did you and Quentin meet?" Carol asked brightly.

"I was in Europe, dancing as a prima ballerina in *Swan Lake*." Leigh's gaze fixed itself over the lunch crowd, clearly seeing something else.

Five years earlier, London

After her evening performance, Leigh dressed in an unadorned apricot silk cocktail dress. Men liked the bare back, and most of the donations would come from men. *Why was that?* she pondered.

Throwing a green velvet cape around her shoulders, Leigh walked regally to the waiting limousine. As she rode, she hummed the music from the second act. She had been mulling a change to the final solo; one that would enhance her performance.

The after-show party at the Ritz was in full swing. On Leigh's entrance, the conversation stopped. Applause started in the back of the room and spread throughout.

Leigh approached the host and curtsied. "Thank you for your hospitality, my lord."

The benefactor took her hand and kissed it. "Leigh, I'd like you to meet one of my contacts in the States. He enjoyed your superb performance tonight, as did I." He turned to the man beside him in the receiving line. "May I present Mr. Quentin Pryor from Los Angeles, California."

Quentin took Leigh's hand and bowed over it. "Your dancing was mesmerizing," he said hoarsely. His dark eyes held hers. Leigh's whole body drew to *en pointe.* Tingles perked her breasts.

Whoa, Leigh cautioned herself. It had been a while since she had ended her last affair, and she had to be careful. Her body couldn't betray her again! Romantic alliances took so much from her: passion, energy. Her dancing suffered. That was to be avoided at all costs. Dancing was her life force.

Still, she couldn't ignore this man's magnetism. Leigh's performance had been described many ways: brilliant; sensual; original. Never mesmerizing. Maybe it was the culture difference. But she didn't think so.

Leigh's post-show weariness vanished as she returned Quentin's smile. "Thank you for attending." She tilted her head and rested her hand on his arm. He covered her hand with his.

Chapter 32

"HAVE YOU GIVEN ANY THOUGHT to our housing project, Leigh?" Mora asked after the waiter had delivered their salads. "I understand you're an expert on design."

"Me? Oh no." Leigh picked at her salad. "I imagine you heard that from Quentin?"

At Mora's nod, Leigh continued, "He says that to tease. I told him in a moment of honesty that his house is ugly: all gray stone, small windows. California has *so* much sun,"—Leigh spread her arms wide, wincing slightly—"one needs to have lots of big windows." Leigh brought her hands back close together. "We Europeans have little windows; less sunshine."

Mora wondered how Quentin had taken the "ugly" comment. He could certainly dish out criticism to others, but he didn't seem the type to take kindly to it himself. And "teasing" could be a powerful backhanded weapon and a subtle but effective means of control.

Carol put down her fork. "We'd like you to become a member of the raffle house decorating committee. We want the house to be pure." At Leigh's puzzled expression, she continued, "You know, not a hodgepodge of different styles."

"Oh, I know what you mean! I've seen houses that are Victorian, Tudor, and Arts and Craft all in one. It does distract." Leigh laughed. "Actually, it's quite ridiculous and gaudy."

Mora warmed to Leigh's enthusiasm and to her finally showing some assuredness. She was quite different—more real—without her husband around. "Then you'll help us?"

"I don't think so." Leigh sighed. "My commitments for Quentin keep me quite busy. I'm afraid I just don't have the time." She twisted her napkin, then unfurled it and returned it to her lap. "He expects me to be available for entertaining his clients—on short notice."

"Don't worry, Leigh. I'll ask him myself," said Mora. "And he *won't* refuse."

Mora and Carol waited with Leigh until the valet brought her Mercedes, and then made their way to Carol's van in the handicapped slot.

Carol pushed the key into the ignition but didn't turn it. She turned to Mora, her eyes wide. "Did you—?"

"I saw your eyebrows at lunch!" Mora fastened her seat belt. "She *did* tell us two different stories about her stiff posture the night of the benefit."

"Why would she lie?"

"I don't know." Mora settled in her seat. "But she didn't want to continue that conversation."

"And that makes me want more. You?"

Mora searched in her tote for her sunglasses. "Of course. You know, I really like her. She's so engaging: English accent, proper ways of saying things."

"She *is* fun to talk to." Carol started the engine and revved it. "But . . . I wanted to hear more about the real her. At least she opened up a little bit."

Mora nodded. "And being reticent is okay. Perhaps her culture or her celebrity cause it." Despite Mora's placating words, she too was searching for answers, her suspicion growing.

"Did you notice her eyes tear when she talked about how she met Quentin?"

"Hey! Who's the psychologist here?" Mora laughed. "I noticed." Was Leigh homesick? Was the marriage in trouble? This wouldn't be the first time she had to tread carefully before diagnosing marital dynamics.

As if reading Mora's thoughts, Carol said, "*My* marriage would sure be in trouble if my husband talked down to me the way Quentin talks to her in our meetings." She pulled out of the parking lot onto Palos Verdes Drive. "She's an intelligent and artistic woman. Is he afraid she'll outshine him?" Carol shrugged. "But then, I let Reggie speak for me whenever we went out socially."

"Quentin *could* be an introverted man in an extrovert's job who compensates for his fear of people by dominating them." Mora had seen signs that Leigh loved her husband. She certainly went out of her way to please him in meetings, bringing him coffee, nodding and smiling while he spoke. But she'd also seen pain, lots of pain, as the former dancer rose from a chair or reached for her purse. She had to be honest; it could be arthritis, but...

Carol looked at Mora squarely. "I hate to say it."

"Don't."

Ignoring Mora, Carol pushed forward. "Her putting up with Quentin's behavior, along with the lies about her stiffness at the dinner, make me suspicious."

"Of?" Mora wanted to build a dam to hold back her own flood of thoughts. Unacceptable thoughts.

"*You* know. Erin already said it."

Erin's joking observation the other day *couldn't* be right. How could this man have accepted an honorary job with the BWEF if he was abusing Leigh? He must be terribly nervous, if he was. Though that *could* explain even more of his behavior.

"Leigh must have been independent when she was dancing and traveling all over the world," said Mora. "It's hard to believe she'd let herself be controlled." Of course, Mora had been the same way.

Carol pulled down the sun visor. "I suppose I *could* be projecting my experience onto others again."

"Maybe," Mora replied thoughtfully. "But maybe not," she admitted. "I think Leigh may be heading toward divorce—or worse."

"Then what's next? We have to do *something*!" Carol pounded the steering wheel with her fist, jumping when the horn sounded.

Mora sat quietly, and then said, "I think I'll inquire discreetly into Quentin Pryor's background. Call on him at work; have Erin ask about him at the marina." She gripped herself hard with crossed arms. "What a horrid thought: Quentin—an abuser."

Mora wanted to kick herself. Had she been so flattered when the bank suggested their CEO that she'd overlooked his personality? Had the bank done the BWEF a favor, or created its worst possible nightmare?

Chapter 33

Lucky—how he hated that name—awoke sweating. He threw back the covers so the circulating air could cool his steaming body.

The nightmare lingered. He was suffocating, drowning. The tang of rubber brushing against his face still permeated his bandaged nostrils. He'd had the sensation of bouncing from wall to wall, then floating over the clouds and falling endlessly into a deep, watery abyss. He gulped a reassuring breath, thankful his lungs were working. His heartbeat slowed. It all felt so real. Was this a dream—or a memory?

He considered ringing for the psychiatrist the hospital had brought in to help him. But he was afraid to. He couldn't shake the feeling that he had something to hide.

Chapter 34

"MOM, WHAT TIME IS DAD flying in tomorrow?"

Taylor felt the blood drain from her face. Thank heavens her son was on the phone and not with her in her kitchen.

"Wh-wh-why do you ask?" She fished an ice cube from her drink and rubbed it on her neck.

"I'm going to the beach late tomorrow morning and thought I'd save you a trip to the airport."

Oh gosh. Was tomorrow *really* the day Marshall was due back from his trip? Taylor had been so wrapped up in her own feelings about Marshall's death, she'd forgotten about how it was going to impact her children—or about how to tell them. They deserved the whole truth, but obviously that wasn't possible.

"Mom, are you there? This cell phone has been giving me trouble. Can you hear me?"

"I h-hear you, R…Rob."

What could she say? That Marshall wasn't coming back? She sighed. She couldn't give Rob any clue that she knew his father wouldn't be at the airport to be met.

"Are you sure tomorrow is the day?" Taylor said. "He usually calls to confirm I'll meet him, and I haven't heard anything."

Taylor racked her brain: If Rob went to the airport, he'd know his dad wasn't on the plane. Maybe *she* should just go—avoid dealing with this for now. No. She'd still have to tell her kids he hadn't come home; otherwise it would look too suspicious. Maybe it was best to let things unfold naturally.

"Rob, I'd appreciate your picking him up. Th…That's real thoughtful of you."

Taylor felt sweat dampen her hair and pour between her breasts. She'd have to compose herself before she faced her children in person.

"But you don't know what time?" Rob asked.

"Like I said, I depend on him to call before he gets on the plane. You may have a trip for nothing." She gulped her lemonade and then coughed. "Stop at the office on the way to the beach. It won't be much out of your way. You'll find his schedule on my desk calendar." Taylor let out a deep breath. "And thanks again, Jungle Baby."

"Will do. And you're welcome, Wilderness Mama."

Taylor hung up the phone and began pacing. *What now?*

Should Taylor report Marshall missing? She'd done that once before, only to have him slap her around after he got home—claiming he'd embarrassed her in front of the same park rangers that he depended on for referrals. Taylor shuddered. This time Marshall wasn't coming back. She honestly couldn't decide which was worse.

Taylor turned her mind back to her pressing problem: what story to present to the public—and especially to her kids. *If only they'd find his body!* Then no story would be necessary.

Focus, Taylor, focus! There was no time for "if-only's" and second-guessing now. If she reported Marshall missing, she'd have to answer a bunch of questions to the authorities and to the nosy press. She wished she could lie low—but she *had* to do something. Marshall was due home tomorrow. The kids might even decide to report him missing!

If only she weren't so poor with words—her inappropriate bluntness with Marshall had incited cuts and bruises. Taylor reached for the phone. Mora would know what to say!

Chapter 35

CAROL CHEERED TWO GROUPS of men playing volleyball on Torrance Beach. She and Mora had taken their bag lunches to the park above the sand for some sun-worshipping. The breeze off the ocean gently messed Carol's hair. "You know, I really miss being around men. Don't get me wrong: I'm not interested in dating. It's just— when I was married, Reggie's friends came around. When I was in training, we had lots of guys in the camps with us. Now I have lots of women friends but no male friends. Like I'm living a half-life." Carol put a partially eaten sandwich back into a Ziploc. "Is that normal, considering everything?"

Mora nodded. "You're a woman, with all of a woman's drive. Of course it's normal." She waved her hand as if presenting her friend to the public. "Here we have Ms. Carol Ewald, a lovely, vibrant, resourceful woman any man would want." She laughed. "Want me to ask the players to come up here so you can get a closer look?"

Carol punched her friend. "Don't you dare!" She bit into an apple. Swallowing, she said, "I saw an ad for a wheelchair basketball coach at the VA—for men who have lost one or both legs. I'm thinking about applying. I played basketball in high school."

"Go for it, gal!" Mora gave Carol a high five. "Does it pay much?"

"I'll volunteer. I don't need money, just networking with men." Carol suddenly pointed. "Look! Dolphins in the surf."

The women watched two young surfers approach the dolphins, only to have the sea creatures dash away from their outstretched hands.

"Mora," Carol said as the fins disappeared down the coast, "don't *you* miss having men in your life?"

"I miss intimacy, but I have many men in my life."

Carol leaned over and stared into Mora's eyes. "Been keeping secrets from me?"

Mora broke Carol's gaze to look down at her vibrating phone. It was Taylor—she should probably get that.

"It's just that I can't talk with you about *my* men," she said, lifting her phone to her ear. "They're clients."

Carol wheeled alongside Mora on the Torrance Beach overlook. She looked over her shoulder to make sure no one was within listening distance. "So I've been dying to tell you about the prep work I've done for our emergency meeting this afternoon."

Mora trotted beside her friend. "Did you get to Quentin's office?"

"I have a date this week with his appointment secretary. I told him I need to put our board meetings on his schedule." She shrugged. "That's all I could think of for an excuse."

"As his secretary, I'd have suggested you do it over the phone." Mora kicked at a rock.

"He did. I said our schedule was so complex, it would be easier to come in to compare dates."

"Will Quentin be there?"

"No. Made sure of that." Carol rolled down the incline. "I could have sworn the receptionist's voice almost sang when she realized her boss would not be in."

Mora unzipped her jacket. "You set a good pace, friend!"

Carol stopped and swiveled to face the water. She waited until Mora dropped herself onto the bench and began stretching her tired legs.

"In addition to that, I've been researching!" Carol announced. "Quentin has been married before."

Mora wiped her sweating face. "We *knew* that. Twice, in fact. Besides, at his age—charming man, handsome, high-power job—it would be most unusual if he hadn't been." She loosened her shoelace. "What happened with the exes?"

Carol hesitated. "I'm not sure we're talking about the *same* former wives. Quentin divorced his second wife almost ten years ago. This woman died only six years ago."

"Died? As in, dead?"

"I copied this off the microfiche at the library."

Carol pulled her jacket around her. Although she didn't know the dead woman, she'd felt bereft when she read the story.

"Tell."

"Name was Dorothy. They'd been married not even a year. She died in a fall at their home in the Palisades."

Quentin doesn't act like a widower, thought Carol. But then, what *would* a man act like? Especially one who'd found a beautiful, world-famous new wife?

"Was Quentin there when it happened?" Mora's face paled.

Carol shook her head. "The housekeeper found her at the bottom of the stairs when she got to work. Said Quentin came in the back door afterwards. Sweaty from his morning run."

"What did the police report say?"

"Accidental death. But evidence of prior falls, old bruises, healed break." Carol looked over her shoulder and swallowed hard. "The paper quoted an anonymous neighbor who believes Quentin pushed his wife." Carol shivered. "If that's true, the BWEF is about to go into sudden-death overtime."

Chapter 36

LUCKY'S GROUCH WON OUT over cheer this morning. The emotions of his nightmare still lingered, though he could barely remember the dream.

Uh-oh, here she comes again to evaluate the sickie for her report.

"How's my favorite patient today?" Nurse Sandy Malik touched Lucky softly on his shoulder as she adjusted his blanket. Her face wore a familiar smile as she searched her patient's eyes for signs of change—and, he was sure, recognition. His face was still fully bandaged from his reconstructive surgery, but at least he had recovered his voice.

"How would *you* be if you couldn't remember who you were?" he growled through his wired-shut jaw. *Crap.* Had he always been such an angry person?

Lucky felt dependent on this lady, and others here at the hospital, to get him well, to bring back his memory. He wanted desperately to know what he'd been up to when this all happened. What crimes he may have committed.

"I feel like I should be outdoors." That should sound like progress.

"Do you think you had an outdoor vocation?"

"Hell, I don't know!" *Geez.* No wonder nobody was banging down the hospital door looking for him.

"Hey, hey, there. I didn't mean to upset you." The nurse handed him his juice and rubbed his shoulder gently. "I was just following some clues."

Lucky wedged the juice straw between the surgical wires and took a sip. "Clues?" he muttered.

"Well, the hikers *did* find you on the bank of the river—practically naked—and your money was in a waterproof pouch."

Lucky nodded. He realized the significance of the pouch—but was still on edge about what that large sum meant.

"Also," Nurse Sandy continued, "your legs have a shorts tan line."

Lucky examined his battered limbs as best he could through his solid mask of bandages. With his muscular legs and fading, but still apparent, tan, he *did* look like someone who worked outdoors. He rubbed his bandaged left hand against his knee to relieve the itch of a healing wound.

Nurse Sandy took his blood pressure. "Do you remember carrying a cell phone? We didn't find one on you." He shook his head. At least he remembered what a cell phone *was*.

She continued in a reassuring tone, "But of course, if you were going down in the Canyon, only a satellite phone would carry a signal. And those are expensive!"

Sandy pushed the wheelchair next to his bed. "Forget trying to remember, Ducky Lucky. Let's do what you suggested: go outdoors. It's a great idea! We can go for a short walk and sit on the veranda. It's not too hot yet this morning to enjoy being outside, even if it is officially summer."

Lucky swung his legs to the side of the bed and tried to stand. Head spinning, he sat down suddenly.

"Take it slow. You may be dizzy from the meds." She balanced him with a firm grip on his elbow and guided him into the wheelchair.

He shrugged off the arm she placed around his shoulders and kicked off the light blanket she'd placed over his knees. *God, I hate bossy women!* Now, where had that come from? A woman must have screwed him over badly at one point.

Lucky gripped the wheels of the chair and headed toward the door. Apparently accepting this small demand for independence, Sandy released her grip on the chair, but she walked close to him as he rolled along the hall. Breathing heavily, he finally dropped his hands and let her propel him to the staff patio. He couldn't believe he was so weak that a woman had to push him. He slumped in his chair, exhausted.

Nurse Sandy said nothing but adjusted an umbrella to shade him.

"Forgive me for being so nosy," she finally said. "I just want to know who you are, so I can find out if you're married."

Lucky wanted to respond to her flirtatious smile. Somehow he knew he liked blondes. But besides the problem of his bandaged face, the nurse's joking tone and engagement ring belied her words.

Lucky sighed deeply. "I've been here three whole weeks. You'd think by now a wife would have come looking for me."

His words made sense, he realized. Why did he think he *was* married—but at the same time not married? He shook his head to clear it. He kept dreaming about blond women. Women with blank faces.

"Maybe they didn't know where you were going, where to look for you. Or maybe they think you're on a long wilderness trip."

Sandy sat down facing him and crossed her shapely legs. His eyes followed her movement, his groin responding. At least part of him was still alive.

"My fiancé is a reporter for the local paper," she said. "Maybe when you're a little better, I can ask him to do an article about you, run it with your picture? Maybe he could even get it on the national news wire."

Lucky shivered. He had that same sense of unease he'd felt that first day. Like he'd been doing something wrong.

"No one would recognize my new face anyway," he grumbled. "Why bother?"

"Do you have any unusual birth marks, tattoos? He could take a picture of *that*."

"Well, you would know that better than me at this point, wouldn't you?" Lucky felt a new surge of anger at his own ignorance and impotence. He shrugged it off quickly and grabbed Sandy's hand. "The problem is," he said with as much flirtatiousness as he could muster, "you might find out I'm *not* married after all. I'd give your fiancé a run for his money."

Chapter 37

"How could the Battered Women's Escape Foundation hire a man who abuses his wife?" Carol's words rang out like a death knell over the somber group.

The OC members had gathered at Carol's house.

Mora had first given the floor to Taylor to discuss the impending Marshall issue—it had been a tricky one to navigate. Mora inhaled deeply. *Just take one thing at a time,* she reminded herself.

"How could we go that wr...wrong?" asked Taylor. "It just can't be!"

Mora's hands turned to ice. She didn't want to face this possible truth. And *she* was the professional; she should have recognized the symptoms early on, back in the interview process.

Carol raised her eyebrows. "As a group, we've seen many sides of Pryor: businessman, charmer, ruthless verbal aggressor."

"To be fair," said Taylor, "we haven't *seen* him attack Leigh with anything other than cruel words."

"True." Mora exchanged a knowing glance with Carol. "But have you noticed the difference in her when he's not around?"

Erin turned to Taylor. "You've complained about how *you,* a successful business woman, shut down your assertiveness when confronting your husband." She waited for Taylor's nod. "Leigh is the life of the conversation during those rare times she's with us alone. She suppresses her real joy so deeply around Quentin that it erupts when she has an outlet—time away from him."

"Weren't you that way when Benning was alive?" Taylor's jutting chin and crossed arms punctuated her defensive tone. "I remember one time when you two came to d-d-dinner at my home. You sat there and let him d-discount every solitary thing you said."

Erin looked down at her hands. "By the time I met you, we'd been to a shitload of marriage counseling and fertility clinics."

Erin looked up at Mora, who returned her gaze with a supportive half-smile but didn't speak. Mora had known Erin almost as long as Carol; it had been a while since she'd seen the plucky contractor in this state.

"I knew he wouldn't change," Erin continued. "His ego just wouldn't let him believe he was infertile, or raise another man's child—even one conceived through artificial insemination." Erin sighed deeply. "It was just easier to let him blame me. Easier to let him win than to fight all the time—followed by being slapped around when we got home." Her eyes softened. "Sometimes when he dominated me at a party like that, he'd even give me *loving* sex instead of wham-bang coupling." Erin visibly shook herself to escape her unhappy reverie. "But thanks to you all—and to Benning's plunge off that cliff in Colorado—I'm learning to live life to its fullest now."

Carol cleared her throat. "Ladies, we wanted to discuss Quentin this afternoon."

Always the practical one, thought Mora. She respected Carol's ability to keep the group on track.

"You said his ex-wife d-d-died under suspicious c... circumstances?" Taylor shivered. "Is Leigh in d...danger?" Taylor's extra-shaky demeanor and pale complexion concerned Mora; she looked like she was about to crack. Hopefully, the group's proposed resolution would help things work themselves out.

Mora couldn't hide her concern. "Well, Carol and I told you how she walked at the fundraising dinner. *And* her disparate stories about it."

Carol pushed up her sleeve and pointed to her arm. "Plus, I've been meaning to mention that I saw a *huge* bruise on her arm when she reached for something and her sleeve moved up. I'm sure she didn't know I could see it."

"We have to help her!" said Taylor. "She's such a nice woman, and—"

"Oh God! Of *course,* our first consideration has to be Leigh," Erin broke in, "but we also have to consider the impact on the BWEF. Can you imagine what would happen if it got out that our finance chairman is a wife beater?"

Apprehension spread throughout the room.

Mora stood up. It was time to take charge of the conversation. "I'll personally look into Quentin's background and counsel Leigh," said Mora. "She may be looking for someone to talk to. In any case, I'll keep close tabs on her, make excuses to see her alone—*and* with Quentin."

"What about the BWEF?" Taylor's tight raspy voice echoed her concern. "W-What if we have to let him go?"

"If that comes about, Taylor, *you'll* take over the finances from him. Erin, you'll continue with our remodeling program, and Carol, you'll supervise the shelters *and* their budgets. It'll be hard work, but we're used to that." Mora reached out a hand to each of them. "We can't compromise *all* we believe in—not at this stage. There are too many women out there who need our help. Maybe including Leigh."

Chapter 38

QUENTIN PRYOR AROSE, smoothed his sleeping wife's hair on the pillow, and tiptoed to his dressing room. God, she was a prize. He wadded his silk pajamas into a ball and tossed them into the clothes hamper with a jump shot. His workout clothes were laid out for him. He pulled the soft white T over his head and faced the mirror to pull it into an exact horizontal line across his hips. He felt vigorous this morning. But he needed his workout to calm him for the stress of the day ahead. After getting his coffee, he set the elliptical machine to level five.

Quentin propped the *Wall Street Journal* against the book rack, but instead of reading, he thought about Friday morning. *Why doesn't Leigh do what I tell her to? Doesn't she know it hurts me to have to discipline her?* Quentin blew out a breath of air. *I should be careful. If I can believe what my first wife said, being hit too much is what drove _her_ to ask for a divorce.* Quentin threw the *Wall Street Journal* on the floor and mounted his treadmill.

Damn Leigh. How could he concentrate when he had to think about her?

Quentin wiped his sweating brow, stumbling as his concentration shifted. When they'd married, Leigh had said she trusted him to know what's right. To invest her money the best way. Why had she tried to insist yesterday that he explain their monthly investment report to her? She knew it made him angry to have his judgment questioned. Fear clutched him. She *couldn't* be thinking about leaving him. His second wife had started asking about finances before *she* filed for divorce. Fortunately, that's all she'd done before she died. He couldn't let Leigh get that far.

Quentin increased the elevation on the machine. He needed an extra hard workout this morning.

Then there was Leigh sneaking off to teach those harbor kids how to dance. The P.I. he'd hired had had no trouble following her to that children's club and watching her through the window. Said the guy at the office seemed to like her, but he didn't see any funny business going on. Still, Leigh *did* seem more relaxed on those days.

Guess she misses the ballet. Don't know why she liked all that hard work. She used to be so tired in London after a performance.

What was he to do with her? He really didn't like hitting her, but that seemed to be the only way he could get her attention.

Quentin shut off the machine and stomped toward the shower. The aborted exercise routine served only to irritate him.

As he passed their bedroom door, he glimpsed Leigh snuggled under the comforter. She was so beautiful! He winced as he noted the bruises on her arm. Maybe he should send her to a psychologist. No, that wouldn't do. She might mention making him mad enough to hit her. He'd have Kyle send her roses when he got to the office. His efficient assistant would remember what color she liked best.

Quentin stood under the hot stream, trying to scrub off the sour remnants of guilt. *Doesn't she know I love her? Maybe it's associating with those women at the BWEF.*

If only the bank's board of directors had listened when he told them he wasn't the one to become involved with the organization. He understood that the bank wanted to attract more women-owned businesses into their customer base, but... *It's just plain boring, dealing with these tear-jerking women. Overly emotional ladies who think they can help other girls who don't know how to please a man.* But enough of that; he was trapped into helping them for the rest of his year's term.

Quentin soaped up a hard loofah and scoured his shoulders.

Although some of the women owned firms smaller than the enterprises he usually dealt with, he *could* scale down his acumen to help them—draw them into the bank's clientele. Ladies like Erin, who owned that tiny construction business—and that woman with all the crazy proposals who owned that wilderness store. All of them had been admiring at last Monday's board meeting; and a few had been downright come-hither.

I guess I'll survive; it won't hurt me to donate my talent to please the board. When my term's up, I won't have to spend any more time with them.

He sighed. Compared to the guys he usually dealt with, these were just small shells tumbling in the Pacific surf.

Quentin shut the shower off so abruptly the pipes shuddered. Time to forget his wife and the do-gooders and think about important things.

Chapter 39

"WE *HAVE* TO CONFRONT Leigh now!" Carol motioned Mora into her van. "I've been thinking about this all night and I really think her life may be at stake!"

Mora frowned. "We can't jump to any conclusions, Carol," she said. "But I agree it doesn't look good."

The two drove in tense silence the rest of the way to the Pryor home. They needed to approach Leigh's situation carefully.

As the two waited for Quentin to depart for work, Mora studied the house across the street, glinting in the early morning light. She tried to focus on pointing out features, while silently praying that Quentin was not familiar with Carol's vehicle.

Finally they saw the garage door move. .

"This is it!" Carol gripped Mora's hand as the two watched Quentin's car back out of the driveway and onto the street. As his silver Jaguar disappeared around the corner, Carol let out a breath. "Okay, let's hit it."

Mora laid a restraining hand on Carol's arm as she stared up at Leigh's somber gray stone home. "Let's wait ten minutes. He could've forgotten something."

Carol raised her eyebrows but said nothing.

Finally, Mora glanced at her watch. "Okay, let's go."

Mora helped Carol up the ramp next to the steps, then held her breath as Carol rang the bell.

The cook answered. "Hello, Ms. Rey, Ms. Ewald. Was Leigh, er... Mrs. Pryor expecting you? She's just rising."

"It's okay, Cookie." A tousled Leigh started down the stairs. "You both look so serious. Is something amiss?"

Mora opened her mouth to speak but shut it as Leigh hurried to the landing. "Oh, I'm sorry to be such a clod! Please come in, ladies. Cookie, would you make us some tea? We'll be in my office."

As Leigh led them through the marble-floored entrance hall, Mora took in the paintings, which hung at eye-level on the dull beige walls. They appeared to be original abstracts but somehow not to Leigh's taste. The angled lines and garish colors clashed with the ballerina's graceful stature and simple but elegant dress.

When the women entered Leigh's study, the whole ambiance shifted.

"What a lovely room!" cried Carol.

Mora rubbed her hand over the mahogany desk with turned legs and claw feet. "This piece is handsome. Is it English?"

"Yes, thank you." Leigh looked down and sighed. Catching her in the morning seemed to have moderated her usual façade of brightness.

"I see you've made this room your own," said Mora. In contrast to the rest of the cold, sparse house, the room felt warm and lived in. Two walls were decorated with gold-framed landscapes; Mora recognized the vibrant English countryside. Photographs of Leigh in costume and with European dignitaries hung floor to ceiling on a third wall. The French doors of the remaining wall led to an enclosed garden full of roses, freesias, and fuchsias.

"I don't know how I did it," Leigh said, "but I somehow convinced Quentin that I needed a spot of privacy." She sat down behind the desk. "This used to be a butler's pantry. I come here for comfort—to look at old pictures, watch ballet DVDs." Leigh sniffed the air. "I smell Quentin's aftershave. I know he comes in here to check on what I've been doing."

Mora glanced at Carol and saw the expected eyebrow rise. This was not good.

"What's he looking for?" asked Carol.

Leigh shrugged, her gaze fixing out the window. "I suppose it's a man thing. They're always wondering what we ladies are up to—

right?" She turned back to face her guests. "Please, be seated. Cookie will be in with the tea shortly."

Leigh motioned her friends to the loveseat on the other side of her empty four-foot workspace. Mora wondered if their hostess felt she needed the desk's authority this morning.

Leigh smoothed her tousled hair and then clasped her hands before her on the oiled antique surface.

"I'm sorry we got you out of bed," said Carol. "We wanted to catch you before you went off to dance with the kiddies."

"Oh, I'm not doing that this morning." Leigh glanced at the clock on her desk. "Quentin has a working lunch here today, so I've hostess duties." She looked up at the sound of a light knock on the door frame.

"Thank you, Cookie dear. Just set the tray on the desk. We'll serve ourselves." Leigh stood and reached for the hot beverage. "You need to get back to the luncheon preparations."

After serving them all tea, Leigh returned to her seat. "So, ladies," she said, "what is this about?" Leigh inhaled the steam and huddled her hands around her cup, as though needing its warmth.

Carol looked at Mora, who nodded.

"We're here to talk about something that is bothering us," Carol said. "Something in our conversation the other day at lunch."

"Oh? Something about *me*?" Leigh's teacup rattled slightly in her hands and she set it down.

"Well not *you*, per se. Just something we want to ask you about." Carol squirmed in her chair.

"I don't mean to be rude," Leigh said, glancing nervously toward the grandfather clock in the corner, "but I hope this won't take *too* long—I need to consult with Cook about today's luncheon. Quentin stepped out to buy a special wine at a store in Manhattan Beach. I need to get dressed before he returns, in case some guests come early." Leigh's lips trembled slightly. "He'll want me especially well-turned-out for this luncheon. He's— *We're* giving it for a prospective client. One the mayor recommended to the bank." Leigh gulped her tea. "Quentin will be particularly anxious. His connection with the mayor is sacrosanct."

Carol glanced at Mora, her eyebrows raised.

"We're concerned about your physical health," began Mora. Leigh looked at her warily. "The first night we met, you said—"

"Oh, the garage door is going up!" Leigh jumped up from the desk. "Quentin is home earlier than I expected. I…I'm very sorry, but I need to get dressed. This luncheon is top priority—to both Quentin and me." Leigh placed her napkin on the serving tray. "Perhaps we can discuss this later? Cook will show you out."

Leigh practically ran from the room, only to bump into Quentin.

"Dearest, you should be dressed," said Quentin silkily. "*Our* guests will arrive in an hour." Quentin bussed his wife on her cheek. "You run off. I'll show *your* guests out." A firm grip on Leigh's elbow steered her toward the stairs.

Quentin turned to Mora and Carol. "A little early to call, isn't it? Especially without an appointment."

If Mora hadn't honed her psychologist's impassive look, Quentin would have seen fear on her face, so disturbing was his tight smile. Had they caused more harm to Leigh by coming here?

"Good morning, Quentin." Mora tried to smile but found her lips frozen. "You're right. This was a bad time to call. Carol and I got an early start looking at homes for a friend, and on impulse we stopped to ask Leigh about the area architecture." She turned to follow Carol to the door. "We'll make an appointment with her next time."

"I see no need for you to discuss architecture privately with Leigh at all," said Quentin, leading them to the door. "She *is* knowledgeable on the subject, but certainly your questions may be posed during breaks at our regular meetings. There's no reason for you to interrupt her important social engagements. Don't you agree, ladies?" Quentin's squint and lopsided smile made Mora's stomach turn.

Back in her van, Carol released a loud sigh. "I'm more certain than *ever* that there's something evil in that marriage!"

Mora nodded. "I'm afraid you're right, my friend. Although he *did* control it in front of us, Quentin was radiating anger. His cheeks twitched and his hands were clenched."

"I wish we could go back in to see if Leigh's okay." Carol inserted the ignition key but didn't turn it.

"Unfortunately, we can't do that," said Mora. "Besides, he wouldn't even open the door."

Carol pushed the button to wash the windshield and then watched the wipers slush the fluid away. "We blew it, didn't we?"

Mora shook her head, looking down at her lap. "I hope not."

Chapter 40

Taylor clicked off the computer, her muddled brain refusing to focus on the Quicken formatting. She had hoped that concentrating on the month-end bills would calm her mind; it had been sprinting since yesterday's impromptu OC meeting. But her suppliers would just have to wait for their money.

She put her head in her hands. If only Marshall would be found— or would be ID'd if he *had* been found. Then she wouldn't have to deal with any of this.

At least she now knew what she had to do. She just hoped she could pull it off.

Taylor's head jerked up at the jangle of the shopkeeper's bell on the front door.

"Mom? Mom? Are you in here?"

Showtime.

"I'm in the office, Rob."

Taylor braced herself as Rob made his way to the back of the store.

"I called you and went by the house to tell you Dad wasn't at the airport. I waited until everyone picked up their luggage to see if his was there. It wasn't."

"Rob...I—"

"Mom, what's the matter? You're as white as soapsuds. Have you heard anything? Is Dad hurt?"

Taylor took a deep breath. "Dad isn't coming," she whispered. "He told me before he left that he was l-leaving us." Taylor blinked back tears that she realized were genuine.

"But—" Rob started to protest. Then his shoulders slumped. "Oh, Mom! So that's why you've been acting so strange? You should have told us."

Taylor looked up at her son, the pain of *his* loss beginning to hit her. "I know. I guess I was just h…hoping he didn't mean it, like b-b-before." Taylor jumped up and hugged Rob tight. "Besides," she said, talking into his shoulder, "I…I didn't know what to say."

Chapter 41

"MORA SPEAKING." Mora's cell had rung as soon as Carol pulled back onto Palos Verdes Drive West. *It's Taylor,* she mouthed.

Mora listened intently for several minutes.

"Taylor," Mora finally interrupted the rambling monologue, "I believe you could use some company. Carol and I just came from Leigh's. We'll stop by your house so we can discuss all this further—okay?" Mora paused. "We'll see you in a few."

Carol looked at Mora. "Sounds like it's time for today's crisis number two."

Mora nodded. "Let's just hope we do a better job with *this* one."

"This m...mess keeps getting bigger!" Taylor paced beside the swimming pool, where she'd hastily thrown together a snack for herself, Mora, and Carol. "I talked to R...Rob about Marshall's not coming home. Now my grown ch-ch-children want to treat me like an invalid. Rob made me leave w-w-work and wants me to stay in. And my daughter is threatening to engage a n-n-nurse to sit with me at n–night—in case I get depressed over Marshall's leaving us."

Mora held up a finger while she finished chewing a bite of cheese she'd just popped into her mouth. "Maybe you can take advantage of your downtime to grieve," she said. "And having a nurse nearby *wouldn't* be such a bad idea."

"But how can I even *start* to grieve until they find h...him?" Taylor shook her head. "It's breaking me up that I can't tell my k-k-kids the truth. If they'd just find his b...body and identify him, it would give me—and them—some c...closure."

Carol reached for a carrot stick. "If he had been found, you'd think the papers would be looking for his ID. Or at least he'd be on the Internet sites for missing people." She sipped her lemonade. "Have you looked there?"

"No. Erin has. I didn't want to do it on my computer; the k…kids might see it."

Mora nodded. "Finding his body *would* be ideal. But Taylor, for your own health, you need to accept that he may not be found. Or, if found, not identifiable—ever. You *need* to move on."

Taylor looked down at her hands. "What if I'm n…*never* able to move on and be normal again?" She shook her head to clear it. "I'm going crazy."

"You're not crazy, just stressed." Mora thought a moment. "I'd suggest outside counseling, but not being able to tell the whole story may stress you more."

Carol squeezed her friend's hand. "Are you okay with the kids running the store?"

"Definitely. They do admirably well." Taylor smiled fondly. "As they should. I've kept them with me in there from the time they were born. Marshall was gone on his trips so much, and I didn't want them to be raised by babysitters."

Mora slurped the last of her iced tea. "Do you get the store under Marshall's will?"

Taylor sucked in her breath. She hadn't thought about that. Even if they *found* the paper she'd signed, the one giving Marshall sole ownership of the store, would he have willed his assets to her? *Damn it!* It was *her* store! He wouldn't *dare* do otherwise. Taylor's thoughts competed as they raced inside her skull.

"The store is, and has always been, all mine," she said with a great deal more certitude than she felt. "I started the company long before we married. That's how I met Marshall: He came into the store for supplies and then hired me to fly one of his whitewater groups to the Canyon."

"Are you *sure* the store's is not tied up in community property?" asked Carol. "Shouldn't you consult with the BWEF family law attorney to be sure?"

Taylor hit the table with her fist. "No!" That's all she needed. An attorney looking for a paper that may have been filed about the store.

"Thanks, Carol. But I have my own attorney for the business. He's made sure it remained my property and not community property."

From the beginning, Taylor had felt uneasy enough about the marriage to protect her business—separate it from Marshall's. The troubles she and Marshall'd had, even after the children were born, had strengthened her determination to keep it set apart. If only she hadn't been so weak as to sign that transfer paper the last time he beat her. Could it be that she'd been *too* protective of the store, and that's what had caused Marshall to steal it from her? After all those years of marriage, had it been reasonable of him to expect her to trust him? She gave a mental shrug. Well, she hadn't, and he'd proven her right.

"Now that Marshall is gone, have you discussed his abuse with your children?"

Taylor was caught off guard by Carol's bluntness. But she knew Carol wasn't being rude; she just cared. Taylor shook her head. "No. They've seemed to deny it exists, and they haven't asked me about it, even now."

"Could you bring it up with *them*?" asked Mora. "As a precursor to their finding out that he's never coming back?"

Taylor shook her head again—this time more vehemently. "I won't ever discuss it with them unless they bring it up. I want to let Rob, in particular, treasure his memories of his father, untarnished by Marshall's behavior with me." She paused. "Rob enjoyed the wilderness trips with his dad—even though Marshall was brutally critical of him at times. And R...Ruth has her own unhappy memories. I can't saddle her with mine."

The three of them contemplated the problem, saying nothing.

Finally Mora spoke. "Taylor, you need to work," she said. "It will be therapeutic, especially because you love that store."

Carol's eyes twinkled. "You can tell the kids it's what the doctor ordered!"

For the first time that day, Taylor smiled. "Thank you—I agree. And it's nice to have some support." She jumped up to clear the table. "In fact, I think I'll head over there right now. We just got a shipment of climbing equipment in from Santa Fe."

Chapter 42

LEIGH WAS STRUGGLING with her earring when she saw Quentin's reflection in the dressing table mirror. Her body chilled. She sensed that Mora and Carol's visit this morning had angered him. Hopefully not to the striking-out stage. She hated feeling her whole being cower in front of him, as it was doing now.

"Why did those women come here when they knew I would be gone?" Quentin's mouth turned down and a frown creased his forehead.

"I don't know that that was the case," said Leigh. She smiled at her husband in the mirror. "I've never discussed your work schedule with them. Have you?" *Oooh,* why had she said that?

Quentin grabbed her elbow and pulled her up. "You are *not* to see them again. Is that clear?"

"Oh— Okay…if you wish, dear." Leigh was willing to promise anything right now to prevent an explosion. She tried to pull her arm from his grasp, only to have him wrench his grip tighter. "Does that mean you don't want me to attend the board meetings either?" *Oh God, let him at least permit that outing.* She looked forward to the normal human contact.

"Well, I did promise I would bring you. You can go, but only if I am going to be there. Understood?" Quentin tightened his hold on Leigh's arm until she whimpered.

"Oh, yes, of course," she whispered.

"And one other thing: You're never to discuss our marriage with them. You hear?"

Leigh grimaced in pain and nodded.

"I want you to say it." Quentin tightened his vice grip on her arm.

"Yes, Quentin, dear." Leigh swallowed hard. "I won't go to the BWEF meetings without you, or speak out without your approval there…and I won't discuss our marriage."

"Just *remember:* I have the knowledge to bankrupt that organization you and your tear-jerking friends think is so wonderful." Quentin released her arm. "Believe me, I won't hesitate to do just that if you disobey me on this."

"Now," he said, helping her on with the dark-olive silk jacket, "put on your stage smile, and come down and greet our guests."

Chapter 43

"SHARON, IT'S ERNEST HAZELTON. Joe and I were hoping you and Mike—Cailin, too, if she's available—would join us after supper this Friday, for our game night." Sharon felt her heart race and then her stomach churn. She hesitated. "Ernest, what a nice invite. Could you hold on while I ask the kids?"

"Mike, Mike!" Sharon rushed over to the couch and pulled the earbud from her son's ear. "Ernest and Joe want us to join them to play games this Friday. Wanna go?"

Mike bit his lip and swiped at his eyes with his sleeve. "Okay, Mom."

"Cailin?"

"Oh, Mom! They're babies. Karen wants me to go to a show with her and Jessie."

Sharon nodded and returned to the waiting phone.

"Thanks, Ernest. Sounds like fun. What time?"

Sharon hung up the phone and returned to preparing dinner, her mind in a quandary. A part of her felt so happy about Ernest's invitation…but she hated living in fear of upsetting her children.

Sharon made a decision: she and the kids could use more therapy. She had to understand their needs—and her own—and they all needed to learn how to deal with life in a single-parent household. Especially if the single parent started dating.

But where should she go—what therapist? They needed someone experienced in this kind of thing, one who understood. Maybe someone at a shelter?

Sharon turned the pasta sauce to simmer and went into her bedroom. She grabbed her fanny pack off her nightstand and dumped it on the bed. The woman she'd met at the BWEF marathon had given her a business card. She was a psychologist.

Ah, here it was: Mora Rey.

Chapter 44

"Of course I remember you, Sharon. You're with the Sheriff's Department, right?" Mora punched the speaker button on her phone, her senses on full alert. She set aside her preparations for this afternoon's BWEF meeting.

As Sharon launched into her family situation, Mora felt her shoulders relax. She pulled a clean tablet toward her and picked up her pen. "Well, Sharon, I don't have a *lot* of time in my schedule right now." She drew a stick-figure family: one woman and two kids, a boy and a girl. "But, I tell you what, let's make an appointment for the two of us to talk, and if I *can't* help, I'll refer you to a colleague who can." She had to navigate this meeting carefully!

"What? Oh, I'm sorry I didn't say sooner. There's no charge for the first consultation. What times of day are you free?"

Mora looked at her calendar. "Actually, Sharon, I could squeeze you in right now if you're interested." *Might as well get it over with.* "Great! I'll see you in twenty minutes."

Mora contemplated her predicament. She shouldn't see Sharon at all—other than to refer her. But it wouldn't hurt to have the inside track with law enforcement. She created a new patient file on her computer.

"Mora, thank you for seeing me on such short notice!" Sharon leaned against the doorjamb, breathing hard from her dash up the stairs.

"No problem, Sharon. Let's sit over here by the window. The flowers in the courtyard are much more fun to look at than my cluttered desk."

She seems nice. Like someone I could talk to. But she's rich, and busy. Maybe I can't afford her. Sharon took a deep breath. What did she have to lose?

"As you know, I've spent time in a BWEF shelter and my ex is in prison. You met my kids at the marathon."

Mora nodded. She drew a legal pad to her lap and twisted new lead into her mechanical pencil. "Yes, I remember them well. They both seem compassionate and responsible. You want to talk about them?"

Sharon sat back in her chair and thought about what she should say. She put her elbows on her knees and leaned forward. "They, especially my son, keep asking if Sean—he's my ex—and I are going to get back together." She sighed deeply. "I just met a man I'd like to date." She shifted in her chair, looked out at the garden, and then back at Mora. "They make me feel so guilty—wanting a new life. I don't think I can handle that without some help. So I—"

"Sharon, let me assure you that both you and your kids are normal. All families of divorce go through this." Mora put down her pencil.

"Oh, then you don't think we need counseling?" Sharon frowned and scooted to the edge of her chair.

Mora held out her hand. "Hold on a minute. I didn't say *that*." She paused.

"Oh, well, can I make an appointment for them? And do you think we should do family counseling, or individual?"

Ms. Key looked like an interview subject, thought Sharon. Like she was searching for words so as not to incriminate herself.

"I usually limit my practice to the abused spouses in BWEF shelters." Mora smiled at the troubled mother. "You've moved on from that point."

Sharon squirmed uncomfortably. "Then I've wasted your time. I'm—"

"You haven't wasted my time or yours. Your concern for your children is real. I'll take your family's case if you can be flexible about the times we meet."

"Sure. I was going to ask you the same—my shifts and all." Sharon sat back, her whole body relaxing. Then she sat forward. "Will it be expensive? I can't—"

"I receive some funding from the BWEF, so my rates are low, and we can set up a payment plan. Besides, you'd be surprised how quickly we resolve family issues like yours. Let me get my calendar."

Chapter 45

"I'M YOUR FINANCIAL OFFICER, not your chief beggar!" Mora recoiled from the force of Quentin Pryor's words. All she'd done was ask him to solicit the bank's contractor customers for pro bono help in making a few changes to the house they'd purchased to raffle. With his attitude toward the whole project, she should have known better.

"He's terribly busy, Mora," interjected Leigh. She glanced at Quentin. "I've entertained most of those men," she said tentatively. "*I* could call on them."

"*Entertained* them?" Despite Quentin's teasing smile, Mora detected a definite sneer in his voice. Was that fear in his eyes, too? "I hope, my dear, you don't mean in the sexual sense."

Leigh blushed and looked down at her lap. Mora pursed her lips. She could not put herself between the two. It was not the time.

Leigh lifted her head. "You jest, dear!" She smiled sweetly. "You *know* I meant they had been to dinner at our home." She paused. "At *your* invitation." Mora cheered silently.

"We can phone them together, Leigh," Mora said quickly. "From my office. It probably won't take a personal visit." Mora wanted to support Leigh's independence. Quentin's verbal abuse was getting worse in their meetings; Mora estimated it wouldn't be long before he forbade Leigh to come with him at all.

"I solicited for the ballet, often—in London. I imagine the pitch is similar here," said Leigh.

"Perfect. And your home is beautifully decorated, too. You'll know what kind of help to ask the builders for."

"I don't think so," said Quentin, with a laugh that didn't meet his eyes. "My *ex*-wife designed our home's interior. It's so well done, I saw no reason for Leigh to bother herself with redecorating."

"Ooh! That man makes me so mad!" Erin held open the door of her pink Ford pickup so Mora could deposit her purse onto the passenger seat. "You *know* I'm right about him."

Of course Mora agreed, but she wanted to be absolutely sure before she confirmed her friend's suspicions. "I agree that he's a *verbal* abuser," she said over the roof of the truck cab as Erin walked around to the driver's side. "But we still can't be sure he's a physical abuser— a life-threatening one."

One thing *was* certain: Quentin Pryor was not an easy man to work with. Mora slid into the cab and reached for her seat belt. Surely there was someone more personable at the bank to help the BWEF. Why did it have to be Quentin? She shivered.

"Mora, you're the psychologist," said Erin, climbing behind the steering wheel. "You *must* see what I'm seeing. She had a bruise on her wrist this morning, under the silver cuff bracelet."

Mora pushed her hair from her forehead. "Even if it's true, Leigh has to *tell* us that Quentin physically abuses her before we can do anything. Then she has to agree to our help."

"Oh, she will eventually, the way things are escalating." Erin started the ignition. "That's if Quentin doesn't kill her first."

Chapter 46

EYES SHUT TIGHT, Leigh stretched luxuriously and snuggled deeper into the silk comforter, waiting for a signal that Quentin had left their Palos Verdes home. She listened intently to the sounds of his rigid morning routine: the chink of the weights as he finished triple rounds on each weight machine in his gym; the thump as he dropped a heavily weighted bar to the rubber mat; and the slap as each foot hit the treadmill in his daily climb up an artificial mountain. She heard the slush of the shower as he scrubbed.

In another thirty minutes, Quentin would be gone for the rest of the week and the entire weekend, traveling to meet with his clients: the western states' elite builders, promoters, and producers. On these trips, he managed the affairs of these executives and met with bank branch officers as well. Leigh welcomed each minute he was so-absorbed—minutes she could dance, sing, and choreograph future exercises.

While her husband readied himself in his custom-appointed dressing room, Leigh remained still in her cool silk nest. She couldn't chance his spoiling her mood—wouldn't give him an opportunity to find some necessary chore for her to do. Not *this* morning.

Thinking about the ballet class she would teach in a little over three hours made Leigh smile: young faces in an array of hues from varied ethnic backgrounds; boys and girls both—eager to turn their awkward bodies into graceful dancers. And with Quentin gone, there'd be no need to devise some errand that would take her from home.

Leigh relaxed as she heard the hum of the garage door motor come to a stop and the roar of Quentin's Jaguar down the drive.

Graceful feet reached from under the covers and glided into red satin mules. Leigh pirouetted her way to the bathroom, humming the music from *Swan Lake*. She fluttered her arms, imitating the movement of the elegant bird's wings.

If only I could dance all *the time, instead of just when Quentin is away. I can't believe I hide it—me, who's danced since I was a toddler.* Leigh sighed. *How did I get myself into this mess? I should have realized Quentin only pretended to be interested in my performance. At the time, I thought I needed to marry. How wrong I was.*

The pain of giving up dancing hurt Leigh's heart. Was Quentin's teasing about her need to express her passion escalating? Or was she just becoming less tolerant?

Leigh shook her head. She'd have to think about it tomorrow. Today was dancing day!

In a flowing amber tunic above her black leotard, Leigh tapped the bell on the reception desk.

"Is that the Ballet Lady, come to sprinkle us with culture today?" the gruff voice called to her from the office behind the lobby of the Boys and Girls Club. "Come on back!"

It was dance day at the gym, courtesy of the Harbor Ballet School. Portable barres and a boom box had been transported here just for Leigh's session. She allowed herself to feel free. Coming here was her salvation.

"Hi, Gordon, how many future stars do I have today?" Leigh walked through the swinging gate to the manager's office, her feet gliding over the frayed gray-green linoleum.

"Let's see. Twelve, in all. You have two new ones: brothers eight and ten years old. Their parents are Russian émigrés who came here when the kids were toddlers. The parents want them to take ballet, like the Kirov." He grinned. "But you should expect *them* to be wary. They may have been born in Russia, but they're typical U.S. boys now. Afraid they'll be sissified taking dance lessons, and sure to be teased by their schoolmates."

Leigh loved working with young boys. Their powerful bodies—even at an early age—allowed them to jump high and lift a partner.

"I'll start them on muscle-building exercises. They can brag about how hard they work out." The dancer laughed. "I proved it to Juan and Sergio last year. Igor, Asad, and Bastiaan, too. Soon, the two new ones will be believers." Leigh felt herself unwinding. Just being here calmed her busy thoughts. Her whole body itched to dance.

"I notice that the kids in your class are beginning to relax," said Gordon as he reached into the key locker on the wall behind his desk. His burr haircut, neatly pressed jeans, and starched shirt reflected his recently completed stint in the infantry. "It's like they've finally found some beauty in their drab existence, and that gives them hope."

"Hope?"

"Hope that they can climb that mountain of poverty in front of them and the ugliness of our streets that goes with it—into, uh, into a meadow full of wildflowers." He spread his arms wide, indicating the expanse of a flower glen.

"Gordon, that's poetic!" Leigh took the key he offered and smiled brightly, despite the tears pooling in her carefully made-up eyes. "And it's true. Dancing here disguises ugliness for me, too."

Leigh turned towards the scuff-floored room that served as her dance studio when it was not hosting a basketball game or a community meeting. She ignored Gordon's look of disbelief. Her careful façade: poised face, manicured nails, emerald engagement and wedding rings, and dancer's carriage served her well this morning. If only she could confess to someone that the perfect life she and Quentin presented to the public was all a farce.

A ragtag assemblage of youngsters, aged seven to twelve, faced Leigh. Socks in various states of cleanliness covered their feet in lieu of the ballet slippers that neither they nor the club could afford. Leigh worried about the lack of shoes. A letter to the local papers should bring donations of outgrown ones. Perhaps she could put a notice on the dance school bulletin board. Dance academies in Torrance and Lomita, too. If she had discretionary funds Quentin didn't know about, she'd buy them herself. But he controlled her investments and would never approve. Leigh clapped her hands and waved the children into straight lines in front of her.

"We shall begin our warm-up session with plies," she said when they had quieted. Smiling at the two new boys, she added, "Like squats, only with your legs in a different position; they develop your thighs and calves." The boys nodded but didn't otherwise respond. "Then we'll move on to the foot and leg positions, and arm exercises."

Leigh pushed the button on the CD player and took second position, facing her giggling charges. As the music started, she lowered her body in a fluid movement. "Now *you* try. I'll walk around and observe." She raised her voice to be heard above the music. "Don't be alarmed if I put my hand on your arm or leg; I'll just be adjusting your body so you can get the feel of the correct position." Leigh sensed that an unexpected touch would startle, and perhaps frighten, a child whose turf was the city streets.

As always when she danced, Leigh's senses sharpened. She felt the air swirl around her as she moved. Dancing was *her* life force. She wondered where these children found theirs.

When the squatting, turning, and jumping warm-up exercises ended and her students were subdued and sweating, Leigh announced: "Time for our ten-minute respite. Don't forget your body needs lots of water after all that exertion. When you're rested, we'll work on our recital." She smiled as her class formed itself into a squiggly line at the drinking fountain.

"What's a re–sit–al?" Sergio asked, approaching his teacher, eyes curious.

"It's a performance—a show—for your parents and friends, so they can see what you've learned." She smiled and patted the bench beside her, inviting him to sit there.

"Did you dance ballet for money?" Sergio looked at Leigh wide-eyed. "Like a movie star?"

Leigh nodded.

Sergio pointed to her neck. "That's a big bruise! I bet it hurts. How did you get it? Did the doctor give you anything for it?"

Leigh struggled to keep her emotions corralled. "Oh! It was an accident, Sergio. I did something stupid, something I shouldn't have." Leigh pulled the neckline of her tunic to re-cover the ocher blemish at the base of her long slender neck. "It doesn't hurt though." She patted the inquisitive youngster's arm. "You know how bruises look worse, the older they are."

Leigh danced her way to the door of the club. When she got home she could go to her office—her haven—and work on the routine she was composing for the children.

Days like this made Leigh realize just how *much* she missed dancing: the discipline, the floating to music. Could it be she should put Quentin behind her and return to the dance full time? Flushed and satisfied after the teaching session, her whole being shouted "Yes!"

Leigh laughed as she pushed through the front doors, surrounded by admiring preteen boys. "Okay, guys, see you next week." Her eyes followed the swaggering youths until they rounded the corner.

"Leigh, over here!"

Leigh started.

"Mora, Carol. What are you doing here?" Two faces peered at her eagerly through the passenger window of Carol's van.

"We came to steal you for lunch. Hop in!" Mora jumped out and opened the sliding door to the back seat.

Leigh looked at her watch. Then she remembered it didn't matter—she was free!

"Sure, why not?" She hurried toward the van.

True, Leigh had been looking forward to working on the ballet and then a long soak in the tub. But having lunch with friends was good, too. Leigh missed having women friends. Friends she could invite to tea at the kitchen table. Friends she could share her secret dreams with.

Chapter 47

Mora smoothed the napkin in her lap as she scrutinized Leigh's face. Leigh looked unusually happy and relaxed—it must be from the dancing, thought Mora.

Mora still had trouble believing that *anyone* could hit this beautiful woman. Let alone Quentin. How could someone of his community and career status need to govern with physical blows at home? And how could he face himself: volunteering to help the BWEF? Certainly, he was in denial. But she needed to find the answer to the complex man.

This wouldn't be the first time Mora had encountered an abuser who was well-founded in their community. But why hadn't she spotted any symptoms earlier? Had she been blinded by Quentin's charm? His financial expertise? Expertise they needed badly if they were to grow.

Mora felt sweat forming on her upper lip. She had to tiptoe here. What if other supporters heard of their goof—hiring a wife-abuser to manage money for the BWEF? Mora still didn't want to believe this was the case, but she owed the organization—and Leigh—her due diligence. She had to know.

"Leigh," she began, "I'm so glad you could join us today. Nowhere to rush off to?"

"Not today!" Leigh grinned. "Quentin's away on business until Monday. As much as I love having so much attention, I sometimes welcome time away from him." She frowned and looked at Mora. "That doesn't make me a bad wife, does it?"

"Makes you a normal one, in my book."

Mora laughed at Carol's droll commentary.

Carol grasped Leigh's hand. "Mora and I are going to her Arrowhead cabin this weekend. Join us?"

Mora cocked her head and tried to catch Carol's eye—what was the woman up to now?

Before Leigh could reply, Carol continued, "There are even paved trails, so I can hike with you and Mora."

Leigh looked back and forth between her new friends. "Oh, I don't want to intrude."

"Please come. It's just a girls' sleepover. We'll be back by Sunday afternoon. And you won't even have to drive. I'll pick you up in my van."

Leigh hesitated. "Well…Quentin *will* be out of town. So what the heck—thank you!"

The waiter arrived with their lunch and the conversation lagged as the women ate. After their coffee was poured, Mora stirred hers but then pushed the cup away. It was time to get to it.

"Leigh," Mora looked at her earnestly. "I— We've been wondering…do you have any *other* problems with Quentin that you'd like to talk about? That we should know about?"

"How— I mean…to what are you referring?" Leigh's eyes widened. Mora could swear she saw fear in them. Leigh regained her composure quickly though. She spoke kindly but firmly. "I'm sorry, ladies, but I don't choose to discuss Quentin with you. We *both* relish our privacy." Leigh picked up her coffee cup and stared into it contemplatively.

Carol raised her eyebrows, while Mora sipped her water.

Mora could see that the door was closed on this discussion— for now. She now appreciated Carol's foresight in inviting Leigh to Arrowhead for further probing.

The rest of the meal was completed with awkward small talk. Mora and Carol returned Leigh to the Boys and Girls Club, both remaining silent until Leigh was in her own car, driving away.

Carol spoke first. "Well, that was…enlightening."

"Yeah, but her reaction still doesn't prove anything." Mora bit her lip. "This weekend, though, I'll find a way to give Leigh our verbal pre-revelation domestic violence test. I'll get her to tell me the truth."

A worried crease marred Carol's brow. "You'd better," she said.

Chapter 48

"I'M GOING HIKING, Lucky. Any pointers?" Doctor George had removed his white coat. His feet were clad in hiking boots and his T-shirt was sleeveless.

Lucky turned from the window where he'd been watching the sun rise behind the hills. "Watch out for snakes—especially the rattlers sunning themselves in the early morning. They'll feel the vibration of your footsteps before you see them." Lucky's recently unwired jaw fell open and his eyes widened. "Where did *that* come from?"

"Sounds like you *have* spent a bit of time in the great outdoors. Anything else coming through?"

"Shit, no. I feel like I'm a brand new baby with everything in the world to learn." Lucky laughed hollowly. "Well, at least I can walk now, and talk—I don't have to learn *that* all over again."

Something still nagged at Lucky—something he wouldn't *want* to remember. Maybe that's why his brain insisted on remaining a blank sheet of paper.

"I don't think I'm up for a hike yet, though!" he said, mustering joviality.

Doctor George nodded. "You're probably right." He put a hand under Lucky's chin and turned his head. "Your face is healing nicely. I just wish I could compare it with what you looked like in your former life." The doctor patted his patient on the shoulder. "I have to be going. See you next week."

"Doc, wait—before you go." Lucky grabbed the doctor's arm. "How's my money holding out? The money you found in that pouch?"

"We haven't sent you a bill, yet, Lucky. But so far, you're probably still in the black. Given your situation, the hospital has donated a lot

186

of their services and is charging cost for the rest. I'm donating my fees to the cause as well."

"Oh." Lucky squirmed—he was sure he didn't deserve all this kindness. Not trusting himself to speak, he bowed his head in acknowledgment. The doctor patted his shoulder one more time and walked out.

Lucky returned his gaze to the window. Maybe losing his memory was a good thing. If he *had* been a shitty person in his previous life, maybe this was his chance to start over—to be someone else.

Lucky wandered to the full-length mirror and turned to and fro. *Gad, I'm ugly: Splotchy skin, swollen cheeks, scars. At least my eyes are the same. Women always said they were my most attractive feature.* Lucky started at the realization. *Now, how did I know that?*

He *did* know there was nothing wrong with his sex mechanism. Nurse Sandy's swaying had made him hard. Maybe a good lay would bring him out of the funk he was in. Would he remember how to perform with a woman? He damn well wanted to try.

Chapter 49

As Mike and Sharon walked to the Hazeltons', Sharon felt a mixture of excitement and tension. She at least felt better about the situation after Mora told her that a group outing was the perfect way to ease into this situation before tackling a one-on-one date with Ernest.

"So, what games do you suppose we'll be playing tonight?" she asked Mike. It would be fun concentrating on winning a game instead of work.

"I talked to Joe. He promised to teach me a new game that needs at least three players."

"What is it?"

"Clue."

Chapter 50

QUENTIN PRYOR YANKED THE COVERS off of his sleeping wife. "Get up and get my breakfast."

"Quen dear, ask Cook; she knows what you like." A sleepy Leigh reached out for the silk sheet to re-cover her lace-clad body. Then she froze. Her husband's ire at the change in his Saturday household routine filled the room.

Quentin doubled his fist and punched her in the shoulder. "I said, 'Get up!'" He pulled her arm until she was upright. "Cook isn't here. What did you do, give her the day off again?"

This was her own fault, Leigh realized. Quentin had come home late last night, three days early from his Boise trip. In her disappointment over having to cancel her upcoming weekend with the girls, she'd forgotten she'd suggested to Cook that she sleep in this morning.

"And I told you last night that I'd be going sailing today!" Quentin was building himself into a full-blown rampage. "And *every* Saturday until the race in September. Got that?"

"Yes, dear. I'll remember: *every* Saturday." She pulled on her peignoir. "I'm sorry I didn't know. I'm sure you were so tired from your trip that it slipped your mind—but it's all right. It won't take long to poach you a couple of eggs." She padded to the door in her bare feet.

Quentin's face turned red-hot. Leigh realized that instead of soothing him, she'd only added to his anger. She should have kept quiet and let him vent on her. She *was* his wife; he could rant at her. If only he would do it without hurting her.

And—*darn it!*—she'd been looking forward to her time away from Quentin, and from this mausoleum he called home. Leigh immediately felt guilty for questioning her husband's tastes, on top of relishing his absence.

Quentin pushed her through the door. "It's your job to see that all of my needs are met. Now stop blabbing and get my breakfast. I'll need a sandwich for lunch, too."

Leigh ground fresh Hawaiian Kona coffee just the way he liked it. *At least he won't be around to annoy me today. And,* she realized excitedly, *I won't have to cancel my trip to Mora's cabin after all! I'll just drive myself and meet them a little later.* Leigh hid behind the open refrigerator door and texted Carol to let her know she'd meet them there. When Quentin entered the kitchen, Leigh stuck her cell phone into the egg carton and closed the refrigerator door.

The timer for Quentin's eggs sounded as he sat down at the table. Leigh could feel his eyes on her as she slipped the eggs from the poacher to his plate. Her hands shook, but she held onto the dish. His silence terrified her almost as much as his rampages. She needed this trip to the mountain.

As Leigh's shaking hand poured coffee into her husband's cup, some of the hot liquid splashed over into the saucer. She set the pot on the counter and clasped a hand to her mouth while she reached for a napkin to blot the spill with the other.

It was too late.

Like a cat, Quentin sprang from his chair and gripped her arm. "You just can't get anything right, can you?" he sneered.

Leigh dropped into a ragdoll pose. *Please, oh please, oh please.*

Quentin wrenched Leigh's arm behind her back and pushed her in front of him to the bedroom, punching her in the lower back with his free hand. He threw her on the bed, grabbed the lace of her nightgown, and tore it to expose her breast. Leigh held her breath as Quentin pinched her nipple and was finally forced to cry out. Quentin let go of her and rose. He unzipped his trousers to release his swollen penis.

Chapter 51

At Mora's Arrowhead cabin, Carol opened the curtains as the morning sun broke through the clouds.

"I thought Leigh was going to meet us here by now," said Erin, pacing the Navajo rug on the floor of the pine-paneled room. "It's already nine o'clock. Are we sure she's coming?"

Carol looked up from her computer. "Well...her text was a little vague." She wiggled in her chair. This was not one of her good mornings. The pain wouldn't stop. Carol wheeled to the window. She didn't want to voice it aloud, but if Leigh didn't get here soon, she was going to leave. She needed the Jacuzzi today.

Carol reached into her stash bag and pulled out an energy bar. They were fattening, but she needed one—now. Only two left; she'd have to pace herself.

Taylor pushed her hair behind her ears with both hands. "Didn't Leigh say she had to wait until Quentin left to go sailing?" She marched from one edge of the room to the other, her hiking boots shaking the wood floor.

"Yes," said Erin grimly. "And as we *all* know, Leigh doesn't make a decision without him."

Carol turned away from the pair to peel the wrapper from her treat.

"Are you eating a-again, Carol?" asked Taylor. "I thought you w-w-wanted to lose weight."

"Yes, I'm eating again. I'm hurting today and want comfort. Do you have a problem with that?" Carol whirled her chair to face Erin and Taylor. "And will you *both* stop that infernal pacing? Taylor, your stomping about in those boots is giving me a headache."

Mora entered the room with a carafe of coffee. "Ladies, now is not the time for such interchanges." She set the pot on the table and checked her appearance in the sideboard mirror.

Carol wheeled across the room with a big sigh. "You're right, Mo. We need to agree on our intervention before Leigh gets here." She shoved the last of the chocolate peanut butter bar into her mouth. "I, for one, think he's definitely abusing her and that we should push the issue today—even if she resists us."

"She *has* to admit to Quentin's abuse before we do anything." Taylor marched from the window, sat on the bench, and tapped her fingers on the table. "And we all know how hard it is for *any* woman to accept that, let alone *admit* it." Taylor shifted her position, crossed her legs, and then uncrossed them. She bit at a cuticle and then sucked on it when it bled.

"Taylor, you don't have to instruct us in the obvious." Warmth flushed Carol's face. She needed a pain pill but didn't want the dulled senses that came with it. She'd will the pain away—or just ignore it.

Erin stretched toward the ceiling and then bent over to touch her toes. "We all know how dangerous it is *not* to accept it. It took me four shitty years to admit it to myself. Eight damn years after that before I got the nerve to ask for help." She laughed and swirled her arm as though she were waving a banner. "Thank heavens for Courtesy Accidents."

Taylor jumped up and strode back to the window overlooking the winding stream below. "You all can laugh about Courtesy Accidents. I can't."

"Taylor, just because they haven't recovered Marshall's body doesn't mean you can't rejoice that he's no longer in your face." Erin brushed her hands together. "He's all gone, down the river."

Taylor gasped. "S-S-Stop it. I can't take it. Marshall was a living, breathing human being. N…Not just a b-body."

Carol looked at Erin and shook her head. Erin seemed to enjoy shocking others. She had to admit that most of the time she appreciated Erin's sense of humor, her directness, but this morning it irritated. Was it because Carol was tense about Leigh, as they all were?

Mora put her arm around Taylor. "Come sit down. I'm sure Erin didn't mean to hurt you. We all regret that Marshall's body hasn't surfaced." She pushed Taylor down on the bench and massaged her shoulders.

"Shouldn't we call Leigh?" Taylor asked. She warmed her hands around her mug of hot chocolate and stretched her neck.

"Perhaps she needs more time," said Carol reaching into her bag to answer her cell phone. "Hello. Hello!" Carol struggled to hear and moved her chair closer to the window for better reception. She cupped her hand like a megaphone and shouted into the phone. "Please speak up." She looked at her phone. "I have three bars; it should be louder." She pressed the speaker button.

"Carol, it's Leigh. I'm going to be a bit tardy today. I don't feel too well, but I'll be there. I simply need to locate my map and get dressed."

"You don't sound too good." Carol shook her head. Leigh often spoke softly, in that refined tone of hers, but this was different. Carol tapped the volume button to its highest setting. "Are you sick? Do you need to see a doctor?"

"No, I'm just slow this morning. Quentin…I mean, I had to make breakfast for Quentin and I spilled the coffee. I'm just—"

"Leigh, you're rambling. You shouldn't be driving. The road to the cabin curves all around." Carol combed her hair with her fingers.

"I'll have my cell phone in the car; I'll pull over and ring you if I start to feel off."

"Are you sure? I can be at your home in an hour and a half." Carol raised her eyebrows at Mora. *She's hurt,* she mouthed. She shrunk down in her wheelchair. She could feel Leigh's pain. Would the memory of being abused ever fade?

"No!" Leigh's whisper turned into a squeak. "I mean, Quentin doesn't like me to have anyone in the house when he's absent. And he'd *know*." Taking a noisy breath, Leigh continued, "I just wanted to let you know I'll most certainly be there, but just a tad later than anticipated." She inhaled noisily.

"Leigh, I'll meet you in an hour at the Vons market at the bottom of the hill. You can leave your car in the parking lot."

Carol heard Leigh release her breath. Was that a sob? "Okay," Leigh whispered. "And Carol—thank you."

Piloting her SUV up the mountain, Carol observed a slumped, quiet Leigh, giving her time to collect herself—though not too much. Whatever had happened in the Pryors' stone prison, she *had* to get Leigh to talk about it.

"It sounds like you had a rough morning, Leigh," she began sincerely. "To be honest, I'm concerned."

"I'd rather not talk about it just now." Leigh's face was ashen; her eyes puffy.

Of course, it wouldn't be that easy, Carol chided herself. Mora would know how to handle this.

"What did Quentin say about your joining us this weekend?" *Shoot!* Another bad pass. Quentin was the same subject.

"I didn't tell him. Since he wouldn't be home." Carol was glad to see Leigh's rigid posture relax, though her face was still creased.

At least that shows she can be independent—but it also proves she feels the need to hide things from her husband.

Leigh pulled her seat belt to loosen its pull across her shoulder. "Oh, look—a deer." She gasped as she jerked her upper body to watch the animal jump down the mountain.

Carol pulled into a lookout and turned off the ignition. She couldn't wait for Mora. A good coach addressed problems immediately. "Okay. Game time!" She turned to face Leigh. "I'm going to be blunt: Did Quentin hit you this morning?" She raised a hand to quell Leigh's protests. "No use denying it; you're moving like a ninety-year-old grandmother. You can't hold your purse in your left hand, and your neck is turning a vivid purple."

"Don't tell anyone, please!" Leigh's grip on Carol's arm was iron-strong. "He told me if even a whisper of his chastising me got out, he'd ruin the BWEF. That he had full control of the BWEF funds and the power to *bankrupt* them—without your ever knowing about it until too late." Leigh's eyes pleaded with Carol. "I'm so sorry I brought this on you. He said he'd destroy your wonderful group if I told anyone." Leigh sniffed loudly. "Besides, I've functioned perfectly all right after worse beatings."

As Leigh used the powder room in the cabin, Carol turned to the waiting committee. "We're almost too late. He beat and raped her."

"The bastard! What triggered it this time?" Erin picked up her diary and studied it. When she didn't get a reply, she looked up to stares from her fellow committee members. "Right," she said. "We all know that the immediate triggers don't matter, just the fucking results." She paused. "I guess what I'm really asking is did he beat her up because he found out we suspected him of abuse?"

Carol shook her head. "Don't think so." She dropped her car keys into her purse and threw it on the couch. "But listen to this: He said he'd hold her hostage in the house *and* bankrupt the BWEF if this gets out."

"Son of a bitch!" Erin slammed down her coffee mug, sloshing coffee onto the mission oak table. She wiped it immediately with her sleeve. "That shithead intimidates me; he's got so much we need." She plopped down. "And I don't doubt his ability—or willingness—to carry out his threats."

"We're d-damned if we help her and d-damned if we don't." Taylor threw her notebook down and stomped to the back window. "I *knew* he was evil, the way he treated us. Like we didn't know anything because we're women." She turned to the group, her eyes flashing. "He had the same stony look Marshall would get when I challenged his thinking. You know, the look that means 'I'm going to hit you if you don't shut up.'"

"So we save one woman and leave many others to suffer?" Mora's voice was calm but her eyes blazed. "Is that the tradeoff?"

"What do we want the BWEF to do? Play wimpy like we all did in our marriages to men like Quentin—or go out there and beat the bastard at his own game?" Carol's anger drove her pain away.

Erin snapped her fingers. "If we offer Leigh a Courtesy Accident, we protect both Leigh *and* the BWEF." She turned to Mora. "I'll do a more thorough job with this one."

Taylor's face blanched. "Better than the botched-up job with M-M-Marshall? Is that what you mean?" She shrugged off Erin's comforting hug. "I'm sorry. I just wish…"

Finally Mora spoke. "Are we or Leigh in *immediate* danger?"

Erin pounded her fist on the table. "Damnation. Of course we are! But that's the chance we take working with wives of powerful men." She paused. "I took the *ultimate* risk to help Taylor." Her head pivoted as she glanced at each woman in the room. "I'm assuming because you're here that you'd all volunteer to do the same for Leigh."

Carol's mind whirled. This was happening so fast. Was killing getting to be too much of a knee-jerk response? As much as she loved the OC, Carol realized, one of these days they would have to stop. Perhaps this should be their last accident. That might be a relief. She could sure use the extra time and emotional energy.

Taylor shivered. "*I* couldn't. N-Not until Marsh…"

Erin's eyes blazed and then softened. "You probably shouldn't be here, Taylor. Especially if you're not sure about offering your services."

"It's not that. I just c-couldn't—you know."

Carol reached for a cookie. "Couldn't murder?"

"Carol!" Mora tuned to Taylor. "We don't expect that of you right now." Mora rose. "Call me when Leigh's calmed down and rested." She opened the French doors, stepped onto the redwood deck that ran around three sides of her cabin, and closed the door behind her.

As soon as Mora exited, Erin sprang into action. She pulled maps from her tote. "We know some about Quentin's habits already. I have marine charts here and also some road maps for his L.A. to Sacramento drives." Carol was a bit surprised by Erin's state of readiness, but it *was* time to act on this, one way or the other. This morning's abuse had been major. "I'd bet a bucket of nails he gets some juicy lovin' on those trips," Erin continued, grimacing, "but that's beside the point. Once we know his schedule, we can research more online."

"Whoa, there Erin!" Taylor refolded the marine map and laid it on the bench beside her. "I...I have to say, I'm g-grateful for what you did for me, but we h-haven't even *asked* Leigh yet."

A lithe figure appeared in the doorway. "Asked me what?"

Chapter 52

THE WOMEN WERE HUDDLED around Leigh when Mora walked back into the great room. She stood in the doorway so as not to disturb them.

Carol patted Leigh's hand. "*Don't* worry. No one, including Quentin, will hear a squeak from us. Your secret's safe." Carol sipped her iced tea and waited until the distraught woman sat. "Let's get this game on the field. We're a whole team, Leigh. You're not alone."

Taylor cradled one shaking hand in the other and turned to Leigh. "I kn-know you're a private person. I am too. But I don't mind telling you: M-Marshall abused me, in every way imaginable."

"We *all've* been victims of spousal abuse." Carol's gesture took in the other women. "We know what it feels like to be a punching bag." Carol pressed her fingers to her temples, massaging them. "And we all dreamed for a long time of escaping our brutal men. But until we came to the BWEF, we didn't have the means." Carol dropped her hands to her lap. "We see fear in your eyes, Leigh. We're feeling it, with you, right now."

Mora sat across from Leigh and spoke quietly. "We want to wake you up from your nightmare." She reached out to clasp the dancer's hand across the table. "Every minute, seven percent of the women in our country are being abused. Statistics tell us that your situation is bound to worsen; spousal abuse is an escalating disease." She paused. "A disease that doesn't cure itself if neglected."

Mora sat quietly, allowing Leigh to absorb her words. When Leigh relaxed, she continued softly, "The Outreach Committee will find you a place to live, in a BWEF shelter—or elsewhere if you choose."

"But I can't go to a shelter! What would I say to my friends? What would my neighbors say if they found out? I'd be so embarrassed."

Mora leaned towards Leigh. "*Everything* is kept in strict confidence. You can tell your neighbors anything you want, or nothing. The BWEF tells zero."

"*Any* new game brings fear of the unknown," said Carol. "That's why we'll put you in the best training program—to learn, or relearn, finances; find a job if you want one; and look for a place to live. We'll even introduce you to activities where you can meet new friends in your own economic strata." As Carol counted the benefits on her fingers, she watched for signs that the dancer was at least considering their advice.

"The BWEF provides all you need—including psychological counseling—to live on your own," said Mora.

Carol shook her blond curls and turned conspiratorially to Leigh. "Plus, at the shelter, you can have a private room *and* bath. You don't *have* to socialize." She smiled. "But most women join in right away— they enjoy the instant team spirit in connecting with others in the same situation."

Mora nodded. "That tends to happen when the dam of withheld confidences finally breaks."

"Plus, there are *always* kids to dance with at the shelter," said Erin. Mora smiled at her friend. Erin negotiated with her heart.

Leigh rubbed her right ear. "If I went to a shelter, I'd have to abandon all my beautiful belongings, the garden I toil so hard on. Once I leave my home, I may *never* be allowed to return." Leigh crossed her arms. "*I* put in the new pool; *I* decorated my office with the antiques I collected all over Europe."

"*Th-Things* don't matter when your life is in danger," said Taylor. "Well…personal things, anyway."

"And we'll help you hold on to them," said Carol. She displayed her buff arms. "I can tug as good as anyone."

"But why should *I* have to be the one to walk away from everything I've helped build up?" Leigh had relaxed some, but her eyes still held the wary-cat look. She sat like one, poised to leap away.

"You said on the way up here that Quentin threatened you." Mora nodded at Carol's change in tactic. "What did he say?"

"He said he'd kill me if I told anyone that he had to *hit* me to make me do things right." Leigh looked at her lap. "He claimed it was my fault he did it—that I hold my life in my own hands." Leigh swallowed a sob. "I know he's right, but—"

"Wrong!" burst out Taylor.

"Shit, no way you should believe that!" Mora heard the frustration in Erin's voice.

"We want to help you truly hold your life in your own hands," said Mora gently. "You *shouldn't* have to give up what's yours—in fact we *may* be able to insure you won't have to give up anything."

For the first time all day, Mora saw hope emerge in Leigh's eyes.

"H-How do I go about it, then?" she asked. "What's next?"

Mora pulled some papers from her briefcase. She looked at her Outreach Committee members and received barely visible nods from each of them. "First is a psychological test, so we can understand *you* better."

Chapter 53

"I FEEL LIKE I'm two divergent women married to two different men." Leigh sat forward in her chair, her face troubled.

Mora was careful to maintain a neutral expression. It would not do for her to show her own emotions.

"Can you describe these four people to me?"

Leigh sat back in her chair and reached for a Kleenex. She and Mora had moved out to the deck while the others prepared a snack.

"I'll start with me." She wiggled in her chair, and then sat tall and said, "When I was dancing—before I met Quentin—I was assertive, independent, talented, graceful, wealthy, outgoing, and popular." She laughed. "If I do say so myself!"

Mora smiled. *This* was the real Leigh—the Leigh she yearned to see in her full glory.

Leigh slumped. "Since my marriage, I fear conversing with others; I'm awkward, clumsy." She pointed to her purse on the chair beside her. "I have little spending money, and I don't know where the remainder of my money is, what it's doing." As she spoke, Leigh seemed to shrink further into her chair. "I'm shy, and I rarely go out. I don't recognize myself anymore." Leigh sighed and glanced at the closed door, as though expecting Quentin to walk in at any moment. "I have no time to myself!" she whispered. "And I can't seem to find an original thought in my head. I *hate* who I am, Mora! I feel helpless and hopeless."

Mora reached for Leigh's hand, but Leigh didn't reciprocate.

Leigh's eyelids drooped. "As much as I want to believe you can help me, I honestly don't think there's enough of the old me left to begin to form a new one."

Mora walked over and put her arm around Leigh.

"The foundation is there, Leigh. I guarantee you that. We can work this out together. And we will." Mora squeezed Leigh's shoulder. "I suspect you've repressed everything you like about yourself to make peace with Quentin."

"You know!"

"You forget: I have expertise *and* experience. Now, tell me about the two men you're married to."

Leigh grabbed another Kleenex and dabbed at her eyes. "In the days after I met him at that party," she began, "Quentin was magical. He was around constantly, sent flowers every day, called me during intermissions, dropped in during rehearsals." Leigh straightened and smiled softly. "And the gifts! Emeralds, and little remembrances: a gold charm shaped like ballet slippers; antique opera glasses." She brushed at her again-welling tears. "He even introduced me to his London broker so I could invest my money more wisely."

"You enjoyed all that attention?"

"Oh, yes! I felt smothered with love." Leigh's shoulders squared and she sat tall.

Obviously, that was his intent—smothering her. Mora rose unobtrusively and walked to the railing. "Had Quentin been widowed long when he met you?"

"Just nine months." Leigh twisted a tissue into a tiny ball. "But we delayed our marriage for six months while he settled his late wife's estate."

"What made you decide to marry him?"

"He was so masterful. He knew where he was going, where he wanted *us* to go as a couple. Where he wanted me to go." She moved her arms back and forth charging ahead.

"Was he a good lover?"

Leigh hesitated. "Yesss…most of the time." She lowered her voice again. "Sometimes he had trouble, but I just assured him it was okay. That I loved him no matter what."

Mora sat down on the chaise lounge. "Tell me about the other Quentin."

"It's unbelievable—he's changed so since our marriage. I don't recognize him at times."

"Describe him. As you see him now." Mora focused her psychiatric radar. She felt desperate to get a handle on the extent and frequency of violence in the Pryor home. Before it was too late to get Leigh away—too late to save her life.

"He's as rigid as a fire poker. Never relaxes, always the perfectionist. His clothes are immaculate. He keeps laundered shirts in the office so he can change midday."

"Does he demand the same tidiness of you?"

"Yes! Don't get me wrong, Mora, I like being neat and tidy. But I can't even trundle around my house in tights and a dance tunic anymore. I have to be dressed, ready to entertain, at all times." Leigh smoothed her skirt.

"How does he know how you dress while he's at work?"

"His gardener reports to him each evening what has gone on around the house."

How insecure he must feel about his marriage.

"What else can you tell me about him?"

"He's so controlling! He dictates our schedule: who we see, what we eat, even the entertainment we go to."

"You do go to the ballet, though." Mora made the assertion, hoping it was true—fearing it wasn't.

"No. He falls asleep during the first act. Says it's a waste of money to go."

"You don't go alone." It was a statement, not a question.

"That's forbidden. I go hardly anywhere without him." She smiled secretly. "Except when I say I'm going to exercise and teach the kids at the Boys and Girls Club instead."

"Leigh, have you considered leaving the marriage?" Mora held Leigh's eyes with her own.

"Divorce? Separation? No—I mean yes. I *have* thought about it, but I decided against it." She dropped the shredded tissue and reached for another.

"Why is that?" Mora leaned forward.

"If he even suspected I was going to leave, he'd attack me—maybe even kill me." Leigh clasped her hands together to stop their tremor. "What if I was debilitated? I couldn't even live on my own!" Color drained from her face. "No, I just can't do it! I can't." Her swan's neck bent, and her chin rested on her chest.

"I'm going to be blunt, here." Mora paused until Leigh looked up at her. "You have to take action soon. If you don't get out, Quentin's physical violence *will* escalate until he cripples or even kills you. This is a very serious situation, Leigh."

"As long as I stay with him, I'm relatively safe though, aren't I?" Leigh pleaded.

Mora steeled herself. She had to be convincing.

"Even in light of what happened this morning, I recognize that as an outsider, I don't see everything between you two. But it seems to me that your husband is demanding more and more control over you and that his violence is escalating. There can be only one outcome to all of that." Mora paused to let Leigh absorb what she'd just said. "We can find a shelter for you today; there are several vacancies right now." She fished her day book from her tote.

"But he'd find me!" Leigh grabbed Mora's hand. "I didn't even think of it before! The police chief is one of his golfing buddies—all he'd have to do is ask. Or he'd hire a private detective."

It's OC time.

"Actually, Leigh, that's very astute of you. In fact, that's exactly what happened to Helen Neil—the friend we honored at the BWEF benefit, the fundraiser where we met you."

Leigh's eyes widened. "Wow—you *see*. I'm trapped! Ohhh!" Leigh broke into sobs. "I feel so stupid and…alone."

"You're not alone—or stupid." Mora paused, swirling circles on her notepad. Was it premature to offer Leigh the Outreach Committee's services? Was it safe to confide in her?

Mora decided against it. She wasn't even certain of Leigh's commitment to end the marriage. As she administered the rest of the Courtesy Tests, she'd have to be sure to watch Leigh carefully.

Chapter 54

LUCKY STROLLED THE GROUNDS of the small hospital. He was happy the doctor had decided he was finally okay to be alone at times— as long as he checked in with the nursing staff.

This morning, the nurses and doctors had bet candy bars on the Dodger-Diamondbacks game. Lucky had been tempted to enter the discussion, but he didn't know *why* he knew Dodger statistics and he feared their probing questions. Had he been part of the team? Or just an avid fan?

A string of numbers kept running around in his head: 2478. It couldn't be a batting average or home run figure, but he knew it meant something. He'd even dreamt them last night. Was it his address? If so, on what street? In what city? Or part of his social security number?

Lucky hit the side of his head. Why wasn't his brain working? He hurried back to his room to keep an appointment the nurses had set up for him.

Lucky clenched his teeth as a rotund gray-haired man wearing a clerical collar approached him. He fought the urge to run and swallowed hard. He'd agreed to the visit when the nurse suggested it, but his reaction to seeing the cleric enforced his strengthening conviction that he had done something wrong. Something damning. Lucky pried himself out of the fake leather chair.

"I'm Tim Townsend, pastor at the Baptist church down the street." The cleric offered his hand. "You must be Lucky."

"Yes, sir." Lucky lowered his eyes as he shook the preacher's hand. "Of course, that's not my real name. I have amnesia." His mouth opened in a cooked grin.

"I know. I hope to help you with that."

Lucky cocked his head. "You're an expert on mental problems?" *All this guy wants is to charge me up with religion and baptize me in his church.* "Reverend, I—"

"Call me Tim, Lucky. Shall we go to the chapel?" Without waiting for an answer, Tim led the way.

Lucky put a hand over his rumbling stomach and followed.

"May I say a prayer for you before we start?"

Lucky shrugged, his eyes dark and brooding. "Sure, I guess so." He bowed his head. He wasn't sure he wanted a prayer, and for sure he felt he didn't deserve one.

"Lord, we ask that you'll be with us as we search for clues to this man's background so that he may rejoin his life and continue to serve you. In Jesus' name, we pray. Amen."

"Amen." Despite this man's obvious agenda, Lucky felt comfortable responding—like he was used to praying.

"Lucky, do you pray for the Lord's guidance?"

Lucky shifted uncomfortably. "Uh…no, can't say I do. At least not since I woke up here." He scratched his ear. "Never thought it would do me any good."

"The Lord always listens to your prayers."

"Even if I don't deserve it?"

The reverend laughed. "Especially then. He forgives us our sins." Tim opened a small notebook. "Let's start with what you remember about church. Like, do you remember sitting in a pew with your family?"

Lucky's forehead crinkled. His hands formed fists as he tried to bring up the past. "I remember my twin granddaughters being baptized." He grinned. "Both of them cried all the way through it." *Whoa.* If he had granddaughters, he must have children—and likely been married.

"Great start, Lucky. Think about what you see in the church; that might tell us what religion you practice."

"There weren't many people there." *Just relatives?* "Most of the pews were empty."

"Were there cloths on the altar? Kneeling benches?"

Lucky shook his head. "I don't remember."

"Do you think you have a church home?"

"How should *I* know?" Lucky shifted in the pew. "I don't even know my *real* home, let alone a church one."

The chubby cleric reached into his back pocket for his handkerchief. He blotted his eyes and then his sweating chin. "Right."

Lucky bit his lip and then blurted, "I don't go to church because I'm not a good person."

Tim seemed unfazed by Lucky's outburst. "Oh? Why is that, Lucky?"

Lucky's face twisted. "I know I've done cruel things—but I can't remember them." He pounded his fist into his palm.

Pastor Tim placed a firm, calming hand on Lucky's arm, waiting for him to settle down. He spoke quietly. "What else can you tell me about your granddaughters?"

Lucky smiled wistfully. "They like the wood animal figures I bring them when I get back from a trip."

"Well, that's a good start. Any idea what store you buy them from?"

"No—I mean, I don't buy them." Lucky's right hand curled, holding an imaginary knife. He sliced at his index finger in a whittling motion. "I carve them with my camp knife."

Chapter 55

Taylor clapped as her twin granddaughters modeled bathing suits she'd pulled from the store's stock. "The sea green becomes you," she said—obviously meaning both of them, their black hair and green eyes promising mature beauty.

Taylor smiled broadly, but she couldn't help ruing how long Marshall's behavior had deprived her of these beautiful young women's company. Why hadn't she seen through Ruthie's excuses about bringing her friends to the house? Her withdrawal from family activities, her sudden shyness—Taylor had mourned her young chatterbox's recession into a glum silent teen. Her mother's guilt would never be assuaged.

Today's outing was the first mission in her Grandmother Campaign to make it up to Ruth and to see her granddaughters. She planned to do lunches, bi-weekly shopping trips, and special rock concerts in Hollywood.

Taylor felt closer to her daughter already. She and Ruth had begun family counseling last week after Ruth's disclosure, and Ruth's reticence was already fading. She was beginning to accept her dad for what he was. And unlike Rob, she'd seemed relieved when Taylor had told her Marshall wasn't coming back.

The twins draped teal beach towels around their shoulders, posing for a perfect picture. Taylor sighed. Her guilt about Ruth was *beginning* to subside. Hopefully her remorse about Marshall's Courtesy Killing would diminish, too.

Chapter 56

A T THE KITCHEN SINK, Sharon handed Cailin a skillet to dry. "You missed a fun game last night."

"Mike said he had a good time. You learned Clue. Said you won." She laughed. "I told him you should have, with your job." She reached for another dish.

"How did your brother feel about the date itself?" *She'd* enjoyed herself immensely, but she'd been watching for Mike's reaction most of the evening.

"Wellllll…"

"Well what?"

"He said he wished it was time to go see Dad. He misses him when he sees how much fun Joe's dad is."

Damn. Sharon was afraid of that.

"Short of not dating, any recommendations about what I should do to make him feel better?"

"Mom, I don't know. He has to realize you're going to date and get married again."

"Date, yes. Married, I'm not so sure. I've seen how sour a marriage can turn."

Chapter 57

Mora stacked the new BWEF brochures coming off the color printer. "I'm anxious to see how Quentin acts today with Leigh." She, Erin, Taylor, and Carol commiserated while the printer duplicated their booklet, outlining the symptoms of spousal abuse.

"Should be fascinating," said Carol grimly.

"I can just picture him being downright loving to her." Taylor shivered. "Sug-Suggesting she sit next to him. Offering to h-hold her hand."

"Yeah, so the shithead can control her!" Erin stomped over to the printer, as if standing over it would make it go faster.

Carol stacked more paper into the printer drawer. "Or like he's wooing her. Reg did that when the guilt hit."

Taylor turned to Mora. "Were you able to finish the pre-counseling with Leigh? How did the BWEF test go?"

"The what?" Erin looked perplexed.

Mora opened her briefcase and pulled out a stapled set of papers. She held it up so that Erin could see it. "The new test we administered with Leigh at the cabin. You remember!"

"Yes, but…"

"Carol nicknamed it the 'Before Widowhood Emotional Frailty' test," explained Taylor.

"Just between us, of course." Carol was obviously proud of her linguistic wit. "So, do you think it's safe to offer Leigh our special kind of help?" she asked.

Taylor sat down next to Mora at the table and reached for the results sheet.

"Her test showed strong commitment to making things right," said Mora. "Putting her world in order, so to speak."

"Still…" Carol glanced at the test results Taylor passed along to her. "We've known her just four months."

"I think she's safe," said Taylor. "She comes across as a genuine person who wouldn't go back on her word about the confidentiality of our methods. Plus, we *have* to help her!"

"Of course, helping her is our priority." Erin sealed a box and stacked it next to the doorway. "But we also *can't* have people finding out that our damn finance chief beats his wife!"

Mora walked back to the copier, so the others couldn't see her face as she considered Erin's comment. It was true that Mora had doubts *whenever* they started with a new client. But in this case, she couldn't be sure her judgment was sound. *Would* they be acting for Leigh, or for the BWEF—and their own reputations?

The former was acceptable. The latter, she wasn't sure of.

"What concerns me"—Mora stacked some more completed booklets in a cardboard box—"is our responsibility in this matter."

"Our responsibility to the BWEF, with an abuser at the financial helm?" Erin closed the box and stacked it with the others next to the door.

"That, but more urgently, our responsibility for Leigh." Mora shook her head. "Now that we know she's being abused, we *have* to prevent her being hurt." Mora felt the burden of her profession; it required her to intervene. But how could she, without endangering Leigh further?

"I'm always concerned at this point in our planning," Mora added. "I want to be *completely* sure our good works won't collapse."

"So, what's the bottom line here?" pressed Carol.

Mora straightened and faced the group. "Leigh feels strongly about keeping her word, about loyalty, and she's deeply troubled by her marital situation." Mora shrugged. "In fact, her emotional makeup is ideal. She feels trapped, desperate."

Chapter 58

MORA SWALLOWED HER SURPRISE at the dramatic change in Leigh's demeanor as the dancer bounced into the ladies room of the BWEF offices.

"Whew! Mora! Isn't this a *beautiful* day?" Leigh's face beamed.

"If you don't look lovely! Your face is full of color; you're full of energy. How nice to see you this way." Mora clasped her friend's hand. "What's brought this on?"

Leigh swirled in her gossamer dress. "I'm in love!"

Mora resolved to remain calm, in spite of her dismay.

"Anyone I know?" Mora clenched her jaw and motioned for Leigh to sit on the makeup bench. She took a seat on the adjacent sofa.

"It's Quentin! We made up last night. He brought me flowers, took me to dinner, and *then* to the ballet. He even stayed awake to discuss the show with me at intermission!" Leigh put her hand over her heart. "When we got home, he made love to me so tenderly. Just like when we were dating."

Mora clasped her hands and leaned toward Leigh. "And how did all this make you feel?" She wanted to shake Leigh and yell "Don't fall for it!" but she restrained herself. With effort she kept her face serene.

"I told you: I'm in love all over again." Leigh swirled again and finally settled into the bench opposite Mora.

Mora sighed. "Leigh, Leigh. I hate to disillusion you, but this high won't last. Quentin's romantic actions are part of a domestic violence *cycle*. He can't have changed overnight. Surely you can see that." Mora leaned forward so her face was close to Leigh's.

"With all due respect, Mora. I *don't* see that." Leigh straightened, her back a strong wall. "He was *really* sorry for what happened over the weekend. I *know* everything is going to be okay this time." Leigh's joy sparkled in her eyes.

"Just three days ago," Mora pushed on, "we were considering the options you had in ending your marriage."

"Mora, I've decided—" Leigh looked up at Mora earnestly. "I don't *want* to end our marriage. I was just being overly critical. Quentin pointed that out to me last night when I—"

Mora's head jerked upward. "So you *talked* to Quentin about divorce?"

"Oh no! Nothing like that. It's just— Mora, after last night, I realized I could never leave Quentin. He's such a big part of my life. Besides, everything's okay now."

Chapter 59

SHARON TURNED from the clothes dryer as Cailin came into the kitchen.

"So, Mom…what's Joe's dad like?"

Hmm. Here it comes.

Sharon trundled a basket of clean laundry into the living room and handed Cailin a bundle of T-shirts to fold.

"Well, let's see… He's a little taller than me, athletic, hazel eyes, brown hair."

"Mom!" Cailin threw a green T-shirt at her. "You know what I mean."

Sharon did know, but she wasn't sure she was ready to discuss this with her daughter—or anyone for that matter. She took her time peeling the shirt from her face.

"Well," she finally said, "he's fun to be with, jokes a lot." She tossed the shirt onto the pile in front of Cailin. "Why?"

"*You* know why." Cailin stopped folding clothes and put her hand on her hips. "Are you going to date him?"

Sharon was silent.

"Mike says he likes him," Cailin reassured her, "and that I will too."

It was early times, but Sharon was heartened by the endorsement. Especially if she continued to see Ernest.

"Well, hon, you can tell me what you think about that yourself." She smiled at Cailin. "Ernest's coming to dinner soon."

Chapter 60

"PLEASE DON'T BE ANGRY with me, Quentin. I just had to go practice—I needed the expression dancing gives me." Leigh slipped off her ballet slippers and glided barefoot across the bedroom, her body still feeling the flowing grace of the dance she'd just completed. Quentin followed.

Leigh turned to face him. Seeing his pallor, she stifled her euphoria.

"'I just *had* to go to dance practice,'" he mimicked Leigh in a sarcastic falsetto. "You sound like a little kid who thinks the world spins around her, just to give her everything she wants." He folded his arms. "Well, I have news for you. You're a grown woman now, responsible only to me. Do you understand that?"

Quentin clutched the folds of Leigh's tunic and tore it off her. "I don't want you wearing this revealing costume ever again! To think you'd even consider demeaning me by wearing this tart dress in public. It shames you—and infuriates me."

"Quentin dear, please calm down." Leigh tried to smile naturally. "I'm a born dancer. My need to dance drove me long before I met you. It has nothing to do with you." She reached to smooth his hair. "Besides, I thought last weekend after we made love, you said you were proud of my dancing."

"Oh, grow up, Leigh!" Quentin smirked. "Things said in the heat of sex aren't always true, you know."

"But I believed you!" Leigh's cry came from her core.

"Here's something you can believe." Quentin slapped her on the back of the head and threw her facedown on the bed. He yanked down her tights and entered her violently.

Chapter 61

CAROL WIPED THE SWEAT from her face and reached for her water bottle. Was that a twinge of feeling in her left foot? The tingle was enough to set her dreaming about walking again.

She rolled her chair to the pool and levered herself onto the lift. She pressed the button and the mechanism lowered her into the warm water. The swim would be her reward. She deserved it after a two-hour workout. Carol relished the feel of water swirling around her body, the strength of her arms pulling her along. She squinted against the piercing sun. She looked up as she heard the back gate clang against its post.

"Carol, I need your help." Leigh had let herself into the backyard and stood at the edge of the pool. The dancer's face was desperate. Her eyes red. She cradled her arm against her body.

Carol swam towards the side of the pool and rose from the water with the aid of the lift. She didn't like the pallor in Leigh's usually vibrant face. As Carol hoisted herself from the lift into her wheelchair, Leigh slumped to the ground in slow motion.

Carol reached for the cell phone that she'd left on the arm of her chair.

"No. Don't call anyone—please." Leigh rose slowly, holding onto the chaise lounge. "I just felt weak for a moment. I'll be all right." Carol pressed the end button.

"What happened?" Carol shivered in the warm sun. She'd been in Leigh's situation; she knew the conflicting thoughts slicing through the fingers of pain. Wanting help but not calling for it, fearful it would cause a new barrage of beatings.

"Quentin doesn't like me dancing, or wearing my dance clothes in public, but I did it anyway." Leigh paused. "And when he got mad, I decided to stand up to him."

Carol whirled her wheelchair and pulled up next to Leigh. "That took courage."

"I don't know where I got the nerve. But I shouldn't have done it." Leigh massaged a heavy bruise on her hand.

Carol reached for her towel and rubbed her hair dry, leaving a cap of wet spikes. "I have some Cokes in the cooler. I think a little sugar and caffeine would go well right now."

Carol pulled the drink cans from the ice surrounding them. "So what happened then?"

"He twisted my arm, threw me on the bed, and…you know."

Carol paused. "He raped you again?"

"Actually, he bashed me on the back of my head." Leigh swallowed hard. "He may have raped me after that, but I think I must have fainted." She raised a shaking hand to her forehead. "When I woke up, he was gone, and I drove over here."

Carol set a tray in her lap and added potato chips and a bowl of salsa. "You should have called. You're in no condition to drive."

As an afterthought, Carol rolled herself to a tree next to the patio and picked two low-hanging nectarines, plump and white with a muted blush.

"Leigh, you're really going to love these—they're just perfectly in season!"

Leigh didn't respond.

Carol swiveled around. She took one look at Leigh and forgot all about their snack. "Leigh. Leigh. Hang in there." Carol rushed to her friend's side and clasped her hand, the lunch tray tottering precariously on her lap.

"I'm sorry, Carol. I—" Leigh closed her eyes again.

"Leigh, you're drifting in and out." Carol made a decision. "Leigh, I have to call someone. I can't handle you myself." She slapped Leigh's hand. "You understand?"

Leigh nodded. "I'm just so dizzy. I don't know what's the matter with me. My head…"

Chapter 62

MORA WAVED SHARON to a chair next to the window. "Glad we could fit you in today." As her client settled in, Mora put her own guard up. She could never fail to remember Sharon's occupation. "So Sharon, what's going on?"

"Mora, I wanted to talk about my dating."

Mora made a note and looked up. "What concerns you? Mike and Cailin object to it?"

"No. Thank heavens. Ernest's son is Mike's best friend. And so far Cailin's being very supportive."

"Then it's *you* we need to talk about?"

Sharon nodded. "I'm nerv—" A loud ring tone interrupted her.

Mora held up her hand to Sharon. "I do apologize, Sharon. That's my emergency line." She fished into her tote for the phone. "Mora here." Mora turned to look out the window as she listened to Carol's play-by-play recounting of her visit with Leigh. Finally, she'd heard enough. "Thanks for calling," she said tersely. "I'll come right away."

Mora looked up at her client.

"Sharon, I am *so* sorry! One of my patients is in crisis. I'm going to have to reschedule you." Mora led Sharon to the door and all but shoved her out.

"I completely understand." Sharon nodded. "Mine's a problem but definitely not a crisis."

Chapter 63

"SHE LOOKS LIKE HELEN DID right before she died: so still, so white, so bruised." Mora lifted her head from her hands and turned to the doctor who entered the room. "Is she going to be all right?"

"She's badly traumatized," said the doctor, shaking his head as he reviewed Leigh's chart. "Possible skull fracture, brain injury, apparent rape. She said she hit her head." He looked at Mora and Carol in turn. "Were you there when she did?" As the two women shook their heads, he continued, "We're trying to contact her husband for permission to operate, relieve the pressure on her brain—if it becomes necessary."

Mora glanced at Carol and found the expected raised eyebrow.

"Did you contact the bank?" Mora asked, struggling to remain calm.

"Yes. They said he didn't come in. Thought he was en route to Sacramento. We've left messages there with the people he's scheduled to meet and with his daughter who lives there. The bank gave us her number."

"What happens if he doesn't contact you?" Mora's fists were clenched. Her thoughts racing with self-incrimination.

"If it becomes a life or death situation, we'll operate without it." The doctor made a note on his clipboard and departed.

Once they were alone, Mora let her held-in tears flow. "I've been here before! How could I let this happen again?" She smoothed Leigh's hair. "I should have talked you out of your euphoria. Made the OC's Courtesy Offer earlier. I guess I was trying too hard to be careful, to protect the OC. Now look what's happened!"

Carol pulled up next to Mora. "It's not your fault. We're all to blame. *I* should have called for help as soon as she collapsed by my

221

gate." Carol's eyes teared. "I just didn't think about how badly he could have hurt her."

Mora grasped Carol's hand and reached her other hand to Leigh.

"Leigh, dear, we'll get you through this, I promise." Mora squeezed her friend's hand. "Then we'll make *sure* this never happens again."

Mora sat by Leigh's bed and tried to focus on a professional article about counseling children in abusive families. She couldn't remember one word she'd read, even though she'd gone over the same paragraph five times. With a snap, she closed the magazine. At least they hadn't had to operate on Leigh. They'd know more when she woke up and could take some tests.

"Mora, is that you?" Leigh's voice was barely a whisper.

Mora leaned over the injured woman. "I'm here. Don't worry. Carol's coming too." She fluffed the pillow behind Leigh's head and pulled the covers up to her chin.

"Water? My mouth's so dry."

Mora lifted the pink plastic cup and touched Leigh's lips with the straw. Leigh drank greedily and then lay back with a sigh. "Quentin?"

"I understand the clinic is trying to find him for permission to operate."

Leigh grabbed Mora's hand. "Tell them to stop. I don't want him here."

"They won't tell him where you are."

Leigh nodded. Apparently exhausted, she went limp. Her eyes closed and she quickly drifted back into sleep.

Mora rummaged through her tote for a food bar. She was hungry, but she didn't want to leave Leigh's side, just in case Quentin showed up. And she couldn't leave the clinic until Leigh was well enough to make decisions on her own. She opened her cell phone and called Carol.

"I'm on my way up right now. I've brought back some things Leigh might want. How is she?"

"I think she's going to be okay—as long as we can keep Quentin away from her."

"I'll spell you on that one. Has she said anything?"

"Not much. I'll keep you posted."

Carol slapped her cell phone closed as she entered the room. Mora felt a rush of relief. She needed emotional support. After all that had happened with Hel—

"I want help."

Mora's head snapped up. A wide-awake Leigh whispered through a tight raspy throat.

To Mora's expert eye, Leigh's face reflected an array of emotions from despair to shivery fear, and then relief. Mora worked to keep her own facial expression impassive.

Carol squeezed her friend's foot. "Glad to see you awake, gal."

"Sorry for causing you all this trouble. I shouldn't have come to your house."

"Oh yes, you should have! I wouldn't have forgiven you if you hadn't." Carol held up a tote bag. "I brought you some slippers, a toothbrush, and a book to read. And some body lotion." She dropped the bag on the bed where Leigh could reach it. "Cookie gathered everything for me. Said to give you her love."

"Thanks." Leigh reached out a hand for the bag but gasped and fell back.

Chapter 64

Leigh's eyes followed Erin as the builder touched each Outreach Committee member's shoulder as she toured Leigh's room at the clinic. As she faced each woman, she asked: "Did *you* ever wish your husband would just disappear from the earth?" She waited for each to nod before moving on to the next.

Finally, Erin turned to Leigh. "What about you, Leigh? Have you ever imagined that?"

Leigh stared at Erin, hard—and then her ballerina's heart leaped into a grand jeté. Had Erin just asked if she, Leigh, had thought about what life would be like if her tyrannical husband suddenly vanished—like a rabbit into a hat? Was this a game, or did Erin have magical powers?

Leigh giggled. The thought was too much. And once she started, she couldn't stop. As Leigh released the sorrow and strain of the past two days, the giggle exploded into a full-blown laugh. Rivers of tears flowed. Soon, Taylor Whitmore's booming chortle, Carol Ewald's snort, and Mora Rey's "ho ho" joined hers. The joyful but sad sounds echoed through the room.

Leigh couldn't erase the image from her mind. "Have I ever thought of splashing my husband with vanishing ink?" she finally replied to Erin, the only woman in the room to have remained stoic. "With each and every one of his punches!"

Leigh gasped. What was she saying? Her heart was dancing again, this time spiraling in unending circles. Finally she was able to steady her erratic heartbeat. In a quivering voice, she queried, "Why do you ask?"

Leigh wiped her face with a tissue. Her eyes darted back and forth, examining each of the faces around the room. "And why are *you* all laughing?"

"We're all chuckling because we're abuse survivors. Believe me; we've all wanted our husbands to vanish." Leigh's heart settled into a quiet glissade. "That's why we invited you to meet with the Outreach Committee."

Leigh looked at the strained expressions on the women around her and stopped laughing. She realized their question was serious. What were they thinking?

"The Outreach Committee has one bylaw that's non-negotiable," Carol said.

"What's that?" Leigh asked, still wary but starting to glow with hope.

"Absolute confidentiality about the Outreach Committee's activities and a mandatory membership in the OC for at least one year." Carol paused. "I guess that's really two bylaws."

"We don't want you to make any decisions today," Mora said. "But you should know that several women in your circumstance have in the past relied on our discretion. You'll need to consider carefully exactly what the committee does. We'll explain it to you in a minute. But first we must have your pledge of complete confidentiality. You may not talk about what we will tell you ever again. Not even to the three of us. In public, we'll deny telling you anything about the Outreach Committee's unique activity. We guarantee to assist you, and then we expect you to join us in freeing others in the same situation."

Leigh's heart skipped a beat. What was Mora about to propose?

"I pride myself on keeping confidences." Leigh sipped some ice water. "I promise that whatever you tell me, I will hold it here only." She pointed to her head.

Erin sat on the foot of the bed. "We've chosen you to help next. With our system, you'll be completely free, live without fear, and won't go through a messy divorce. Everything you own will remain yours."

Under the covers, Leigh's feet moved from first to third position and back. She couldn't keep still.

They were offering her a way to wake up from her nightmare. But how?

As Erin launched into a brief narrative about what *exactly* the Outreach Committee would do for her, Leigh's facial muscles remained composed; but her expressive eyes did not. Leigh's eyelids narrowed, then flew open wide. The pupils of her dark-brown eyes receded in fear. She shook her head and blotted the film of perspiration from her face. It was as if Leigh truly realized for the first time that theirs was the only way.

"Whatever your decision, Leigh," said Mora as the group prepared to leave, "please know we are all here to help you. We've all been at the exact stage of indecision that you're in right now."

"I think I'm st-still in that stage," said Taylor. "Even though it's t…too late to change my mind."

Carol rolled herself close and squeezed Leigh's hand. "Think ahead, about what you can do for your community, the arts, the poor kids who dream of being dancers but can't afford shoes, let alone lessons."

Leigh nodded and attempted a smile. "Thank you all for comforting me. I've felt so lost for so long. I didn't know which way to turn." Her smile emerged, genuine and bright. "I have four new friends for life."

Erin jumped up and embraced Leigh. "You're damn right we're friends for life." She winked. "'Til death do us part!"

Leigh put a hand on Erin's. "I need— No…I *want* you to do what you said."

Looking around to ensure no one was listening, Carol asked, "You mean…?"

Leigh nodded.

"Okay, but I want you to be absolutely sure."

"I have no other option. I *am* sure."

Chapter 65

Taylor followed Mora to her car in the hospital parking lot. "Mora, I've been thinking hard about what Erin said in there—you know, about moving on." Taylor twisted her car keys on the key ring. "Do you think I should file for divorce?"

Mora opened her car door and motioned Taylor to sit with her. "How would the kids accept that?"

That's one thing Taylor loved about Mora: you could throw anything at her and she would volley it without missing a beat. You didn't have to pussyfoot around.

Taylor had already considered Mora's question long and hard. She sat down in the seat Mora proffered. "It would make Rob sad," she replied, "but he knows I've tried to hold the family together. And he'd continue loving his dad." She fought to keep her tears at bay. "It's so sad—to know he won't be seeing his dad again."

"And Ruth?" Again, Mora didn't linger on something that couldn't be changed.

"She'd say good riddance. But as you know, she has different memories of her father."

Mora nodded.

Taylor shook her head. "I still can't get over how stupid and guilty I felt when she told me." She swallowed a sob. "I don't know how I'll *ever* forgive myself."

Mora sat quietly until Taylor regained control. Taylor always felt reassured by Mora's calm presence in the face of distressing situations—and people.

"To be honest, Taylor," Mora finally said, "I don't think you'd stand up in divorce proceedings right now. You are much too shaky—and guilt-ridden."

Relief of a sort filled Taylor. She agreed with Mora about her ability to withstand a contact with the law—even in divorce court.

"What if the kids ask why I don't file?" Would she be able to answer them so they'd believe her? Should she tell them Marshall said *he* was going to file? She had made honesty with her kids a priority when she was raising them. It was killing her to deceive them now.

"I suggest you start by talking to the BWEF family law attorney about your divorce concerns," said Mora. "From there, you can explore your options and decide what to tell your kids."

"Wouldn't that endanger the OC?"

"No. You'd just be talking to her about divorcing a man who said he wasn't coming back. Nothing more." Mora hugged Taylor. "You don't have to *do* anything. You're a widow now."

"But my kids don't know that—and to tell you the truth, I'm not sure of it either. I won't feel at peace until I've been notified of Marshall's death."

Taylor's heart thumped so hard it hurt.

Chapter 66

LUCKY STRODE THROUGH DOWNTOWN Flagstaff alongside Dr. Malick, the major stockholder and chief administrator of the hospital where Lucky was staying. The good doctor had invited him to lunch at the local Tio's restaurant, just half a mile from the hospital.

The short walk outside the grounds invigorated Lucky. For the very first time in memory, he felt as though he actually might *be* lucky. Life was improving.

As the two men sauntered down the main thoroughfare, Lucky stopped short. The administrator smacked into him and immediately jumped back.

"Oh, pardon me, Lucky! What is it? You want to shop the sporting goods store?"

Lucky's mouth turned down into what was becoming a habitual half-moon. But remembering how he'd looked in the mirror that morning when he'd practiced his facial expressions, he forced a smile. "Uh...no thanks. It's just that it looked familiar somehow. Like I used to spend a lot of time there or something." He shook his head. "But never mind—I've lost it now."

"Hey, don't sweat it, pal. With that tan you came in with, you must have *loved* the outdoors. You want to try a game of tennis next weekend? I have a court at my place."

No, damn it. What I want is to go home. Does this guy think a stupid game of tennis is going to cheer me up? Lucky stopped himself. Here was this man—this doctor—treating him so nicely, putting him up in the hospital for practically nothing, and now inviting him to be a guest in his home. Had he always been so rude?

"I don't know, Doc. I mean, how will I ever repay you for your generosity toward me? I don't feel worthy." Lucky realized this was the truest statement he had uttered since arriving here.

"Think nothing of it, Lucky. You seem like a good-natured—not to mention, good-*looking*—fellow. I'm sure you have a great life waiting for you somewhere, too."

Lucky rubbed his jaw and glanced at himself in the shop window. He had to admit, he did look good. But he didn't want to look just *good*. He wanted to look like *himself* so he could find out who he really was. Get back to his own life. No, he wasn't convinced it was the "great life" the doctor spoke of, but if nothing else, it was surely less boring than the one he was living now.

And the money. He probably hadn't earned the stash they'd found on him honestly. But somehow, he knew he made lots of cash. How bad could his life be?

"So, Lucky, what do you say? Join me for a match this weekend?"

"Well, Doc, I don't know if I know how to play tennis, but I'm up for giving it a try."

Lucky shrugged. If he couldn't find his way back to his old life, he might as well start forging a new one. Tennis with rich doctors seemed like a good place to start.

Chapter 67

WITH LEIGH'S AGREEMENT to join the OC, Mora felt her usual mix of emotions: fear and elation. The latter prevailed. She'd be able to help another woman in peril. She gripped Carol's hand. Also, as usual, Mora worried that they would make a mistake, get caught. But she was willing to take that risk. This was Leigh's *life* they were saving.

"You'll have to help me with how to behave around Quentin until we do this." Leigh sighed.

"We hope to keep you away from him," said Carol.

Leigh shook her head and then winced. "You needn't do that just now. When he gets back from Catalina, he'll regret that he hurt me. He'll treat me like gold for a spell."

Erin turned from the window. "I think Leigh *should* go home. If she doesn't, Quentin will hire a PI to find her and that probably means following *us* too. We can't have that!"

"Well, I admit, he will be less suspicious if you go back to him in the meantime," said Mora. "But you have to be careful! Carry a panic button with you when he's around." Mora reached for her purse. "Now, let's plan our next meeting—after you leave here. We'll need to know everything there is to know about your husband before our OC agent approaches him."

Chapter 68

"HEY THERE!" A tanned, slender, graying man entered Lucky's room. "Remember me?"

Lucky stared at the uniformed man blankly. Then fear enveloped him. The law was here to take him away. And he didn't even know what he'd done wrong yet. Best to play it cool; let the man do all the talking.

"Uhhh...should I?" Maybe this was another test the hospital was pulling on him—hoping to jog his memory.

"The name's McConnell—call me Mac. I'm a ranger on the north rim of the Canyon. I heard about you and thought you might have been in one of my tour groups. That seeing me would help you remember."

Lucky felt his gut relax—a little. "Thanks, man." He exhaled. "I appreciate that. Do *I* look familiar to *you*?"

"Unfortunately, no—but my wife who works in admissions here figured it was worth a shot."

An awkward silence filled the room.

"Umm...bring me something to read?" Lucky dipped his head toward the magazine the ranger was holding.

"Oh, this? It's just something I brought to look at while I waited for my wife to get off duty—in case you were in therapy or something." He flipped through the pages. "It's the Wilderness Outfitters catalog."

"Wilderness Ou—" A firecracker exploded in Lucky's brain.

"Man, are you okay? You're face just turned as white as your bathrobe. Does the store's name mean something to you?"

Lucky hesitated. Was this a link to his past? He cautioned himself from revealing too much. It was just too dangerous—he felt it.

"Nah…" he covered, "just a queer name. They probably don't even know what *true* wilderness is!"

Lucky accompanied the ranger back to the office to pick up his wife.

"Say, could I borrow that catalog from you?" Lucky donned his most charming, breezy smile. "I'll need some clothes if I'm ever going to get out of this hospital!"

"Sure, pal, have at it." Mac handed him the cheery full-glossy booklet. "Their stuff's too expensive for me, anyway. I just use it for a wish book."

As soon as he was out of Mac's sight, Lucky sat in a blue leatherette chair in a lobby alcove and leafed through the Wilderness Outfitters catalog. As expected, he saw pages of outdoor clothing and equipment; but nothing special that sparked his interest—or memory. He turned to the back cover. A staff picture showed five people standing in front of the store. He squinted at it. Anger—followed by fear—encompassed him.

The catalog also featured knives—and guns.

Had he killed one of these people?

Chapter 69

IN MORA'S OFFICE, she and Leigh completed their calls soliciting funds for the rehab of the raffle home.

"You're a super fundraiser." Mora had enjoyed listening to Leigh's sales pitch to some of Quentin's contractor clients. "I think we've raised enough pledges this afternoon to more than cover any contingencies." Mora looked slyly at her companion. "I wouldn't tell him this, but I bet you are as good as or better than Quentin at this sort of thing."

Leigh turned and glanced toward the closed door between Mora's office and the BWEF lobby. "Shhh. He's in the conference room making business calls on his cell." She grimaced. "I think I told you he forbids me to come here without him." She looked at the door again and leaned across the desk towards Mora. "He thinks the BWEF ladies will tie up all my time and leave none for him."

Mora grimaced. They both knew Quentin had fears other than his wife's depriving him of her time volunteering.

"What did you tell him about your hospital stay?"

"Just that I went to the ER 'cause I was dizzy. Told them I'd tripped on a paving stone in Carol's yard and hit my head."

"He accepted that?"

"Yes, he did. Even seemed relieved at my made-up story."

Leigh's eyes softened. "I appreciate your compliment. If only he'd let me do more!" She smiled and then bit her lip. "Are we still on for Arrowhead next weekend?" she whispered.

Mora nodded.

Leigh blew out a sigh. "Okay, I'd better get cleaned up. Give me a minute." She reached for her compact.

Mora watched silently as Leigh powdered her face, attempting to cover the tears that had erupted.

At a loud knock on the office door, Leigh raced to the restroom off of Mora's office. Mora waited until Leigh was gone before she opened the door.

"Quentin. You must have finished your calls." Mora waved him in. "We've just finished ours." She smiled at the scowling man. "You'll not be surprised, probably, but Leigh convinced two of the three contractors to work with us for free."

"Took you long enough. I made eight calls in the time it took you to complete three." He looked up as Leigh entered the room, her face freshly made up.

"Come, darling. I need to take you home and get to the office."

Chapter 70

LUCKY ROAMED THE BANK of the Colorado River. This was the most comfortable he'd felt anywhere, he realized—like he belonged here somehow. His eyes were drawn to a rubber raft floating by, filled with obvious tourist neophytes.

"Lean left to take us away from the bank," shouted the man in back.

"No! Lean right!" called out Lucky, to everyone's—and his own—surprise. "Otherwise the current will run you right into the rocks!"

The guide's eyes followed Lucky's gaze and he realized his mistake. "Lean right, lean right!" he urged his confused crew.

Lucky's shoulders tensed as he watched the rowers follow the new direction and pass by unscathed.

"Hey thanks, man!" The guide called back to him. "I owe you!"

Lucky lifted his hand in an "it was nothing" gesture. And it *was* nothing, he realized. Spotting that current had been as natural to him as breathing. How did he know so much about rafting? It made sense that he'd been on the river at some time. Maybe even on a raft.

Somehow the thought of river-rafting, while comfortable, also made him uneasy. Was it because of his recurring drowning nightmare? Or was it something real? The very question caused his heart to rev. He decided to stay away from the river until he could recall for sure.

Not knowing was tearing him apart. Part of him wanted to make amends for whatever had brought him here with all that money in his pocket. The other part of him wanted to yell at someone, someone who had done him harm.

But who?

Chapter 71

"Now, TELL US QUENTIN'S HABITS, from the time he gets up in the morning, to the end of the day when he drops into bed."

Leigh shivered. Should she—*could* she—go through with this? Pale-faced, she sat with Carol and Mora in front of a fire in Carol's den. She felt weak from the hospital stay, but going home had given her a big boost. With Quentin in his "I'm sorry" mode, life had been rather calm this week. Thankfully, he'd told her this morning that he'd be in Sacramento this weekend. Hopefully, arrangements for her safety could be made during that time—one way or another.

Carol poised her fingers over the laptop resting on her knees as she waited for Leigh's response. Her cheeks reflected her dahlia-red blouse as she concentrated on the screen.

"Are you sure you should be typing this up?" Leigh pulled a thick eggplant chenille shawl around her cold body and dried her sweating hands on her wrap. Southern California's "June gloom" depressed her. The conversation and her own dread chilled the room even more.

"Don't worry; I save only to an external device." Carol waved a thumb drive and plugged it into her laptop. "When it's appropriate, I'll use the information to write a glowing BWEF public relations piece about Quentin. If anyone opens the database, it will track only to the PR file. No one can trace any of this information to any of us. Besides, I've installed software to make it virtually impossible for anyone other than me to unlock the data." She patted Leigh's knee. "Take a deep breath. Relax. We've plenty of time."

Mora leaned over and took Leigh's hand. "Right now, we're just gathering information about Quentin to get a feel for what the *theme* of the article should be."

Leigh sighed. *Yes, think of this as an article interview.*

Mora lowered her voice. "We can't know how we can help *you* until we know all about Quentin's surroundings, the environment that makes *him* what he is. We won't move forward without that information."

"After our plans are firm," Carol added, "we'll prepare the 'article' and the flash drive will be yours. You can smash it with a hammer if you want."

Leigh settled into the soft cushions, took a small sip of her hot tea, and set her chattering cup and saucer on the glass coffee table. She swallowed with a large gulping sound. "Quentin rises at seven a.m. He has his coffee in the kitchen and then works out in his gym for exactly one hour and thirteen minutes."

"What equipment does he have in there?" Mora asked.

"I don't really know. Let me think." Quentin forbade Leigh from distracting him while he exercised. And she didn't exercise there; he didn't want her to change the settings on the equipment.

She smiled ruefully. "He complains I've gotten flabby, but he won't let me use his gym—*or* dance." A tear glistened, swelled, and coursed down her cheek. "So I guess he's right about my being out of shape."

Carol raised an eyebrow at Mora and turned to face Leigh. "How could anyone think *you're* out of shape? You're as trim as a high school cheerleader."

Leigh shrugged, trying desperately to remember *something* from her last walk through Quentin's home gym.

She began speaking as though hypnotized. "There's a leg press and a couple of machines for the upper body." She snapped her fingers. "Of course. The treadmill and the stair stepper. He uses those all the time."

Carol tapped on her keys. "Okay. Your first assignment is to go into Quentin's gym and write down the information from the machines' permanent labels: Name, manufacturer, and model." Carol pointed to her screen. "I'll print out a simple chart you can fill out, so you won't miss anything."

"Okay." Leigh twisted her single auburn braid. She'd have to find a time when she was *sure* Quentin wouldn't return unexpectedly. Maybe this weekend.

Carol consulted her notes. "It also might prove helpful to know his height and weight."

Leigh frowned. Quentin was vain about his height. Wore elevator shoes even. Without them, he was shorter than she was wearing high heels. And his weight was *never* discussed.

"We don't have to be exact," Mora said, reading her thoughts. "You can just look in his closet for some clothes sizes and we'll extrapolate the information ourselves."

"He has them made. But I don't think I should call his tailor." Leigh tied the ends of the shawl, pulling it tight around her. "He'd find out."

"You could measure his clothes: the sleeve and inseam lengths." At Leigh's frown, Carol said brusquely, "If that's too much trouble, never mind. We'll guess, from what we observe."

"You'll see I've asked you for the settings on the machines." Carol pointed to the chart she'd printed. "It's important for us to know how strong Quentin is." Leigh nodded, but a tear traced a path on her cheek.

Carol pumped her arm to display her bicep, pushing on despite Leigh's distress. "I've worked out on about every machine he could possibly own. I'll know what each is for and how it should be set for one of Quentin's size."

"Now, tell us," Mora said gently, "what else does Quentin do in his spare time?"

"We're really interested in activities where he might be alone," Carol added bluntly.

"We obviously don't want to interrupt his business activities for our 'interview,'" Mora explained, "and we won't want our 'discussion' to be observed or overheard."

"However, that doesn't preclude our approaching him anonymously in a crowd," broke in Carol. "*If* we have no other option."

Leigh inhaled deeply. This was going to be even harder than she thought. "Well…" she began hesitantly, "Quentin *used* to play golf and tennis almost every weekend, and swim in our pool every evening. Now, there's mostly just the sailboat."

Leigh looked out the window, reflecting on how much she usually welcomed his time away from home. But if the activities turned out badly, she suffered on his return. At those times, she wished he had no hobbies at all.

"Is he an accomplished sailor?" Mora's words broke Leigh from her ruminations. "I haven't seen him at the Yacht Club regattas, or in their classes for that matter." Mora poured herself another cup of coffee.

"He taught himself." Leigh's eyes glistened. "Quentin never takes lessons from anyone, ignores instruction books." Leigh stood, pointed her toe, and stretched to touch it in a fluid movement. "In that respect, I guess he's like most men. He says he learns more from figuring things out for himself than anyone could ever teach him." She tugged at her coral tunic, then returned to the couch and sat on its arm.

"I guess the 'Dummy' books weren't written for him," said Carol dryly. She glanced at her screen. "What else can you tell us about his everyday stuff?"

"He drives to Century City every morning, and then walks a few blocks from his parking garage to his office at the top of the bank building. The bank would prefer to send a limousine for him, for security if nothing else, but he says the walk clears his mind for the day's activities." Leigh paused. "I suspect he doesn't want to have to be civil to the driver that early in the morning."

Leigh stretched her arms in front of her, hands clasped. "Even a *minute* of stretch exercise erases my waking up dourness." She flushed. "Quentin is entirely the opposite. He's a decided night person and waking to exercise—which he insists upon doing—makes him a raging bear." She hesitated. "I avoid him in the mornings. He hits me hardest then." She bit her lip. "It was a morning beating that made me miscarry last year."

Leigh mentally waved off Carol's moan and Mora's "Oh, sweetie." That misery would *never* leave her. She mourned her child badly. Leigh looked down at her hands. "He wanted me to get an abortion; his blows to my abdomen saved him the money." Mora moved to the couch and enveloped Leigh in a warm hug. "We're here to help you get through this."

"That means so much," said Leigh, wiping her tears. "Let's go on, shall we?"

"Of course," said Carol. "But this actually could be important. Did the hospital call the authorities?"

"No. I told them I'd fallen. Quentin was so solicitous and exuding so much authority, they wouldn't *dare* suspect him." Leigh's eyes glazed as her thoughts drifted. "I don't know what makes him so angry all the time. I've wondered if he dislikes his job, but he says he looks forward to going to work, all the contacts he makes." She sighed. "He *could* be afraid they're going to replace him. I know he doesn't get along with some of the people on the board of directors." If Quentin had a job in a less tense environment, Leigh wondered, would he act differently with her?

"What time does he go to work? Does he keep bankers' hours?"

The tapping on the computer keys was the only sound in the room as the two women waited patiently for Leigh's response. Leigh felt the emotions emanating from the two women. They apparently understood her pain and confusion.

"Every day he leaves the house at exactly 9:02 a.m.," began Leigh. "I know, 'cause that's the time I turn on music and practice my ballet."

241

Leigh's eyes filled with tears, and she smiled wanly at her companions. "I have this dream of opening a dance studio for preschool kids," she said softly.

"Well, that's a *great* dream," said Mora. "Tell us about it."

Energized by the support—by *allowing* herself to dream for the first time in a long time—Leigh jumped up and pirouetted for Mora and Carol, her shawl becoming a diaphanous scarf trailing from her hand. "In addition to my dance lessons for inner-city kids, I also help out when I can with dance classes for the disabled." Her brown eyes shone with golden highlights. "It gives them balance and confidence. I'd like to give that gift to so many *more* children." Leigh pirouetted again—dreamily. She knew now that she *couldn't* live her life any longer without dance. She and ballet were one.

Carol looked up from her computer and smiled. "I'd *love* to help you with the disabled," she said. "Of course, I don't know beans about ballet, but I sure know the wheelchair culture! Maybe I could go with you sometime. Learn about the physical challenges—and possibilities."

"Of course, Carol!" Leigh hung her head. "But it will have to be when Quentin's out of town. Or after…" She couldn't bring herself to finish the sentence.

"Does Quentin travel often?" Mora asked in a professional tone. Leigh reluctantly returned to her seat. "We may want to discuss 'the article' some time when he isn't here."

"About once a month he goes to visit the out-of-state branches. He's in charge of all the western states: California, of course, Oregon, Washington, Idaho, Arizona, and Nevada. He schedules his bank visits a month or so in advance—but I don't find out he's going until the morning he leaves."

Leigh drained the last of her tea and accepted a refill. "Well, so far, this isn't too hard," Leigh admitted. "I thought you'd be asking me lots of questions I couldn't answer—or that were too painful."

"Remember, we've both been in your shoes," said Mora. "We know a lot about your life without asking. What we *don't* know is the routine that Quentin keeps—and what keeps *him* going."

Mora looked at Carol. "Anything else?"

"What foods does he avoid?" asked Carol. "Any he's allergic to?"

Leigh saw where this question was heading and felt a bit queasy. "Well, let me see: He doesn't eat beets. I found that out the hard way, when we were first married—he threw them at me. I had to trash my yellow silk blouse because I couldn't get the red stain out of it." Leigh thought for a minute, her fingers caressing her pant leg. "He told me once that he's allergic to okra, but I'm not used to eating it so I've never had a problem with that." Leigh shivered. "Isn't food too obvious? And too close to me? I mean, wouldn't they suspect me if he was sickened by food? I thought you—"

"We just want to cover all the bases." Carol tapped on her keys a final time and removed the flash drive. "Let's talk about next steps."

Mora rose and walked to the window. She circled the large room and peered into the hallway from each of the three doors.

Finally she said to Leigh, "Carol and I will discuss the information you've given us. We may come back for more. We'll call for a lunch appointment each time we need more details for the article. Under *no* circumstances will you discuss any of this with either of us on the telephone. Is that clear?" Mora's pointed look willed Leigh to respond.

"Yes." Leigh nodded emphatically. "Does that include *all* activities of the Outreach Committee?"

"Yes!" Carol and Mora both spoke at once.

Chapter 72

TAYLOR STOOD LOOKING OUT at the crowd, nervous, but so proud to see that her house raffle venture had pulled in so many. She pulled at the jacket of her blue and white seersucker suit and moistened her lips.

The sun beat down on the parking lot of Malaga Cove. It was only nine a.m., but the day had already shown signs of setting heat records.

The crowd gathered for the house drawing appeared oblivious to the temperature. Clutching their tickets in moist hands, they danced from one foot to another. Taylor was excited, too. Not only was this a first for her, but for the BWEF. Just think of all they could do with the funds they'd received!

An enlarged color photograph of the home with its red-tile roof, tropical plants, and unobstructed view of the Pacific Ocean was positioned at the entrance. Only those holding raffle tickets were permitted near the stage. Static and electronic whistles echoed across the lot as the loud speakers were tested.

Finally, Taylor stepped up to the podium and raised the microphone to accommodate her almost six-foot height.

"Good morning. Don't we have a beautiful day for our lottery drawing?" Holding her hands up to quiet the crowd, she waited patiently. Finally, after much shushing among themselves, the ticket holders grew silent.

"We'll start with the monetary winners: first, the two-hundred-fifty-dollar winners, then the five hundred and one thousand. When I call your name, take your ID to the table on my right and they'll write you a check. You'll be asked for your Social Security number, too." She made a face. "For the IRS."

Taylor drew the first name from the basket in front of her.

"And now, the moment you've all been waiting for. Our grand prize: A beautifully furnished home with its panoramic ocean view, large gardens, new appliances. It's move-in ready: recently painted in and out—even the four-car garage. Perfect for our lucky winner's family living—and celebration party." Taylor turned to the black-clothed security guard next to her. "The envelope, p-please."

Eager eyes followed her every move. The emotions: hope, anxiety, elation, were palpable. Taylor ripped off the end of the envelope and shook out the card inside. She read it and locked eyes with Mora, sitting in the front row. Tailor steadied herself and looked back out at the crowd. "The w-winner of our fabulous home is...C-C-Claire Finehold, of London, England!"

Four excited women sat around the conference phone in Mora's office. Mora dialed and they listened to the electronic sounds as the call was transmitted overseas.

"Hello?" a sleepy voice answered.

Mora motioned for Taylor to speak.

"Oh, Claire, I'm sorry! We've gotten you up in the middle of the night. This is T-Taylor Whitmore, and I'm here with Erin, Mora, and Carol."

The group heard some shuffling, and Claire cleared her throat. "Taylor! What a pleasant surprise. You *have* woken me, but I enjoy talking to you ladies anytime!"

"We all miss you."

"I miss you, too. Is that why you're calling?" She lowered her voice. "Or is this about...a new, uh, 'operation'?"

Taylor sat up straight. "N-no...Actually we're calling to tell you some *happy* news!" Taylor smiled at the other committee members. "As you know, we had our big house r-raffle today—Operation Castle." Taylor tipped her head toward Carol. "We had a mind-blowing turnout."

"That's right!" The force of Claire's enthusiasm could be felt through the phone line. "I'd forgotten this was the big day. I'm so glad to hear it went well!"

"There's m-more," said Taylor. "Much more." She paused for dramatic effect. "The grand-prize winner of the beautiful home on the Peninsula is…you!"

"Congratulations, friend!" broke in Mora. "We're all so thrilled for you."

"Yes!" chimed in Erin. "Now you have no damned excuse not to come visit us more often!"

"Hear, hear!" said Carol.

As the four women beamed at each other, the other end of the line remained silent.

"C-Claire?" Taylor said tentatively. "Are you th-there? Aren't you ex…excited?"

"Of course…" Claire answered slowly. "Actually, though, I'm excited for *you*. When I bought my ticket, it was with the intention that, if I won, I'd donate the home back to the OC, to sell for Operation funds or to give to the BWEF for a shelter—your choice!"

Taylor looked at Mora, Carol, and Erin, who all appeared as stunned as she felt.

"That's an overly g-generous donation, Claire," Taylor finally said. "Are you s-s-sure you want to do that?" Taylor's voice had lost its celebratory tone. This was a serious decision.

"I'm sure," replied Claire, her tone also somber. "As you know, I moved to London before I could complete my obligation to the Outreach Committee. I've been troubled by that."

Taylor looked at the others, her brow furrowed.

"Consider it payment for services rendered," said Claire, "three years ago."

Chapter 73

MORA TRIED ONCE AGAIN to push aside her feeling of failure, but she couldn't.

"It's *my* fault he's here. I was the one who asked the bank for help."

"The bank appointed *him* though," Carol reassured her. "He—and we—didn't really have a choice."

But Mora wasn't letting herself off the hook that easily. Quentin could *easily* make good on his threat to bring down the organization, using the power of attorney he'd been given over their bank accounts and investments. If he destroyed the BWEF's finances, it would be *her* doing. She closed her eyes and shook her head.

"Plus"—Carol's eyebrows started their acrobatics—"*no one* would have suspected someone at CEO level of being a wife beater!"

"Bankers are notorious for having dictator characteristics," countered Mora. "Something *else* I should have thought about. It's obvious he feels much more competent in his career than he does with women." Mora felt a chill that wasn't explained by the air-conditioning.

"Well, the bottom line is that we've got to take action *soon*." Erin strode into Mora's office, followed by Taylor. "Leigh is in danger and so is the BWEF. The sooner Quentin is taken care of, the better."

Mora had purposely not included Leigh in this evening's meeting. At this point in Leigh's Widow-Hood Anticipation Training (the OC's tongue-in-cheek reference to "WHAT" do I do now?), it would be too risky for her to participate—for all of them. She took a deep breath and let it out slowly. "Where are we?"

Carol opened her laptop and inserted the "PR" file she and Mora had created during their meeting with Leigh. They'd updated it with details Leigh had slipped to them yesterday at the weekly BWEF finance meeting.

"He's a tough one." Carol shifted in her chair and rubbed her knee.

"He's an intelligent, self-serving man," said Mora. "We'll have to be extra careful so he won't sense our intent."

"Yeah—a real chameleon," said Erin dryly. "Every time I see him, he's a different person. I don't know whether to flirt with him or give him the finger—though I know which he deserves." Erin crowded close to Carol and read the screen.

"Maybe we could follow him on the golf course."

Taylor pushed up the sleeves of her red-and-white-striped T-shirt. "Too many people—even on a weekday."

Mora continued her soul-searching. *Had* she been fooled by Quentin's charm? Abusive men enchanted—until they trapped their prey. Succeeding, they reverted to type. Mora closed her eyes and shook her head. Even with her expertise, she had not spotted Quentin's true nature until it was too late. Even then, she had needed convincing.

"The golf course would be easier logistics," said Carol. "We could catch him when he's ahead of his foursome."

"The course he plays is relatively flat. Someone might spot our agent." Erin leaned over Carol's shoulder again. "What else does Quentin Pryor do with his time?"

"What about another seduction?" said Carol, paging down the computer screen. "Do you think someone could entrap him on a business trip out of town?"

Mora frowned. "Unfortunately, it doesn't sound like we'll have ready access to his itinerary—with his being so closed-mouthed to Leigh about his schedule." She waved her hand dismissively. "Besides, I'm not sure how easy it'd be to get him to actually lower his guard."

Carol nodded. "Well, what about you and me, then?" she said to Mora, her eyes bright.

"Wh-What do you mean?" Taylor's perplexed tone reflected Mora's own confusion.

"Mora and I could corner him on a trip to Mammoth Mountain," explained Carol. "Teach him some of our 'cliff-jumping' methods."

Despite the sick humor of it all, Mora giggled. The other women joined in. Mora gave a mental shrug. Sometimes laughter *was* the best stress reliever.

"Well, as much fun as that sounds,"—Mora smiled again—"perhaps we should consider some safer venues."

Carol smiled and consulted her notes. "Hmm…Leigh said Quentin has been sailing a lot lately," she said. "Alone."

The laughter stopped abruptly as the women considered this possibility.

"Taylor, you're an underwater genius." Carol set the computer aside. "Could you find him at night in a marina?"

Taylor paced the room, pulling books off the shelf and then putting them back. "M-M-Maybe," she said slowly, "but I'd run the risk of others spotting me."

Mora observed Taylor's body language warily. "Taylor," she said, "I have to say that I don't think you're ready for this."

Taylor faced the room. "Well…I guess it depends on exactly w-what 'th-this' is." She finger-combed her hair, worn long today "I know I have to pay back your favors." She smiled at Erin.

"And?" Mora felt bad putting Taylor on the spot, but they had to know where each other stood—for safety's sake.

"Well…the truth is, I don't know if I *c-could* perform a Courtesy Killing. Ever." Taylor lowered herself into the straight-backed chair. "I know Marshall deserved what we did, but I can't help it. I'm still feeling so guilty." She looked down at her hands. "And to top it all off, I can't even m-mourn him since I don't even know for sure that he's dead."

The room went silent as the ladies allowed Taylor's words to sink in. Mora had suspected as much, but she hadn't known how honest Taylor would be with the group—or herself.

"We *do* recognize that not everyone can do *every* job," Carol finally said, looking down at her lifeless legs. "What *would* you be willing to do? If we encountered Quentin near the marina on Catalina, for example, we'd need a pilot to fly in the point person; a dive master; and an equipment supervisor. Could you do one of those tasks?"

"I *could* do all of them." Taylor rose again and walked over to the window, apparently lost in thought. Finally, she turned and surveyed the group. "R-Right now, I'd like to l-limit my help to outfitting and m-maybe flying someone in and out of Catalina. W-Would that work?"

Mora smiled. "Taylor, that would be a great start." She paused. "But of course, we still need a point person."

"Well, I guess Claire's out now," said Erin. "She finally paid off *her* debt—at least sort of. And it was about time!"

Carol opened her folder and withdrew Claire's "press release" sheet. "Former Superintendent of Schools in Illinois," she read, "Claire Finehold is an experienced educator and an adventurer. She is an avid sailor and diver, and has traveled solo across the Pacific." Carol shut the file. "It's too bad—she would have been perfect for this operation. Maybe we could ask her anyway?"

Mora shook her head. "Claire's awaiting a new grandchild," she said. "I don't think we can wait long enough for her to come back to the States."

"Well, who then?" asked Carol. "*I'd* do it, but somehow this Op just doesn't seem up my particular alley!"

"What about me?" Erin asked.

The women looked at each other.

"Don't look so fucking surprised." Erin put her hands on her hips. "There's nothing in our rules that says I can't do two in a row."

"But—" Mora hesitated.

"I know, Mora. I'm concerned too—that it might be dangerous. But this is important to Leigh *and* to the BWEF." She looked directly at Mora. "Besides, maybe having someone experienced would be a benefit."

Mora considered this. Erin *did* have a point. But would it be wise to use her again so soon? She seemed genuine in her willingness, but it really *could* be dangerous—not just legally, but emotionally.

"Before I became a construction contractor, I owned a dive shop in Oxnard," Erin reminded them.

"Do we have any indication that Quentin dives?" Carol reached to take Quentin's PR file from Mora.

"Well, if you'd rather, I could just flirt with the bastard and get him to take me on a boat ride." Erin's laugh echoed in her periwinkle eyes.

Carol practically choked on the water she was sipping. "No way, lady! Remember how he acted when you went to his office? You're much too assertive for him."

Mora looked on silently, thinking about all Erin had accomplished. This was one woman who had surely come into her own since being widowed!

"Erin, are you really volunteering for this?" Taylor paced from the corridor door to the restroom and back, twisting her hair and biting her lip. "I know it's my turn, but..." Her words trailed off.

"I thought we'd settled that," said Erin. "You can contact the marina for Quentin's schedule on the boat rental, fly me in and out of Catalina, and outfit the dive. I'm willing to do the rest." She flapped her arms. "I can't fly and *you* can," she said bluntly. "You can't kill and *I* can. It's that simple—okay?"

Taylor looked at her feet. "I g-guess so."

Mora exchanged a silent look with Carol, her friend's eyebrow raised in its usual fashion.

"Well, I guess it's settled then," said Erin. "Let's get to work!"

Taylor drove around the beach area until she found a still-functioning pay phone. After glancing over her shoulder to make sure no one was within listening distance, she consulted her Day-Timer for a phone number and then dropped her money into the slot and dialed.

Taylor tapped her foot as she waited for someone to answer.

"King Harbor Yacht Club. May I help you?"

Finally!

"Hello. Yes, I apologize, but I need to confirm a r-reservation. Y-you know, for one of your craft made by my boss. Oh! I mean, he didn't make the b-boat, just the reservation." Taylor coughed. "I-I'm so embarrassed to say that I didn't write it down when he told me." She lowered her voice in commiseration. "*You* know how it is. You think you'll remember something and then you don't." She giggled. "I don't d-dare ask him. He'll get mad. You know?"

Taylor could practically hear the girl at the other end of line nodding.

"Oh, so *you* have one of those, too. Sure I can help you. Who'd you say your boss is?"

"Oh, I guess I didn't say." Taylor couldn't believe her dingy-secretary act was actually working! "He's Quentin P-P-Pryor—you know, of W-Western States Bank."

"Yes, we know Quentin." At the girl's words, Taylor smiled; she was almost there! "But I remember his assistant I talked to before was a really nice man."

Taylor froze, feeling physically sick. She moved to hang up the phone but stopped herself with her hand mid-swing. She *had* to make this work. This was her only shot.

Taylor wiped her face with her sleeve and returned the phone to her ear.

"What did you say? Oh, a nice man. Yes, he still is; that is, I'm Mr. Pryor's a-assistant's assistant—if you know what I mean."

"Oh," the girl said sympathetically. "That makes it even worse, doesn't it? Okay. Do you know *about* what time the reservation was for?"

"Well, actually," Taylor stood up straight to try to emit confidence. "I'd appreciate his b-boat reservations for the next two months. I'm re-re-doing his electronic schedule and I want to check *everything*." Taylor held her breath. Was she pushing her luck?

"Have you got a pencil and paper?"

Guess I really do sound ditzy. Taylor didn't have to pretend to fumble for her pen, which in her nervousness she'd dropped to the floor of the phone booth.

"Okay, I'm ready." She balanced her notepad on the tiny shelf under the phone.

"July twenty-fifth and every Saturday in August. Does that help you?"

"Oh yes. It does t-tremendously. Oh, one other thing: Could you please verify whi-which boat and the times?" Taylor felt sweat dripping off her forehead.

"The Rio, seven a.m. Saturday 'til dark on Sunday; Catalina is the destination for all of them. We've reserved docking space for him there on Saturday night for those weekends." The receptionist coughed. "My other phone is ringing. Is that all you need?"

Taylor let out a breath. "Yes. Thank you so v-very much. I didn't catch your name."

"It's Josie."

"Josie, you have *no* idea what a lifesaver you are."

Chapter 74

L UCKY LEAFED THROUGH the Wilderness Outfitters catalog for what seemed like the hundredth time.

Maybe he should just call them.

Twice, he picked up the telephone receiver and returned it to its cradle. What was he afraid of? His whole body broke into a cold sweat.

Taking a deep breath, he pulled the phone to his ear and dialed.

Chapter 75

TAYLOR DOODLED ON THE MESSAGE PAD in front of her, consumed with the pending Quentin intervention. She drew a plane, followed by a sailboat, and then heavy bars across a small window. What would happen to *her* if Erin were caught? Sure, she could claim ignorance of Erin's plans, but that would substitute a good friend for herself in the hot seat. And would the authorities then ask her about Marshall?

Taylor dropped her pencil and put her head in her hands with a moan. Her life had become too complicated. She couldn't blame anyone but herself. She'd married an abusive man and then asked the Outreach Committee to arrange his death for her. So *what* if someone else had orchestrated the accident that had maybe failed to kill him? It was still her fault she was in such turmoil.

At the beep of the phone ringing in the store, Taylor raised her head and wiped her face with a tissue. She peered over her reading glasses as her son entered. "Is the phone for me?" She reached for the instrument on her desk.

"No." Rob plopped in the visitor's chair. "At least I don't think so. It rang twice, and then the third time I could tell someone was on the line, but I couldn't hear anything. I told him to call back."

"Him?"

"Yeah. Somehow, I know it's a guy."

Chapter 76

I<small>T TOOK TWO WHOLE DAYS</small> for Lucky to build up the courage to call the 800 number at Wilderness Outfitters again. This time a woman answered. He listened closely as she identified the store, but still he said nothing.

"Hello. Is s-someone there?"

She sounded friendly. Familiar? Yes and no.

He remained silent, not knowing why he'd called. What he had expected to learn. He heard a raspy breath intake. Either the connection was bad or she had a cold. He coughed reflexively.

The woman gasped. The phone slammed into the cradle.

Lucky rubbed his ear. The racket was painful.

Chapter 77

"Hello? Hello!" Mora pressed the phone to her ear. "I'm sorry, I can hardly hear you."

"It's T-Taylor. It's h-horrible."

"Wha—"

"M-M-Marshall. I have to see you."

Mora sighed. All they needed amidst everything was an emotion-flooded emergency; she should have known this operation was too much for Taylor. "Taylor, take a deep breath." Mora paused. "Is this something we can discuss over the phone?" she asked pointedly.

"No!" Mora recoiled from the shout.

"Okay, Taylor. I need you to relax. Why don't you come on over to the office? I'll put the teakettle on. *Wait*—are you safe to drive?"

"I...I don't know. I'll call a c-c-cab."

"Never mind. I'll come to the store." At this point, Mora didn't want *any* records of OC member visits. Not even taxi logs.

Her sensors at red alert, Mora struggled to maintain the speed limit on the way to Wilderness Outfitters. Was this the beginning of the end she knew was inevitable?

"H-H-Horror movie!" Taylor let the door fall shut behind Mora and dissolved into her arms, sobbing.

Taking pains not to disrupt Taylor's embrace, Mora bolted the door and turned the sign to Closed. She led Taylor along the hallway to the store office and helped her into a chair. Spotting a plaid throw, Mora tucked it around Taylor's sides. It was the middle of summer, but the woman was clearly in shock.

"Tea first, then talk. You stay right there." Mora entered the employee break room, which connected to the office. She rummaged up the kettle, cups, tea bags, and a plate of cookies.

Adrenaline-pumped as she was at the moment, Mora knew she would need the tea to stay alert once she crashed back down. Plus, she hadn't been sleeping well lately.

"Okay, what happened?"

Taylor's face lost some of its pallor with a few sips of tea. "Like a dream, only it wasn't."

"Tell me."

Mora studied Taylor's mannerisms. First she put her hand over her eyes, and then she twisted her hair. She finally opened her mouth to speak, only to close it and clear her throat.

"You know that whatever you say is safe with me. It's just between the two of us."

Taylor looked around the room, staring at each entrance. "M–M–Marshall's going to walk in any m–minute," she whispered. "I know it."

Mora sighed in relief. Was that all? She took Taylor's hand. "Taylor, that's a completely natural reaction. After the death of a loved one— for *any* reason—you always expect to turn around and see them again. It takes a while for that feeling to go away."

Taylor looked at Mora, her eyes tormented. "This is d–different," she croaked.

Mora squeezed Taylor's hand. "I know Marshall's body hasn't been found—" began Mora.

"Not that," cut in Taylor.

"Then what?"

"You see, today…" Taylor paused to brush the hair from her eyes. "I'd been working around the shop, rearranging inventory—W–Wait. Back up. Over the last few d–days, Rob's answered a couple s–s– strange phone calls here at the store. You kn–know: the kind where you know someone is there, but they don't t–t–talk?"

Mora nodded but said nothing.

"So today, the phone rang, and I picked it up and gave my normal greeting. Taylor gasped. "I h–heard b–breathing, and then—" Taylor put her hands over her ears. "And then a c-c-cough."

Mora waited.

"And?" she finally said.

"And…" Taylor's voice dropped to a whisper. "It was him."

"Taylor, listen to me." Mora squeezed her hand. "You are in a heightened state of anxiety. It's perfectly normal to imagine things. Things you don't want to have happen."

Taylor shook away Mora's grip. "N–N–No, you don't understand!" she said. "It was *r-r-r-really* him. I'm not imagining it!"

Mora smoothed her friend's hair and rubbed her back. "What makes you so sure it was Marshall?"

"N–Nobody coughs as annoyingly as he does. It sounds like… like a wh–whooping sneer." Taylor threw off her wrap and jumped up to look out the sliding door. "Wha-What if he survived the wa-waterfall?"

Chapter 78

AFTER TRYING HER BEST to calm and comfort Taylor, Mora headed home—utterly exhausted after a full week. Thank God it was Friday! Still, her busy mind wouldn't rest.

Was it *possible* Marshall was still alive? Mora rejected the thought. Taylor was under so much stress, she was becoming afraid of her own shadow. Poor thing.

Mora's stress was heightening too, between the Marshall situation and gearing up for the impending Courtesy Killing of Quentin. It was taking all of Mora's professional training to try to manage everyone's emotions—including her own.

Perhaps they should postpone the move on Quentin? Mora felt a chill not explained by the balmy night air. Ignoring the threat to the BWEF, Mora had to think about Leigh.

Leigh had been so independent during her dancing career. As she'd become successful, she had even helped finance a renowned ballet school whose graduates were accepted in notable troupes around the world.

Mora sighed. Knowing *that* made it all the more heartbreaking to see Leigh now, fearful and subject to Quentin's every whim.

Career women challenged Mora the most. Oh, she knew them inside and out. They were just like she'd been. It still hurt to think of the years she'd wasted being a punching bag to an insignificant bully.

They *all* had: Taylor…Erin…Claire…Carol…Helen.

Mora slammed on the brakes. Lost in thought, she had missed the brake lights in front of her and had almost rear-ended the light-blue Prius she'd been following.

Thinking of Helen renewed Mora's resolve. It didn't matter the risk to herself, or the OC. She simply *had* to rescue Leigh. And despite the current issues, she was confident they could carry out a successful dispatch operation.

Mora's biggest concern was Leigh—they'd have to act before she changed *her* mind.

Chapter 79

CAILIN COLLINS TIPTOED into the apartment without turning on the light. She grunted as she bumped into the couch in the darkened living room. *Oh, that's all I need,* she thought, swiping at a tear.

"Is that you, Cai?" A soft whisper came from her mother's bedroom.

"Yeah, Mom. Sorry I'm half an hour late. Game ran overtime."

"I trust you, honey. Was your date with Paul fun?" Cailin tiptoed to the window and sneaked the curtain to the side so she could see out.

"Not the best, Mom. Our team lost, so he wasn't in a very good mood."

"Want to join me in bed and tell me about it?"

"Nah. I'm tired; I need a shower. Nothing really to tell."

"Okay. Good night, hon. I'll sneak out in the morning. Ernest and I are meeting for breakfast. Don't forget your book report is due on Monday."

Cailin closed the bathroom door behind her and turned on the shower. She stepped under the hot water, grabbed the bar of soap, and began to scrub herself vigorously. The sound of the water masked her sobs.

Chapter 80

MORA REY FRETTED ANXIOUSLY all night. Still running through scenarios in her mind...*What if Marshall was alive? What if Leigh changed her mind? What if Quentin bankrupted the BWEF? What if, what if, what if?* She struggled to come up with contingency plans for all the possibilities.

Watching the sun crack over the horizon, Mora pounded her forehead with the heel of her hand. No matter what else was going on—even if the OC was on its final run—of one thing she was sure: Quentin had to go. The BWEF could go on without him. But it would die if he stayed.

Glancing regretfully at the glowing clock next to her bed, Mora picked up the phone.

Chapter 81

$\mathint$HARON WAVED GOODBYE to Ernest as she pulled out of the restaurant parking lot.

He was a fun man, polite; why was she so hesitant about more dates? She'd used the work excuse this time; said she'd check her schedule. *I wasn't playing hard to get—I'm damn afraid.* She needed that talk with Mora.

As Sharon entered the living room, she saw Cailin start to rise and then fall back onto the sofa. "Cailin, hon, you were asleep when I left this morning. Have you been dragging all day?" Sharon put her purse on the coffee table. "I could understand if it was a school day, but this is Saturday, your favorite day to bob around."

Sharon walked to the couch where her daughter was stretched out, facedown. She sat next to her hip and nudged her over to make room. "You on your period? Need a back rub?" Without waiting for an answer, she pressed her hands into Cailin's back muscles, only to feel her daughter wince.

"Hey, what's going on here?" Sharon lifted the girl's T-shirt and gasped. "You're all bruised. Who did this to you?" A knot formed in Sharon's stomach. "Was it Paul?" *My little girl. This can't be happening.*

"Oh, Mom, he wanted to have sex after the game. Said it would, like, make him feel better. He was bummed about losing." Cailin sat up cautiously. "He held me down on the seat and started pulling my clothes off." Sniffling loudly, she continued, "He got mad when I, like, reminded him that we had agreed to wait."

Sharon's guilt blossomed. She had waited too long to get counseling for the kids, and *now* look. This was her fault.

264

"Is that when he hit you?" Sharon couldn't stop her own angry tears from flowing. "I'm going to have that young man arrested right now." She reached for the phone.

"No! Mom, please. He didn't mean it." Cailin clenched her jaw, looking every bit the defiant teen. "Just 'cause you're a sheriff doesn't mean you arrest everyone who makes a mistake." Cailin swiped at her face with a crumpled tissue. "It was *my* fault; I should have realized how depressed he was." She sat up straighter, testing her sore spots. "He missed the basket that could have won the game—and with scouts in the bleachers, too. I guess the coach really lit into him in the locker room." She grabbed her mother's hand. "I *know* he loves me. He was just mad about the game, and because I didn't understand how important it was to him."

Sharon remained silent, internally berating herself. She *needed* to spend more time with the kids. If only she didn't have to work shifts, she could keep roughly the same hours they did with school and activities.

Sharon cupped her daughter's chin. She turned it toward her so that Cailin was forced to look her mother in the eye. "Listen to me; I know what I'm talking about—both from what I learned at the shelter and from being a sheriff. *No one,* whether they love you or whether you love them, has a right to hit you or force you into sex." She held her tongue on the question she wanted desperately to ask: Had Paul succeeded? Was her daughter no longer a virgin?

Instead she said: "This is my fault, too, you know. I should have continued your therapy after we left the shelter." Sharon bowed her head. "Your blaming yourself is all wrong; Mora would back me up on that." Sharon rose and kissed her daughter. "And I *will* get you whatever help you need. But first, I'll put a rice-filled pad in the microwave to heat. That should make your sore muscles feel better."

When Sharon returned, Cailin had regained a small bit of her composure—and typical teen resistance.

"Mom, Paul isn't like Dad; he wasn't drunk! Just because *you've* had bad luck with men doesn't mean I can't handle myself."

It just __may__ be, my love, because you learned self-hatred from me while you were growing up. She tried to tone down her sentiments.

"Oh, honey, I wish it was that simple. The part I played in what happened between your dad and me—and the part you *appear* to be playing with Paul—is having a poor opinion of yourself: what you're worth as a person."

Sharon paused to place the warm pad around Cailin's shoulders. "Otherwise, you would never even *think* of considering his brutal actions your fault."

"But I love him!" Cailin's erect posture dissolved into a sobbing, shapeless lump in her mother's arms. Sharon's stomach tightened.

"Honey. I'm not telling you that you don't love Paul. I can only tell you that you are a talented, intelligent budding beauty. A girl with too big a future to throw away on someone who hits you." She smoothed hair out of her daughter's eyes. "How did you get home?"

"I ran. We were just parked down by the pizza parlor, on the dark side street."

"Was anyone else in the car with you two?"

"No, we don't double-date. He likes to keep me to himself."

Sharon sighed. "I'm beating around the bush. Did he rape you?" She held her breath, not wanting to hear Cailin's answer.

Cailin shook her head.

"Sweetie, I have to know the truth. If you and Paul *did* have sex, we need to get you to the ER for a DNA swab, have you tested for pregnancy—get you a morning-after pill." Sharon's rambling thoughts spilled out.

"Mom, stop!" Cailin patted her mother's arm. "I didn't give him a chance to do that to me. I jumped out of the car when he tried to pull down my cheerleading briefs." She became contrite. "Mom, I had on my new ones; they tore when I pulled away."

Sharon shook her head. "Of course we'll replace them, hon—but that's the least of my concern right now. Did he follow you in the car?"

"He had to find his keys and get into the front seat before he could do that." Cailin giggled. "I ran so fast they should star me on the girls' track team." Sharon smiled despite herself. Maybe it *wasn't* too late to work on Cailin's self-assurance.

Cailin sobered. "After I got inside, I saw him drive up, look up here, and then drive on. I didn't turn on the light."

Sharon reached again for the phone.

"Mom, don't turn him in, please! *Please!*" Cailin tugged at her mom's arm. Sharon hesitated, grasping the cordless handset. She was torn between her job and her doubts about her parenting skills. Had Paul made a one-time mistake that shouldn't ruin his life? Would turning him in alienate her daughter forever?

Cailin's anxiety was mounting. "*Please* don't do this. I'll be so humiliated. It will ruin my life at school...my friendships... everything!"

Sharon sighed. She couldn't risk driving this wonderful child away. "I'll agree, on two conditions."

"What?"

"That I talk to his mother about this, and that you break up with him." Sharon cradled the receiver.

"*But Mom!* If I have to break up with him, I'll die!" As Sharon again grasped the phone, Cailin grabbed her mother's arm. "Okay! Okay! I'll *think* about breaking up with him. But..." As Sharon put the phone down again, an ocean-deep sigh escaped her daughter. "Mom, what should I tell him? What can I tell my friends?"

"It's simple. Tell Paul the truth: that his behavior was unacceptable and you're not going to tolerate it. If you can't do that, just tell him the relationship is no longer working—period. He'll know why." Sharon hated to sound so insensitive, especially after what Cailin had just been through, but she knew she had to take a hard line here.

"Now," she said, fixing Cailin with a stern gaze, "pick up the phone and call Paul, or go to the computer and send him an e-mail. I'll give you a half-hour or I will do it for you. And I don't think you want that."

Now that she'd said her piece, Sharon softened. "I won't suggest what you tell your friends; that's up to you." She adjusted the hot pack on her daughter's back. "I only hope that if you *don't* tell them about this, then if one of your girlfriends starts dating Paul, you watch carefully for signs of abuse."

Cailin nodded thoughtfully. "But what should I do if I see those signs?" She wrinkled her forehead. "They'll think I'm just jealous, if I say anything to them about it."

Sharon rose from the couch. "You say, 'Mom, Paul is hurting someone else.' And I'll have him brought in."

Chapter 82

WILDERNESS OUTFITTERS MUST BE a prosperous place. Its online store was filled with all kinds of hiking, rafting, and hunting equipment and clothes—even more variety than the catalog had offered.

For the second weekend in a row, Lucky had taken Dr. Malick up on his offer to visit his home, and he had spent a beautiful Saturday afternoon playing tennis. He'd lost, but not by as much as the first time. Seems he knew how to play.

Now, while the doc was busy cooking steaks on the patio, Lucky took the doc up on his offer of a computer to surf the web. He kept returning to the page of rubber rafts, choosing one he liked and then searching for paddles to outfit it. He was a rafter—no doubt about it. But that still wasn't getting him far.

Finally, Lucky clicked on a Customer Comments link. A woman's photo appeared on the screen. Hmmm…a pretty blonde. He felt his groin stir. He scrolled to the bottom of the page to view the caption:

Erin C.

Chapter 83

THE RACING SLOOP slowed as its sole occupant lowered the sails one by one. Fatigue overwhelmed Quentin Pryor, spent from a hard day fighting wind and waves—and from the disciplinary scene with his wife that morning.

Thinking about it, he shook his head. He'd chosen all his wives because they could be an asset to his career. Leigh bested the others in that regard. Realizing he loved her had been a surprise; he'd not loved his first three.

He moved the tiller to direct the boat away from the center of the channel so he could anchor before lowering the mainsail. The water patrol had assigned him a mooring spot. He motored to it, angry that it was so far away from the center, which he preferred. He'd learned on other trips that it was first come, first choice. His influence didn't matter here.

As the anchor took hold, Quentin's thoughts returned to his wife. He wished Leigh wouldn't insist on her independence. When she did, she deserved what she got. Her bitchy ways angered him; his necessary discipline depleted him.

The calm waters inside the breakwater were a pleasant respite. As the sun settled behind the horizon, he turned on the running lights.

Clad in a black full-body wetsuit, Erin Craig dropped into the water from a black rubber raft and approached the sloop. After positioning and clearing her mask, she inventoried the rest of her gear and then waved Taylor off.

She kept her eye on the *Rio* as Pryor maneuvered. She reviewed their plans to commit him to the deep and shivered in anticipation.

If she were honest with herself, she thrilled at yet another challenge. Although it had been a few years, she still relished *her* release from the tyranny of abuse—*and* celebrated her ability to give that joy to another woman.

Erin focused on the reason for her mission: If she didn't disable Quentin Pryor permanently, he would surely kill his wife. Leigh was her friend, and society didn't need the likes of him. Besides, he'd threatened to break the BWEF financially.

He may be a whiz at finances, but in the world of relationships he's illiterate. Erin's conscience was not an issue.

The diver's sturdy legs kept her abreast of the Rio as she waited for Pryor to turn his back. The darkness and the rough water concealed her head from even the closest boaters. After Pryor turned on the running lights, Erin waited until he ducked under the mainsail to lower it and then pulled herself aboard.

Water splashed Pryor's neck. He swiped at the wet spot and turned toward the stern, scowling. Erin reached up and pushed the boom towards him with all her strength.

"Hey!" yelled Quentin. "What the fuck—" He landed in the water with a loud splash. Their carefully calculated plan had worked! Erin looked around to be sure no one had heard his cry. Hearing only party conversations echoing over the water, she ducked under the boom and back into the water.

Quentin floated face up, entwined by his lifeline, which had twisted around him, pinning his arms to his body. Erin sized up the situation. She hadn't taken the lifeline into her planning; still, it was working perfectly. She grasped the twisted lifeline in one hand and pushed on Quentin's shoulder with her other. She flicked off the blood that was oozing from the gash the boom had made in the back of his head. *Damn!* The lifeline had shortened in the tangle around him and was preventing his total submersion. His struggles increased. The blow from the boom *should* have stunned him. She tried again to push him under the water. The lifeline held taut.

"I know you. You're…"

She had to shut him up. Erin held Quentin's head in a firm grip with her right hand and reached around her body with her left for her diving knife. With a sharp snap, the cut lifeline parted. As she turned to fit her knife into its sheath, Quentin butted her face with his head.

Erin jerked back, gasping with pain as flashing lights filled her head. Her nose felt like it had been hit with a sledgehammer. She gagged from the blood that flooded down her throat. Quentin pulled on the lifeline. If she didn't subdue him, they were all in real trouble.

Erin gave a strong kick to maneuver herself into position against Pryor. Floating on her back, she aimed both legs toward the banker's head. With all her might, she let out a two-legged kick—right at the spot where the boom had hit. Quentin let out a shudder and his flailing limbs grew slack. His continued curses were lost in gurgles as he labored to keep his head above the cold salt water. Erin swam over to his weakened form and with both hands pushed hard on the top of his head.

Erin held Quentin's head under the sea until long after bubbles stopped rising to the surface. She had to be sure.

Winded, Erin floated on her back. Quentin had been stronger than he looked. Sure, Leigh had told them he worked out, but Erin never dreamed he would almost drown her. She floated for several minutes more, trying to regain herself. Finally, she turned onto her side.

Erin winced as salt water entered her nose. Painfully, she side-stroked toward the Rio and held on until her breathing steadied. Then she swam toward her meeting place with Taylor, two coves north—her breathing hindered by the swelling in her nose. Erin stopped every few strokes to try to spot Taylor's flashlight from the shore where they'd agreed to meet. They'd sleep in their tent near the airport and fly out at first light.

At last! Erin adjusted her course toward the beam of light and rotated onto her back to relieve the stinging in her nose. Boy, she'd have a shiner to explain. She was too tired to think up a good story now. But she had a wealth of wild ones she'd used to explain the bruises from her husband's "love pats." Plus, she was in construction—that should help.

After what seemed hours—but was probably only fifteen minutes, Erin knew—Erin's kick hit the sandy bottom. She dropped to her knees in the shallow water and sat back on her heels, blowing out her raspy breath.

After five minutes she felt stronger. Wavering on her feet, she labored her way to the shore and to Taylor's welcome. As she approached the beach, Erin smiled and brushed her gloved hands together. *Another* job well done. Operation Commander complete.

It hadn't gone exactly as planned, but she'd succeeded.

PART IV

Operation Cover-up

Chapter 84

SHARON HESITATED AT THE DOOR to Mora Rey's office. She *was* being pushy—coming by with no appointment, and on a Sunday. But where her kids were concerned, she would do anything. She squared her shoulders and knocked.

"Come in!" Mora's cheerful voice alleviated some of Sharon's nervousness. She entered the office and closed the door behind her.

"Hello, Sharon." Mora sat behind a desk stacked with file folders. She removed her reading glasses and rose to greet her visitor. "I thought our next appointment was for this Tuesday?" She paused, surveying the deputy up and down. "Oh! Is this a law enforcement visit?"

Sharon blushed and looked down at her uniform. "Oh no, I'm on my way to work. It's about Cailin. My visit, that is." Maybe this wasn't such a good idea. "I apologize for not calling—"

"No apology necessary. You look upset. What is it?"

"It's my daughter."

Mora looked around Sharon towards the door. "Is she with you?"

"No, I've done something for her that I need your advice on."

"Sounds serious." Mora motioned Sharon to a chair.

"Her boyfriend hit her 'cause she wouldn't have sex with him."

Mora's face maintained a professional calm, but Sharon could guess what she was thinking. *The same thing I would think,* she berated herself. *How could I let this happen to my own daughter?*

"What did Cailin do or say?"

"She got out of the car and ran home." Sharon smiled shakily. "Thankfully, he didn't rape her."

"That's a relief." Mora's eyes locked with Sharon's in sympathy. "So what did you do that you want to talk about?"

"My first thought was to report him, of course, but Cailin didn't want me to. And I was afraid I'd lose her if I did."

Mora let out a breath. "And now you're feeling guilty because you didn't."

Sharon nodded. "I love her to pieces, but I have a duty—not only to my job, but to my daughter. I can never allow her to fall into the same cycle of abuse I was in."

Sharon started as her cell phone vibrated. "It always makes me jump," she said ruefully. Sharon removed the phone and squinted at the text message. "Oh, dear. We have a floater off Catalina—I'll have to go. My partner's meeting me at our helipad."

Sharon turned as she went through the door. "Mora, I'll be in touch again soon to make an *appointment*."

As the deputy left, Mora stretched upward to release her nervous tension. *A floater off Catalina. Whew! That was quick.* Mora exhaled as she lowered her arms. At least Leigh wouldn't suffer like Taylor had.

Mora's own phone vibrated. She looked at the caller ID. *Perfect timing,* she thought.

"Taylor, are you there? Is Erin with you?"

Mora heard muffled noises in the background.

"Taylor? What's happening?" Mora held the phone away from her ear and stared at it.

"Hi, Mora. It's Erin. We're back at Torrance Airport. Taylor is shaking so damn hard she dropped the phone."

Mora tensed. At least Taylor had gotten them on the ground before she'd started disintegrating.

"Take her home and stay with her, will you? It's dangerous for her to be alone." Mora paused, not wanting to say too much over the phone. "And I happen to *know* I'll soon be needed elsewhere."

Mora let Erin absorb the news.

"Shit, of course I'll stay," Erin finally said. "I'll be *damned* if I let anyone spoil my good work."

"Carol. Get ready to start the telephone comfort tree." After hanging up with Erin, Mora leapt into action. Cradling her cordless phone between her shoulder and chin, she pulled casseroles from the freezer as she talked—food always kept there for an occasion such as this.

Mora's mood was somber elation, if that were possible. Death was never something to celebrate, but Leigh's freedom from abuse certainly was.

"Come get me in thirty minutes," she told Carol, snapping open a hamper and placing the rectangular dishes inside. Mora tugged her T-shirt from her shorts as she stepped into her dressing room. "I'll shower and dress so I'll be ready when I get the call." Mora's tone was stern. "I don't want her facing the authorities alone."

Chapter 85

SHARON AND HARRY REACHED the Catalina waterline just as the crime scene technicians were finishing. Sharon was glad the no-doubt engorged corpse was already in a body bag.

"Do we have an ID yet?"

In answer, the investigator handed her a driver's license enclosed in a see-through evidence bag.

"Quentin Pryor. That name's familiar somehow."

Harry unzipped the black bag and looked at Pryor's bloated face. "Drowning?" Harry looked around at the silent shoreline. "Where is everyone?"

"They're probably on their way back to the mainland or drinking at the clubhouse." The resident sheriff's deputy pointed to a low building up a path from the water. He nodded toward the body. "He was found floating next to his boat." The deputy pointed to a sloop bobbing on its anchor rope. "We looked it over. The guy had on a separated lifeline but no life vest. The mainsail boom was swinging in the breeze, so I'd guess it hit him and pushed him overboard."

Sharon was relieved. Pryor's *accidental* death meant she wouldn't have to arrange a sitter for her kids tonight. She retrieved her notebook. "Who discovered the body?"

"A man sailing in from Los Angeles." He pointed to a bench on the path to the club. "He's sitting over there. Pretty shaken up."

"He know the vic?"

"Said not. Just never seen a dead person before, I think."

"What else can you tell us?"

"That boat we're studying—the Rio—was rented to Pryor for the weekend."

"Anyone see him come in?"

"Not that we've found. I'll ask around, though, when I finish here."

Sharon turned to the local deputy. "Where did this Pryor come from? Does he have a vacation pad here?"

The short gray-haired man shook his head. "Probably not. Sooner or later, I get to know all the residents. I don't remember him. The body is wrinkled but evidently hasn't been in the water long enough to be fish food. I can pretty much tell what he looked like."

Harry waved his hand at Sharon. "Come on, partner. We have next-of-kin duty. Copter's waiting for us. The victim's license has an address on the Palos Verdes Peninsula."

Sharon cringed. The worst part of the job. She knew she could act with compassion—she'd done it so many times before—but she always dreaded it.

Best to get it over with.

Sharon drove the black-and-white around the circular drive in front of the Pryors' gray stone edifice.

A rosy-cheeked woman in a white uniform answered the door.

"May we speak with Mrs. Quentin Pryor, please." Sharon showed her badge and took a deep breath. Deaths were hard, even to those so rich they could afford this mansion.

Sharon could handle most of her duties objectively, but her emotions always floated to the surface with a death. Losing both her mother and father at the same time had done that to her. She felt tears threatening and brushed them away.

"She's just gone up to change. May I tell her why you are calling? Or perhaps *I* could help you?" She smoothed her apron with work-red hands. "I cook for the Pryors."

"It's official business. You need to let us in." Harry's voice was soft but firm. The woman opened the door and led them to an informal room at the rear.

In short order, a slender woman entered, wearing a dancer's leotard and tunic. Her auburn hair was damp and frizzy around her face. Sharon admired the woman's regal walk. She herself was a plodder. And clumsy.

Concern creased the older woman's face.

Harry motioned to the settee. "Please sit down, Mrs. Pryor."

After Leigh had settled and picked up a frosty glass, Harry spoke again. "I'm afraid we have some bad news for you about your husband."

Sharon's shoulders relaxed. Harry was going to notify her.

"Quentin? He went sailing yesterday. If you need to speak with him, I'm afraid you'll have to come back tomorrow." At Harry's solemn look, Leigh's eyes widened. Her face paled, then crumbled. "Has he had an accident? Is he okay?"

"He was found dead, floating in Catalina Harbor."

Leigh dropped her drink and did not seem to notice its contents splashing on her clothes and the Oriental rug. She bent over and hugged her knees. "Quentin is *dead*? But that can't be!" Leigh's shoulders shook. The cook put her arm around her employer.

Sharon knelt in front of the distraught woman and took her hands. "Is there someone you'd like us to call to be with you, Mrs. Pryor?"

Leigh raised a chalky face and nodded.

"Who would that be?" asked Harry.

Leigh looked at Sharon. "I don't know…"

"I'll call Ms. Rey," said the cook.

Chapter 86

"WHAT ARE WE GOING to tell the press?" Carol asked, her eyes on the road. Mora tried to focus on Carol's question. But she wondered how Leigh was handling Quentin's death—and more importantly, the questions from the police. Even if Quentin's death was anticipated or welcomed, the torment of the first few hours could cause Leigh to babble and not realize what she was saying.

"I'll send the PR bio we prepared when Quentin took office as Finance Chair—plus a message of condolence. They'll lead their stories with the details of his accident. Our material adds a bit so small the reporters may not use it."

Mora steadied a clipboard in her lap and jotted down a brief paragraph.

"How does this sound?" She held the board up to the light. "The Battered Women's Escape Foundation is deeply saddened to hear of the untimely death of its honorary finance chairman. During his short tenure, Quentin Pryor donated his valuable time and raised a generous amount of money for our organization. Our deepest sympathies are extended to his wife, Leigh."

Carol reached over and squeezed Mora's hand. Mora looked back at her gratefully. Carol was Mora's rock and understood what Mora was going through without her needing to say it.

Carol steered the van into the drive at the Pryor residence. "Every little mention of the BWEF is valuable to us, but you're right that they may not deem it worth mentioning." Carol braked at the already-open gate to the Pryor residence and pressed the call bell. "Ms. Rey and Ms. Ewald to see Mrs. Pryor," she announced, before proceeding on.

"The sheriff must still be with Leigh," said Carol as they approached the deputies' car.

Mora tensed. It had been unnerving enough to have Sharon in her office when the call about Quentin's body came in. If Sharon was here *now*, Mora didn't want to violate her privacy by acknowledging her counseling visit in front of others. But would it be suspicious *not* to? Mora sighed. Best to let Sharon take the lead on that one.

Mora reached for the car door handle. "Park here, in front of the steps. I'll push you up the ramp." Mora slipped out of her seat, touched the gold angel pin on her shoulder, and walked to the open rear door of the van.

As Mora pulled out a white wicker hamper of baked goods and casseroles, Carol deftly unclamped her chair and wheeled it to the lift that deposited her on the ground next to the van's sliding door.

Mora set the food basket on Carol's lap. Carol smiled as she looked up at her friend. "We make a good team, co-chair."

"Hello, Ms. Rey, Ms. Ewald." The cook received them at the door, her face clouded. "Leigh is in the sunroom with the sheriffs. She's very distraught. I'm glad you could come so quickly."

"We were already— I mean, I'm glad we live close by," said Carol.

Cook accepted the basket that Carol held out to her. "Thank you *so* much. If it's like England, this will be the first of many food offerings. Meals are *so* difficult when everyone is sad."

As the cook led them to the sunroom at the back of the house, Mora felt the woman's tension. Surely the longtime servant knew about the abuse in the Pryor home. But Mora had sensed the employee's loyalty to and protectiveness of Leigh, and was counting on her discretion in the matter. She prayed she hadn't miscalculated.

A tall, slender man in his fifties came forward when the women entered the room. Mora recognized his uniform as the same one worn by Sharon.

"I'm Deputy Adler and this is Deputy Collins." He stepped to the side to reveal Sharon seated on a wicker settee. "Is one of you Mrs. Pryor's friend, Mora Rey?"

Apparently Sharon had chosen *not* to divulge her relationship to Mora. Fair enough. Mora would honor her client's privilege. She nodded and hurried over to Leigh.

"Leigh, dear. I am *so* sorry. What a horrible tragedy." She gave Leigh a hug and felt the woman trembling. "But please know you do not have to go through this alone. Carol and I are here to help you in any way we can."

Sharon made her way to the door. "Now that your friends are here, Mrs. Pryor"—Sharon nodded almost imperceptibly to Mora—"we'll be going. Again, our condolences. Here's my card if you need to contact us."

"It will be a few days before we complete our investigation." Harry followed Sharon to the doorway. "And we *will* want to talk to you again, when you can think more clearly, about your husband's activities."

Leigh looked up at Mora with alarm. Mora squeezed her hand.

Leigh straightened and faced the deputies. "Certainly, Officers. I'll do whatever I can to help."

Chapter 87

LOS ANGELES—*RENOWNED BANK PRESIDENT DIES IN BOATING ACCIDENT,* the headlines screamed across the wires. *Quentin Pryor, CEO of Western States Bank, was found floating near his rented sloop, the "Rio," in the harbor at Catalina Island. A sailing enthusiast, Pryor was alone when he died, apparently the victim of a boating mishap.*

The article continued. *The Los Angeles County Sheriff's Department, which has jurisdiction for the island, reported that Pryor wore no life jacket.*

Quentin Pryor had been prominent enough that the wire service included tidbits about his life's work and the charities he supported, including the Battered Women's Escape Foundation. The article concluded: *Sheriff's deputies notified Leigh Pryor, Quentin Pryor's fourth wife, of his death upon her return from the San Pedro Boys and Girls Club where she had taught ballet classes that afternoon.*

Sharon Collins perused the article about Quentin Pryor's death as she waited for Harry to join her at her desk. So far, they'd discovered no evidence of foul play. Pryor had simply been knocked out by the mainsail boom and fallen overboard, after being arrogant or stupid enough to go sailing without a life jacket.

Why in the world had the coroner ordered this back to the Sheriff's Department? Why had their brass agreed to take it? Disgusted, Sharon threw the paper on her desk. Of course, she *knew* why. Pryor's prominence in the community would put pressure on the men and women at the very top of her department. She'd waste many hours proving an accident so no one could point a finger at the boss, who'd already announced for re-election next year. They *did* know Pryor's wife wasn't with him on the trip and appeared to have an alibi—at least for Sunday morning. They'd check with the Boys and Girls Club to be sure, but she'd had on dancing clothes when they met with her. Maybe he'd had someone *else* in the boat with him—another woman? They could look for evidence of that. She wondered if he and Leigh had any kids.

Sharon's scattered thoughts were interrupted by the arrival of her partner at their cubicle.

Harry Adler slapped a stack of folders on his cluttered desk. "Well, it looks like we have ourselves a fucking politically prominent vic this time. Wouldn't you know—just when I can't find my desk under all the stacks of unsolved cases."

"Quit yer bitching, Harry. You know it won't help."

Harry grinned. "You sound just like my mother!"

"Sorry. After a couple of days off, it's hard to get my head out of mom-mode."

"Does the coroner have doubts about the actual cause of death?"

Sharon shook her head and looked at the clipboard in her lap. "According to the weather report, the seas were calm inside the breakwater, where the boat was found. The victim's gear had a place to connect a lifeline, and one was found trailing from the body." She read aloud: "Probable death by drowning. The open wound on the back of the head and bruises on his neck insufficient to have caused death, probably occurred when the unsecured boom hit him. Rope marks." Sharon looked up, puzzled. "'The mainsail was down and the boom was swinging as the boat rocked.' What's the boom?"

Harry drew a picture of a sailboat for her. "The sailor moves the boom so the sail can catch the wind. Usually it's tied down after it's moved."

"The blood alcohol level was .02," she continued reading from the report, "well below the legal limit. While homicidal drowning is relatively rare, accidental drowning also seems improbable under circumstances of clear, shallow water; near-zero blood alcohol level; and calm seas. A malfunctioning or tangled lifeline may have held him underwater." She put the report down.

Harry stretched and yawned. "Sounds on the surface like a royal time-waster." He paused. "But, you know—despite my own cynicism, I have a niggling feeling that there's something about this case that hasn't come out yet."

Sharon and others in the department respected Harry for the accuracy of his gut feelings. Was he right once again?

Seated at her desk, Sharon continued flipping through the morning's paper—an unusual luxury. Buried in the Sports section, an article about Marshall Whitmore's prominence as a trip guide caught her eye. Sharon read it with interest.

She remembered Taylor telling her at the marathon that her husband led small groups on trips to the wilderness. Reading of the adventurer's precise rules and stiff pre-trip training absorbed Sharon's attention. She'd always wanted to go on such a trip.

Taylor hadn't mentioned much more about her husband, other than to say he was gone a lot. She'd ask her more next time she saw her.

"How does a wife cope with a man who's gone so much like that?"

Sharon started. Harry had snuck up behind her and was reading the article over her shoulder.

Sharon looked up at him. "Me—" Sharon recovered herself. "I'd have welcomed Sean's disappearing for days."

"You maybe could have gotten away from him sooner."

Sharon nodded thoughtfully.

"Still," said Harry, "I feel sorry for women who *love* their husbands and have to spend so much time away from them, rear the children by themselves."

"I don't know." Sharon shook her head. "It could be worse. Too much togetherness is brutal."

Chapter 88

LADEN WITH A BACKPACK of trail mix, sandwiches, and water, Lucky followed the park ranger along the trail at the edge of the Grand Canyon. It felt good to loosen his muscles, feel the sun on his back. He relished the feeling of the wilderness: the aloneness, tuning into the universe, and challenging his body.

Lucky loved everything about this canyon: its range of color, its depth, the history told by the streaks in the rocks. He felt like he'd spent a lot of time here—but not hiking. Oh, this was okay, and he liked that the ranger had asked him along on his inspection hike, but it wasn't the way he enjoyed the Canyon the most. It took a trip on the river to experience the full grandeur of this national treasure.

The river. There it was again. He just *knew* that the river was the key.

Chapter 89

SHARON COULDN'T HOLD HER TONGUE any longer. "You know I respect your judgment," she said as she and her partner made their way up the Peninsula, "but I still think that visiting Mrs. Pryor again so soon is uncalled for." Harry had insisted they go.

"Oh? Why is that?" Harry flipped on his left-turn signal.

"It's unnecessary and insensitive."

"And you feel strongly about this?" Harry gave her a sidelong glance. Obviously he was teasing her.

She often wished she had Harry's grasp of their job, but she wasn't going to let insecurity stand in the way of what she felt was right. She and Harry had agreed that their conflicts should be out in the open, if they were to do a good job. She glanced at her partner and was encouraged by his relaxed posture and twinkling eyes.

"I think she's obviously very shocked and upset," she went on, "*and* that we shouldn't add to her misery."

"I agree she's grieving, but that doesn't mean she didn't kill him." Harry shrugged.

"Oh, wait up now." Sharon brushed a stray hair back from her face. "Do you really think she would be grieving so strongly if she had hated him enough to kill him?"

"Maybe she's grieving the loss of his income, her privacy—her freedom if she's guilty of offing him."

"Oh!"

"Well hello, Sharon. Good to see you." Carol Ewald swiveled her chair out of the entryway so that the deputies could enter the Pryor mansion.

Inside the massive double doors, the slate-floored foyer of Leigh's home was filled with hotel-lobby-sized arrangements of gladiolas, birds of paradise, and lemon leaves. Conspicuous cards identified Quentin's many business acquaintances who had sent them. Andrea Bocelli's voice soothed visitors with sacred arias piped into the downstairs rooms through the built-in music system.

"Sounds and smells like a funeral home," Sharon whispered under her breath to Harry.

Carol faced them and nodded toward Sharon's gun. "I assume you're here in an official capacity?"

Sharon nodded. "Yes, Ms. Ewald. You remember my partner, Deputy Adler? We'd like to speak to Mrs. Pryor." Sharon turned to Harry. "I don't know if I mentioned it yesterday, Deputy Adler—Ms. Ewald and I met that weekend I ran in the BWEF marathon."

Harry raised his eyebrow at Sharon but said nothing. Guess she'd have to deal with that one later.

Carol rolled her chair back a few feet and stopped, blocking the entrance to the hallway.

"May I ask why you want to see Leigh? She's terribly upset right now—has been since you brought her the bad news yesterday. She hasn't slept."

Sharon looked at Harry. If Leigh were a suspect or at least a person of interest, Harry would say this was the ideal time to catch her off guard.

"We'll be as brief as possible," said Harry.

"And don't worry," said Sharon, "we'll be as gentle as we can."

Carol rotated her wheelchair. "Mora, Erin, and I came to help Leigh with immediate things." She spoke over her shoulder. "You know, like the press statements and funeral arrangements." Carol rolled quietly through the downstairs hallway.

"It's just a routine follow-up," said Harry. "The coroner asked us to look into Pryor's death—because he died alone."

And because the rich and powerful get better treatment than us working stiffs, Sharon added silently. She hoped her face didn't betray her mixed feelings about their being here. That wouldn't be fair to Harry—or the grieving widow.

"I don't understand why the L.A. Sheriff is involved. Quentin died out at Catalina, didn't he?"

"Yes, ma'am. The Los Angeles County Sheriff has jurisdiction out there—and especially because of Mr. Pryor's respected, uh, position, they want to make sure this case is handled correctly."

Sharon tilted her head to Carol in a way she hoped was reassuring.

"Well, of course." Carol nodded. "That makes sense." She waved her hand, motioning them to follow. "Leigh is in the solarium."

As they followed Carol through the palatial home, Sharon took a quick but observant glance into each room. Anxious to get to the widow, she'd ignored them on their first visit, but her training insisted she take in all the details of the victim's home. *That living room is as big as our corner basketball court,* she thought. *My kids would have those white couches battleship-gray the first week.* She admired the life-size oil portrait of the deceased. But where were the pictures of the other family members? His kids? His wife? *Oh well,* she concluded, catching up to Harry and Carol, *each to his own vanity.*

Carol led the officers into the glass-walled sunroom where Leigh sat with Mora and Erin.

"These are the things you need to attend to in the next week." Mora pointed to a page in the notebook on her lap. "The next page shows things to think about in the next mo—" She stopped when she saw the deputies.

"Hello, Deputy Collins. Deputy Adler, is it?" Sharon couldn't quite read the expression that passed over Mora's face.

"Hello, Ms. Rey," said Harry. "I seem to have interrupted something."

"As members of the BWEF Outreach Committee," Mora explained, "we have a 'separation' counseling program for women we

work with. To give them tools to go on with life as a single person."
She clasped Leigh's hand. "I thought Leigh might benefit from some
of that advice—given her situation."

What a great idea for a new widow! Sharon remembered receiving
that counseling. It helped her look to the future: set goals, find a job,
education.

Harry glanced at the other woman in the room.

"Hello, deputies. You may not remember me—I'm Erin Craig.
I work with Leigh and Mora on the Outreach Committee and—oh,
and with Quentin." Harry nodded. "We wanted to be sure Leigh had
someone with her, since she and Quentin don't have family in the
area." Erin approached with her hand out, seemingly oblivious to
their frank looks at her taped nose and black eye.

Sharon remembered the welcome emotional support she'd
received at the shelter from women like these. Her family all lived
back East and couldn't afford to travel to L.A. Her first days alone after
being married for so long had seemed like an endless walk in a hot
desert—a scorching marathon, no matter the reason, but especially
for someone who had been totally dependent, never daring to make
a decision of her own.

Leigh rose with her hand extended to greet the two deputies.
A green shawl was wrapped around her shoulders, giving little color
to her paper-white complexion.

"Good morning. May I ask what brings you 'round?" She halted
and looked at Carol. At Carol's nod, she motioned to the deputies.
"Please excuse my manners; I feel just beastly today. Have a seat over
here." As she gestured towards the heavily-cushioned wicker chairs,
her shawl slipped from her right shoulder. Harry reached to retrieve
it but stopped when Leigh cowered as if expecting a blow.

Harry's scratch of his left ear signaled to Sharon she should take
note and they'd discuss it later. She returned the briefest of nods.

293

Sharon sat where indicated, facing the other ladies. She tugged on her belt to accommodate the position of her cuffs and club against the back and arms of the body-swallowing chair.

"If you'll excuse me a moment," said Leigh, "I sent Cook on an errand, so I was about to fetch some tea on my own from the kitchen. Would you fancy some? We have coffee, as well."

Sharon nodded and looked at Harry, who held his finger up in agreement. "Yes, that would be nice. We're both coffee drinkers—black."

Sharon made a mental note to talk to the cook later.

"I'll help you." Mora followed Leigh from the room.

Somehow Sharon felt like she was observing a well-rehearsed play. But then, she couldn't dream of ever rising to the social strata of these women. She pushed herself from the deep cushion. "I've changed my mind about my order. I'll just follow them to the kitchen."

Sharon saw Leigh and Mora turn into a brightly lighted doorway at the end of the hall. She hurried to catch up with them.

Erin picked up the morning's paper from the table next to her and turned Pryor's front-page photo toward Harry. "The picture doesn't do him justice. Quentin is—was—a driving force in the banking community, and also quite charismatic." She stopped talking abruptly, suddenly tongue-tied with the officer.

Harry nodded. "Yes, ma'am. His prominence is one reason we feel compelled to follow up so promptly on his death." He cocked his head. "Pardon me, Ms. Craig, but that's some black eye you've got there. Are you okay?"

Erin put her hand to her face. "I'm terribly embarrassed, but I'm otherwise fine." Thank heavens she'd practiced her story this morning in front of the mirror. She and Mora had decided that Erin needed to be here today. Especially since Taylor was too exhausted to come.

"What happened?"

"I own a construction company. I got rushed and didn't check my tools before I started work—something I constantly drum into all my workers." She touched her nose. "The hammer head flew off and gave me this shiner—and a broken nose." She giggled. "My crew had a good laugh over it when I told them. I'll probably never hear the end of it!"

Harry nodded, apparently accepting her story. *Phew.*

"Ms. Craig, have you known the Pryors long?" Erin set the article down and blinked her eyes several times before replying. She had to concentrate. There was no room for screw-ups.

"Actually, no. I met Quentin about four months ago, when he became our honorary finance chairman—for the Battered Women's Escape Foundation, that is. A month or so later, Leigh joined our board as an advisory member." Erin thought back to that fateful fundraising dinner. She'd actually been attracted by Quentin's magnetism, his confidence, as had the others. "He is—uh, was—a charming man."

"Mrs. Pryor seems dependent on you all. Are the other ladies her longtime friends?"

Erin didn't like the path the deputy was going down. "Are you asking: Does Mrs. Pryor have a lot of other friends?"

Harry nodded.

"I don't know about that," said Erin. "You'll have to ask *her.*" Erin smiled and waited for the deputy to say something else. Better not to ramble on and risk a slip-up.

"I wonder what your thoughts are about why two people need such a large house as this," said Harry.

"I understand the Pryors entertain lavishly for business purposes." Erin smiled softly, relieved by the deputy's change in tack. "I sensed Leigh was thrilled to work on our small committee so that she could make some friends who weren't her husband's clients." Erin felt herself stiffen. She had to be careful not to raise questions about the Pryors' relationship; the deputies simply *couldn't* find out that Leigh's husband had abused her.

"Pryor must have been popular if he did a lot of entertaining here."

295

"I can't speak to that. I interacted with him only at our office—and then, only once a week." Erin surreptitiously wiped her sweating hands on her pants leg. Why had Carol left her alone with this nosy man? She had to keep him distracted. "Are you familiar with the activities of the BWEF?"

"A little…yes."

"You need to know what we do in order to understand the organization."

"Tell me about that."

Erin took a deep breath. "We help women in trouble. In our work, we often interact on a high emotional level; every case can really tear us up. Sharing that brings us together as close friends." Erin shivered suddenly. "That, and having lived with an abusive spouse."

Chapter 90

L EANING AGAINST THE WHITE GRANITE COUNTER, Leigh frowned at Mora, her arms crossed. "You know I'm so pleased to have you as a friend, especially under the circumstances. But you rather misled me when you said there would be no investigation!"

Mora checked over her left shoulder and lowered her voice. "You know Quentin was alone on his sloop. They probably have to look into any healthy person's death when there are no witnesses." She continued back in her normal tone, "I'm sure they want to close the case as quickly as you do."

Mora filled two mugs with coffee and set them on the enameled tray Leigh had set out. She spooned tea into the teapot, poured boiling water over it, and covered the china pot with a quilted tea cozy.

Seeing Deputy Collins approach, she took a deep restorative breath and hugged Leigh.

"Go ahead and cry." She patted Leigh's back. "It's *good* for you," she added meaningfully. Mora handed Leigh a tissue from the box on the counter. "You know," she said loudly, "one or more Outreach Committee members will stay here with you until you're comfortable being alone."

"I'm sorry to interrupt you," said Sharon, "but I decided I'd love some sweet iced tea if you have it. I find sugar provides a good boost under these circumstances."

"Of course; I'll get it." Mora smiled at the deputy. "Sorry for the delay, Sharon. It's a tearful, worrying time—*I* know." Seeing the deputy's confusion, Mora hesitated then continued: "My husband died suddenly, too."

As Sharon murmured her condolences, Mora mentally kicked herself. Why on *earth* had she brought up Sherman's accident? No need to get the deputies thinking along *that* line!

Passing by the large formal living room, Mora loved how the peach and sage décor provided a visual transition from the room to the lush green of the estate grounds that surrounded the pool and tennis court. If only the lives of the people inside could be so peaceful.

Erin sighed as the other women joined her, glad for the interruption. Adler's questions had unnerved her.

Carol returned at the same moment with a bouquet of coral roses, which she set on the end table. She shooed Leigh to relax on the sofa and took over helping Mora.

"Did you two know the deceased, uh, Quentin, well?" Harry's voice was casual as he spoke to the women now serving beverages. He nodded his thanks to Mora as she handed him a mug of coffee. He left his notebook in his pocket.

Erin was relieved the interview remained low-key—and at Harry's attention being directed away from *her*.

"Not what I'd say *personally*," replied Carol. "Our relationship was purely a business one." She hesitated as Mora placed the tray carefully on the coffee table.

Erin, who'd made her escape to the couch with Leigh, flipped her ponytail over her shoulder and reached for a cup of tea. "Damn, I could use this! I feel like I've been up all night."

"You have, Erin, just for me." Leigh smiled softy. "You must be just knackered by now. Here, have a biscuit."

"You four good friends?" Harry asked. Erin frowned and glanced at Mora. Why was he so tied up with who was friends with whom?

"All of us on the BWEF Outreach Committee spend so much time together," Mora answered quickly. "And dealing with battered women, we become quite close."

"My husband considered everyday women friends a waste of my time," interjected Leigh.

Erin squeezed Leigh's hand, willing her to silence.

"But," Leigh attempted a smile, "he was quite keen on my involvement with the BWEF. Making new friends was a real gain!" She squeezed Erin's hand back, even harder.

Erin smiled at Leigh and relaxed a little. So far, they were all on the same page with their answers.

"We came to help Leigh get through the worst days," Erin added.

Although Harry seemed to accept all the women's comments at face value, Erin's eyes followed his as he observed the group's interplay over the rim of his coffee mug.

And Sharon, Erin couldn't figure out. She wasn't really saying much; just watching. *They make a good team: he talks while she snoops.*

Despite Leigh's obvious—and quite genuine—stress under the situation, could the deputies sense her underlying relief that her spouse was gone? Erin could see it in Leigh's small gestures; her relaxed posture. But then *she* knew what that relief felt like. Plus, unlike the deputies, she'd seen how Leigh acted before Quentin's mur— *accident,* she corrected herself.

The beverages distributed, everyone settled back in the sunroom's white wicker furniture. Erin was amazed how the flower-garden print brightened even the brown of the sheriffs' uniforms.

"Mrs. Pryor, I'd like to talk to you about your husband's activities before he went sailing last weekend," said Harry.

So *now* they were getting to it. Erin curled her toes. She straightened and shifted her legs.

"When did you last see him?" Harry asked.

"It was Saturday morning," replied Leigh, shakily, "when he left to go sailing."

"Was he planning to meet anybody—that you know of?"

As Leigh shook her head, Sharon threw Harry a glance. Erin squinted at the deputy. Now, what was that about?

"When he left that morning, did he seem upset about anything?" Harry continued.

Leigh's hand shook as she lowered her teacup. "Well, a lit—"

"Deputy, please! Leigh is quite exhausted, physically and emotionally. Can't this wait?"

Erin welcomed Mora's interruption. Leigh prided herself on being honest; they had warned her not to talk too much.

"This won't take long." Harry sipped his coffee, unfazed. "What was it that upset him?" he asked, not unkindly, his eyes centered on Leigh's face.

"I didn't get up to fix his breakfast. I forgot Cook had asked to come in later that morning."

"What happened then?"

"I got up and cooked his eggs."

"Was that all? Did he kiss you goodbye?"

Shit! Talk about a sneaky question! Erin struggled to keep her face neutral. They'd have to be careful with this guy.

"N–no…he'd gone off on another tangent by then." Leigh paused and looked at Mora, who nodded almost imperceptibly. "All I did was query as to when he would return." She stifled a sob with her damp linen handkerchief. "He, he…" She swallowed loudly. "He lost his temper." Leigh's tears spilled. "I just wanted to know so I could have dinner hot when he came back. He always gets…uh, got, upset if it was late." She reached for another handkerchief tucked into her pocket. "I didn't get to tell him I love him," she sobbed, "like I usually do."

Good girl! Erin almost slapped her knee. *Just like we rehearsed—except for the part about his getting upset a lot, of course.*

"Sharon, not to change the subject," Carol interrupted, pointing toward the deputy's chair leg, "but there's a spider near your foot; be careful. We seem to have so many this year. I don't know where they are all coming from."

Sharon raised her foot over the spider as it moved slowly across the floor.

"Oh, please don't harm the poor creature!" exclaimed Leigh, wiping her face. She handed Harry a magazine. "Let it crawl onto here, won't you? And then pop it outside. It doesn't deserve to die; it's done nothing wrong." The group watched in silence as Harry accommodated Leigh's wishes.

Once the spider had been sent on its way, Sharon took over the discussion. "Tell me more about this Outreach Committee," she said. "I heard you all talking about it at the marathon, but I still don't know what you do."

The four members looked at each other and Erin nodded to them. She would take the lead on this one. "Well," she said, inhaling deeply, "we make special efforts to help others in unique situations: women in abusive relationships with wealthy, influential men."

"Does your husband support the organization as well?"

Erin followed Harry's gaze to her broad gold wedding band, which encircled the ring finger of her right hand.

"No. Unfortunately, I'm widowed." Erin avoided elaborating, having hoped for the subject not to come up at all. She snuck a quick glance at Mora whose face remained impassive. But then, Mora was good at that.

"Did he support your activities in the organization when he was alive?" Harry pressed on.

Erin centered a strong gaze on the officers. "I had just joined the Outreach Committee when he died."

Sharon stood to signal to Harry that she felt it was time to leave. The poor widow had had enough for one day. Sure, a suspect often spilled something under stress, but Leigh was a victim—not a suspect. "Mrs. Pryor. Again, our condolences. We may have to talk to you some more about your husband, but we have enough for now."

Leigh gripped Sharon's arm. "Can you tell me when Quentin will be sent to the mortuary? I need to plan his funeral; all his co-workers have been ringing me up."

Sharon glanced at Harry, who nodded. "The coroner may want to do an autopsy," she said gently, "depending on what we find."

Leigh's face paled. Erin squeezed her hand. "It's okay. They'll be looking for health problems that could have caused his death, or to verify he drowned."

Sharon kept her voice low. "I'm sorry for the delay, Mrs. Pryor. But it's nothing to worry about. Just routine."

Leigh pushed herself from her chair, clasping its arm to steady herself. "I'll show you out," she said. "Cook has yet to return."

"Mrs. Pryor," Harry said as they neared the entryway, "may we have a private word with you?"

Sharon looked at him in surprise. *What now?* Leigh motioned them into a small office.

"I didn't want to bring this up in front of your friends, but how did you get that bruise?" Harry pointed to Leigh's right arm.

Leigh pulled her sleeve down over her hand. "Silly me! I tried to move a couch, but it was too heavy and I lost my balance and fell against it." She smiled slightly. "Quentin, the love, called me a clumsy c— cookie when I did such things. Said he couldn't understand how one who was so graceful on stage could be so gangly at home." Tears blossomed and overflowed.

Sharon fumed silently. Harry's interrogating Leigh like this was so disrespectful of her grief. But Harry *was* a good investigator—she had to give him that.

"Thank you," said Sharon, shooting Harry another look. "We'll be leaving now. But if you need anything—"

"Or find out any more about your husband's plans for last Saturday," interjected Harry.

"—please give us a call," Sharon finished.

Harry handed Leigh his card.

Chapter 91

"YOU KNOW, these women haven't known Mrs. Pryor—or the victim—for very long," Harry launched in as soon as Sharon exited the Pryors' gate. "Just since the victim started working with the Battered Women's Escape Foundation a couple of months ago."

He paused while Sharon turned left onto Palos Verdes Drive East.

"Don't you think it's odd that they're the ones comforting her?"

Sharon slowed for a stoplight. "Well, maybe they know what it's like to suddenly go it alone. A couple of them said they were widowed. I'm sure that's why she called for them." Made sense to Sharon. She remembered how shelter workers always had good advice for her. "It's like a sorority: widows and divorcées truly relate to each other as no happily married women ever could." Her eyes glistened. "A lot of emotional pain. Fear, too, of being on one's own. Terror, even."

Harry twisted around to reach for his ever-present pretzels in the back seat. "It didn't seem funny to you that there were no neighbors there, or friends outside the organization?"

Sharon considered. "Now that you mention it, I suppose it's a little bit strange." She took the pretzel Harry offered. "Maybe they haven't heard yet—or are waiting to be invited. Who knows how these high-society types operate." She shrugged. "Maybe sending those gigantic flowers is enough."

Harry chomped on a pretzel. "I suppose you have a point with that one...but those bruises on Leigh's arm,"—he swallowed with a loud gulp—"they must have hurt. Could she have gotten them on the boat at Catalina?"

Sharon banged her hand on the steering wheel. "Oh, come *on*! We already know where she was. And she explained the injuries."

Sharon remembered her own days hiding humiliating bruises from her friends. Wow, wouldn't that be— "Harry!" she interrupted her own train of thought. "Do you *really* think a woman who wouldn't let me kill a spider could kill her own husband? Be honest."

Harry shrugged. "You know the first rule in a murder investigation." He looked over his shoulder at a passing LAPD car.

"I know, I know. It's usually the spouse. But..."

"But what?" Harry crunched on another pretzel. "Maybe she hired someone else to do it, because she couldn't. She certainly has enough money."

"But didn't you hear her say how every poor creature deserved to live?" Sharon turned to Harry, triumph on her face.

"No." Harry said sternly. "That's *not* what I heard. What *I* heard her say was that the spider had done nothing to *deserve* to die."

Chapter 92

"HARRY, I'M NOT AT ALL ENTHUSIASTIC about continuing to pursue Leigh Pryor." Back at the station, Sharon shoved her purse into her office drawer and locked it. She wished they could go on to other, less emotionally charged cases. But she knew this case took priority.

"Is that because you don't think she did it, or because I now find out that you're buddies with Leigh's friend, Carol Ewald?" Harry tapped his knuckles on his desk.

Damn! Sharon was chagrined. *She knew she should have mentioned that sooner. Now it could become an issue.*

"Oh, so *that's* why you were staring at her when Mora was talking?" she shot back. Heck, the best defense was a good offense.

"Was I that obvious? I must be losing my touch." Harry's face creased into a wolfish smile.

"Come on! You were *not* lusting after her; that wasn't your expression."

"Well, now that you ask…I had a feeling that their conversation— you know, the talk about handling grief—was all an act." He waved a hand in Sharon's direction. "Now, don't ask me why. You women aren't the only ones who have intuition. We male detectives have it too."

"What set you intuiting?"

"Like I *said,* the part about grieving. Rey and Ewald both seemed to be experts on the subject."

"Why wouldn't they be? If you were suddenly left alone to handle your family affairs, you'd become an expert *real* fast. Believe me, I know."

"But *you* weren't grieving. That's what I'm talking about."

"Now wait just a minute! I *was* grieving—maybe not for Sean, but for the life I thought I was going to have with him. It wasn't easy!" Sharon slammed her desk with her fist.

"Okay, okay. Cool down. I'll give you that."

Harry headed into the lunchroom and reached for a coffee cup. "I just can't shake the feeling that I was being scammed."

Sharon sighed. "You're going to drag out this investigation, aren't you?"

Harry spooned sugar into his coffee. "Yes—at least for a week or so."

"It's a good thing I'm your partner, here to keep your big head deflated. That poor woman just lost her husband in an accident and now you're gonna add insult to injury."

"Just following a hunch, partner. Are you on board?"

"Do I have a choice?"

"No."

Chapter 93

"WELL, ONE THING I LEARNED at the Pryors' yesterday is that we didn't learn *anything* about the victim." Harry entered his report into the computer.

Sharon looked up from scheduling her kids' supervision. "Yeah, *if* this is a homicide, we need to know what made him tick—and what *his* world was like." She grinned. "We could go to the bank and pretend we want to deposit our lottery winnings." She shook her head. "Naw—one look at us and they'd know we were poor."

Harry grinned. "I'll meet you at the car at ten o'clock. Until then, I need to attack this paper pile."

Harry pulled into a visitor's slot underneath the bank building. He noted the twenty-minute time limit but knew the black-and-white was in no danger of being towed. He and Sharon took the elevator to the marble-tomb lobby and conferred with the guard. The chief of security arrived in short order to escort them to the executive suite via the express elevator.

Harry took in his surroundings. Bureaucracy screamed at him. *Looks like the victim worked in pure plush.* He wondered if the bank was as profitable as the offices suggested. He shrugged. He guessed they needed to be lavish. *He* sure wouldn't want to trust what little money he had in the hands of a firm with shabby carpets and dirty walls.

Upstairs, the deep pile carpet customized with the bank logo muffled normal office sounds; but not the voices of those gathered in front of Quentin Pryor's dark office. Nearing, Harry saw a young man addressing the group. He wore a black suit, gray shirt, and black-and-gray-striped tie—suitable after the death of his employer.

"Who would've thought Mr. Q would have drowned? He was always so in control of everything he did." Was that sarcasm?

"After the way you bitched about him, 'Kyle baby'—" The woman cut her comment short, clearly sensing the new arrivals. She turned from the group and approached the deputies.

"I apologize. I didn't hear the elevator." Her cultured voice shook a little. "Our routine is a little disorganized today; our CEO, Mr. Pryor, was killed in an accident this weekend."

"Yes, ma'am," said Harry. He presented his badge for her verification, even though they were in uniform. "With your permission, we'd like to look through Mr. Pryor's office, talk to a few people, see what sort of person he was."

The receptionist sat down behind her desk, looking bewildered.

"Sir, I can't let you into his office; I'd lose my job. He'll be very—" She stopped talking and caught the eye of the security captain who nodded. "I...I guess he isn't around to get upset about it. Let me go to the key safe in the storeroom. I didn't open his office this morning, since he…" She jumped up. "Excuse me; I'll be right back."

Harry watched the woman escape to the recesses of the office. He doubted the employees in his own workplace would be this muddled with the death of an official. They were well-programmed to do what they did, no matter what.

"At least she didn't question why we're investigating an accident," whispered Sharon. To her, the surroundings seemed to call for a certain amount of quiet decorum—in addition to wanting to be discreet around the employees. Harry rolled his eyes as Sharon tugged at her uniform sleeve and swiped the tops of her dusty shoes on her pant legs.

The receptionist led the deputies to a small conference room adjacent to Pryor's office. Harry took in the amenities, which would provide a comfortable setting for their interviews of Pryor's staff: deep-maroon leather chairs, a china coffee service on the credenza, a connection for their laptop computer centered on the table. Even a fax machine. A large window overlooked the downtown skyline to the east, today obliterated by a layer of haze.

Depositing their portfolios on the conference table, Sharon and Harry returned to Pryor's office. "Any sign of an appointment calendar?" Harry asked as Sharon opened the center drawer of Pryor's desk.

She shook her head. "It's probably all electronic these days."

The deputies opened drawers with the keys the receptionist had left them; they admired the bottles of wine and brandy in the hidden bar and looked down at the people on the street, twenty-two stories below.

"I'll go tell security we're ready to start our interviews," said Sharon. "I'll make sure he asks them all to stay, even if it's getting near to lunch hour." Harry nodded his approval.

While he waited, Harry looked for family pictures. He found none. According to what he'd read about the banker, Pryor had two children and at least as many ex-wives. He could understand the ex's pictures not being around, but what about snaps of the kids or the current Mrs. P? She sure was a looker—and a dancer with the ballet. You'd think some of her performance pictures would be here.

Their first interviewee, Kyle Norbest, appeared in the doorway. He was the sharp-looking man from the foyer.

"You wanted to see me?" Kyle adjusted his tie and flexed his neck as though his collar were too tight. Harry rose and shook the young man's hand, noting the jumbo-sized Band-Aid on his palm and Kyle's wince as his hand was gripped. *A strange place for a bandage,* thought Harry. And his presentation was too soft. An aspiring executive's handshake should be all firmness and bravado.

He looked up to see Sharon wink as she noted his concentration on the interplay. Harry often bragged to his peers about how much he could tell about a man from his handshake. Assessing women's handshakes was still new though. He was working on his theories there.

Harry reintroduced Sharon and himself as he motioned to the conference table. "Have a seat. This won't take long."

He waited as the young man perched himself on the edge of the chair, dressed his cuffs, and aligned the crease in his trousers.

"The coroner asked our department to verify that there was no foul play in Mr. Pryor's death, since he died alone."

Kyle's right eyebrow shot up. "No foul play?" He swallowed and licked his lips. "I wouldn't be so sure about *that*."

Harry and Sharon looked at each other in surprise.

"Oh?" said Harry calmly. "What makes you say that?"

Kyle leaned forward in his chair. "The bank covered it up," he whispered, "and even used it to their advantage." He paused and sat up straight. "Everyone in Western States hated Quentin Pryor's guts."

After Kyle had gone, the receptionist came to check on the deputies.

"Do you have everything you need?" she asked, refilling their coffee cups.

"Well, actually, Ms….uh, Ms. Applewood," said Sharon, consulting her notes. "We may as well talk with *you* while you're here. Please sit down."

"I don't think I know anything you'd be interested in," said the mini-skirted bottle-towhead. She fluffed her hair. Sharon noted with amusement that Applewood sat at such an angle to afford Harry a clear view of her shapely legs.

"Tell us first, what you do here," said Sharon. "We're just trying to get an idea of the routine in Mr. Pryor's office." When panic appeared on the young woman's face, Sharon leaned forward. "Why don't you just start with what you do first thing when you get here."

"Well, I come in and go to the restroom to check my makeup." She blushed. "My boyfriend brings me to work and, like, he kisses me goodbye at the door." She grimaced and smoothed her hair. "One day I didn't know my lipstick was smeared and Mr. Pryor sent me to wash my face. I borrowed makeup from my friend, but it was the wrong color, so I spent the rest of the day looking freakish." She bit her lip and looked down. "He, like, docked me an hour's pay, too." Her sophistication slipped as she talked about her punishment.

Sharon's cheek twitched as she struggled to hold back an expletive. "Then what do you do? After you tell your boyfriend goodbye and check your makeup?"

"I go through all of the office and turn on the computers, printers, and copiers, so they'll be ready when the rest of the people get here." She pressed her index finger to her pursed lips. "Then I make the coffee for the staff—plain supermarket brand—and after that, I brew Mr. Pryor's coffee with his special blend in here." She grinned and leaned toward Harry conspiratorially. "If there's no bottled water for his coffee, I take a bottle from my desk and fill it in the restroom, so he'll *think* I used bottled water."

"What time did Mr. Pryor arrive for work?" Sharon had recovered from her shot of anger about the lipstick incident.

"At exactly 9:47 a.m. We, li— We set our clocks by him. The bank opens at ten. It wouldn't do for him to walk through the lobby *with* the customers."

Sharon smiled. "What are your duties after his arrival?"

"I stand up and say 'Good morning, sir,' when he steps off the elevator. Then I sit at my desk, answer the phones, sort the mail, and greet visitors."

"Do you stay at the desk all day?" In spite of her youthful demeanor, Ms. Applewood knew her job and seemed efficient.

"All except for the ten-minute bio-breaks and a half-hour for lunch."

"Just half an hour?" Sharon was shocked. It would take that long to get to a restaurant from this floor.

"Yeah. That's something new. I used to go to the pool at the second-floor gym during my lunch hour, but Mr. Pryor didn't like me coming back with wet hair—and sometimes late 'cause I had to wait for a shower."

Ms. Applewood pulled her chin in and turned her mouth down. *"It just won't <u>do</u>, Ms. Applewood,"* she mimicked her employer, *"to have you sitting at the reception desk with wet hair. From now on, consider that your lunch hour will be <u>exactly</u> thirty minutes, and your hair will always be dry and properly set. Any infractions and you will be dismissed."* The woman's hand flew to her mouth. "Oh! I shouldn't make fun of the dead. I'm sure Mr. Pryor meant well, you know—grooming me for better positions."

"Did Pryor have a lot of visitors?" Harry jumped in, allowing his partner to recover her composure after the latest revelation about Pryor.

"Yes, sir. That's all he does—did—all day is meet with folks. I don't even know why he had a computer in here. None of us ever saw him, like, *use* it."

"Recently, have any of his visitors seemed angry with him when they walked out, or did you hear any angry words?"

"Oh yes, sir!" The grin broke out again. "It got to be a game with those of us who sit between QP's office and the elevator. We'd bet beforehand about how the visitors would look when they came out of his office. We'd, like, analyze their facial expressions."

"Oh," said Sharon. "What was there to notice about them?" Once this lady relaxed, she'd let it *all* out. "Were they smug, angry, smiling—what?"

"Some were lipstick-red, some were biting their lip so hard it looked like they'd cut it off; a couple were as white as cottage cheese." She paused. "I probably saw, like, one smile a month—if that."

This woman was a good observer. Probably honed her skills at the reception desk. Sharon found herself liking her, and appreciating her candor.

The receptionist was followed into the interview room by Loretta Wilson, the executive office's chief of staff. Medium height, slim, she was dressed in a brown business suit and beige silk shirt. She arrived dabbing at red-rimmed eyes.

Harry rose and pulled out a chair for her, across from Sharon.

"You seem upset," said Sharon. "Would you like to come back another time? After we've interviewed a couple of your colleagues?" She was torn between compassion and expediency. She knew upset people were apt to tell more. She consulted her notes and looked up.

"Oh, no." Ms. Wilson sat chimney-straight on the edge of the plush chair, as if it were hardwood with a straight back. "It's just that I miss him so!" She swiped at pooling tears.

"By him, you mean Quentin Pryor?" Sharon hoped her disbelief wasn't exposed by her expression or tone of voice.

"Of course. He was *such* a lovely man."

At least someone here saw a good side.

"Lovely, in what way?" asked Harry.

"He was always so polite, so understanding when I had to leave for the dentist—that sort of thing."

Wow, that was a switch!

"Did you see him socially?" Harry asked. Sharon frowned at him.

"Oh, no! Please—I didn't mean to give you that impression." She hesitated. "It's just that he was such a dynamic, caring executive." She blinked and rubbed her right eye. "You see, I worked for other executives before I came to the bank. Believe me, Mr. Pryor stood well above most of them."

"Oh? How so?" asked Harry.

Sharon suppressed a smile at Harry's feigned innocence.

Loretta opened her mouth to answer…and then closed it.

Chapter 94

"WELL, WHAT DO YOU THINK?" Sharon maneuvered the car around the garage ramp and pulled out onto the busy street.

"I think the little lady manager protested too much," said Harry, once they were back on the road. "Those tears were more than grief for a good boss." He looked over at Sharon who was pulling onto the access ramp to the 405. "You wanna bet there was good old-fashioned office sex in their relationship?"

"You aren't suggesting that all women in power positions sleep with their bosses to get there, are you?" Not that Harry ever acted that way, but Sharon couldn't help but pose the question.

"Of course not. I wouldn't dare with *you* as a partner!"

Sharon had to smile.

"But I do think she loved the man," Harry continued. "Or thought she did."

Sharon nodded. "I agree. But women *can* love their bosses, and mourn their deaths, without sexual relationships."

"Okay, true…but you can't honestly tell me you think we should ignore this. Love spurned is a powerful motive for murder." He turned on a jack-o'-lantern smirk.

Sharon shook her head. "Of course we shouldn't. Why don't I call on her at home and discuss this relationship with her, woman to woman?"

"Then you can bash your male colleagues together all you want, huh?" Harry dodged the fist aimed at his arm. "Seriously though, I think that's a good idea."

Sharon squared her shoulders at the compliment.

Harry leaned over and pulled a Coke from the cooler at his feet. Popping the top, he said, "Meanwhile, I'll tackle QP's personal assistant, 'Kyle baby.'"

Sharon looked up the office manager's address on the employee list they'd acquired from the bank. She'd strike while the iron was hot and stop by on her way home from work.

A disheveled Loretta Wilson met her at the door. Sharon smelled wine on her breath. "What do *you* want?" Loretta had apparently left her manners at the office.

"I just wanted a woman's perspective—on Quentin Pryor." Sharon turned on her best commiserating-girlfriend tone. "Without my chauvinist partner looking over my shoulder." Harry would forgive her misrepresentation of him.

Ms. Wilson emitted a loud groan and nodded. She opened the door further to admit Sharon.

Loretta led the way into a small but neat living room. Gold-framed oil paintings hung over the fireplace and velveteen sofa. *Western States must do all right by Ms. Wilson.* Sharon wouldn't mind an apartment this lavish.

Loretta motioned Sharon to a chair next to the fireplace and sprawled onto the couch. Her red silk robe gaped open and she pulled it back around her. She picked up the full wine glass sitting beside her and downed half of it; then she crossed her arms over her large breasts and stared at Sharon.

Sharon wasn't going to get one bit of help from this woman. She bit her lip and looked down at her notes.

"We need to know more about what Quentin Pryor was like as man, as a person." She looked back up in time to catch the agony on Loretta's face.

"As I told you, he was a perfect gentleman in the office." A long sip lowered the wine level further.

"From what Ms. Applewood said, he wasn't so polite to *her*."

"Well, she deserved her reprimand and punishment. Young people these days take all kinds of liberties in the workplace. Treat it like a walk on the beach."

"Did she flirt with Mr. Pryor?"

"Oh, no! He wouldn't have permitted that." She tapped her fingers together around the glass. "Nor would I—as office manager," she added hastily.

Might as well go in for the kill. "What was your *personal* relationship with Mr. Pryor?"

"What are you asking?" Loretta's hand shook as she refilled the glass from the drink trolley next to her. She gulped the wine and then sat up tall.

"Did you see him socially, outside the office?"

"Yes, of course. I helped him—*and* Mrs. Pryor—when they entertained clients in their home." She pulled a limp handkerchief from her kimono sleeve and patted her eyes.

"Are you and *Mrs.* Pryor friends?"

"Well...not really. You may as well know: I thought she was rather stuck up with that accent and all—and the way she walked." Sharon waited while Loretta emptied the bottle into her glass.

"Did you ever see Quentin socially *without* Mrs. Pryor?"

"Hey, Lady Sheriff. I don't like what you're suggesting about me."

Sharon's intuition was on alert. Was the drunkenness an old habit? Or was it because of her boss's death? She decided on the latter. In addition to the emotional loss, this poor woman was probably afraid of losing her job.

"You must be dreading the upcoming changes at the bank, with Mr. Pryor gone."

"Oh, yes." She scrubbed her face with the damp handkerchief. "Most executives bring in their own office managers and assistants. I'll probably be out on the street."

Sharon uttered soothing sounds and then forayed again into the fray. "How about business outings?" She felt a burst of inspiration.

Loretta slammed her glass on the table. "Fine! I guess you'll find out soon enough."

Jackpot. Harry would be so proud.

Sharon decided to use Harry's tactic of not responding to Loretta's outburst. She was actually a little surprised at how well it worked.

Unprompted, Loretta began speaking. "About once a month," she began, "I went with him on his out-of-town trips." She patted her well-cut mousy-brown hair, its perfect shape a sharp contrast to the disheveled appearance of the rest of her. Sharon suspected it was so doused with hairspray, it would take a heavy hand to disarrange it.

"Were you lovers?" Sharon's voice was filled with a tone Harry often called her "empathy come-on." She just hoped it didn't convey her utter disbelief of Pryor's ability to attract women with anything but his fortune.

Loretta sighed and nodded. "Before he met Leigh, I suggested that he marry me. But he said I was too old; that he'd never marry me, even though we were so compatible, so exciting in bed." Her head pillowed in her hands, Loretta sobbed, her tears spilling over to raise blood-red spots on the kimono. With a dreamy look she continued, "We went on a trip just last month." She waved a hand over her robe. "He gave me this when he brought me home—as a thank-you gift."

Sharon drove away elated. She'd pulled the truth from Loretta. Then she sighed. Harry would lord it over her; he'd suggested the intra-office romance. Plus, despite feeling proud, the situation disturbed her. Pryor toyed with women.

Of course, his death changed all that. No matter what front he'd put forth while he was alive, his true nature would come out in their investigation. If he had medical or drug abuse problems, they would be known when the autopsy was performed. Death revealed all; it afforded no privacy.

In the end, Pryor could only hope that the tombstone engravers would be kind.

Chapter 95

"THERE'S A YOUNG LADY TO SEE YOU, Collins." The desk sergeant spoke politely into the phone.

Must be someone important, thought Sharon—*or a real beauty.* Otherwise, he'd be mouthing off at her like always.

"Send her back."

Sharon assembled her paperwork, stacked it, and closed the Quentin Pryor file. They'd never finish this investigation with all these interruptions.

Sharon looked up to see a tall, slender brunette with the bearing of a gazelle. Her rumpled black suit brought a sallow tone to her face. Her gray eyes sparked anger. She stopped at Sharon's desk.

"Deputy Collins? I'm Adrienne Pryor—Quentin Pryor's daughter."

Well, this made the next step easy. Sharon stood and offered her hand to the young woman. Diamonds flashed on the manicured hand that reached to take it.

"Ms. Pryor, I'm so pleased to meet you. I'm sorry for your loss." Sharon motioned Adrienne to the chair across from her desk. "How can I be of assistance?"

"Actually," said Adrienne, still standing, "I'm here to assist *you.*" She placed her hands on her hips. "I came to give you information about my father's murderer."

Sharon stared at the woman before her. She cleared her throat.

"We haven't proven it was homicide," she said, motioning her visitor again to a chair. She watched as Adrienne brushed the plastic cushion with her linen handkerchief before sitting.

"I take it, from your relative ages," Sharon continued, "that Leigh is not your mother."

Adrienne exhaled loudly. "Thank God she's not! It would be obscene to have a murderer for a parent."

Sharon tilted her head but said nothing.

"Leigh's the one who did it. She killed Father. There's no question." Adrienne dabbed at her eyes with a corner of the linen square.

Sharon picked up a soft rubber ball and squeezed it rhythmically. This was going to be a long one.

Adrienne continued, "That snobby Leigh with her snooty English accent, she was jealous of me, upset that Father didn't include her when he and I met for lunch." She grimaced. "I'm sure she's said all kinds of awful things about me."

The dabbing continued. Sharon noted that the handkerchief *was* wet and that tear streaks marked the once perfectly made-up face. At least her tears were real.

"I don't mean to be unkind," Sharon said, "but Leigh has not mentioned you." Sharon dropped the stress-reliever ball and pulled a blank sheet of paper from the stack at the corner of her desk.

"Tell me why you think Leigh murdered your father. Was she with him on the boat?"

Adrienne scooted forward in the chair. "Hell, I don't know. What does that have to do with anything? I tell you, she did it." The long, thin face reddened.

"What evidence do you have that Mrs. Pryor killed your father?"

"Don't call her that! 'Mrs. Pryor' was my mother."

Sharon picked up the ball again and squeezed it—hard. "I apologize. What evidence do you have that *Leigh* Pryor killed your father?"

"Evidence? That's your job. I'm sure you can find it. She's so dumb, I'm sure she left lots of it."

Sharon sighed inwardly. She wished Harry were here to help her. Was Adrienne's hostility just conflict with a stepparent, or was

319

there more? Even if no evidence of Leigh's guilt turned up, they'd be obligated to investigate. The accusation had been made.

"Okay, well why don't we focus on *why* you think Leigh killed your father. What motive did she have?" Sharon glanced at the clock on the wall above Adrienne's head.

Adrienne snorted. "Isn't it obvious? For his money, of course. That's the only reason that gold digger married him in the first place."

Sharon had had similar thoughts about Loretta Wilson, but she had felt that Leigh's grief over Quentin was genuine.

However, this Adrienne *could* prove to be valuable to their investigation. Sharon needed to milk this discussion for all it was worth.

"Who *is* your mother?" she asked Adrienne. "Is she still alive? Have you seen her recently?"

"No." Adrienne answered the last question first. "Audrey—she wouldn't let me call her Mother—married a horse-racing promoter. She lives in Australia." Adrienne sniffed.

"When did you last see your father?" Sharon smiled at the young woman. She didn't want to sound as though she were interrogating a suspect. "Do you live nearby?"

"I saw Father two weeks ago when he came to Sacramento to speak with the governor about the banking bill he was promoting. I live there and work in the governor's office. My dad and I dined together." Adrienne clenched her lips to stop their trembling.

"How often did you see him?" Sharon sat forward in her chair and rested her chin on her hand.

"About once a month. He had many contacts in the capitol area and traveled there often." She paused to blot her eyes again. "I acted as his hostess when he entertained the legislators and lobbyists." She raked her lower lip with her teeth. "I don't know what I'll do without his visits."

She seems genuinely grief-stricken, Sharon's soft side told her. *But it's more likely she's missing her cash cow,* deduced her cynical side, *rather than her lively conversations with Daddy Dearest.*

"Do you have other family in California?"

"No. That is, unless you count my half-brother, who *could* still be around here. I have no children, which is a blessing, since my ex would have passed some terrible alcoholic genes to them." She sighed.

"Your ex? I didn't realize you'd been married—your last name being Pryor. Is he still in the area?"

"I must have sensed the marriage wouldn't last. I never changed my name to his."

"What *is* his name?" Sharon picked up her pen to make a note; another potential to check out.

"George Whimp…le." Adrienne giggled. "He was truly a wimp!"

Sharon sighed. This was getting more like a soap opera every minute. "And where does he live now?"

"He doesn't. He died of pneumonia before the divorce was final."

Sharon crossed George off the list.

"So, tell me about your half-brother."

"David? I wouldn't bother with *him*. He's the black sheep of the family. He's the son of Father's *second* wife, Estelle; they divorced years ago. I haven't seen David since he was in high school, since he was sent to Juvenile Hall."

A kid in juvie? Of a paragon like Quentin? The plot kept thickening here.

"Can you give me your brother's full name? I'd like to check his current whereabouts."

Adrianne sat up straight. "Quentin David Pryor—the Third, to be exact. Father disinherited him years ago. I *should* be Father's only rightful heir now." The voice was cultured, but its whine gave it a childish air.

Ah, the money again. Adrienne doesn't share well.

"Okay, let's get back to why you came here. Tell me more about your father."

"My dad was my best friend in the whole world. Loving. We really got along great until he married that Leigh woman."

Another point for Quentin on the Likeable side of the scorecard; Sharon had begun a mental tally. So far the pros were still winning. It was only the office staff who disliked him. *And potentially hundreds of clients,* she reminded herself.

"What kind of a father was he when you were growing up? Did he spend a lot of time with you and your mother?"

"My parents separated when I was a year old. But after that, he spent every other weekend with me until I went away to college, to Smith. He and Audrey never saw each other and she didn't talk about him to me—ever."

"So I guess she never discussed their marriage."

Adrienne shook her head. "Nope. She'd not even say his name— not even a 'your dad.' When it came his turn to see me, she'd just remind me to pack my clothes for my 'weekend away.'" Adrienne paused. "So I guess you could say their relationship hadn't been good, if she acted like that."

Sharon nodded. She couldn't feel sorry for this woman, in spite of her obvious grief. She was too spoiled and self-centered. But still, that must have been a rough situation to grow up in. "Well, at least she didn't run him down to you like many divorcees do."

"True," said Adrienne continuing her stream of out-loud thoughts. "Except by omission. Even as a young child I sensed she didn't want to hear about him, so I stopped telling her about my weekends away." She swept her hand in front of her body. "She used to examine me all over when I came home, though; like she thought I'd been in a mud pool or something."

Sharon narrowed her gaze. What she was saying sounded—

"Did your father ever hurt you? I mean physically?"

The gazelle frowned. Then she smiled slowly. "We had a very close physical relationship; he was loving and kind to me, hugged me often. I never was afraid of him. I knew he would protect me, not hurt me."

Sharon nodded, still uneasy. If Quentin had ever abused his children—or his wives—well that...

"Did your father talk about his life with Leigh? Did they get along well?" Sharon hated to pursue this, but she had to ask.

"I wouldn't let him talk about her when we were together. I just wanted to talk about him and me."

Sharon raised her eyebrows. *An awfully close relationship for a grown daughter.*

"Did Quentin ever drink?" asked Sharon.

"Of course." Adrienne shrugged.

"Did his mood change drastically when he did?" Sharon continued.

Adrienne's demeanor shifted. She pulled herself up to her full sitting height. "What are you implying, Deputy Collins? My father was a pillar of the community and a member of the best social set. They *do* have social functions where alcohol is served." The indignant tone and set lips did not become Quentin's daughter. Her features took on a harsh, brittle edge—aging her at least five years. Was she being overly defensive of Dad?

"What you asked, that's slanderous," Adrienne continued. "Why, he told me at our last dinner he had just been made the financial head of the Battered Women's Escape Foundation. They wouldn't hire a man who couldn't hold his liquor. Leigh must have started the rumor as a ploy to distract suspicion from herself."

The interview left Sharon with no real clues but another person to interview—the son. And one question: *Did Adrienne truly believe Leigh was guilty, or was she revenging her father's marriage to the dancer?*

Chapter 96

SHARON WEDGED HER AGING HONDA CIVIC into a barely long enough spot at the curb. "Well, baby, you're going to need a hinge in the middle to get me out of this tight squeeze." She patted the steering wheel. The door creaked, metal on metal, as she pushed it open. *I guess it's okay to put halfway houses on crowded streets,* she thought. *If the ex-cons can't leave home, they don't need cars.*

Taking her badge from her shoulder bag, Sharon rang the doorbell. A pale young man with a sullen expression answered the door. She held up her badge.

"Who you here to see, Officer?"

"I'm looking for Quentin Pryor the Third." Her records showed he had been assigned as a manager to this home last month.

The young man examined her badge closely. "You got to surrender your weapon, Ms. Deputy."

"I'll keep it, thank you. I'm not here on a social call. Please let me in." Sharon's smile belied the firmness in her voice.

The man, tall and rail-thin, had a well-worn tan. His pressed jeans looked new, but his faded red sweatshirt had seen better days. He stepped aside and waved her in.

"Now," said Sharon, "if you'll lead me to Mr. Pryor…"

"Can't do that."

"Oh?" Sharon tilted her head. "Is he at work?"

"No." The man snickered. "It's just that I haven't heard my stuck-up name for quite a while. My friends and my charges here all call me Three."

Sharon sighed. Guess she'd found her man.

"Okay, Three. We need to talk privately. Someplace in the yard, in the breeze?"

"Yeah, come on in. We'll walk out through the kitchen."

Three grabbed a cold drink from the refrigerator, leaving a quarter behind in a cracked dish on the counter. He offered it to Sharon, who shook her head. They settled on the patio under a faded umbrella.

"You're not here to tell me that my dad's dead; I already read about it in the paper." He paused. "No one at the bank would remember I exist, let alone call me. Though I'm sure they called poor deluded Adrienne." He took a deep breath and exhaled noisily. "Tell me why you're here."

"Just routine, Quentin."

"Please call me 'Three.' I don't like being called by my dad's name." The young man's jaw tightened.

Sharon sighed inwardly.

"Three, I'm just following up on your father's accident, making sure there was no foul play." She shifted in her chair. "Tell me about him."

"As a man—and as a father—only one word describes him."

"Oh?"

"Bastard."

Sharon suppressed a smile. The single word clearly embodied a host of emotions.

"So tell me, Three, what was your dad like when you were growing up?"

"He's the reason I ended up in juvie."

"Please, do tell." Sharon leaned forward with interest.

"You probably won't believe me."

"Try me."

"My piece-of-shit four-door broke down the day of the senior prom. I was desperate for wheels and too embarrassed to ask my date to drive. I asked my dad if I could drive one of his cars that night, and almost fell over when he said yes."

"How does this relate to your being incarcerated?"

"Don't push me, Dep. Collins. I'm getting there."

Sharon tipped her head to him and sat quietly, waiting for Three to continue his story. The shabby overstuffed chair felt heavenly against her tired hips.

"Turns out he was plastered on vodka when he told me I could drive his Porsche. When he went out after I left and found it missing, he called the cops. They arrested me as we arrived at the prom; right in front of all my friends—and Sally, my date."

"Didn't he withdraw the charges when he sobered up and you reminded him that he'd loaned you the car?"

"Denied doing it." Three's eyes went stone cold. "After that, I never said another word to him ever in his life. And he never tried to contact *me,* either." Three stared at the garden wall. "Believe me, Ms. Deputy," he said, finally looking at Sharon, "I feel nothing but pure joy that my dad is dead. Couldn't happen to a more deserving person."

Chapter 97

HARRY WALKED INTO Kyle Norbest's office. "Have you had lunch yet?" Norbest looked at his calendar. "We don't have an appointment, do we?"

"No. I just dropped in. Thought you and I could chat at the café down the street." Harry raised his eyebrows and nodded towards Loretta Wilson who had stopped working to listen.

"Sure. Just let me close my computer and I'll meet you downstairs. I can rub your nose in the Padres' win over the Dodgers last night." The assistant grinned. "And I might even let you buy!"

Nibbling on a French fry, Kyle said, "What's so important you didn't want Ms. Loretta to hear it?"

"I thought maybe you'd want to fill me in on Pryor's disillusioned clients without an audience." This guy was sharp, figured Harry. If he killed Quentin, he'd have covered it up well, and they'd have to dig deep to prove it. His deputy's instinct told him, though, that the kid, while grossly unhappy working for the bank CEO, was ambitious enough not to endanger his future with a criminal act. But that didn't mean he wouldn't reveal some corporate secrets to get revenge. Harry sipped his Coke as he waited.

"Where do I start? There must be hundreds of them." Kyle bit into his burger and put it back on the plate. "It would be easier to tell you about the happy ones. I could count them on my toes."

"Which of Pryor's turndowns did you think were wrong?"

"You mean which ones could have made it, if only the bank had come through?"

Harry nodded, his eyes on the young man's tapping fingers.

327

"The worst—and most recent—wrong I can think of is Angelo Dimitri. He wanted an extension for his loan to compensate for rain delays. Just two months, but that idio— uh, Pryor, turned him down."

"I'll start there. Where's Dimitri's office?"

"I don't know offhand, but it's in Manhattan Beach. When we get back to the office, I'll give you a full list of Quentin's clients and recent appointments—including their unhappy outcomes."

Harry nodded and sipped his soda thoughtfully. Would the list of potential suspects never stop growing?

Sharon and Harry clumped up the stairs of the DM Homes construction trailer. "Sir, may we speak with you a moment?" The deputies approached the open door of the builder's office.

Angelo Dimitri was a self-made man. His homes blossomed all over Southern California. His wrinkled forehead and downturned mouth expressed his extreme displeasure at looking up from his desk to see the deputies.

"Bethie, where are you when I need you?" he mumbled. "Sorry, my assistant is at the dentist this morning. I didn't hear you come in." Bracing his shoulders, he turned on a marketing executive's smile and changed his tone. "How can I help you, Officers? I assume you're not here to buy a home."

Good save. Harry shook the builder's hand. Firm handshake.

Harry introduced Sharon and himself. "We're assigned to investigate Quentin Pryor's death."

Dimitri patted his paunch. "Don't get my stomach in an uproar. I never want to hear that man's name again."

"He drowned." Harry looked at him sternly.

"And that's supposed to *concern* me?" Dimitri looked skyward. "QP would *delight* in my being bothered by the sheriff." He waved toward the hardwood side chairs. "I may as well listen. Sit down and tell me about it."

"We understand you were a friend of Pryor's and also one of his clients at the bank," said Sharon. She took in the building plans that papered the wall and littered the floor.

"No one I know would call that bastard a friend." Deep lines rippled across the executive's face. "Just last month, in fact, he turned me down when I asked for a loan extension on my Manhattan Beach project."

That jibed with Norbest's interview statements. Harry shifted in the hard chair. There was no love lost here.

"An extension? You wanted more time to pay it back?"

Angelo Dimitri leaned his leather chair back, placed his feet on his desk, and steepled his hands. "Sir, ma'am"—he nodded toward Harry and then Sharon—"please get to the point of your visit. I'm a busy man."

Sharon smiled. "We're investigating Quentin Pryor's death at the request of the coroner; so we're talking to his friends and business contacts to profile him." She shrugged. "We need to understand your relationship with him and your thoughts about him as a person."

"He was a bastard, with a capital B!" Angelo dropped his feet to the floor and sat tall. "But I'm repeating myself." He looked at the ceiling for a moment and continued. "He was a mean, selfish, insecure man who got his jollies by finding the most vulnerable spot in a person—or a business—and exploiting it."

Harry studied photographs of the builder with his influential friends on the office wall. He pointed to a picture of Angelo on a dock with a sailboat in the background. "Looks like you went sailing with him."

"Purely a business trip—believe me. I have to use those ear patches when I go out on any boat so I won't toss my breakfast. Besides, that was before I asked for the loan extension."

Harry nodded. Seemed like Dimitri was telling it like it was. "Were you able to get a loan elsewhere?"

"Of course." The man smiled. "I switched banks. Got a bigger loan at lower interest with no problem—from a firm that knows how to treat a valued customer."

"So you feel Pryor was unjustified in refusing to extend your loan." Harry was beginning to understand the person behind the success of this construction company.

"DM homes are highly sought after. I have a long list of qualified purchasers for this new tract. I can't take time to deal with a little Hitler; I have a business to run." He stood and shoved loose papers into a file folder. "Now if you two will excuse me, I'm past due for my next appointment."

Chapter 98

"ANYONE WHO *LIKED* THIS PRYOR?" Harry asked. They'd have to expand their interviews. *Damn!* He fisted the stack of files on his desk.

"Adrienne, his daughter with his first wife," said Sharon. "She told me, you know, they had a great relationship, saw each other often."

"She sincere?" Harry twirled his pencil.

"Said she missed him; lots of tears." Sharon looked down at her notebook. "Said Pryor called her his angel.'"

"Other kids?"

"The son. The one running the halfway house. Calls himself Three." Sharon shrugged. "Won't use his dad's name."

"You believe his dad loaned him the car he allegedly stole?"

"Yeah. A lot of anger there." She flipped through her notes. "Can you imagine—turned in for grand theft auto by your own father?"

Harry shook his head. "Nice dad." He'd been lucky. His own dad had spent hours with him, fishing, hiking, talking about how to act on a date. He still missed his gentle ways.

"I *will* say Quentin Pryor's a chameleon, all right." Sharon spoke around a peanut butter cookie she'd snatched from her partner's desk. She wanted to remain neutral, but she couldn't help but distrust the dead man.

"Or a con," said Harry. "The ladies of the BWEF talk about how he helped them run their organization. How pleasant he was in explaining everything to them."

"And his daughter and wife loved him," Sharon interjected. "Though his son…" She reached for another cookie.

Harry moved the cookies to the far side of his desk. "Then we talk to the office staff, and at work he's a real tyrant."

Sharon chewed thoughtfully. "The office *did* seem well-run," she mused.

"True." Harry sipped his coffee. "But it was *fine* after he died. The staff didn't *need* to be yelled at to do their jobs."

Harry could be right there.

"Of course, it could be the management style of the bank." Harry straightened his belt. "They're known for their dictatorship. They *say* to prevent theft."

Sharon nodded. Not that she agreed with that reasoning.

Sharon reached for another cookie, only to have her hand slapped. "We've talked to the people who worked for Quentin," she said, pouting and cushioning her hand, "but not with the man *he* reported to, this Coughlin. Shouldn't we do that?"

Harry picked up his hat. "Good call! Let's go without an appointment. Catch him off guard." He locked his cookies in his desk and winked at Sharon.

An expensively suited gatekeeper stood in the path to the Board Chairman's door. Her smile contrasted with the furrows in her forehead. "Officers, do you have an appointment with Mr. Coughlin? I don't see it on his schedule for today." Sharon bet the assistant had many years of protecting her boss from unwanted intrusions.

"I understand he's busy, but we hoped he would give us just ten minutes." Sharon held up her case book. "It's about Quentin Pryor's death."

"Ma'am, we just want to close our case," said Harry.

The assistant returned Harry's smile with a slow one of her own. Sharon marveled at her partner's way with women of any age.

"I'll ask. Please be seated." She motioned to the red leather chairs lining the reception area.

Twenty minutes later, the assistant returned carrying a stack of file folders. "He'll see you now."

Once they'd been ushered in and had refused an offer of coffee, Sharon nodded to Harry to begin the conversation. Harry scooted forward in his chair.

"Mr. Coughlin, sir, first let me express our condolences on the death of your CEO. You must miss him." Harry always knew the right way to start an interview. Sharon hoped she was learning from him.

Coughlin nodded and pointed to a stack of folders on his desk. "We're culling candidates for his replacement. This stack just came in from our head hunter." He folded his hands on his desk and waited.

Cool cat. Not flustered. Sharon admired that. Powerful people seemed to need that talent to move up.

"Tell us, please, why Quentin Pryor was working with the Battered Women's Escape Foundation."

Sharon wished she'd accepted coffee so she'd have something to do with her hands while Harry interviewed.

"The women asked for the bank's help in managing their finances." Coughlin looked down at a clock on his desk.

"Wasn't Quentin rather high up in your organization to be doing community work?" asked Harry.

"We ask all of our executives to do pro bono work. It familiarizes the community with the bank. And..." Coughlin brushed a hand over his forehead.

"And?" Sharon couldn't help jumping in.

Coughlin looked up at a painting across from his desk, then back at Sharon. He cleared his throat. "Sometimes, when an executive gets as high up in an organization as Quentin, he—*or she*—forgets that the people on the street are the ones who keep the bank alive. The community thriving. Because of that, the bank has a policy of assign— er, loaning our executives to worthwhile nonprofits." The executive shrugged. "They asked, and we provided Quentin. It's as simple as that." Coughlin picked up a gold pen and tapped it on his desk.

"Was Quentin pleased with the assignment?" Harry asked.

Coughlin gripped the pen so tightly his knuckles whitened. "Of course. It came directly from me."

"Thank you, sir, for your time."

The deputies shook Coughlin's hand and let themselves out.

In the foyer, the assistant glared at them, her blue eyes snapping. "You took *fifteen* minutes. Now I'll have to rearrange his schedule *again*." Harry didn't attempt to charm her this time.

In the elevator, Sharon raised her eyebrows. Harry looked around the enclosure and shook his head. "In the car."

"Coughlin was hiding something," Sharon burst out as soon as Harry had turned out of the bank parking lot onto the busy thoroughfare.

"Good girl! I knew your radar was picking up something. What was he hiding?"

"At the very *least:* Quentin didn't want to work with the ladies, but Coughlin forced him into it."

Harry nodded. "You're improving with each case." He puffed out his chest. "'Course it's 'cause I taught you so well." He pulled up to a stoplight and turned to Sharon. "And at the most?"

Sharon tapped her fist on the dashboard. "Coughlin felt Quentin needed compassion, humility, when he worked with people and that the charity might give him that."

Harry whistled. "Very nice, partner. I'll make a chief detective of you yet!"

Chapter 99

SHARON PUSHED A YELLOW PAPER in her partner's face. He took off his reading glasses and looked up. "What's that? Your grocery list?"

"More delicious than that. It's a list of suspects in the Pryor case."

Harry shot her a sidelong glance. "I thought you were pushing for a finding of accidental death." He twirled his glasses. "What's changed your mind?"

"Nothing—it *was* an accident. But you're not going to believe me until we check the alibis for all these people." She'd worked on the list at home last night when she couldn't sleep.

Harry grabbed the paper and put on his reading glasses. "From the office," he said, perusing the list carefully, "you have our unfairly treated receptionist; our somewhat-spurned office manager; and our beaten-down personal assistant. Those *should* be easy to track."

"Then we have the five clients he turned down for loans last month." Sharon had been surprised at Harry's ease in obtaining this confidential information from Kyle Norbest. The young man sure must have hated his boss.

"Then there's family." Harry scrunched up his face as he read. "You have Pryor's kids and two ex-wives but not Leigh." He looked at her over his glasses.

"We already have an alibi for her—even though she doesn't need one. She was at home. She taught the kids in ballet class Sunday morning; I verified it with the Boys and Girls Club."

Harry shook his head.

"What?"

"Have you verified her alibi from the night before—at the time of death?"

"Well…I—"

"You didn't." Harry groaned.

"No, but…"

"No buts, Deputy Collins. That's lazy cop work. And you know it." Sharon fell silent.

"All right!" Sharon grabbed the list and headed toward the coffee machine. "I'll see what I can find out."

"You do that," called out Harry. "And you'll convince me a lot more if you find witnesses who *aren't* in that charity. Those friends of hers aren't exactly neutral parties."

Sharon stopped short and nodded. *Damn.* He'd caught her—again—letting her personal feelings cloud her work. She'd been cautioned about it in her last job review.

"Even though you like her," Harry continued, "Leigh Pryor's the most likely suspect, given her probable inheritance."

Sharon swallowed hard. "You're right. We need to follow the money."

Followed by Harry, Sharon stepped off the elevator and surveyed the opulent reception area. The law firm of Bacon, Doth, and Smith occupied the entire twenty-first floor of the Western States Bank building. The receptionist led them down a long hallway decorated with walnut-framed renderings of nineteenth century U.S. courthouses. The two-inch-thick carpet was guaranteed to muffle the most strident steps—*if* the grim-faced receptionist were to permit a disgruntled client past her desk.

Brian Doth extended a limp hand to meet Sharon's and motioned her to an oak hardwood chair on the opposite side of his desk. She knew Harry would have derogatory comments about the lawyer's handshake.

Harry took a chair a little behind Sharon.

"Humph. What can I do for you, Deputy, uh—Collins," Doth asked, glancing down at the card she had given him.

Sharon took a slow breath and willed her nerves to calm. Harry had pressed this interview onto *her,* despite her protests. Was she ready?

She had to be.

"We're here to investigate Quentin Pryor's death. I understand from his assistant upstairs that your firm represents the Western States Bank and that you also were Quentin Pryor's personal attorney." Sharon leaned forward in her chair. She decided not to mention Kyle's insinuation that the CEO had been thinking of taking the relationship elsewhere.

Perched stiff-backed, Doth looked down his nose at Sharon. "I'm not aware that—humph—Mr. Pryor's assistant was *privy* to the nature of our relationship. Our clients demand and get complete confidentiality here. He certainly didn't get that information from *me*." Doth's defensiveness made Sharon wonder what he felt he had to prove to her…or to the bank, his firm, or to the Pryor family.

Sharon decided to ignore his complaint.

"We're here to find out who inherits Quentin Pryor's money." Sharon reached into her pocket to retrieve her notebook and pen. "We can get a warrant," she added when Doth looked prepared to challenge her. *No need to be afraid of this windbag.*

"Humph." Doth toyed with the pencil on his desk, considering his course of action. Finally his shoulders slumped. "We're reasonable people. You won't need the warrant."

Woo hoo! She'd won the first skirmish with this arrogant little turd. She imagined she could feel Harry's pat on her back.

Doth pressed a button on his phone console. "Bring in the Quentin Pryor probate file." He had hardly turned back to face Sharon before the door opened and a young woman entered with a thick manila folder in hand. She placed it precisely on the center of Doth's desk. Sharon watched with a mixture of bemusement and disgust as Doth's gaze fixed on the assistant's long legs as they returned to the door.

After a few moments of silence, Harry cleared his throat. Doth started, as though he had momentarily forgotten the deputies' presence. Then he opened the Pryor file and perused it.

"First of all," began Sharon, "how much is Quentin's estate?"

"I don't have the final figures on that yet." Doth said stiffly. "Humph, these matters take time, you know."

Doth's condescending attitude made Sharon squirm. "Your guess will do for our purposes—today." She forced a smile in his direction.

"Well, it's, you see, it's..." Doth finally looked up at Sharon. "We've *estimated*—only an estimate, you understand..."

Sharon nodded. Was the man ever going to get to the point?

"Well, it's considerable. About twenty million."

Harry let out a low whistle.

People have certainly killed for less, Sharon had to admit. She forced herself to remain straight-faced.

"Who gets what?"

"Quentin David Pryor the Third is bequeathed the amount of ten thousand dollars, to be paid on the condition that he is not in prison or in a substance abuse facility. If either of those is the case, it is to be held in a trust fund administered by Western States Bank until the young man's return to society." Doth looked up. "I understand he is currently managing a halfway house in the city."

Sharon didn't confirm or deny Doth's intel.

"And the balance?"

"The balance of the estate goes to his daughter by his first wife, Adrienne Pryor."

Wow—I guess Quentin and his daughter <u>were</u> really close, thought Sharon. To thoroughly examine the money trail, they'd have to check on her finances. Was she in need of money?

Harry cleared his throat, urging Sharon forward.

"What about Leigh Pryor?" Sharon asked. "His wife when he died. Doesn't she inherit part of the estate—by law?"

"Are you an attorney, Ms. Collins?" Doth looked at Sharon with such disdain she felt like a child. "Of the California Bar?"

Sharon straightened her back. "I'm not. But I know my rights as a married—and divorced—woman."

Doth grunted again and began flipping pages in the thick Pryor file. "If I remember correctly, she waived her rights to her statutory share of the estate in a prenuptial agreement." He pulled a short document from the file. "Yes, here it is."

Sharon steeled herself. "I'll need to see that," she said, reaching for the document. Doth hesitated but reluctantly handed it over.

Sharon took her time reading the prenuptial agreement— all four pages. She couldn't allow Doth to bully her into missing something. When she finally looked up, Doth was glowering at her. *No surprise there.*

Sharon pointed to the first paragraph. "It says here that the agreement expired on April first, this year." She pretended to look at her notes. "Wasn't Quentin Pryor killed on June sixteenth?"

Doth grabbed the document from Sharon's hand. "Let me see that! You've misread it, I'm sure." He hooked his rimless glasses behind his ears and examined the document. As he read, his face turned a smoky gray. "It expired—as you said—two months ago." He paused. "You don't suppose…"

Before he could finish, Sharon stood and held out her hand. "Thank you, Mr. Doth. We'll come again if we need more information from you." She glanced at Harry. "But until then, I don't suppose anything."

"What a pompous man!" Oh, how Sharon had relished pointing out to him his error. "Of course, a *good* lawyer would have already known about the expiration date. Especially from a file he had supposedly reviewed recently." Sharon wrinkled her nose. "Do you think he's incompetent?"

Harry shrugged. "Maybe. But, you know…the *real* question is—"

"I know, I know." Sharon sighed. "The real question is: Did *Leigh* know about that expiration date?"

Harry pointed a finger at her. "Bingo!"

Chapter 100

"I FEAR I WON'T BE ABLE to live up to others' expectations of me." Leigh spoke softly to Carol as the two lounged poolside in Carol's backyard. "I just want to hide myself in a cave. So I don't have to put on a public face."

Leigh *needed* privacy. In London, she'd loved the public life that came with her dancing, but she'd also insisted on maintaining a strictly private one, too. One her friends had helped her to hide.

"What expectations won't you be able to meet?" Carol slathered her body with sunscreen and then leaned back in the lounge chair, her eyes still on Leigh.

"Yours and Mora's, for example." Leigh wished she could just enjoy life as her friend did: no cares in the world. "I fear I can't just pick up my life and go on, like the two of you did. When I start to make plans, my thoughts always turn to Quentin's incessant drumming about my ineptness in doing even the most menial of tasks." She cradled her head in her hands. "When he was here, I didn't have to work, pay bills, take the car to service, or make any decisions. It no doubt seems odd, but I miss him when I have to do those things." Leigh sighed. "All he needed do was crook a finger and people magically took care of things for him. They jumped to meet his every whim." Leigh shrugged. "They ignore *me* more often than not—until they realize I might have money."

Carol nodded her understanding.

Leigh's eyes widened and she grabbed Carol's arm. "You don't suppose people were *afraid* of him—as I was?" She pressed her trembling hands on the chair arms. "I'd always assumed he commanded their respect. But perhaps I was misreading it."

Carol smiled broadly. "Congratulations! You're beginning to heal!" She gave Leigh a high five. "You're now looking at the *real* cause of your problems with Quentin: his need to control you in order to feed his own ego."

Leigh waved her hands as though she were dancing.

Carol turned somber. "Now, don't get me wrong. I know just what you're feeling," she said, nodding. "I had the very same fears and frustrations when *my* husband died. I was in a panic, almost, at times."

"*You* were? Why, what nonsense!" Of all people—except maybe Mora—Carol was the person Leigh least imagined not taking charge of her life. She squeezed Carol's hand. "Perhaps you can help me get around all the anxiety?" It felt so good to not be alone after all.

"Not completely," said Carol. "But I *can* advise you to remember that you don't have to do everything. Or at least not all at once."

"If you please, can you explain?" Leigh leaned forward, her eyes riveted on her friend. She had a long list of things she had to look into, stuff Quentin had insisted he did best—in fact, that included everything but what she put on in the morning. No, that wasn't true. He often dictated that too.

"The car won't rot if it isn't serviced today, if you don't feel like it." Carol smiled. "Some morning when you wake up with a smile, just call the dealer, explain your new circumstances and tell them you'll depend on their help in servicing the car. They'll pick it up and leave you a loaner."

"Why, it sounds rather simple when you put it that way. Quentin would insist on hovering over them while they worked on his car."

Carol wrapped a towel around her wet hair. "One thing I've found is that people in the service business want to be helpful, and most of the time they do a good job."

Leigh twisted a strand of hair, untwisted it, and then curled it around her finger. "What about finances? I managed fine before we wed, but Quentin took over afterwards. I don't even know how much money I have."

Carol's face twisted into a frown. "I thought you told us at the cabin that you have a trust fund from your mother. What about that? And what about Quentin's estate?"

Leigh shook her head. "Who knows? We signed a prenup, and Quentin called me a gold digger when I asked about his will." Leigh sipped from her water bottle and set it down so forcefully, water spurted on her. Wiping her arm on the towel, Leigh continued, "My trust fund alone would only support me in this money-draining stone prison for a year."

"You don't need to stay in the stone mausoleum," replied Carol, patting Leigh's arm. "You could sell it and live off the proceeds—at least the part that doesn't belong to the bank. Besides, didn't you say the will reading was next week? You'll find out soon enough, I expect."

Leigh frowned and bit her lip. "Indeed. There's another thing I'm dreading. I presume the deputies are planning to be there. Should I be concerned...about, you know?"

"I don't see any reason you should be." Carol squeezed Leigh's hand. "Now, back to our original subject: What about life insurance? It may even pay double since your husband's death was an accident."

"But it wa—"

"Hush!"

Chapter 101

"SO, HOW MANY POTENTIALS are we at now?" Harry rose from his chair and hiked up his belt.

Sharon counted on her fingers. "Ten?"

Harry nodded. "Let's start a whiteboard. Rank in order of probability who could have been with Pryor on the boat."

Sharon threw down her marker. "We have all these people who *might* have motive—and maybe even opportunity—to kill Quentin Pryor, but we still have no indication this wasn't just an accident, you know."

Still on her campaign to drop the case. Harry would have to keep a watch on Sharon with this one.

"Wrong—as usual." He smiled and pulled a bag of peanuts from his pocket. "Here, have some brain food."

He poured peanuts into her outstretched hand.

"Okay, smarty, whatcha got?" She stuck a peanut in her mouth.

"Some people didn't like Quentin Pryor, true." Harry tossed a peanut in the air and moved under it to catch it in his mouth. "And now we got evidence changing that accident to a probable homicide."

Sharon paused mid-chew. "What?! You holding out on me, partner?" She stomped her foot. "What's the deal—you trying to seem more important? Smarter? Powerful?"

Yikes! There she goes. Harry threw up his hands. "Honest, I just found out ten minutes ago."

"And you were going to tell me...*when?*"

Ignoring Sharon's question, Harry said, "Forensics found that the lifeline holding Quentin was cut; likely with a diving knife."

"So?" Sharon wiped her forehead with the back of her hand. "Couldn't Pryor have cut it himself? You did say he'd gotten tangled up in the cord."

Harry nodded. "All well and good. Except one thing."

Sharon looked at him expectantly. "And that one thing is…?"

"Pryor had a knife still attached to his belt." Harry pantomimed pulling out a knife from his belt. "I find it doubtful he would take time to re-sheathe it while fighting for his life."

Sharon remained silent, her expression still dubious.

"Oh, one more thing," said Harry, pausing for effect. "The holster was snapped shut."

Sharon's eyebrows shot up into her furrowed brow. "So we're almost *definitely* looking for Quentin Pryor's murderer?"

Harry lunged at her with his invisible knife.

"Looks that way."

Chapter 102

SHARON SCRUBBED THE FLOOR of her kitchen, then vacuumed the whole apartment. It had been a *long* week of interviews, and the housework gave her time to process all the information about the Pryor case—*and* to put off the phone call she needed to make. It would not be pleasant, telling Paul's mother that her son had abused Cailin.

Sharon *should* have reported Paul to the authorities immediately. But that would have alienated her from Cailin. Their relationship was the tenuous one of all teen girls and their mothers. Added to that was Sharon's own insecurity about being a good single mom.

Sharon shoved the vacuum into the overstuffed closet and reached for the phone.

"Hi, Marjorie. It's Sharon Collins, Cailin's mother."

"Hello, Sharon." *Oh-oh, she knows why I'm calling.* Sharon could tell from the flatness of Paul's mother's voice.

"Is this a good time?" Sharon forged ahead. "I need to talk with you." Sharon held the phone with one hand and made a fist with her other.

"If it's about your daughter spreading rumors about Paul, you're right—we do need to talk."

Sharon plopped down on the sofa. "*Excuse* me?"

"Paul said he asked Marsha for a date, and she said she couldn't go out with him 'cause Cailin was spreading vicious rumors about him." Marjorie's voice broke into coughing. "I don't know what she said, but that sounds like slander. If it continues to happen, I have a mind to sue both you and your daughter."

Sharon bit her lip and swallowed. "Actually, that *is* why I'm calling."

"Oh?" Marjorie's voice took on a defensive edge.

"But there's no slander. What happened is that Paul *hit* Cailin—because she wouldn't have sex with him." Sharon tapped her fingers on the phone table.

Silence. And then: "So she teases him and then says no?"

"You may not know it, but Cailin and Paul agreed to hold sex until they married."

Marjorie scoffed. "You believe that and I have a plot on Torrance Beach to sell you!"

Sharon cringed at Marjorie's putdown—and the implication of her words. But she *did* believe in her daughter.

"Marsha must have seen Cailin's bruises in the gym showers and come to her own conclusions." Sharon ignored the hiss from the other end of the line. "But whether you like it or not, Paul *did* hit Cailin after last Friday night's game."

"You lie! Cailin is just trying to get back at Paul for breaking up with her."

"But she brok—" Sharon refused to get involved in a he-said/she-said argument. She took a deep breath and continued with a calm voice. "You *need* to talk with your son about how to treat women," Sharon continued. "He should never hurt them—for *any* reason." She paused. "Paul is an ambitious young man with a future—*if* he keeps out of trouble. That's one reason I promised Cailin not to report him, *for now*. But be assured, I *will* turn him in immediately if I hear of his hurting anyone else. I'd recommend you talk to him tonight."

Marjorie's voice lost its edge. "Well, then..." Sharon held her breath during the long pause. "You can consider the matter discussed!"

Sharon winced as Paul's mother slammed the phone into its cradle.

Now what? Well, vowed Sharon, *if Paul doesn't straighten up immediately, I make good on my threat. That's what!*

Sharon's hands went back to her cleaning—and her mind to the other reality she could no longer avoid: Quentin Pryor apparently *had* been murdered. The heat on this investigation was about to be turned waaayyy up.

PART V

Operation Courage

Chapter 103

LEIGH STRETCHED as the sun filtered through the lace-curtained window. Something was different; she paused before she swiveled her legs to the side of the bed. Then realization dawned: she was alone. The sounds of the treadmill and shower were missing from her morning. Gone, too, was her fear. She no longer had to start off the weekend tiptoeing, awaiting signs that her husband had gotten up in an increasingly rare cheerful mood.

It had been exactly one week since Quentin had been ki—*since he was in an accident,* she corrected herself—and she was finally starting to feel some positive effects.

Leigh slipped her long slender feet into satin mules and pulled on a pale-green peignoir. She would have coffee and read the morning headlines before she dressed. Then she'd go to the dance studio to practice. Quentin had not permitted lounging in the morning—not even on a Saturday. In the realm of his strictly organized existence, lazy, unstructured mornings were a threat of senility.

"Good morning, Cook." Leigh smiled at her longtime friend. "You keep that antique so beautifully polished; we should use it more."

"With all due respect, ma'am, you could entertain your lady friends with a spot of tea, now that the mister is gone." Cook rubbed at a yellow spot on the side of the otherwise gleaming sterling water dispenser, the centerpiece of a ten-piece Victorian tea service that Leigh had bought in London following her final dance performances. "I could make those little tea sandwiches you fancy."

"Cook, that's brilliant!" The dancer pulled her foot from her slipper and flexed her toes as she stood at the kitchen counter. "I've missed your full English tea." She picked up her mug of coffee and studied the dark liquid. "Do you suppose you could cobble some of those little cakes I fancy, too? You know, the ones you found at Harrods."

"Of course, I could, Ms. Leigh. I still have my book of recipes— even though the mister didn't like to try new foods." Cooks hands flew to her mouth. "I'm sorry, ma'am, I don't mean to be disrespectful of the dead." Cook wiped her hands on the towel hanging from her waistband.

Leigh set her mug on the table and crossed the room to hug the gray-haired woman who'd been with her for many years. "I'd never assume you were being disrespectful; that just isn't like you." She hugged Cook again. "You're just being observant—and honest." She looked down into the older woman's face. "We both know I made a terrible mistake when I married Quentin."

Cook held Leigh at arm's length. "Those bruises are almost gone from your pretty arms," she said, "and the pain lines have disappeared from your face." Cook smiled broadly. "The good Lord works his wonders in many ways."

Chapter 104

"**W**HO IS IT?" The muffled voice came over the intercom at the gate of the suburban home.

Sharon smoothed her pink sweats and looked up and down the street. She spoke quickly and distinctly into the speaker. "It's Sharon Collins, come to say hello to the matron." She heard the click of the electric lock as the gate moved to the right, just far enough to admit her. As Sharon walked up the familiar stone walk, she admired the new moss-green stucco and the white railings on the wraparound porch. She smiled at the shrieks of children splashing in the backyard pool, remembering her own children learning to swim in the very same facility. It felt good coming home. She'd regained life here.

The polished old oak door swung on quiet hinges as Sharon stepped into the entrance hall. "Sharon! Are you here to question one of our residents?" The woman who spoke enveloped the deputy in a bear hug, which was returned with gusto. Sharon often thought of hugs when she thought of the shelter. They were everywhere.

"No, Matron. I just want to talk with *you*, get a feel for the place again."

"Coffee?" The matron could have been the poster woman for the perfect housemother to abused women and children: smiling pink face; plump, short arms permanently curled into a hugging position; gray hair tucked into a bun; and a no-nonsense air about her. She led the way into a brightly lit cavernous kitchen, centered by a pine-plank table. She pulled out a chair for Sharon. Seeing the woman who'd rescued her gave Sharon a feeling of being tucked in safely for the night.

"I'd love some. I'm so down about Cailin's problems—and a new case—I'm cold to the bone." Sharon shivered and pulled her sweat jacket around her, even though it was summer.

"You sick?" The matron peered at Sharon as every mother does when she suspects her child is ill.

"I think it's regression." Sharon smiled ruefully. "Cailin's boyfriend hit her the other night 'cause she wouldn't sleep with him." The matron's eyes reflected Sharon's pain. "I talked to the boy's mother this morning and she refused to believe it. Slammed the phone down." Sharon rubbed her ear.

"You didn't turn him in?" Matron prepared the coffeepot.

"No. I promised Cailin I wouldn't if she stopped seeing him. But she knows I'll have him brought in if I hear he did it again." Cailin had been a real trooper. Breaking up with a popular basketball star wasn't easy. She could face all kinds of harassment for it.

"Why?"

"Why didn't I report him?" At Matron's nod, Sharon continued. "He'd always been super with her 'til this happened, and…and I didn't want to lose her trust. Not now."

"I understand." Matron patted her arm. "I think you're doing a wonderful job raising those kids alone. I trust your judgment." She rose and looked out the window at the kids playing on the patio. "You do what you have to do. Those kids are important."

Sharon nodded mutely.

"You mentioned work was bothering you." Matron never missed anything. That's why Sharon had to come here today.

"I have a case where the deceased and his wife were involved with the BWEF." She looked around at the familiar room. "You've redecorated. I like the cornflower wallpaper; it's so cheerful." She grinned. "You must have put some of your guests to work again."

"Is she badly hurt?" The matron poured crockery mugs full of her famously strong coffee and offered a pitcher of milk. At the blank look on Sharon's face, she said, "The domestic violence victim you were talking about."

"Oh, this case isn't DV. It's an unexplained death." Sharon sipped the bracing brew, added sugar, and drank again. "Probable murder." She wiped her lips with the paper napkin. "Besides, they're rich. You don't find violence in those homes."

"Don't you believe that!"

The matron's anger startled Sharon. This calm women had never shown such emotion in her presence.

"Matron, what's upset you so much?"

"You came here after she'd gone." The matron's eyes shone. "But Helen Neil was one of our guests."

"The movie star who died?"

Matron nodded and wiped her sweating face and neck with a tissue. "Her director husband found out our address from one of his city government chums and came for her."

"You didn't stop her?"

"She said she wanted to go with him to protect the other women from his anger." A tear slipped down the troubled woman's cheek. "Next I heard, she was in intensive care and not expected to live."

Sharon walked around the table and hugged the woman. "I'm so sorry."

A pigtailed girl came running, breathless, into the room. "Matron, Matron, my mommy is crying. I don't want her to cry." She looked accusingly at the matron, her dark eyes flashing. "You said we'd be happy here, but Mama's worried about what will happen to us. Says it's her fault we're in here—and that we'll *never* be happy."

The matron stooped to look into the worried brown eyes. "Sometimes we have to cry to get over the things that hurt us and brought us here," she told the troubled young girl, "before we can go on to be happy." She smoothed the frown lines from the coffee-colored forehead. "You go on and play on the slide in the backyard. I'll look in on Mom in a little bit. See if she needs to talk."

The ever-caring woman watched her charge run to the gaggle of kids on the patio and then seated herself opposite Sharon. She continued to watch the children, listening to their welcome of the newcomer.

"Where were we?" She finally turned to face Sharon. "Oh, yes. The accidental death case."

Sharon lifted her mug for more coffee. "The husband is dead, under suspicious circumstances. The wife is a nice lady; I feel sorry for her. She's from England and doesn't seem to have friends here." Sharon centered her mug on its coaster. "Her husband fell overboard while sailing—or more likely, was pushed. I need to investigate, even consider the widow as a suspect, but I'm fighting myself to keep focused on the case." She smiled ruefully. "From what we've learned about him, he wasn't a very nice man. He must have been hard to live with."

"If that's the case, at least the poor wife is at peace."

Matron's comment brought an unbidden thought to Sharon: *Would Quentin's verbal abuse at work have flowed over to his behavior at home—perhaps even manifesting itself physically?* Sharon practically scoffed at herself aloud. No matter *what* Matron said about rich folks, given the couple's ties to the BWEF, the idea bordered on the ridiculous.

Matron reached for her notebook. "Does she need a donation of clothes, toys?" The kindly woman's pale blue eyes softened in empathy for yet another woman starting out on her own.

"Matron, you're always ready to help. Without you, I'd still be doing escape-and-come-back yo-yo returns to my angry drunk of a husband." Sharon patted her mentor's dry, work-reddened hand. "Like I said, this widow is rich, no kids. Seems to have plenty of money—*and* plenty of rich friends to help her out. In fact, she's on the Outreach Committee of the BWEF."

"That's a high and mighty one," the matron said. "I work with the Referral Committee; they send us the poor abused waifs and their children, day and night. *And* with the Oversight Committee, the one that checks our books, nutrition, and cleanliness. But that Outreach Committee is a snooty one. I don't know *what* they do."

"I'm not sure either, except I know the members are personally very close to one another, and they concentrate on bringing rich women into the BWEF. I met a couple of them at the marathon they organized."

Matron sniffed. "I suppose those ladies *do* serve the community too—and everyone comes out for their race." The matron smiled. "Did I tell you your old roomie, Marigold, finished in twenty-third place?"

Sharon smiled. "*That* should boost her self-esteem!"

The matron nodded. "I wish all our guests could succeed like that, in the marathon or elsewhere. Gives them the push to go out on their own, like you did."

Chapter 105

LUCKY DROPPED COINS into the pay phone in the hospital lobby. "Wilderness Outfitters. How can I help you?"

"I'm a client of yours and I'm looking for information. Does my voice sound familiar to you?"

The young woman's tone was puzzled. "No, sir, I'm sorry. Should it?"

Lucky sighed. "I thought you might know me as an old customer. Oh, never mind." Lucky's voice sounded different—even to his own ears. Somehow he remembered enough to know that. It was caused by the alteration in his facial structure, the docs said.

"Sir, don't hang up. I'm a little new here. Is there something you wanted from the store?"

She was right—maybe he should try a different tack.

"Uh, yes…I understand you carry river rafting equipment."

"Oh yes, sir. Let me call Rob to the phone. He's our expert on that."

Rob? Why did he feel like he should know that name? Panicked, Lucky slammed down the phone. *Now what?*

Chapter 106

HARRY TWISTED THE EMPTY PEANUT PACKET and lobbed it into the wastebasket. Given the turn of events in the Pryor case, he and Sharon were meeting on a Sunday to get a jump on things—crime didn't wait for weekdays.

Sharon reached for the whiteboard marker. "Okay. It's time to do this investigation right!"

Harry smiled. *At last!* Sharon was changing her tune.

Harry counted on his fingers. "Starting with the office, there's Ms. Applewood—the receptionist he made go home and change clothes." Sharon wrote as he dictated. "Our buddy Kyle, the admin assistant. And all the builders whose loans Quentin refused—arbitrarily, according to Kyle."

Sharon had to scribble to keep up with Harry's thoughts.

"Next, there's family: the son...the daughter..."

Sharon stopped writing and peered at him over her reading glasses. "Are we sure we should keep her?" She tilted her head. "Ms. Adrienne *really* loved old Dad, you know."

Harry rubbed his thumb and forefinger together. "Maybe she needed his money—all of it."

Sharon nodded but added the name at the bottom of the board.

"Hey, you forgot the office mistress."

Harry waved his hand back and forth. "What's her name again?"

"Loretta Wilson." Sharon wrote the name on their list and put an asterisk next to it. "Boy, did *she* sob over Quentin."

"What's that star for?

Sharon looked up, as though surprised at Harry's question. "She's the murderer."

Harry's eyebrows rose. "That so? Just because she loved the man and can't tell anyone about it but us strangers?" He cleared his throat. "I don't think so. Erase it."

"Men! You're all alike, you know. Didn't you hear me say she'd asked Quentin to marry her? The beast turned her down."

Harry rubbed his ear. "His marriage didn't end the affair."

Sharon sighed and shook her head. "Loretta needs to get a life! Especially if she thought Quentin Pryor was good husband material."

Harry laughed and tossed the eraser at Sharon. "Be reasonable, partner. If every scorned woman murdered a man who didn't want to marry her, there'd be few of us left." Harry shook his head. "You're not getting the whole picture."

"What picture is that?" Sharon crossed her arms.

"It wouldn't do Ms. Wilson any good to knock off her lover, but…" He pointed to Sharon to add another name on the list. "It sure would help Leigh Pryor if *she* offed hubby because he was seeing Ms. Loretta on the side."

Sharon lowered her marker. "You're going to have to prove that one to me, you know." She stooped to pick up the eraser Harry had thrown. "I just can't believe Leigh Pryor could kill *anything*—let alone her husband."

Chapter 107

"MORA, LET'S TAKE OFF OUR SHOES and walk down to the surf. I need to get my feet wet." Erin leaned down so her face was level with the open driver-side window of Mora's car. "I'm desperate to talk to you," she whispered.

"Sure. The surf would feel good on my feet, too."

Erin and Mora watched as a dog walker trotted by with her three charges. Mora swung her feet out and slipped off her shoes. "Let me put money in the meter and we can go."

The two women walked in silence. The cool water contrasted with the warm sand they'd dashed across in their bare feet.

"What's up?" Mora asked.

Erin hesitated. She felt about to burst, with fear, anxiety, or whatever it was called. "I'm having these rushes of feelings in the middle of the night," she finally said.

"Dreams?"

"Yeah, sweaty ones. And I'm too young for hot flashes." Erin kicked at the surf. She wasn't sweating now.

"What's in your dreams?"

"I'm back in the Canyon, experiencing it all over again."

"Tell me what happened there."

"You know the plan we made, Taylor and I."

Mora nodded.

The plan was etched in Erin's brain. She'd gone over it many times, trying to figure out if she'd done anything wrong.

"It went like clockwork. But…" Erin's voice drifted off. What was she doing here on the beach talking to a shrink? She'd become her own person the last few years. She should be able to deal with her feelings herself.

Mora stopped and faced her. Waiting. She showed no signs of impatience, however.

"It happened so fast." Erin words came in a rush. "I didn't have time to feel. It was if I was a robot, going through my computerized program."

Erin took off jogging along the shore a ways, leaving footprints in the hard sand. She stopped and waited for Mora to catch up.

"When did your feelings come back?" Mora asked, not missing a stride.

"A week later, in my dreams—and every night after that."

"Does the same dream come back?"

"Yeah."

"Tell me about it." Mora's hand on her shoulder felt comforting, her voice calming, nonjudgmental.

"I drive to the rim, park the rental car in an unobtrusive space, retrieve my pack from the trunk, and start walking." Erin felt like a travel agent as she recounted her story in logistical detail. "I set up a campsite and wait for Marshall to arrive. When he does, I—"

"I'm still not hearing any emotion," Mora cut in. She stopped to pick up a shell and brushed the sand off it.

Erin watched her friend's hands. Her own were gripped into fists. She flexed them and dipped them in the cool water.

"That's part of what bothers me. I *didn't* feel anything—then. I just walked through my script like an actress."

"Have you thought that your body went into automatic pilot so you could succeed without your emotions interfering?"

"You mean so I wouldn't sabotage myself?"

Mora nodded.

Erin's face broke into a wide grin. "Well, I sure didn't do *that*. Marshall's gone and so is Quentin. And that's what I set out to do."

"Tell me what went wrong with Quentin."

"What do you mean?" Erin frowned at Mora. "Everything went according to plan. Well, mostly."

Mora indicated Erin's still-bruised face. "Want to tell me about *that?*"

Erin described her last harrowing minutes with Quentin.

It had taken her a while, but Erin was proud of how she'd met the problems with Quentin head on and completed the mission. "And we know *he's* dead," she said proudly.

Mora picked up another shell and tossed it into the surf.

"Distancing yourself from uncomfortable acts is normal behavior, Erin. Is that the only thing bothering you?"

Erin shook her head.

"In my dreams," she told Mora, "I'm tying myself to Marshall's raft with Quentin's lifeline."

"But what *emotions* are coming out in your dreams? Fear? Remorse? Shame? Guilt?" Mora's voice was calm, her demeanor caring but professional, as she looked into her friend's eyes.

"That's what *really* scares me."

"What?"

"The emotion I feel. It's— It's elation. I got a real high killing those beasts!"

Chapter 108

"Y OU DONE ANY VOLUNTEER WORK with the shelter people?" asked Harry. He navigated a corner while he awaited his partner's response.

Sharon tensed. She sipped her coffee and considered her answer carefully.

"No. Got big guilt feelings about it, too. Hoping to fix that soon." She glanced at her partner. "Why?"

"I'm curious. Mrs. Pryor's friends *said* they met the vic and his wife at meetings. But they seem to be very close with her. I want to know more about this Outreach Committee they're on. What women do there that makes them such good friends."

Sharon tugged at her ear. "They saved my life: Bringing me into the shelter."

"These same women?"

"No, I just met Carol and Mora recently."

"So I know about the shelters. What else does the BWEF do?" Harry looked over at his partner. "Besides the marathon we all pledged money for you to run."

"Oh yeah, the marathon." Sharon bent her head. "Well, to be honest, I walked part of the way." She laughed. "They have *lots* of events like that to raise money for the various committees."

Where was Harry going with this? If this was a backhanded way to tell her she needed to exercise more… Naw, he'd just come out and tell her to join a gym.

"I just want to know more about them. Saw in the Peninsula paper that they raffled off a house recently. That took some organization, some real estate smarts, and frankly, some guts." He licked his fingers and pretended to count money. "Two hundred and fifty bucks for *one* raffle ticket. The paper said the money was going towards the shelters *and* their other charities. What other charities?"

Sharon let out a breath. "I don't know, Harry. The shelter is the only help I took. I could ask when I volunteer."

"Might be a *good time* for you to volunteer—learn about Pryor's work for them. Could be important."

As the pair continued their journey up toward the Peninsula, Harry spotted a group of waving people outside the small chapel in Alpine Village. "Hey, a wedding! Let's drive through the parking lot." He slowed down to take the sharp turn.

They watched the happy couple dodge handfuls of eco-friendly birdseed and then climb into a limousine. The gray day hadn't dampened their spirits.

"That's something *I'll* never do again," Sharon said as they followed the limo down Torrance Boulevard. One bad marriage was enough for her life. Sure, it gave her the kids, but been there, done that. But that didn't mean she couldn't date.

Sharon's heart lifted at the thought of Ernest—but sank again. This Pryor investigation was becoming all-consuming; she barely had time for herself and her kids, much less dating. She could only hope he understood. Well, if he wanted to be involved with her, he'd *have* to.

Harry eyed her speculatively. "*If* you ever got so stupid as to consider it, what would you investigate in a man?"

"I'd need to know what he thought of his mother," said Sharon. "Or maybe a sister."

"And that'd tell you…?"

She finished her coffee and dropped the reusable travel mug behind her seat. "If he ridiculed them, it might tell me his father was an abuser—or at least that he doesn't respect women."

Harry nodded, his eyes somber. "Not that it *bothers* me, but it seems like you're biased against *all* men."

"Not *all!*" She punched his arm. "Not you, of course."

"Thanks for that!"

Or Ernest.

Sharon turned in her seat to watch a woman chasing a child on the sidewalk. She laughed as the woman caught the little boy and hugged him until he squealed.

"Now it's your turn, partner. *If* you were single, what would you need to know about a future spouse?"

"I'd find out if her mother cheated on her father." Sharon felt Harry's pain. His voice didn't disguise how he still felt about his first wife's infidelity.

"You don't think cheating is hereditary, do you?"

"No, but cheating in the home has to rub off on the kids, subtle as it may be. Kids pick up a lot more than we think they do," said Harry. "When they watch their parents—or feel the atmosphere in a room."

Sharon knew this was true. Her kids had definitely perked up when their dad was no longer causing *her* unbearable pain.

"A big job, raising kids," she said. "I wouldn't take a billion for my two, but they're such a responsibility!"

As the deputies looked across the median strip, a blue SUV filled with a large family sped by them in the opposite direction, far exceeding the speed limit.

"Reckless driving is a different form of abuse," said Harry. "Maybe I'd ask about their driving record." He glanced in the rearview mirror. "Good! Smokey just pulled in behind that speed demon."

"Great idea—I'd ask if they ever had a DUI or had their driver's license yanked," said Sharon. "Road rage must be a reflection of *something* in their emotional makeup." She smiled. "Wonder if our victim Pryor had any of those? We'll have to look."

"What about pets?" asked Harry, smiling at the antics of a yellow Lab as it cavorted with two kids on the library lawn.

"Sean wouldn't tolerate pets, so I'd make sure my future husband liked animals, probably before the second date." She'd been thrilled to see the mixed-breed dog and a cat at Ernest and Joe's home. "Of course, we've had cases where the family pet was abused along with the wife and kids." She shook her head. "How can anyone abuse an animal or a child? What does it get them?" Sharon turned to her partner with tears in her eyes. "I guess I'd also want to know if they ever gave a pet to the pound because it was inconvenient to take care of it."

"That could apply to wives, too."

Sharon's eyes flashed. Harry raised a hand to cut off her tirade. "I don't mean sending wives to the pound, but like cheating on them when they get pregnant."

The deputies pulled up to the Pryor estate and Harry spoke into the intercom. When the gate opened, they drove through and parked in the arrival courtyard. Today's overcast sky darkened the mansion's granite exterior to a smoky hue.

"Okay, partner," said Harry. "Let's go find out more about the Pryor marriage that's ended so conveniently just after the prenup expired."

Chapter 109

LUCKY FELT HIS GUT relax a little. Another day, another resolve. By the end of the day, he'd know where Wilderness Outfitters fit into his life. With numb fingers he again dialed the 800 number he'd found in the catalog.

"Wilderness Outfitters, Taylor speaking. How may we help you?"

Lucky coughed. "Remember me?"

"N–N–No!" A sob echoed before the phone was slammed into the cradle on the other end.

Who was this Taylor? Clearly a woman, though she had what he considered a man's name.

Lucky wiped his sweating hands on his pants. Of one thing he was sure: *Taylor remembered him.*

Chapter 110

"THANKS FOR SEEING US, Mrs. Pryor," said Sharon.

"Please call me Leigh. Mrs. Pryor is so formal…besides, Quentin's gone. I have to get used to that." Leigh pulled her yellow cashmere cardigan around her. She led them to the solarium and motioned for them to sit on the couch. Sharon noted a change in the ambience of the room. Flowers and bright cushions had been added since their last call.

"Ma'am, tell us about your marriage." Harry's eyes caught and held the new widow's, daring her to evade the question or to look away.

"We were married for years, but in many respects it seems a much shorter time. Of course, other times, it seemed we'd known each other all our lives." Leigh rolled her shoulders back and stretched her neck. She was tense, that's for sure.

"Was it a happy one?" Harry asked.

Sharon hated prying into another person's private life, but she was learning to accept that it was part of the job.

"It was—much of the time," said Leigh. "I've never known such luxury, especially when we vacationed. Top class all the way. When I traveled with the ballet troupe, it was decidedly third class; when we were flush, we took trains instead of buses. Hardly the front-cabin airplane seats I shared with Quentin."

"That's the material side. I was thinking more of the emotional side," said Harry. "Were you close?"

He does know how to interview a suspect. Sharon didn't think of Leigh as a suspect, really, but why did she feel Leigh had purposely evaded Harry's question? Was it her downcast eyes?

"Quentin was most reserved when it came to emotions; unless he was angry, and then he let it all out."

"In what way did he 'let it all out'?" Harry asked sharply, shooting a sideways glance at his partner.

"Would you all like a cup of tea?" asked Leigh, reaching for a bell pull. "I'm feeling quite parched."

Sharon smiled, her eyes on Leigh Pryor. "Ma'am, you were about to tell us about Quentin's temper, how he acted when he was angry."

Sharon felt uncomfortable balancing the thin porcelain cup. She didn't really like tea, but she sipped the hot liquid as she waited for Leigh's reply.

"Nothing, really." Leigh picked at invisible lint on her blouse. "I didn't mean to imply anything. Just a husband's venting to his wife when things didn't go well at the office."

"Did the two of you ever argue over money?" asked Harry.

Leigh's gaze narrowed slightly. "Why would we? We had plenty of it."

Harry cleared his throat. "What I mean is…what about a prenuptial agreement?"

"I beg your pardon?"

"When you married Quentin, did you sign a prenuptial agreement?"

"Er, uh, yes. I did. Wha—What is it about it you want to know?" Leigh seemed bewildered by the question.

"Why did you *agree* to sign it?" Sharon couldn't hide her tone, even if it elicited Harry's frown. Logically, she *knew* that legal documents were needed to protect children and rightful fortunes; still, she couldn't help but feel that prenuptial agreements were barbaric, insulting, and demeaning. Marriage should be founded on trust. If he didn't trust her, he shouldn't have asked her to marry him. Both would be at fault if it didn't work out. Why should one person—usually the woman—be punished and devalued in the dissolution?

"We were engaged to be wed. I loved and trusted Quentin. He said the agreement was necessary to protect his children's interest in his estate." She glanced at each of the deputies in turn. "He said it would protect *my* assets, too." She shook her head as if to clear it. "Why? Should I have refused to sign?"

Instead of answering Leigh's question, Harry posed another. "How long is it effective?"

"Why, I don't know. I assume for the whole time we were married—and in case we divorced, of course."

"You assume. You haven't read it?" Harry's voice dripped disbelief.

"No. We were in the midst of last-minute wedding preparations when Quentin told me about it. We dashed into his lawyer's office and I signed where they told me to."

"The lawyer didn't read it to you or suggest you needed your own lawyer?"

"He started to, but Quentin said he had already discussed it with me, so it wasn't necessary."

"And you signed it then?" Sharon's voice squeaked.

"I trusted Quentin. Why?"

Harry shifted forward and cleared his throat. "Ma'am, uh...Mrs. Pryor, your husband's death is now being investigated as a homicide."

Leigh's cup clattered in its saucer. "Homicide? Are you saying someone killed Quentin? Why would anyone want to do that?" She covered her face with her hands and bent over sobbing.

"That's the question we wanted to ask you." Harry paused. "Did your husband have any enemies?"

Chapter 111

TAYLOR WRAPPED HERSELF in a soft bathrobe. The hot shower had felt good after her traumatic phone call today at the store. Fortunately, she'd kept herself busy so she wouldn't have too much time to obsess over it. She shuffled her feet into bunny slippers. This was going to be a pamper night. Warm soup and then to bed with the romance novel Carol had brought her.

Carol called romances her escape, her salvation. Taylor definitely wasn't in the mood for reading anything serious. Not even a murder mystery. Would she ever enjoy a murder mystery again?

Absorbed in her book, Taylor reached for the ringing phone. "H-H-Hello?"

A dreaded silence followed. It couldn't be. A call to the store she could *try* to write off. A call to her home…

"Wha— Wha— Who is this?" Nothing. "It's you, isn't it?" she squeaked before she could stop herself. The line went dead.

Taylor crumpled onto the bed, her whole body shaking violently. She pulled her knees to her chest, trying to stop the pain in her stomach.

Even though she'd just showered, Taylor went to the bathroom and ran a hot bath, hoping it would calm her. She was frantic. Had she said his name out loud? Had he heard her? What had she done?

She decided she couldn't sit still long enough to take a bath and opened the drain. She was wasting water, but that was a small guilt compared to what she felt about Marshall.

Who had she become? Why had he forced her to do this? Taylor yanked the sash of her robe so tight she gasped. She sobbed into her hands. She had no one to blame but herself for her misery.

The night before their wedding, Marshall had been so possessive, so intolerant of her speaking to other men at the rehearsal dinner. *I knew. I knew.* Taylor wanted to shake herself for being such an idiot. *But I was so enamored of what he said he was. And I didn't want to let our families down. Besides, I thought marriage was the ultimate in happiness. Thought he would change, become sure of me. God, how I regret that. No, I take that back. This agony of a marriage brought me two lovely children.* She clawed at her robe and threw it on the bed. She was sweating all over.

But dammit—he stole the store from me! How could he, when he knew it meant the world to me? Did I kill him over just a business? No. He'd also hit her, hurt her badly. Taylor bit her cuticle, what was left of it. If only she had someone to discuss this rock-hard guilt and fear with!

Taylor called herself a pacifist, but she lied. She was a murderer. Engaging the OC—Erin—to eradicate Marshall. Compared to the boulder in her gut, the relief she felt—or was waiting to feel, she thought ruefully—about Marshall's death was gravel underfoot.

Taylor's thoughts returned to the ominous phone call. Was it someone who saw what happened? Could she have the call traced? She'd have to call Mora immediately.

Taylor reached down and closed the bathtub drain. Half the water was still there. She'd take her bath. She felt gritty and grimy. Ever since Marshall had disappeared, she'd washed her hands over and over, compulsively. It was never enough.

Chapter 112

PADDING BAREFOOT into the kitchen, Mora poured herself a glass of Merlot. She'd had a hectic Sunday: two new women who needed shelter, her beach walk with Erin, a flat tire with the long wait for the AAA truck—all on top of her worry about Taylor's mysterious phone calls.

Was it *actually* possible Marshall had survived his trip over the falls and phoned Taylor? Or was Taylor's post-op remorse causing delusions? Whichever—it threatened the Outreach Committee. Taylor was overwrought, which made her at risk for disclosing confidential information.

Mora reached for the phone to call her co-chairman, knocking over her wine in the process. "Oh, God in Heaven. What else can go wrong?" Grabbing a wad of napkins from the counter, she mopped the blood-red liquid as it dripped from the counter to the floor.

As she picked up her cell phone, it vibrated in her hand. Who would be calling her private line? It didn't bode well.

"Mora Rey here."

"Mora, it's Leigh. I have some simply awful news to tell you. Can you come to call?"

Chapter 113

Monday morning, Leigh Pryor pulled into a slot in the underground parking garage. *You are going to get through this,* she counseled herself. *You are not going to cry. And you are not going to be bullied by that little man, Doth— like you were when you signed the prenuptial agreement.*

Leigh cleared her throat and straightened her shoulders as the elevator took her to the floor that housed the law offices. By the time the lift stopped, she was feeling strong enough to get through the encounter. It was like preparing for a premiere. She had no choice but to be perfect in her performance. If not, the consequences could be…she couldn't allow herself to think about that.

"Leigh Pryor to see Mr. Doth," she said quietly to the receptionist.

"Yes, Mrs. Pryor. My condolences on your loss. Mr. Doth asked that I take you to the conference room; he'll be with you shortly." As they reached the beige-and-white-appointed room, she inquired, "Would you like some coffee?"

"I'd prefer tea. Earl Grey, please."

The receptionist's smile turned friendly. "My favorite. I'll be back with it in just a moment." At least she wasn't a prune like her boss.

Sipping her tea, Leigh continued to fight her internal demons. The deputies were coming to this will reading; if she inherited something, would they arrest her?

Leigh had purposely arrived early in hopes of speaking with Doth privately. She was still adding to her list of questions when he entered. She did not rise but offered him a graceful hand, with a smile.

"My dear Mrs. Pryor, I am so sorry for your loss. Please let me express my deepest sympathy." Doth extended a damp hand to meet hers. He turned and sat opposite Leigh, centering a thick folder precisely in front of him. "How have you been doing?"

Leigh would have welcomed the question if she thought it was sincere.

"I'm getting through this."

"That's good." Doth cleared his throat. "I have Quentin's estate papers here and I'll go through each one of them and answer any questions you may have about them." He coughed. "But we'll wait for everyone to arrive before we start. That way, you will all get the same information at once." He folded his hands on top of the file and looked out the window.

Drat! Leigh had been hoping to finagle a sneak preview out of him to help her retain her composure later in front of the sheriffs.

The receptionist poked her head in the door. "Mr. Doth: Miss Pryor, Mr. Pryor the Third, and two deputies from the Los Angeles County Sheriff are here. Shall I show them in?"

"Yes, please."

Leigh's heart beat a staccato rhythm. Mora would know how a widow *should* act at a meeting like this. If only she'd been free to come. Too late now. Leigh was on her own. She patted her face with her handkerchief.

Adrienne marched into the room, a queen expecting all deference. Her half-brother followed, strolling. Quentin's daughter took the chair at the head of the table; Three sat next to Leigh. Leigh welcomed his show of support for her, little as it was.

The deputies sat together next to Doth, opposite Leigh. Sharon spoke first. "You all may want to know why Deputy Adler and I are here." She glanced around the room. "We're here because Quentin Pryor's death *has* been ruled a probable homicide. The will contents could have bearing on our investigation."

Leigh nodded her agreement, ever so slightly, as Quentin the Third sat stone-faced and Adrienne shot Leigh a none-too-veiled dirty look.

Guess she's not bothered by what the deputies think, mused Leigh. But fear gripped her. Adrienne had always disliked her—been jealous of her relationship with Quentin. Would she cause even further trouble? *If only this meeting, this day, this month, were over!*

Doth opened the folder in front of him and cleared his throat.

"I don't think there will be much to talk about, Mr. Doth," Leigh cut in. "You remember, I'm sure, that I signed a prenuptial agreement the day before Quentin and I were married. I would just like you to explain to me how much of my own money I am left with, so I can make plans for going back to work, moving, et cetera."

Leigh wanted to make very sure the deputies knew she wasn't after Quentin's money. She tensed as she saw them exchange a look.

Doth tilted his head and looked over his glasses at the widow. "Surely you remembered," he said.

"Remembered what?" Leigh frowned. "Remembered that I was too much in love to think that anything could happen to our marriage? That I was too naïve to expect I had any rights in our marriage, or upon a divorce? Of course I remember." Leigh flushed. Had she really said all that out loud—in front of Quentin's children? And the deputies? She folded her hands and looked down at her lap.

Doth glanced at the deputies and then cleared his throat. "Mrs. Pryor, the details of Quentin's estate will *all* be revealed very shortly."

Doth cleared his throat again and looked around the room. "The deceased's CPA and I have reviewed Mr. Pryor's entire estate and we have determined that his assets—including his residence, his other real estate holdings, his considerable stock and bond investments, bank accounts, works of art, and his automobiles—total approximately twenty-one million dollars."

Leigh saw Adrienne's head jerk up. Her face flushed and her eyes sparkled. "That's more than I estimated."

The deputies again exchanged glances.

I wonder how much of that is what I brought to the marriage. Will I get any of it? Given the situation, Leigh no longer even knew what to hope would happen.

"Per Quentin Pryor's will," Doth continued, "the amount of ten thousand dollars will be given to his son, Quentin Pryor the Third."

Three's face flushed, but he continued to draw circles on his notepad and didn't respond.

"The balance—minus the estate taxes. And of course, attorneys' fees..." Adrienne rolled her eyes. "...will be split evenly between his daughter, Miss Adrienne Pryor, and his wife, Leigh Pryor."

"What?!" Adrienne's cry rang out.

"Pardon me, Mr. Doth," Leigh interrupted. "But wh—"

Doth held up his hand for silence. Leigh bit her trembling lip. Adrienne stood as though to leave, then sat back down.

"I know she signed that prenuptial agreement," Adrienne said more calmly. "*I* insisted on it."

"True," said Doth. "However, Mrs. Pryor's prenuptial agreement with Quentin Pryor expired two months before his death."

Leigh felt the blood rush from her face. This couldn't be.

Doth coughed behind a pasty white hand. "California is a community property state. A legal spouse, according to state law, absent a prenuptial agreement or a bequest giving more, is entitled to fifty percent of the deceased spouse's estate." He paused and his lips cracked into a feeble smile. He glanced at the deputies again. "The only exclusion, of course, would be if the surviving spouse were convicted of murdering the other."

Chapter 114

THAT SPITEFUL LITTLE MAN. Who does he think he is—suggesting I murdered Quentin? Leigh felt her heart thump so hard it could break through her ribs. She gasped and raised a hand to cover her mouth. *That's why the deputies were asking me about the prenup! I wish Mora were here; she could tell me if I needed a lawyer.*

Leigh lowered her hand and tried to use her expert acting skills to hide her emotions. She'd had extra practice with that, playing the perfect hostess for Quentin while suffering from his latest attack. She focused on looking surprised, which was not too difficult.

"You incompetent bastard!" Adrienne jumped from her chair so forcefully that it toppled onto the plush carpet. "Why didn't you remind my father of the upcoming expiration and make him renew it? I'll sue you for malpractice—you can count on that!"

Doth looked down at his folded hands.

"And you, you murdering bitch!" She turned her venom toward Leigh. "Why, I'll—" Adrienne stopped midsentence, as though suddenly remembering the deputies' presence.

Leigh saw Sharon raise an eyebrow at Harry, who nodded but said nothing.

"Mrs. Pryor, Leigh," Doth continued as though the interruption hadn't occurred, "since the will noted your rights in accordance with the prenuptial agreement, and not after, we will have to go to probate court for you each to obtain your rightful share."

Leigh struggled to take in what the lawyer was saying. Suddenly she felt the tension leave her neck; her shoulders drooped. She wouldn't be homeless after all! She could live anywhere she pleased— even go back to London.

She hesitated, not wanting to seem too eager. "That will take a spell, won't it?"

"Yes, but since I have handled Quentin's affairs for some time, I can do it as expeditiously as possible, I'm sure." Doth smiled and patted her hand. "I'll see if we can arrange a loan with the bank against the estate, for your living expenses until probate is settled." He leaned forward. "You do realize that some of the assets may have to be sold to divide the estate and/or to cover estate taxes?" He reached for a brief. "I have here an engagement letter for you to sign, so that it will be official that I represent you, as well as your husband's estate." He placed the documents in front of Leigh and handed her a pen. He turned to Adrienne. "I have a similar document for your signature, as well."

"Thank you," said Leigh. "I'll take these with me to read before I sign." She smiled at his sour expression. "I'm sure you counsel all new widows not to sign anything without reviewing it first."

The dour man nodded. "We'll need to get started as soon as possible, though."

"I'll be in touch with you soon," said Leigh. *I probably should hire him,* she thought, *since he's so familiar with Quentin's affairs with the bank. And thankfully, Quentin can't control him from the grave.* But she definitely wanted the BWEF legal expert to check out the papers before she signed.

Adrienne turned to the deputies. "Why aren't you arresting her? It's obvious she did this!" Adrienne pointed at Leigh. "You dancing witch! Not only do you steal Father from me, you murder him and steal half of his money!" Adrienne Pryor's angry fist pounded the table. "You were a destitute has-been dancer when you married Father for his money. That's *why* he demanded the prenup. He *told* me how he had to threaten to not marry you to get you to sign it." The distraught woman stood and leaned over the table, her face close to Leigh's. "Murderer!" she shouted.

Leigh sat rock-still as spittle hit her face.

Chapter 115

TIRED FROM DRIVING ALL DAY, Sharon stuffed files into her desk and locked it. The hot bath she'd promised herself beckoned. She groaned as Harry approached with his "I have a great idea" look.

"Let's discuss and update our suspect matrix," said Harry, pointing to the whiteboard. "We should be able to eliminate several."

Sharon looked at her watch. "But...I...Oh, okay, discuss away."

"I investigated Angelo's alibi and it checks out. He had his crews working late on Saturday to make up time. You can erase him." Sharon drew a line through the builder's name. She wasn't about to *erase* anyone until the case was dropped.

"Kyle Norbest's roommate says he and Kyle were hiking on Mount Gorgonio the whole day Quentin was sailing. Kyle showed me a dinner receipt from Palm Springs for that night." Sharon struck through his name.

"Anyone else?" Sharon rolled her neck and then her shoulders. God, she needed that hot water.

"Mr. Three had weekend duty at the halfway house. He couldn't leave between Friday evening at six and Sunday at eight."

"I'm glad," said Sharon. "I like him for some reason."

"Well, he does seem the most down-to-earth of the bunch," agreed Harry. "Besides, if he wanted to do in dear old Dad, I'm guessing he would have done it long ago. I don't see any incentive *now*."

Sharon crossed off Quentin Pryor III.

"Can we eliminate Leigh yet?" Sharon cocked her head and pursed her lips, awaiting Harry's response. "In addition to her having an alibi, I was watching her at the will reading; she was as shocked as daughter Adrienne that the prenup had expired!"

"I agree Adrienne was shocked. But remember, Leigh's been on the stage." He shook his head. "If she *did* know about the prenup, she had a couple of weeks to practice her surprised act."

"Fine." Sharon slumped in her chair. "At this point, you won't drop her from the list 'til the very end just to annoy me."

Harry raised his lips in a half-smile but didn't confirm or deny. "It's been a long day, partner. Why don't you go on home." He patted stacked files on his desk and grimaced. "I'm going to stay a while, finish up this paperwork. Tomorrow, I want you to talk to Leigh about Loretta's affair with Quentin."

"But what if she doesn't know about it? That's a terrible thing to tell a new widow."

"You apologize to her." He patted Sharon on the back. "Look, it can't be avoided—if you're going to do your job."

Chapter 116

LEIGH SIPPED HER MORNING TEA on the patio, fretting. At the BWEF financial counselor's suggestion, she had called Doth to discuss her inheritance. But didn't that make her seem greedy to get Quentin's money? And therefore more of a suspect? But, Carol had reminded her, she also needed to act how a normal widow would act.

Why, oh why, couldn't Quentin's death have just been ruled an accident like the OC women had said it would be? Would she be looking over her shoulder for the rest of her life? She sighed. *At least I have an airtight alibi. But what about Erin? And Taylor?*

Leigh forced herself to focus on her impending appointment with Doth—bringing on a new set of worries. Leigh hadn't thought about money for the five years that she and Quentin had been married. Even before their marriage, he had refused to discuss finances with her, except to ask her to sign documents. Right now, she didn't even know how much money was in their checking account that he'd balanced every month.

Leigh assumed, from her outburst in the lawyer's office, that Quentin's daughter would challenge the will. Leigh scrunched up her face. So plebian, fighting over money. Maybe she should just let Adrienne have it. That might help alleviate suspicion, too.

But wait a minute. Leigh *had* contributed towards the house, and she had added her antiques, bought before the marriage. Surely, she would win at least those. But how could she prove anything? Besides, didn't she deserve to be left with *something* for putting up with Quentin's abuse all these years? She couldn't mention *that,* of course.

The worried woman looked up as Cook approached. "Miss Leigh, Deputy Sharon Collins is here to see you."

Startled, Leigh broke out in a full body sweat. Wiping her forehead with a napkin, she jumped to her feet.

Sharon followed Cook onto the patio.

Why is Leigh sweating? Sharon had purposely come early to catch Leigh off guard. Seems like she'd succeeded.

"Good morning, Mrs. Pryor. I hope you have a few minutes to talk with me." Sharon put a hand on Cook's arm. "I'd like to chat with you before I leave, too."

The cook glanced over at Leigh, as though seeking permission from her employer. The two seemed to share a silent communication—but about what she wasn't sure—before the cook nodded at her.

"Of course, Deputy," said Leigh, rising. "How can we be of assistance?" Leigh wiped her hand on the leg of her white sharkskin trousers and shook Sharon's hand. She motioned toward an ochre wicker chair with yellow cushions. "Please, have a seat." Leigh grabbed a stack of rumpled newspapers from the seat and handed it to the housekeeper. "I'm sure Sharon would appreciate some coffee, Cookie. Oh, and please bring us some grapes from the fruit bowl."

Sharon nodded her thanks as the elderly woman smiled pleasantly and turned toward the kitchen.

Sharon scooted her chair around so she could face Leigh squarely. She waited until Leigh quit adjusting her clothes and settled back.

It didn't feel right to confront the Loretta issue so suddenly. Best ease into the conversation—start with something more familiar.

"Leigh, I'm a champion of the BWEF," Sharon began. "I've stayed in one of their shelters, and I send women to them." Sharon sat back with her arms relaxed on the chair arms but not taking her eyes off Leigh. "I sometimes attend their group sessions on developing self-confidence."

Leigh picked at a thread on her blue silk tunic.

Sharon leaned forward, trying to connect with her interviewee. "Sometimes I still find it hard to believe in myself. I attend the classes for the same reason an alcoholic attends AA—for reinforcement and support from others in the group, others who understand where I'm coming from."

Boy, am I chattering on. Sharon stopped herself. *Maybe Harry's tactic of silence would work better here—like it had with Loretta.* Sharon grimaced at the thought.

Leigh pulled on her sleeve, still avoiding her visitor's gaze. "I myself am just learning about the shelters," she finally said. "And the services the BWEF offers." She looked up at Sharon, her face earnest. "How long did you stay in one? Was it wretched being around so many women who'd been abused?"

"No, ma'am." Sharon addressed the latter question. "It was solace to feel so safe, and away from the horror of my ex's abuse. I didn't have to explain to the others what I'd been through—they *knew!*" Sharon settled back into the cushions of the comfortable chair and smiled fondly. "I particularly liked the change in my children, seeing them relax and laugh again. They made new friends real easy."

Leigh smiled wistfully. "Quentin and I have no children. I love kids, and I thought Quentin did, too…until after we married." She spoke almost as though in a trance. "Oh, forgive me, Sharon!" she said with a start. "Here I am taking up your valuable time reminiscing. Did you want something special this morning?" She frowned at her watch. "I don't mean to be impolite, but I'm due at the gym to teach a dance class today."

Time to do my job, as Harry says. "Yes. As a matter of fact, I did," Sharon said. "A couple things."

Leigh looked at her expectantly.

"I heard of the Outreach Committee when I was in the shelter, because of the marathon." Sharon nodded her thanks to Cook for the coffee, added sugar, and stirred it in. Hands cupped around the china cup, she continued, "Frankly, I'm curious to learn more about it. You're on that committee, aren't you?"

Leigh tapped her lips with a napkin and folded her arms. "I'm not sure that I'm a proper member. I began sitting in on board meetings when my husband became the BWEF Finance Chair." Leigh shrugged and spread her hands. "I'd call me…an intern." She shook her head. "I really don't know much about it yet." Her hands shook as she reached for the cordless phone next to her on an end table. "Carol or Mora could tell you more. I'll call them."

"Don't bother; I can talk to them later," said Sharon.

Ignoring the deputy, Leigh punched in a phone number and looked up at Sharon as she waited for a response. "Please forgive my nervousness," she said. "I just made an appointment with Quentin's accountant to discuss the disposition of his estate, and I'm simply a basket case. There's just so much to think about—budgets and all."

Sharon nodded, silently pondering what it would be like to have an "estate."

"Mora, I'm relieved you're home." Leigh hesitated with the phone to her ear, listening. "Oh, nothing's wrong, really. It's just that Sharon Collins—you know, the deputy sheriff—is here. She'd like to know more about the Outreach Committee, and I feel I'm too new to it to be accurate about what we do." She turned from the instrument. "If you can stay a few moments, Mora can pop right over. She lives nearby."

Sharon would have preferred to get Leigh's take all on her own, but it obviously wasn't going to happen. She nodded her assent.

"Come 'round." Leigh spoke into the receiver. "Bring Carol, too. Cook has just brewed some coffee."

Leigh hung up the phone and turned to Sharon. "Mora and Carol were working together on the agenda for the next committee meeting. They'll be here shortly." She looked at her watch. "I still have a few moments before I must prepare for the dance lesson."

"While we're waiting, I have something else to ask you about." Sharon looked at her notebook, trying to word her question gently. "I understand you know Loretta Wilson from your husband's office?"

"Yes, of course." Leigh's head bobbed. "She's lent a hand sometimes in entertaining Quentin's clients and business associates at the house."

"What were your husband's feelings about her?"

"His feelings? I'm sure I don't know. He didn't much discuss his feelings—about anything." Leigh squinted at Sharon. "Your question is unusual. Why do you ask it?"

Sharon took a full breath. "I was just wondering if what Ms. Wilson told us is true: that she and your husband were lovers."

Leigh leapt up, her teacup falling and shattering on the concrete. "No! That is *not* true."

Sharon studied the new widow while Cook swept the broken china into a dustpan and brought another cup. Leigh seemed genuinely shocked by Loretta's affair with Quentin. Or was it surprise that the sheriffs had discovered the motive behind her husband's murder?

"Most wives suspect when their husbands are having an affair. You didn't?" Sharon asked.

Leigh blotted a cut on her finger from the broken cup. "N-no. I didn't."

"You saw no change in his lovemaking that might indicate an affair: decreased frequency, demands for new positions, complaints about your ability to please him?" Sharon hated asking these questions; a woman's sex life was so much a part of her core, it should be hers alone.

Leigh's head jerked up and she stared unseeing at Sharon. She spoke as if in a trance. "Well, yes, I saw all those things, but..."

"But?"

"His age and all. I thought it was natural, or he was getting ED, you know?"

"Did he ever compare you to Loretta?" Sharon couldn't help thinking that Quentin was a fool if he found Loretta more attractive than Leigh.

Leigh shook her head. "No. He only mentioned her when we were planning a social affair she would help with."

Sharon believed her.

"Can you suggest a reason for Loretta to *lie* about having an affair with Quentin?"

"He could be very charming when he wanted something, so…"

"So, what?"

"So maybe she's in love with him and fantasizing about it." Leigh paused, looking confused and sad. She looked up at Sharon. "I guess I should say she *was* in love with him."

Chapter 117

"MORA, CAROL, thanks for coming." Leigh's spirits rose. Mora knew how to handle people and Carol was a great observer. "Sharon was asking questions I plain couldn't answer." *And I was scared I'd sic her on all of us if I said the wrong thing.*

Mora sat down next to Sharon. "How can I help you?"

"Tell me about the Outreach Committee," said Sharon, when drinks had been served. "I talked to Matron yesterday afternoon, at my old shelter in Torrance—but she couldn't tell me anything."

Leigh felt her stomach churn, her hands sweating again.

Mora sipped from the rose-patterned Havilland cup and waved her hand. "*That's* no surprise. The Outreach Committee doesn't work with the shelters. We use *other* avenues to help women who refuse to go to a shelter—for whatever reason."

Leigh relaxed into the soft cushion behind her. She knew Mora could handle the situation.

Mora set her cup on its saucer and continued, "I'm sure you already know how hard it is to convince some women to leave their abusive husbands." Leigh looked down at her hands. She was one of those. "And to the women we help, whose husbands have exceptional influence, status is often more important than their health."

"It's part of the abuse cycle," added Carol. "The woman thinks she's useless without her husband. I'm sure you know about that too, unfortunately."

Sharon nodded. "When you're told every day you're worthless, you don't think about yourself," she agreed. "Just tiptoe around so you won't trigger an attack."

As the other three women commiserated and shared sympathetic looks, Leigh worked hard to keep her own expression neutral.

"So tell me, how is working with these women different? The wealthy ones with powerful husbands." Sharon looked at her ragged fingernails and then up at Mora. "I'm afraid I'm not in that league."

"Unfortunately, powerful men get to be so partly because of their extensive network of other powerful men. In spite of all of the precautions the BWEF takes, we find that forceful, wealthy men have the influence in the community to ferret out the location of a seemingly secure shelter. They also have the wherewithal to hire detectives to track down their wives."

"For example," Mora continued, "if your husband was abusing you and he was a business acquaintance of Quentin's, he'd call Quentin—the honorary BWEF Finance Chair—for the location of the shelters. And he'd get it, in return for unspecified future favors, despite Quentin's pledge of confidentiality." She shot Leigh an apologetic look and sighed. "Unfortunately, both would consider the information exchange a normal, and expected, part of their business relationship."

Sharon nodded. "That *does* make sense. Who are your committee members?"

"Carol and I are the most active. Once we help a battered woman escape from her uniquely connected husband, we ask her to serve on the committee for a time to reach out to others in the same situation. Our membership changes as those we help conclude their active participation—though we may occasionally call them back for special contributions, like presenting financial planning seminars. The committee and victims both benefit from this structure because the newest members relate most readily to the raw emotions that the victims are experiencing." Mora turned to her hostess. "Then we have honorary members like Leigh. She joined us when Quentin did." She patted Leigh's arm. "She's added a lot to the committee."

Sharon turned in her chair to face Leigh who had stood to replenish her cup. "Because, of course, Quentin didn't abuse *you,* right?"

Leigh felt her face flush. "I should think not, deputy. What an idea!" She feigned laughter and retrieved a linen handkerchief from her pocket to dab at her eyes. "And of course, we attended meetings *together!*"

Sharon squinted, and then nodded at the dancer.

"But *you* were married to an abusive spouse?" Sharon turned to Mora.

Leigh let out an internal sigh.

Mora frowned. "Unfortunately, yes. Actually, that's why I became active in the BWEF, why Carol and I started the Outreach Committee."

"These men aren't used to failure," Carol explained. "Don't accept it in themselves or others. Their underlings follow their every command."

"But, your husband is dead?" Mora nodded. Sharon turned to Carol. "And yours?"

"Actually, our husbands died two years apart." Carol looked down at her lap. "But…we remember."

Mora added milk to her coffee and sipped. Her smile disappeared. "We keep a close eye on wives of men who appear to the community to be outstanding citizens. To detect which ones are living a lie." She set down her cup. "We approach the wives and try to help them."

"So, I'm curious," said Sharon. "If these women don't go to shelters, how do you help them?"

"Ahh," said Mora. Leigh held her breath. "Well, first, we get them away from their abusive husbands," Mora continued without missing a beat, "to a second home owned by one of us, an out-of-the-way hotel, or a school, for example. Then we help them understand their options. We have a string of adjunct members who counsel these women on *their* role in the abusive cycle and how they can move away from that way of life: job searches, divorce, finances, investments, real estate, and if they have kids, parenting concerns."

"Do many of them have kids?"

"Not really. Regardless of abuse, women in higher social circles tend to have fewer children. Their husbands, and *they,* generally prefer to keep the attention—and money—for themselves."

Sharon shot a glance at Leigh. Must be hard—married to a man like that—if you weren't in total agreement. She couldn't imagine her own life without Cailin and Mikey.

Sharon turned her attention back to Carol and Mora. "I admire you two," she said. "You don't have to work; you have everything and could be out playing golf or bridge every day. But you choose instead to help others." Sharon smiled at each of the women in turn. "I don't know what would have become of me and my kids if it weren't for the BWEF shelter." Carol and Mora sat back in their chairs. "Can you refer me to some clients you've helped?"

Leigh saw Mora and Carol exchange a glance.

Mora inhaled deeply before speaking. "Because of their public and prominent circumstances, we've promised them anonymity if they work with us. If our clients and purpose were known, we'd be less effective in our social circle." Mora rose to pass the fruit bowl. "I hope you understand, Sharon." She paused, frowning. "Not to mention, of course, that they're all quite ashamed. Here they are— or were—successful entrepreneurs, business executives, athletes. It's hard for them to admit to *anyone* that they were emotionally insecure enough to suffer an abusive spouse. That's a long explanation, I know, Sharon. But we feel our insistence on confidentiality *is* necessary."

Sharon did not respond immediately. "If it weren't for my job, I could agree wholeheartedly," she finally said. She squirmed in her chair. "However, I hope you understand that I can't let my own memories of abuse cloud my thinking."

As the women nodded, Leigh shifted uneasily.

"For now, I'll honor what I feel is a valid concern for privacy," Sharon said. "But if I need more specific information later, I'll have to ask you to cooperate."

"Of course, deputy," said Mora. "We appreciate your sensitivity."

Sharon nodded and rose to leave. "Thanks. I admire the work that the BWEF does. And next time I see Matron, I'll be sure to relay what you told me. I know she'll be pleased."

As Leigh escorted the deputy to the kitchen to talk with Cook, she felt as though she'd spent the morning rehearsing a three-act ballet. Hopefully Cook wouldn't trip up her part!

Ignoring the rattles of her aged car as she drove home, Sharon thought about her visit to the Pryor home. Were there really that many abusive men in the affluent executive population of the Los Angeles area? And did Leigh suspect Quentin's affair with Loretta in spite of her denial? And then there was Cook: Why was *she* so evasive when asked if the marriage was a happy one? Or about Quentin's feelings for his wife? That looming home did seem to hold a lot of secrets.

Sharon's thoughts turned toward the institution of marriage. Were any of the women on the Outreach Committee remarried? And what about herself: Would *she* ever be able to trust a man enough to form a loving relationship again?

Things seemed to be on hold with Ernest—though he was being beyond patient with her. She had to ask herself: Was she *really* too busy with this investigation to move the relationship forward—or was she using it as an excuse to avoid getting close?

Chapter 118

LUCKY HAD A NEW FACE, but he needed to search out his old identity—his real one. He admired the surgeon's handiwork in the bathroom mirror: smooth skin, fading scars, straight nose. His eyes were the only thing that hadn't been reconstructed; he stared into them long and hard trying to remember what he used to look like. Finally, he gave up. He couldn't do anything about what he saw in the mirror, so he'd just accept the new Lucky.

But, God, how he hated that name! He'd have to make one up soon if he didn't find out who he was. What about Adam? That signified a new beginning, didn't it? He liked the sound of it. Almost familiar. Adam Marsh. That's what he'd call himself.

His memory was returning in the tiniest of bits. Last week, when he'd called a remembered phone number, the woman had seemed distraught. Could it be because she was missing someone—him? It sounded like the same woman who'd hung up on him at Wilderness Outfitters. She had the same stutter. But if she *were* looking for him, why would she hang up? *Damn!* He wanted to bang his head against the wall.

He flexed his arm muscles. The workout in the gym had brought back that old feeling of being fit. And a readiness to fight. *Yes!* Fighting back was the answer. It was time he stopped being a charity case and faced the future.

The past is past. I can't change what I don't know. Time I moved on. As of today, I'm starting life anew as Adam Lucky Marsh.

Chapter 119

THE NEXT MORNING, Lucky reluctantly bade goodbye to the doctors and nurses at the small hospital that had been his home for three months. Physically, he felt recovered, and he itched to get outdoors.

The psychologist had advised against this bus trip to the Los Angeles area. She'd said the city was so big and sprawling that it might only confuse him instead of clarifying his background. But so what if the trip didn't bring back more memories? At least he wouldn't be wasting time *thinking* about a wrong path.

He didn't have a lot of money with him but enough to get by—with what he'd made doing odd jobs at the ranger station and the hospital.

He still worried that he had done something to deserve all that had happened to him. He hadn't mentioned Wilderness Outfitters to the lady shrink. If the answers he found there incriminated him, he didn't want any links from the new "Adam" to his old identity's crime.

Perhaps he'd robbed the place and that's where his cash had come from. Just in case, he'd better go armed. He'd buy a good knife at that sporting goods store near the bus depot; a man shouldn't be without one. And maybe he could pick up some wood chunks to whittle.

Chapter 120

SHARON SMILED AT CAILIN as her daughter sat down to breakfast across from her. "Cheerleading practice today?" At least Cailin was keeping up in school. The breakup with Paul hadn't sent her into a tailspin.

"Mom! I told you! Today is the tryout for next year. For the football season."

Sharon smiled. "It must be so embarrassing to have a mom who's so out of it." She smoothed her daughter's bangs back and kissed her forehead. "Got the grumps this morning?"

"No. Why do I have to be pleasant all the—" She stopped and hugged her mother. "I'm nervous, that's all."

"About?"

"Paul is the team captain, so he's on the review committee."

"He hasn't been bothering you, has he?"

"I haven't seen him, except in class, and I leave the room in the opposite direction so I don't have to talk to him." She held back a sob. "Mom, he told the other guys on the basketball team that I was so cold to him I was probably a lesbian."

Sharon's guilt returned. If only she'd left Sean earlier. Her daughter might have a better sense of self. Stand up to Paul.

"Oh, honey. That hurts: to have someone you loved talk about you that way." Sharon knew the hurt never went away completely. It stayed around like an aching muscle—flaring up, disappearing for a while, only to come back stronger than before.

"But this one guy on the team, Dave, told Paul that he didn't believe him and they aren't friends anymore."

Sharon pumped her arm.

"Paul's digging himself into a hole, honey. He knows what he did to you is wrong." Sharon sat down. "Are any of your girlfriends dating Paul? Is he behaving himself?"

Cailin shook her head. "He asked a couple of them, but they said they were my friend and didn't think it was fair to date him when I'd been dating him." She paused. "I think they suspect what he did, although I wouldn't tell them."

Sharon hugged her daughter.

"You're well rid of him. I'm so sorry this had to happen, but I'm proud of the way you're handling this, young-un. It's mature and reasonable." Sharon's face broke into a teasing smile. "Did this Dave ask you for a date?"

"Not yet, Mom, but I think he might." Cailin crossed her fingers.

"Do I know him? What's his last name?" After the Paul episode, Sharon vowed to keep a closer tab on her daughter's friends.

"Dave Johnson. He's in the band and on the track team." Cailin's eyes glowed as she talked about her new friend. "Everyone says he's a brain. He says he's not, but he wants to be a physicist." She stumbled over the unfamiliar word.

"Maybe he can help you with your science project!"

Chapter 121

LUCKY *FELT* LUCKY this morning. *Adam,* he reminded himself proudly. The bus trip to Los Angeles had brought him on familiar roads. He'd even been able to point out upcoming landmarks to his seatmate.

Now, standing before Wilderness Outfitters, he had the distinct feeling that he had once *owned* the store and it had been stolen from him. From his vantage across the street, he considered the banner hanging over the front entrance: *ANNIVERSARY SALE! Help us celebrate 35 years in business and save on supplies for your next adventure!* Thirty-five, huh? Adam didn't even know how old *he* was.

Wishing he were back in the cocoon of the hospital, he willed himself to take the next step to finding out more. As he started across Pacific Coast Highway with the light, the front door to the shop opened, and he immediately pulled back to the sidewalk.

He watched as a blond woman entered the store: Erin C. from the website! His body grasped something else about her, though. It reacted with a tremor from his hair to his toes. She was a danger to him, for sure.

And her name *wasn't* Erin—it was Eve. She'd tried to kill him.

Adam's mind whirled. What had he done to make this woman want to kill him? Maybe he'd raped her. If he did, how could he live with himself?

He plotted his next move. He *had* to find out who this Eve, Erin—whatever—was. He called a cab and waited in it at the curb until he saw the blonde exit the store.

"There she is. We're going to follow her."

"You must really like this babe, mister."

They followed her to a home in Torrance. God, this was going to cost him. He instructed the driver to wait around the corner, so he could peek in her mailbox without being seen and find out her last name. *Damn!* She was emptying it from her car!

He'd have to find another way.

"Pick me up here tomorrow morning at eight."

He didn't care *what* it cost.

Chapter 122

ADAM SPENT THE NIGHT on a series of benches along Torrance Beach, moving each time he saw headlights approaching. He made his way back to the blonde's house in the morning and climbed into the waiting cab.

"I hope you're not some freaky stalker, buddy. I could be in real trouble for helping you."

"Nothing to worry about. I'm just trying to find out who she is."

At nine a.m., the blonde finally emerged wearing a black dress and hat. Man, she was a looker!

They followed for several miles, keeping a safe distance. Finally, her car turned into a parking lot. It was a mortuary.

Was she attending a funeral? Had this Eve broad killed someone else?

Well, he'd wait a while and see. Maybe she worked here.

She emerged a short time later and entered a waiting limousine. He tried to see who else was in the vehicle, but the dark glass prevented it.

As the funeral procession filed out of the drive, a sheriff's black-and-white brought up the rear.

Adam's back tensed and his heart pounded staccato. He poked the cabbie's shoulder. "I've seen enough; drop me at the Torrance Pier."

Chapter 123

STANDING AT THE REAR of the sanctuary, Sharon Collins scanned the members of the elite banking community who filed in for Quentin Pryor's funeral. Pryor's body had finally been released from the morgue, though the full autopsy findings were still being processed.

Sharon noted that the men all wore black or midnight-blue Italian suits and their wives, black designer dresses. Watching as they walked down the aisle and sat gingerly in unfamiliar pews, Sharon found it strange that their faces—though they bore solemn expressions appropriate for the occasion—showed no actual signs of grief: no red eyes from crying, no pale faces, no leaning on others for support. Conversations were either about business, the breathtaking stained-glass designs in the church windows, or plans for the evening's activities. Quentin's name was rarely even mentioned.

In Sharon's family, the deceased would be the *only* topic of conversation. Maybe in elite circles, they didn't speak of the dead.

A commotion at the front of the chapel next to the sealed coffin turned heads in that direction. Sharon walked down the side aisle to listen.

"What a wonderful way to desecrate my father's funeral: my thief of a brother and his murdering stepmother sitting next to each other!" Adrienne Pryor stood by the first pew dressed in a rumpled green silk suit, her hair a disheveled mess, face white. "What right does *either* of you have to attend the services for this great man?"

The funeral director and Adrienne's father's attorney rushed to the distraught woman's side and escorted her to the front pew on the opposite side of the chapel, where she collapsed in tears. The business press reporter assigned to the funeral perked up at the scene, but he

399

didn't take out his pad and pencil. Sharon figured his coverage wouldn't carry mention of the outburst, but the gossip columns might.

Three rose and addressed Leigh. "I appreciate your asking me to sit with you, but my sis is right—I don't belong here. Not because of what she said, but because I don't mourn the loss of my father one bit." He let himself quietly out the side entrance.

Leigh Pryor, her back arrow-straight, fanned her hot face with the funeral program. This was turning into more of a comedic tragedy than some of the ballets she'd danced. If only she'd stayed in London! She wouldn't have to deal with all the worry, fear, and guilt she was feeling now. Hopefully, only the Outreach Committee members knew how close Adrienne's accusation was to the truth.

Leigh had often wanted to have Quentin's children to visit, but her husband had refused to even consider it. When she'd asked him why, he'd told her stonily that his offspring were none of her business. Quentin's son actually seemed nice, friendly—now that she'd finally gotten to know him. She couldn't say the same for Quentin's daughter. Adrienne had apparently inherited her father's abusive personality.

Leigh tensed and gripped Mora's hand. Why was Sharon Collins still staring at her?

She wished this was over. She wasn't sure she could take much more of this grieving-widow role. Sure, she'd had years of professional drama lessons, all ballerinas did, but trying to act like she was mourning all the time was hard. Truth be known, she was sorry Quentin had to die and she did miss him in an odd way. But when she thought of her new life, she wanted to dance, not sit here and act bereaved.

She turned toward Mora as she felt a hand on her shoulder. Mora nodded toward Sharon and then bowed her head as if in prayer. Leigh followed her example.

Chapter 124

WATCHING THE HEATED EXCHANGE before the funeral, Sharon decided that both Quentin's daughter and Leigh *were* grieving. It was interesting to see Leigh's continued interaction with family.

At Mora's invitation, Sharon had come early with Leigh and her enveloping entourage of Outreach Committee members. What a wonderful support group the Outreach Committee was. So solicitous. *It's almost as if she doesn't have to speak for herself. They speak for her.*

Sharon thought back to her ride in the front seat of the limousine on the way over, listening to the quiet ruminations of those in back.

Leigh had turned to Mora. "Do you think I should have looked at Quentin in there?"

"Regretting your decision not to?"

"I didn't know if he'd look like himself." Leigh twisted her handkerchief. "It's so confusing. I've never seen someone I loved and lost like that."

"The suddenness of an accidental death makes it seem unreal for such a long time," Mora said quietly.

"I'm not sure what I feel," said Leigh. "My thoughts and emotions are so jumbled."

"When someone dies, we often blame them for dying, so intertwined is our love with our grief," explained Mora.

"I miss him," said Leigh. "The house is too quiet."

Sharon knew what it was like to have your husband leave suddenly; she'd used music to fill the silence. She turned around to comment but decided not to when she saw Mora elbow Leigh in the ribs and tilt her head toward the front seat.

"Oh!" Leigh spoke suddenly. "You know how it is—when you've lived with someone for a few years. You get to know them so well that they seem so much a part of the family, that you stop thinking of them in purely romantic terms." She cleared her throat.

Sharon felt tension in the back seat. It relaxed when Sharon saw Mora's nod reflected in the windshield.

"I can imagine so," said Carol with a nervous laugh.

Sharon was confused. She was trying to get to know these ladies, but they seemed to speak a different language than she did. Shouldn't she expect it? After all, she had been raised on a completely different social level.

"*All* of it will hurt and worry for a while," said Mora.

Sharon turned her attention back to the church. She'd have to finish dissecting the back-seat conversation later.

After the opening hymn, the congregation settled into their pews, rustling service programs and thumping the hymn books back into the racks. A gray-haired minister appeared behind the pulpit and the crowd stilled.

"I'm Dr. William Stover, senior pastor of this church." Sharon had heard of him, seen news articles of his charity work, particularly with children. She'd admired him and his missions from afar. Quentin must have been important to have Doctor Stover speak.

"Quentin Pryor was a self-made success. He grew up in poverty and rose to become the CEO of one of our largest banking institutions, going to school on scholarships and working to support himself while doing so. Our church and its missions have benefited greatly from his advice and generosity."

The pastor turned to face the front pew. "He loved children and was very proud of his daughter and her accomplishments." Adrienne squirmed in her seat as the congregation turned to catch a glimpse of Quentin's offspring. Sharon wondered what the pastor would have said if Three had remained for the services. She assumed that Leigh had written the eulogy.

The pastor continued, "And he was so proud of his lovely wife, Leigh. He often told me about how he'd met her at a ballet performance in London." *Well, maybe she didn't write that part.* She seemed too modest. For sure, Adrienne had not.

"Now, I'd like to introduce Adrienne Pryor, who will talk to us about what it meant to have Quentin Pryor as a father."

Adrienne pushed up awkwardly from the pew and straightened her wrinkled suit. She walked to the podium and stood quietly for a moment, waiting for the audience to settle. She seemed oblivious to the stain that her tear-washed makeup had made on her white blouse. Sharon recognized that the woman was troubled; whether it was by grief or guilt wasn't evident.

"Quentin Pryor was a loving, nurturing father. Because of his help and encouragement, I have a career of which I am very proud." She dabbed her face with her handkerchief. "I didn't see him enough, but I welcomed him into my home just last month. We've always talked about anything: the world, politics, finances, even marriage." She smiled softly. "Of course, he wanted grandchildren, and I am so sad he'll never—" She gulped back the rest of the sentence as an onslaught of tears gushed forth. When she regained her composure, she looked out at the assembled group. "I loved him dearly. He will be missed." Adrienne stumbled down the steps and resumed her seat with a sob.

The closing hymn brought the congregation to their feet and they filed out in cadence with an organ requiem.

As the service concluded, Sharon strolled out into the sunshine ahead of the others. She'd declined a ride to the cemetery with the widow. She wanted to get a good look at the mourners as they exited the chapel and talk with Harry about his observations from his balcony position. He'd take her to the burial, where they would both watch the mourners. She was glad of the change in transportation. She'd been walking on conversational eggs the whole morning.

Not that she didn't have to be cautious around Harry. When she was with him, she was afraid she'd misspeak and reveal her intensely personal defensiveness of the BWEF members.

The majority of those at the church service did not follow the hearse to the graveyard, even though it was close by. A tent covered the open grave and white chairs surrounded it. Sharon and Harry chose to stand in back for a better view. Leigh sat in the center of the first row on the east side, flanked by Mora, Carol, Taylor, and Erin. Adrienne started to head there before transferring suddenly to the west side, trailed by Doth, Kyle Norbest, and Loretta Wilson. Leigh started as Loretta passed by, and Sharon saw Mora squeeze her hand to calm her.

Following a brief ceremony, Leigh laid a single burgundy rose on the casket. After it was lowered gently into the ground, she turned and walked away, holding her head high and not looking back. Mora rose to accompany her.

The pastor turned toward Quentin's daughter. "Ms. Adrienne, would you care to throw dirt into the grave?"

"Yes, I would." She picked up a handful of dark loam from the rim of the canvas-covered mound and threw it, hitting Leigh's back.

Leigh hesitated, and then continued walking, holding onto Mora.

Chapter 125

LEIGH FELT BEASTLY, unable to move a muscle. Her faded terrycloth coverup hung limply on her bony frame.

With the funeral over, the flowers donated, and the food dispensed to the BWEF shelters, she felt truly alone. Blast! She *was* alone. Sure, dear Cookie was at work behind her somewhere in the vast kitchen, but she didn't know all her employer had been through.

Leigh wiped a tear on the sleeve of her robe. Besides the OC group, she had no true confidants—or even acquaintance buddies—in her life. Quentin had driven away all of her old friends; the ones who hadn't drifted away on their own because she was never available.

For the first time, Leigh glimpsed the totality of the isolation that marriage to Quentin Pryor had brought her. Being wed should have brought her twice as many friends, not zero. She squirmed at the thought. Quentin had brought *no* personal friends to their marriage and had felt threatened by any time she spent with hers. Had her husband felt alone? Was that why he'd clung to her so fiercely?

Leigh's thoughts were interrupted by the yard man, who stood before her waiting for her to notice him.

"Pardon me, ma'am. Those women from the Women's Escape Foundation are at the gate." He shifted from one foot to another. "I know you said no visitors, but they insisted I come tell you." He waved his hands. "I'm sorry, ma'am."

"Oh! It's okay." She nodded. "You did the right thing." She rose and slid her feet into rubber sandals.

"What brings you ladies round?" Leigh's puzzled frown greeted Mora Rey and Carol Ewald who waited at the gate, silly smiles lighting their faces. Maybe she *could* do with some happy people around her.

Carol's eyes lit up, but she shook her head. "You look terrible. It's a good thing we came when we did."

Leigh looked down at her faded robe. She indeed looked appalling—just as she felt. "Why is that?"

"It's a secret outing, planned just for you."

"Of course," added Mora, "we planned one that would make *us* feel good, too—selfish gals that we are. You *may* want to change your clothes, though." She winked at Carol.

"I'm not fit to be seen publicly today. I don't feel at all social—except for you ladies, of course." The thought of having to get dressed overwhelmed Leigh, but she didn't want to be rude to her friends.

"You just have to trust us to know what you like," Carol assured her. "*And*—you'll hardly have to say a word."

"How can I dress appropriately, when I don't know what we'll be doing?" Leigh's spirits were lifting. She did rather *like* surprises. And she needed an airing.

"Anything but that sun-faded tent you have on. Something casual and loose," said Carol. "You can see how we're dressed. Oh, and no makeup; we don't have time."

We must be going to the cabin, thought Leigh. *Not such an exciting surprise, but at least I won't be completely isolated.* "I'll just duck in and put on my sweat suit, then," she said. "Won't be a minute."

The trio drove down Pacific Coast Highway and pulled up in front of a classic-looking building with a discrete sign: *The Ultimate Day Spa Experience.*

"Oh, a spa!" cried Leigh as Carol positioned her van in the handicapped parking area. "I dare say you *do* know what I like." She grinned sheepishly. "I haven't had a massage since I got married. Quentin forbade it." At Mora's and Carol's raised eyebrows, she explained, "He was afraid I would have a male do it, and then hanky-panky would follow."

"Just goes to show how unsure of himself he was, as a man," said Mora. She and Leigh waited as Carol maneuvered her chair from the lift and pushed the control to close and lock the door.

"I hadn't thought about it that way," said Leigh. "Just as another control ploy." She nodded vigorously. "I often pitied his employees at the bank. They must have hated working for him—not being able to make any decisions on their own."

The trio entered the spa and were enveloped by its atmosphere. Soft guitar music soothed. Candles emitted dim light and the scent of violets. The water gurgling in a floor-to-ceiling fish tank and the soft ocean breeze wafting through the open window brought the beach inside. At the registration desk, attendants spoke with their clients in subdued voices.

"Mora Rey here with Carol Ewald and Leigh Pryor," Mora announced demurely, pointing to her guests. "Taylor Whitmore and Erin Craig were to meet us here."

Leigh brightened. *All* her new friends would be here!

"Let's see," said the attendant. "We've scheduled you all for hour-long facials, then the fifty-five-minute massage followed by a body wrap, and of course, manicures and pedicures."

"Will we all be together?" asked Leigh.

"I'm sorry, but no," said the attendant with a soft smile. "We put you in individual rooms for privacy and a peaceful, relaxing experience. But we schedule fifteen minutes between sessions to give our specialists a break. You can visit then in the client lounge."

"It will be nice to get a massage again," said Leigh. However, she wasn't sure she wanted to be alone in a room—even with a therapist. She didn't want time to contemplate things, like her part in Quentin's death.

As if reading Leigh's mind, Mora said, "You'll be so absorbed with what's happening to your body, you won't want to talk—or even think!" She hugged Leigh around the waist. "I guarantee it."

"You're a love to have arranged this," said Leigh.

"While we chat between sessions, we can eat the wonderful fruit they provide and sip herbal tea," added Mora.

"And we've reserved the hot tub for our group at the end of the day." Carol sank back into her chair. "I'll be so vegged out, you guys may have to drive home."

"It won't matter," said Leigh. "I don't think I'll ever want to leave!"

"So, what have *you* been up to, Erin? That's quite a shiner you got there."

Erin Craig flexed her sore muscles. Ila, her massage therapist, had comforted her through many hardships—physical and emotional. Erin's face and body were crying for her special lotions.

"Fortunately, I look worse than I feel!" Erin laughed. "After my silly work accident, my broken nose is finally healing. But I *am* sore from gardening yesterday. I helped the residents at the Torrance shelter plant pinks and begonias. They were so enthusiastic that they wouldn't let me rest." Erin smiled; the shelter's lovingly tended flowerbeds rivaled those of the South Coast Botanical Gardens. "In their motivation to create beauty," she added, "they didn't have time to dwell on their misfortunes."

Gardening had once provided Erin solace, after Benning's abuse.

"In my mind, there's no better feeling than planting flowers and watching them grow and blossom." Ila slathered green goo over her friend's body and wrapped a sheet around her. She patted Erin's shoulder. "And with your job and your obvious joy in being alive now, you're a great example."

Erin nodded. It was too bad she couldn't share her rapture in dispatching abusers for the Outreach Committee. Erin's mind returned to her river trip. If only Marshall's body would be found; then Taylor could share in her joy.

"Hey, what you thinking about? Your whole body tensed all of a sudden!" Ila massaged her friend's scalp.

Erin sat up. "Oh, just something I enjoyed doing. Something private."

Lying on the soft table, Leigh Pryor again thanked her friends silently for this luxurious surprise.

"Is this a bruise on your shoulder? Do you want me to skip the upper-body massage?" Jasmine, the esthetician performing Leigh's facial pulled the mist generator so that the spray covered Leigh's face.

Leigh sighed and stretched as the cleansing moisture washed over her. "I'm fine with whatever you want to do. The bruises are old and ugly, not sore." *And when they disappear, there would be no others.* She'd taken a big step in starting her new life.

Leigh swallowed a gasp as an image of herself in an orange jail jumpsuit flashed in her head. She'd had Quentin murdered!

Jasmine examined her client's face through a brightly lit magnifying lens. "You have skin like an actress who wears a lot of heavy makeup." She smoothed cream across Leigh's cheeks. "This should clean and tighten your pores."

"I performed in the ballet," said Leigh. "The bigger the hall, the heavier the goop layer. The makeup often helps to define the character." She giggled. "Some of it's rather quaint."

"Oh, I've watched ballet on TV. Some of the makeup looks like clown faces!"

"If the truth be known, I don't care how my face looks when I dance; it's all in how my body deals with the motion and music." Leigh smiled, cracking the thick layer on her cheeks. "My soul emerges then."

Jasmine smiled at her. "Do your children dance? I bet they're good."

"Oh, I don't have any children of my own."

"You didn't want kids?"

"Why, yes, I wanted them frightfully. My husband made it very clear he didn't."

"Oh, I'm so sorry." Jasmine went silently back to applying finishing touches to Leigh's cheeks.

Leigh still mourned the child lost in her miscarriage. She didn't even know if it was a boy or girl. As tears slipped down her gooey mask, Leigh vowed to forget Quentin, and her guilt, and move on. She'd promised herself that. *She* was in charge now. Today there were many avenues open to a single woman who wanted to become a mother.

Lying on the heated bed next door, Carol worked hard to feel the deft hands of the massage specialist kneading her lifeless thighs. "Does it feel any stronger, Jill? Do you feel any muscle tone?"

"Carol, your legs feel firmer, but I can't say it's muscle." She patted her client on the upper back. "I'm sorry."

"Hey, I don't expect miracles." *One would be welcome.*

"Are you still going to PT? How are you doing there?"

"Oh, Jill, I work so hard! Once a week, I get an hour's therapy, and then I work out twice a day at home for at least an hour." Carol had kept up the brutal schedule since Reggie's death. He no longer dictated her healthcare, and she could afford both a personal trainer *and* PT. She flexed her arm. "I *feel* so much stronger!"

"With that kind of dedication, you'll be walking again before you know it." Jill's probing hands moved to Carol's powerful shoulders.

"When I was training for the Olympics, I'd think about where I wanted to be, say by the end of the week, month, year, then work with my trainer to get through the small goals to the big one. I'm doing the same with the PT."

The masseuse helped Carol turn over and placed a soothing pad over her eyes. The calming ritual of the massage continued.

As she finished, Jill patted Carol's head. "There you go. I'll put your clothes here on the table. Lie there a few minutes, dress when you want. I'll get your wheeled steed from the corral and help you mount."

Carol dressed herself, and Jill returned and put a steadying hand on the wheelchair as Carol moved herself into it.

Carol flexed her shoulders. "As usual, I feel pampered." She pressed Jill's hand. "Thank you."

"You've made such progress since you were hurt. All of us here are so proud of you!" Jill opened the door for Carol and handed her a glass of lemon water. "Too bad your husband isn't around to celebrate with you."

Carol nodded mutely.

Mora tuned out the spa music as the manicurist worked on her hands and feet.

She wondered at the positive effect that the spa treatments had on all of them. Things she'd noted just during their last tea break: *She* felt like she could conquer the world. Carol was more determined than ever to walk. Taylor had not stuttered once. Erin had been singing instead of cursing.

And Leigh—lovely Leigh had chattered joyously.

Taylor rubbed her hands over her smooth legs. The warm wax had felt good. She hated shaving, and now she wouldn't have to for a while.

Her legs seemed slimmer. The only thing good about her stressful months: she'd lost her appetite and five pounds. Marshall loved ethnic foods and they'd eaten out a lot. She hadn't been able to go back to any of their favorite places without him. A knot returned to her stomach.

A massage and then a manicure were next on her agenda, but she wasn't sure they would relax her either. Her stomach hurt and her head ached.

As Taylor dressed in the spa robe and sandals, she took several deep breaths. She had to look at her situation realistically. Either they would find Marshall's body or they wouldn't. There was nothing she could do until they did or didn't—except go on with her life as if nothing had happened.

Taylor pulled on her swimsuit and headed to the hot tub.

Chapter 126

"Boy, you must really have a thing for this broad," said the cabbie. "Did she ditch you or sumpthin'?"

Had she dumped him? Was that what had started all this? He was certain she had hurt him, but somehow it didn't make sense that he'd dated her.

They followed her to the beach cities.

When they got to Redondo Beach, the woman parked her car on Catalina and walked into a small spa. Lucky/Adam (he was still getting used to his own name) held back until he was sure she'd be occupied and then told the cab to wait and followed her inside.

He wrinkled his nose at the perfumed air in the spa's lobby.

"May I help you, sir?"

"The blond woman who just came in here. Uh…Erin?" He wiped a hand across his blushing face. "I think I dated her, but I forgot her last name. Cou…could you tell me who she is?"

As the receptionist shook her head, Adam's eyes followed an older brunette with her hair in a bun. Did he know her, too?

"Sir!" Adam turned back to her. "I'm sorry, but our clientele expect complete confidentiality from us." Her eyes twinkled. "But if you give me *your* name, I'll be sure she hears you were asking about her."

"I…I can't." Adam thought fast. "That would spoil the surprise." He winked at the petite receptionist and sauntered from the spa.

Chapter 127

"THIS IS A BIT of a different atmosphere than our meetings in Arrowhead," said Leigh, verbalizing Mora's thoughts. The women were convening in the private hot tub Mora had reserved to end Leigh's girls' day out. As Leigh lowered herself into the tub across from Carol and Erin, Mora was happy to note the pair's relaxed postures and lazy smiles.

"So, I gather you *like* the new OC meeting place?" Mora said.

"Oh, is this an official meeting?" said Leigh.

"Well, it is in one respect," said Erin. "We have a damned agenda!"

"Oh? I didn't get one. Are there extras?" Leigh looked over to the bench where they'd plunked down their beach bags.

Mora smiled and patted Leigh's arm. The poor woman still thought literally, like Quentin. It would take time for her to mellow.

"Not a written one, Leigh—Erin was joking!" Mora spread her arms wide. "Every once in a while, we gather to celebrate our freedom, remind ourselves how lucky we are to be unencumbered by our former spouses."

"*Pure* freedom! Not many women have that," said Carol, scooting down into the warm water. "We can go where we want, when we want, and spend what we want." She shook her head. "Whoever said marriage was heaven didn't know what they were talking about."

"I can spend a day—or a week—with friends without any shitty recrimination." Erin stretched her arms above her head and leaned back. "Until the customers call to complain that my work isn't done!"

Mora smiled at Erin. Erin always made time for the OC. Even if it meant joining them on a workday. She'd hired enough employees—

most from the shelters—to ensure her customers were happy, whether she was there or not.

Leigh looked around the circle of women. "Thank you to each and every one of you, for your support. And especially you, Mora. Your counseling has helped so much." As the other women nodded, Mora smiled. *This* was why she'd become a psychologist.

Taylor entered the room and dropped her bag on the bench. She approached the group.

"Mora, the…" Taylor started to speak and stopped. Her legs shook as she lowered herself to the edge of the tub.

Mora turned to her. "Yes?"

"The m–manicurist said there was a cute m–m–man asking for Erin but watching me as I walked across the deck to her space. He knew her name but wouldn't leave his own. Did you see him?"

"No. Why?" Mora heard fear in Taylor's voice.

"She said something about him reminded her of my husband, of Marshall."

Mora climbed from the tub and grabbed for her towel. "We all *know* that can't be." She glanced at Erin. "Don't we?"

Chapter 128

SHARON AWOKE Monday morning wishing it were still the weekend. Both the kids had sleepovers with friends last night, so she had invited Ernest over and they'd stayed up late watching a movie. She should know better, but she owed herself some entertainment—plus she couldn't keep avoiding Ernest forever. It had been nice to see him. Nice to have someone to talk to who wasn't involved in the job, or this case.

"So, partner, you've told me what the Outreach Committee does, but..."

Harry's entrance shook Sharon from her morning stupor. She couldn't let Harry pick up on her lack of focus. She wanted so badly to excel at this investigation. And she needed Harry to support her bid for promotion.

"But what?" She looked at him as bright-eyed as she could muster.

"Something's still bothering me." He drummed his fingers on the desk. "What I'm wondering is: Why couldn't Leigh Pryor tell you *anything* about the committee herself?" He rose and began pacing. "She's supposedly part of this committee and is obviously so close to these women, and yet she knows *nothing* about what they actually do. How is that possible?"

Sharon's head started pounding. Harry just wouldn't drop this subject.

"I don't know...maybe what they do is *so* confidential, they don't bring it up at finance meetings—with outsiders like Quentin there."

Harry looked at her over his glasses. She got the distinct impression he was deciding whether to laugh or cry. He did neither, just continued his quizzing. "Were any of the women who are on the Outreach Committee helped by it?"

"Well, they said that the rotating members *are* past recipients of their services. However, Carol's and Mora's husbands actually died two years apart."

Harry's eyebrows rose. "Died? How?"

Sharon shook her head. "I don't know! If you want that information why don't you look into it—or ask them directly?"

Sharon returned to the forms on her desk. Her annual review was coming up soon; she wanted to keep her paperwork current.

"I'll do that." Harry turned on his heel and returned to his desk.

Sharon bit her lip. She knew she should apologize, but *she* was right. She spun around in her chair to face Harry. "Let me make myself clear, partner: we are going in the wrong direction on this Pryor case."

"Not *we*. Me?" He dropped his pen on the notes he was making and turned to face Sharon.

Well, at least I got his attention.

He blinked a couple of times, as if to refocus his thinking. "You've made yourself *quite* clear, but I still don't know where you're coming from."

Sharon balled her hands into fists. "Don't patronize me! You know exactly what I'm saying. These are *good* philanthropic women!"

He combed his fingers through his scraggly burr cut. "I do trust your people skills. And you're a good detective. But, with due respect, I think you may have a conflict of interest here."

Sharon jumped from her chair and leaned over Harry, her nose almost touching his. "That's just not true."

"You have to admit that you *could* be overly prejudiced toward the widow, since she's associated with the BWEF." He curled his lips into an inside-out grimace. "*And* now that you've joined the club."

Wow. At least he'd called her a good detective. A first.

Sharon nodded. "*Could* be, but I'm not." Her cheek muscle rippled as she clenched her jaw.

"You forget: the spouse is *automatically* suspect in a homicide. You're apparently not willing to accept that premise."

"I just think that for some reason you feel you need to focus *only* on her. Is it because she's rich—leads a lifestyle you don't understand?" Harry was usually fair, but she couldn't help accusing him.

"Now I get it. You took extra credit in psychology and you're trying to find a use for what you learned, analyzing my reasons for conducting a thorough investigation."

"Think what you want." Sharon straightened and lifted her chin. "I'm going to a BWEF meeting tonight."

Chapter 129

SHARON STRAGGLED into the community center. She was eager to learn more about the BWEF—and the Outreach Committee. The case took priority, but she also wanted to prove to Matron that these women were *not* snooty. She smiled. More so, she was *determined* to prove Harry wrong about the involvement of the Outreach Committee in Quentin's death.

Sharon stood at the door, looking around, until Mora spotted her and called from across the room. "Welcome, Sharon. Come over here and meet some of the committee chairs."

Sharon waved back and edged her way through the group of women standing at the door. She pulled at her tunic top, aware that her Target chic was a sharp contrast to the designer clothes they wore.

"Sharon, you remember Erin Craig. In addition to the Outreach Committee, she's also our Community Liaison. Her committee puts our name out in front of other neighborhood organizations that can refer women to our shelters."

Mora spoke brightly to Erin. "Here's a *perfect* member for your Liaison Committee. I'm sure Sharon has contacts in the county you've never heard of."

"Welcome, Sharon." Erin squeezed Sharon's outstretched hand with both of hers. "Damn right, we'll be happy to put you to work. Our community education drive starts in two weeks, and we're shorthanded."

"I'll help with that! I could take some brochures with me on patrol, hand them out to social workers, et cetera, when I contact them on domestic violence cases."

"Hell of an idea!" Erin slipped her arm through Sharon's. "Come meet the other members."

She caught the eye of a tall woman listening close by.

"Alyson Zender, I'd like you to meet Sharon Collins. Sharon's a deputy sheriff and wants to help get our word out." To Sharon, Erin said, "Alyson owns A to Z Travel. She helps us with our offshore charity trips."

"Offshore?"

Erin put an arm around Alyson's waist. "Our overseas outreach trips. We bring help to women in third-world countries. Provide information against abuse, female circumcision, things like that." Erin smiled fondly at Alyson. "All Mora has to do is say the word, and this Wonder Woman does all the planning and scheduling for that."

Moving on, Erin said, "Let's talk to Taylor before the official meeting starts." Sharon nodded. "She has information on *all* of the committees."

"Hi, Sh-Sharon, welcome to the BWEF. Let's sit over here out of the w-way of the traffic, and talk." Taylor led her to some chairs in the corner of the room. She beckoned a waiter and ordered a Coke with lime. "What w-would you like to drink?"

"Do you have iced tea?" Sharon smiled as the waiter nodded.

Taylor's hands shook as she laid out a brochure on the low table.

"This is our latest c-community-focused literature about th-the BWEF." She opened the pamphlet to its center. "Here's our list of committees: Community Liaison, Shelter Acquisition, Shelter Maintenance, Oversight, Referral, Finance." She smiled at Sharon. "Is th-this your f-first time to a BWEF meeting?"

Sharon smiled sheepishly. "I'm embarrassed to say that except for running in the marathon, I haven't done *anything* for the organization since they sheltered me."

"Maybe joining us earlier would have brought back p-painful memories." Taylor's voice choked. Tears clouded her eyes.

"Perhaps." Feeling shy at the woman's sudden emotion, Sharon picked up the brochure and read the list of committees. "I don't see the Outreach Committee on here."

"It's n–n–not," said Taylor. "Because of its n–nature, that committee is by i–invitation only."

"Oh? I guess I was hoping…I mean, since I already know Carol and Mora—" Sharon looked down at her scuffed shoes. "Oh, never mind." *You idiot,* she thought. She wasn't the right social status to belong. Score one for Matron.

Taylor must have sensed her embarrassment. "Th–they, umm, the women we w–work with might not be comfortable working with *you*—as a d–deputy, that is," she added hastily.

"Oh, I see." Sharon frowned. They were afraid she might have a conflict of interest, working for the county. Seems like she couldn't win on either side!

Taylor reached for her drink and gulped half of it. "They communicate best with other women who've been i–in their same si–situation."

Sharon nodded.

"Taylor, are *you* on the Outreach Committee?" Sharon didn't remember seeing her at Leigh's with the rest of the committee women.

"Y— No. I— I mean, not really." Taylor shuffled the packet of brochures she held. "I work with them—on financial matters only."

Chapter 130

DRESSED IN HER LEOTARD, Leigh discussed activities and meals for the day with Cook.

"I'm excited, Cookie. Carol wants to get involved with the kids at the club. She's going to talk to Gordon about it today." The two women stood under the porte corchere, waiting for Carol to arrive.

"Miss Leigh, you look as though you're floating; I do believe you're well rid of Mr. Quentin." Cook clasped her hand over her mouth. "Oh, I'm sorry. I shouldn't say things like that."

I wish I could say it, too, thought Leigh. *But I'd better not.*

"It's okay, Cookie dear. I *am* beginning to feel like my old self—now that I can dance all I want."

"I've watched you practicing; you're beauty in motion." Cook took a tissue from her apron pocket and wiped her eyes. "I have to admit, I feel better, too. Sometimes I felt creepy when I was here alone with Mr. Quentin. I don't know why. I thought he was always judging me."

Leigh felt like that too, but she couldn't tell anyone but Mora. It would be dangerous.

Leigh hugged the rosy-cheeked woman. "You're my first and best supporter." She turned toward the drive. "Oh, there's Carol. We're having lunch after the club, so I'll be home mid-afternoon." She picked up her dance shoes and ran down the brick walk.

"The kids are going to be so happy you wanted to join me today," Leigh told Carol, climbing the running board of the Mercedes and settling into the cool leather seat. She strapped herself in and put her bag at her feet. "I don't think they've had an Olympian visit before."

"I've been thinking, since you called," said Carol, "about what I could do to help at the club."

"What did you decide?" Leigh smiled. "Once you see these kids, you'll be hooked into doing something, I know." She valued her new friendship with this plucky woman. Together they could bring purpose to the kids' lives. Make the gangs uninteresting alternatives.

"I decided I could help them with skateboard skills."

Leigh glanced involuntarily at Carol's lifeless legs. "How would that work?"

"Easy. I can show them videos, read to them from books, critique their form." Her tone turned defensive. "I coach the Olympic teams on occasion, you know."

"Carol, you're a marvel! I'm sorry. I didn't mean to offend you—honest. I was just curious. I wouldn't hurt you for the world, you've done so much for me." Leigh touched Carol's arm. "When I get settled with the financial stuff, maybe I can buy some boards for the club."

"We're on our way to a unique friendship, Leigh." Carol turned and smiled at her companion. "Please just accept that I am not hurt or offended by any comment about my disability. I realize my friends have to live with it, too."

"Thanks. I've never had a disabled friend before," said Leigh. "In fact, I haven't had *any* friends, not really, since I married Quentin."

"So this is it," said Carol as she followed Leigh's directions into a parking spot next to a 1930s wood clapboard building. Leigh had to admit, her glowing description of the Boys and Girls Club had not included the rundown building.

"Um, yes," said Leigh, concentrating on unlatching her seat belt.

At the front desk, Leigh introduced Carol to Gordon. She put her arm around Carol's shoulders. "She wants to work with the kids. You may have heard of Carol when she was skiing. She's an Olympian."

"I sure have! I was one of your fans—your late husband's, too." Gordon's smile was broad; his eyes twinkled. "I was a wannabe downhill medalist in my high school days." He pulled his lips into an exaggerated pout. "Those judges weren't too kind, I'm afraid."

"I know the judges you mean," said Carol, laughing. "It's a pleasure meeting you, Gordon."

Gordon's face reddened. "I'm sure the work you'll do here will be even more gratifying than all your contributions to the world of skiing."

Leigh hated to interrupt; it was so genuine a mutual admiration moment. "While you two discuss what Carol could do for the club, I'm going to get ready for my dancers."

"They're all in the gym waiting for you, and practicing—even the new boys."

Leigh positioned the children on the barre and gave them warm-up exercises. She toured the room, moving a small arm here, demonstrating a foot position there. Her eyes twinkled; she stood tall. This was what she wanted to do with the rest of her life. She was heading to the front of the classroom when she heard the door open.

"Leigh, you have another student," said Gordon.

"Oliva!" Leigh rushed to hug the newcomer. "Welcome! Are you coming back to classes at the school?" Leigh had taught at the ballet school in San Pedro where Oliva had taken individually coached lessons. The exceptionally talented young dancer had dropped out when her mother found work and needed an after-school babysitter for Oliva's younger brothers and sisters.

"No, Señora Leigh, mi madre still needs me to sit with the children after school, but when she heard that you were here on Mondays, her day off, she insisted that I come." The dark eyes pooled with tears. "She knew how much it hurt me to give up the dance." The proud head ducked to hide the tears.

Leigh clapped her hands. "Class, I'd like you to meet Oliva Alvarez. She'll be dancing with us. You'll learn lots from watching this very good dancer. If you have problems, I'm sure she'll be happy to help you." Leigh welcomed the power and influence of a peer expert when it came to children who were unsure of themselves and not wanting to ask an adult for help.

"Oliva, would you dance for us? I have some records here; why don't you look through them while we finish the warm-up exercises."

"Sí, yes. I will dance for you. I have music with me." She held up an oversized tote bag. "I have made up a dance for you. I'd love for the class to see it." Her smile lit her entire face. The faces of the other students reflected her enthusiasm.

The delight and awe on the children's faces as they watched Oliva dance delighted Leigh. Maybe she should engage her as an assistant. If the club couldn't pay her, she would.

Chapter 131

"Hi, THIS IS SHARON COLLINS. I'm a past recipient of your services and now a deputy sheriff." Sharon spoke to the receptionist in the office maintained by the Battered Women's Escape Foundation. "I talk about your organization whenever I find a woman who is in trouble. *You* could help *me* by sending me a list of the members of the Outreach Committee. I looked in my old directory but couldn't find it." Sharon paused. "What? Oh, thank you. I'd love a new directory, too. Please send it to me at the sheriff's station."

Sharon tore up the sticky note Harry had given her as a reminder and booted her computer. *Her* main goal was to research Quentin Pryor's former marriages. How long did they last? How did they end?

Mora looked up as the receptionist knocked. "Yes?"

"I just had a call from a deputy sheriff Sharon Collins. She asked for our new directory. Wants it for liaison. Okay to send it to her?"

"Sure. I must have forgotten to give her one at the meeting."

"She also asked for a list of the OC members."

Mora's stomach clenched. She shook her head. "We don't give out the OC members—security." The deputy's increased interest in the OC was bad news.

Chapter 132

SHARON HIT THE PRINT KEY. She couldn't wait to show Harry the information she'd culled from the online records. As he walked into the office reading his messages, Sharon said, "Thirty-one years ago, the Torrance PD called on the Pryor residence—domestic dispute. His then-wife wouldn't file charges."

"Was she Adrienne Pryor's mother?" Harry looked up from his messages and slurped his coffee loudly.

"Could be. Adrienne said her mom and dad divorced when she was small. There's a news article quoted here. Seems the wife and kiddy got very little. There was a prenuptial agreement. She took Quentin to court for child support and won." Sharon pointed to her screen. "His second wife divorced him too—apparently right around the time 'Three' got sent to juvie." Sharon grabbed the completed printout and handed it to Harry. "What's interesting is that after that, Quentin had a *third* wife before he married Leigh."

"Oh?" Harry continued nursing his coffee while flipping through the printout. "Where's *that* one now?"

Sharon paused for effect. "*She* died in an accidental fall at their Brentwood home. Head hit at least a dozen steps on her way down. Fractured her skull."

Harry paused mid-slurp. "Where was Quentin?"

"The maid said he was out jogging and came home just after the fall, all sweaty."

Harry gave up on the printout and leaned over Sharon's shoulder. "Yeah, I *bet* he was." He returned to his desk and booted his computer.

Sharon heaved a sigh. "You have to admit, this *really* seems a stretch, partner. The hubby supports the shelter at the same time he's beatin' on his wife?"

"It's not unheard of." Harry shrugged. "It's common for an abusive husband to present the façade of a perfect marriage. Part of his control. What better way to appear innocent than to support the organization that shelters battered women? You *do* know that abuse is about power and control, don't you?"

Sharon looked up to stare at Harry. "You think he hurt Leigh?" Sharon thought back to the couple of niggling feelings she'd had along that vein. But it *couldn't* be—could it?

Harry shrugged again. "I don't think one way or the other until we talk to her again about those bruises we saw. Her excuse was pretty flimsy, you have to admit."

"But she talked about him like he was a wonderful husband—didn't mention anything like that." Sharon tugged on the collar of her uniform. Was it always this tight?

"If you'd murdered your husband because he abused you, would *you* describe him as a monster?"

Sharon could tell Harry felt bad as soon as the words came out. She had told him once in confidence that she *had* thought of killing Sean.

"No, of course you wouldn't." He patted her back. "Sorry. I stepped over the line on that one." She took his crooked smile as an apology.

"Okay. But you won't change your mind about Leigh as a potential suspect?"

"No. And neither should you. Plus, I need to look into Leigh's friends, too."

"What?" Sharon's shoulders hunched forward. What was her partner thinking?

In answer to her unspoken question, Harry said softly, "Just how far do *you* think that group of women might go to avoid publicity about their finance chairman—the abuser?"

427

Chapter 133

CAROL COULD SEE Mora's flag T-shirt from down the block. She lowered her passenger-side window. "You look especially patriotic today!"

Mora stowed her picnic basket in the back of the van and climbed in. "I *do* believe it's the Fourth of July," she said looking pointedly at her watch calendar, "and Taylor *did* invite us to a picnic to celebrate the country's freedom—and hers."

Carol hoped fervently that the day *would* be a glorious festival. Taylor needed to celebrate and go on with her life as a single woman.

Mora grinned mischievously. "Besides, all *you* need is a torch in your hand, and you'd look like a seated Statue of Liberty in those flowing robes." She pointed to their right. "Turn here for that shortcut to Leigh's back gate she told us about."

Leigh greeted her friends wearing a blue-striped sarong over a matching swimsuit. "Cook made us sour cherry and blueberry pies for dessert. Carol, could you please open the back so I can place them on the flat surface? I put them in a foil-lined box so they wouldn't mess up the van."

"This van has survived many messes, believe me," said Carol. Her stomach rumbled. "Sorry!" She laughed. "I skipped breakfast so I could eat some of everything."

Mora turned in her seat to watch Leigh position the pies. "Box them in between the picnic baskets so they'll make the trip in one piece."

"I'm sure they'll be fine," said Carol. "Hop in. We're due at Taylor's in twenty minutes."

Carol turned on her CD player and "Born in the U.S.A." blasted the interior. The women sang along. Carol turned the van around and headed around the hill.

"I'm surprised Erin didn't call me for a ride too."

"She went early to check out the barbeque for Taylor and make sure there's enough gas." Mora moved her seat belt to a more comfortable position. "Marshall always insisted on doing the barbeque stuff, so Taylor let him and never learned."

"I called Taylor this morning to tell her about Cook's gift and she sounded like she'd been crying."

"I'll keep an eye on her," said Mora. "I'm sure this whole Marshall thing will blow over eventually."

The three women spent the rest of the ride in silence, each lost in her own private thoughts.

Rob greeted the van at the drive to his mother's home. "Mom says to take the food around back to the outdoor kitchen." He reached for a basket as Mora and Leigh unloaded the rest of the cargo.

Rob smiled at Carol. "I'll let these ladies go ahead of us while I help you navigate the stone path."

"Thanks. That time I got bogged down and almost burned out the motor taught me a lesson." If Carol had had a son, she'd want him to be like Rob. "I want to spend my time racing you in the pool, not playing mechanic!" She pushed the button to close and lock the van.

Mora scrutinized Taylor's face as her friend approached wearing a red apron and wielding a spatula. She gave Taylor a big hug. "What a great day! Hot enough for a swim this afternoon and a close-up view of the fireworks from both the Queen Mary and the Redondo barge."

"I hope you brought an appetite! Costco had a sale on rib-eyes and I couldn't resist—in spite of my last cholesterol test." Taylor nodded towards the grill where Erin, clad in a white chef's hat and an apron over her red shorts and tank top, waved a long-handled fork. "Our barbeque chef is raring to go."

"Who all is going to be here?" Mora asked as she and Leigh transferred the cold food from the portable cooler to the under-counter refrigerator.

"My next-door neighbors who just moved here from the Midwest are coming, Rob is already here, and Ruth is coming with her husband and kids." Taylor smiled fondly. "The girls have just finished their intermediate swimming lessons. But,"—she gestured to a man sitting next to the pool—"to play it safe, especially with Carol and the kids here, I hired my neighbor's son who used to be a lifeguard to come keep watch."

Carol joined Mora and Leigh by the pool in time to catch the end of the conversation. "I don't need a lifeguard, friend—unless *you* plan to dunk me."

Mora straightened and put her swim bag on a lounge next to the pool. "How are you doing?" she asked Taylor softly. "Sleeping more?" Her friend's hands were shaking, her color poor. Dark circles outlined her eyes.

Taylor fidgeted with the plastic wrap she'd removed from the fruit salad. "In fits and starts."

"And…?" Mora raised her friend's chin to look into her eyes.

"I'm at the end of my rope, Mo. I *have* to do something soon."

"You know we'll help when you're ready. Find divorce lawyers, financial advisors…whatever you need to move on. Maybe a private investigator to look into the calls?"

"I know what I need," Taylor said somewhat resignedly. "But for now let's enjoy today, our special Independence Day fiesta!"

Chapter 134

"I LIKE YOUR NEW BOYFRIEND; he's so considerate of you."

Dark was settling in, and as the group cleaned up their picnic on the beach to prepare for the fireworks, Sharon stole the opportunity for a quick conferral with her daughter.

Cailin stopped folding the towel they had used for a tablecloth. "I like him, too." She looked down at her hands. "He wants me to go steady."

"I thought you'd decided to date lots of boys for a while." Sharon stowed the leftovers from their supper in the hamper.

Cailin frowned at her mother. "You aren't going to stop me, are you?"

Sharon shook her head. "I trust your judgment. Here, why don't you and Dave take the hamper and umbrella to the car before it gets dark."

"Thanks, Mom." Cailin kissed Sharon's cheek.

Ernest plopped down on the sand next to Sharon. "What was that all about?"

"I told her I was okay with Dave and her going steady."

"What about us?" Ernest put his arm around Sharon's shoulders. "Going steady, I mean."

Sharon's whole body tensed. "I— I…"

Ernest cradled her face in his hands, and Sharon felt herself relax. She smiled softly.

"Does that mean yes?"

Sharon nodded.

Sharon's senses roared as Ernest leaned in and kissed her. Was it possible she, too, had found the right one?

Chapter 135

LAD IN BLACK, Adam rode his newly purchased used red motor scooter up the street. He'd followed Erin to a home here earlier and then gone for a long ride. It had felt good to get out in the open air.

He glanced around, and then stashed his scooter in the trash can alcove to the side of the house. He found the spot almost instinctively. Adam flexed his shoulders and stretched his neck. Sleeping on beach benches was taking its toll, but the early-morning swims helped make up for it.

Adam slid along the wall to the backyard. It sounded like a fairly large gathering. Must be a Fourth of July party.

Adam stood in the shadows, watching and listening. He was able to catch snippets of conversation here and there, but they meant nothing to him.

As dusk settled, the partiers turned their chairs west in anticipation of the light displays to come.

"So," a man asked, "when will your husband be back from his trip? I was hoping to meet him tonight."

"I don't know." The woman who replied looked around the group, chagrined. "To tell you the truth, he has l-left me." She looked at her bare fingers. "I'm filing for d-divorce next week."

Just then, the blonde crossed the patio from the house. "The dishes are done. Time for the fireworks!" Punctuating her words, a green flash spotlighted the yard as its boom echoed around the hill.

Adam beat his ears with his hands as a returning memory flashed in his head. He ran and rolled his vehicle down the driveway. He fired it up as soon as it hit the street.

He had to get away from these people.

Chapter 136

THE NEXT MORNING, Adam motored to the coffee shop on Pacific Coast Highway across from Torrance Airport for breakfast. He liked to watch the planes take off and land as he ate. He kinda remembered eating here and then walking across the road to board a small plane.

As he counted out his change for the tip, he realized it was time to look for a job—*if* he wanted to continue his search for himself. Why not try the airport?

At a large hangar, he approached a wizened old man on a ladder who was laboriously fueling a Cessna 182. "Need help with that?" He'd done this many times: checking the filter for moisture and then topping off the tank.

"Sure do! My helper didn't show up the last two days. I'm getting too old for this crawling around." He stood on the top rung of the ladder and looked Adam up and down. "Don't pay much: minimum wage."

"That's more than I'm makin' now. And I can start right away."

"You're hired." The old man pointed to the back of the hangar. "Put your wheels in that room with the cot at the back." He went back to work. "You maybe want to sleep there. We have lots of early takeoffs to service."

433

Chapter 137

SHARON LOOKED OVER at her partner as they stopped at the red light on Sepulveda. "*You*'ve been awfully quiet all day."

Usually it was the other way around: he did most of the talking. But today she felt perky. Her life was turning in the right direction.

Sharon rubbed her ear. Quiet definitely wasn't Harry's normal state. Truth be told, many a time she wished he'd shut up for a few minutes—to give her some peace. But, of course, she never said anything. They were partners, sure, but he had seniority.

"I was reviewing the Pryor case in my head…" he finally began.

Sharon smiled. As much as she treasured silence, she liked it when Harry shared his thinking with her. Made her feel professional.

"I looked through your new BWEF directory. Then I went to the morgue at the *Los Angeles Times*. Did you know that, including Quentin, five husbands of major BWEF supporters have died in the last twelve years?"

Sharon squinted at the traffic through the spotted windshield. "Why is that strange?"

Harry continued, "*All* were in good health. They all died in accidents—alone."

Gunning the motor, Sharon accelerated to cross the intersection just ahead of the red light. "It's a huge organization that does good work. Those shelters are a godsend to unfortunate women." Where *was* he heading with this conversation?

"I know," said Harry.

"They gave *me* the will to go out and make something of myself," she said. "No way I'd be here right now, if not for them!"

"But I'm talking about women *in* the organization that supports the shelters, not about the shelters or their guests," Harry protested.

"The organization *is* the women. You know that." Sharon blinked. *My bruises are no longer black, blue, and yellow, but they're still with me,* she thought.

Harry pulled a small notebook from his shirt pocket. "Here's another coincidence about those BWEF husbands who died: Two died in skiing accidents. And guess which two? Reginald Ewald and Sherman Rey: the husbands of your buddies, Mora and Carol."

"I *told* you they said they were widows," said Sharon. "So they both skied."

Harry continued his monologue. "Erin Craig is on the BWEF Outreach Committee. He turned a page. "*Her* husband, Benning, took a fall down a cliff six years ago while on a rock-climbing trip." Harry flipped another page. "That's not all—"

"Partner," Sharon cut him off, "you and I both know our coroner is really sharp. Something would have turned up in those investigations by now, if foul play was involved." Sharon rolled her head, pulling on taught muscles. "You've gone back *twelve* years. It's got to be a coincidence the men died accidentally." She admired Harry's tenacity when he was investigating a true crime, but this was heading toward the absurd.

"There's no statute of limitations on murder." Harry eyed Sharon. "I don't know if the accidents were even investigated." He reached for his coffee thermos. "And when we've talked to the members of the Outreach Committee, none of them have even *mentioned* the similarities in all these deaths. That's strange in itself, when we're investigating *another* mishap, don't you think?" Harry returned his notebook to his shirt pocket.

Sharon glowered at him but said nothing.

"Another thing about them," he continued. "In my church, the 'Outreach' Committee looks for new members."

"I know; in mine, too. But this group of women is different."

"Different? Or hiding something? What are these women really up to?"

"Come on, why *wouldn't* they support an organization for battered women?" She knuckled her partner's shoulder. "I think that's *exactly* what they would do, once they were free of their husbands, by death or divorce."

"Death or divorce, huh?" Harry raised his eyebrows. "Seems to be a lot more of the former!"

Chapter 138

Harry tapped Sharon lightly on her shoulder. "Want to go sailing?" "Sailing? Let me guess!" Sharon touched her finger to her cheek. "Oh, I know: You won the lottery over the weekend and bought a boat. Right?"

"Wrong! The crime scene guys just released the boat Quentin Pryor sailed to Catalina."

"And you want us to sail it back to the mainland?"

"Nope. It's already back—in the Redondo marina. I hoped we might get some clues from it."

Sharon interviewed the club secretary at the marina while Harry boarded the boat.

"Was there anything unusual about Quentin Pryor's charter of the Rio?"

"No. I don't remem… Well, only one *little* thing."

Sharon pulled out her notepad. "Little things can make or break a case."

"Mr. Pryor's personal assistant, let's see, a Kyle Norbest, scheduled the rentals."

"And?"

"Later a woman called to check on the rental dates. Said she worked for Mr. Norbest. Wanted to know Pryor's schedule. Said she'd lost the whole thing." The secretary smiled. "I remember her because she seemed like a real nice lady, but she was a bit ditsy and had a stutter, poor thing!"

Sharon joined Harry, wondering why hearing about a stuttering woman had caught her attention. *And* why they hadn't met Kyle Norbest's assistant.

Chapter 139

A TROUBLED TAYLOR paced the main aisle of her store. The last customers had left. She bolted the doors and locked the cash register. It was time to go home. She yawned.

The sleepless nights had to stop. She accepted that. But how to accept the action she must take to make it happen? These women were her friends. They'd done the ultimate to relieve her misery. On the other hand, she had to live with *herself*, didn't she? She had to sleep! She pulled her cell phone from her pocket.

"M-Mora, I need to call an emergency meeting of the OC." Taylor's voice had risen a couple octaves, its normally mellow tones transformed to a squeak.

"What's upset you, Taylor?" Mora's voice was soothing. "Something I can help you with now, instead of waiting for everyone?" Taylor felt herself relaxing. Mora would know what to do.

"I'm t-trying to make a decision that will a-affect all of u-us. E-Everyone on the committee sh-sh-should be there—except C-Claire, of course."

"Then we'll gather. Tell me when."

"Now! T-Tonight, here in my store?" Taylor held her breath.

"Okay—if I can reach everyone. And it may be an hour or so. Will you be okay until we arrive, or should I come over now and make the calls from there?"

Mora was such a good friend. She always had such consideration for others.

"Th-Thanks for asking, but I need some time alone to collect my thoughts." Taylor hesitated. Was tonight too soon? Would she be ready with what she wanted to say? Her tired body swayed and she grabbed the desk to remain upright. Never mind. She'd just have to be.

"What the hell's going on with Taylor?" Erin immediately asked as she settled behind Carol in the van.

Mora turned to face her from the front seat. "I think she's haunted by the Marshall sightings. She needs our support."

Erin worried a hangnail. "You want to know what *I* think?" She went on without waiting for an answer. "I think she's been suffering from a fucking overactive conscience." She laughed without humor. "I'm no psychologist, but that's been my gut feel for quite a while."

The group stopped under the porte cochere of Leigh's house. Leigh joined them with a tin of homemade cookies. "They're chocolate, good for the mood. And I'll eat them, even if no one else does. I skipped dinner for this."

"We may need them," said Mora. "Taylor has a serious matter to discuss with us. A consequential one, if I'm right."

Erin returned to her hangnail. What if the Marshall sightings *were* real? What if he *had* contacted Taylor? Erin hugged herself. If Marshall had appeared, *she* was headed for jail. Damn it all. Saving a friend from misery shouldn't be a crime.

The five women settled into the back office of Wilderness Outfitters. Taylor had coffee waiting and the women dove into the cookies.

Mora sat tall, presiding over the impromptu get-together. "What's happening, Taylor? Why the urgency?" All heads turned toward their hostess. Mora noted the black shadows smudging her friend's eyes. Obviously a lack of sleep. Was there a serious illness, too? A nervous breakdown?

Mora leaned forward as Taylor shuffled the papers in front of her and walked to a corner of the room. She appeared to be distancing herself from them.

"I have s-something to tell you. I know you'll h-hate me, but I c-c-can't help it. I d-don't want to lose you as friends, but I may have to, so…" She coughed and looked down at her feet.

"We're here for you," said Mora.

"We'll stick by you, come hell or high water." Erin raised her fist in the air.

"Taylor, you *know* we support you," said Carol. "We're a team."

"I'm all for you, Taylor," said Leigh.

Taylor shook her head rapidly, as if warding off her friends' love and compassion. Then she looked up.

"I c-c-can't l-live with what I did to M-M-Marshall," she said. "I was wr-wrong to think I could stop his violence with violence of my own."

Mora nodded but said nothing. Erin and Carol exchanged looks.

Taylor continued, "Wha-What I haven't told you is the real r-reason I decided to k-k-kill Marshall." Taylor braced her shoulders. "Marshall beat me and forced me to sign the s-s-store over to him." Her sob echoed in the room. "I actually had someone *killed*— m-m-murdered—over *material* things."

Mora glanced at each woman, assessing her innermost thoughts from her facial expression. The silence seemed to extend forever.

"And?" Mora finally whispered.

Taylor bit her lip. Her face paled. "And…I-I want to confess to M-M-Marshall's murder." Taylor looked down at her shaking hands.

Mora started to get up, but Taylor held out a hand to stop her. "Let me f-finish. I haven't worked out what I'll say, but I w-wanted you all to know that I *will* do it without involving the Outreach Committee. I owe you all that." She gulped a mouthful of air and sat down as if her legs could no longer hold her.

Leigh, Erin, and Carol all looked to Mora. Their eyes reflected the same sorrow and horror.

Mora hugged Taylor. "We've put you through a lot, and I don't blame you for wanting it to end."

"Oh shit, Taylor," Erin interjected. "What brought all this on *now?*"

"Well…it's been b-bothering me for a while." Taylor paused. "Plus, I think someone kn-kn-knows what w-we did—whoever's making th-the phone calls. Or maybe that guy who was a-asking about Erin at the s-spa."

"Worse yet," said Carol, "what if it *is* Marshall?"

Mora's heart hammered. *Could* it be? Was this the end of the Outreach Committee?

"It's s-s-spooky," Taylor said, "but I've th-thought about it, and it *can't* be Marshall. He-he'd be *so* mad at what I did to him, he'd come b-b-beat me up. He'd probably k-kill me." Taylor paused. "And wh-who could blame h-h-him?" She shook her head ruefully.

"Shit, Taylor. If Marshall *is* dead, *you* didn't kill him. I did." Erin's voice shook as she spoke. "*I'm* the one who should be punished for it, not you." Before Taylor could respond, Erin stood and faced the other women in room. "I *knew* about Marshall stealing Taylor's store. I knew she was upset, and I should have talked her into holding off. But I was so caught up in my own eagerness to 'do a good deed,' I didn't even think about what this would do to my friend." She turned to Taylor. "I'm so sorry."

Leigh gasped. "If you two confess, won't the deputies want to investigate Quentin's death even more vigorously? Won't they suspect all of us?"

Carol turned to her. "Yes. Then Reggie's and Sherman's."

"Wait a minute, ladies. Let's keep level heads about us." Mora released Taylor's hand and turned to the group. "We always have Operation Courage."

Taylor looked up in shock. "Operation Courage? Th-That long-range one?"

"Yes, and I'm proposing it as an alternative to your confession." Mora looked around the room. "But it has to be each person's choice. We won't force anyone."

Chapter 140

"WHATCHA DOING, PARTNER?" Sharon popped the ring on a Diet Coke as she approached Harry's desk. She pointed to a yellow pad sprinkled with Harry's shorthand squiggles. "Still trying to prove those nice ladies are axe-murderers?"

"Well, they *are* widows." *Here he goes again.*

"Wealthy women cling to charity work; keeps them busy and in the public eye. I don't think it matters if they're widows or not." Sharon sent Harry a pointed look. "Confess: you can't *truly* believe they're widows 'cause they knocked off their husbands." She poked his chest with her finger.

"That's exactly what I'm thinking *might* have happened. One of the scenarios, anyway. Each one has implied that they were abused by their famous, rich husbands. They must have *wanted* to kill them." He held up a hand to stifle Sharon's reply. "Let me finish. *And* they seem unusually happy and secure in their widowhood." He paused. "*And*, you have to admit, they *are* well-situated with their *inherited* wealth."

"Hey! You *know* that abused women don't have enough self-confidence to plan, let alone carry out, a murder. They stay with the abuser because they don't have the courage to leave and feel they have no skills to make a living without him." Sharon's quiet voice emphasized her statement.

"These women had an additional incentive: Money, lots of money! Besides, their lifestyle may have given them more confidence." Harry slapped his thigh to punctuate his thoughts.

"I'll admit: rich would help. But I read an article the other day about how well older widows and widowers adjust after the death of a spouse. They learn to do things for themselves that the spouse always did for them before. Gives them a sense of accomplishment. The same could apply to abused women. They get out on their own and blossom." Sharon knew she certainly had. Just look at this job: she never in her married life could have believed she could do it.

Harry nodded. "But consider, partner, what confidence they could get if they had a committee of influential women to back them up, encourage them to do away with the abusing spouse, and then take control and build a new life? What about that?"

"Man, you are re-e-eaching today." Sharon's raised eyebrows expressed her incredulity.

Harry nodded. "I'll give you one thing: They're a formidable support group for other women in their social strata. But…I sense something else in these women, something different. Like, there's unspoken communication between them. That's why I want to come back to this."

Chapter 141

"OKAY, IF YOU INSIST on pursuing this line on all these accidents, I suggest we do it in a methodical way. We'll make a chart with timelines, write down who was where when, what was investigated, what was found, and what *wasn't* looked at." Irritated with Harry but forced to admit that—objectively speaking—the situation *did* warrant a little investigation, Sharon dragged a giant roll of graph paper from their supply room. Harry helped her unroll a five-foot piece and tape it to the whiteboard.

"Okay, let's get this over with." Sharon opened the BWEF directory to the list of officers. "For a start, let's assume that all the officers we've met are also on the Outreach Committee." Might as well get this out in the open—make Harry drop it for good.

Smoothing the graph paper, Sharon looked back over her shoulder. As Harry dictated, she topped each column with the information to record for each of the deceased husbands: *Name; Date of Death; Cause of Death; Location of wife at the time of death; Witnesses; Coroner's Ruling; Next of Kin; Beneficiaries; Clues.*

"That's enough for starters," she said as she added a *Comments* column. "Which of the husbands died first? Let's take them in chronological order." Sharon rolled her shoulders. *What tedious work.* Truth be told, she'd rather be out on patrol. But a detective needed to develop *all* the skills. "Read me the dates."

Harry sorted through the news articles. "Rey was first, Ewald was second. Let's start with them." He got up from the desk and joined Sharon at the chart. "Hey. Didn't you say their wives *head* the Outreach Committee?" He shot Sharon a smirk.

"When did the committee form?" Harry asked. "Before or after their husbands died?"

"They indicated that they formed the committee *after* their husbands died, because they had spare time and resources." Sharon kept her face neutral. "Leigh Pryor also mentioned that Mora and Carol have run the OC, as they call it, from its beginning. Leigh thinks Mora and Carol walk on water." Sharon couldn't quite keep the sarcasm from her voice. She had to admit she still smarted over being told she was not welcome on the Outreach Committee.

"Why is that?" Harry rolled the marker between his fingers.

"Oh, gee, I don't know: Maybe they're helping her survive the trauma of her husband's death?" Sharon paused. "They helped arrange the funeral, figure out her financial position, that sort of thing." She tapped her forehead. "Oh, *I* get it now!" She made sure her sarcasm was evident. "*You* think it's because they *helped* her kill him off." She plopped into a chair. "Even *you* have to admit that it's rather fanciful to think that a group of society women are going around bumping off their husbands—are you hoping to make TV Movie of the Week with this one?" Sharon waved her hand in front of Harry's face as though to wake him. "Seriously, partner, you think these women would actually soil their dainty, well-manicured hands—let alone, risk going to jail?"

"No need to badger me, partner." Harry picked up another news article. "Let's finish our chart and map out the coincidences you're pooh-poohing. Hopefully, that thumbs down'll change to a high five. *If* you can be so charitable to your partner, that is."

Sharon crossed her arms noncommittally.

"We'll start with Sherman Rey." Harry smoothed out an article on his desk and highlighted parts as he skimmed. "He and his wife were skiing on Mammoth during a blizzard. The ski patrol told her to go down off of the hill. She didn't wait for her husband *or* tell them he was on the mountain, apparently. Says she thought he was ahead of her."

"Read me the stuff for the chart." Sharon rose and picked up a black marker.

"We've got the article date," said Harry. "The coroner said he died instantly, about four p.m. the day before. Skied right off the cliff." He held up Mora's picture. "Here's a picture of grieving widow Rey.

"She certainly *looks* forlorn and lost." *Of course that could be because Mr. R was such a controlling abusive bastard, she didn't remember how to even think for herself.* Sharon chose not to voice her thought to her co-worker.

"I remember hearing about Reggie Ewald." Harry's attention turned to the next on the list. "I was crushed. He was my hero when I was in high school. He died doing what he loved best, though." He frowned as he perused the news article. "I think that's an overworked phrase, but that's what the paper says too."

"His wife's the one in the wheelchair," said Sharon. "She was partially paralyzed in a slalom accident the year after she won an Olympic gold medal. She surely couldn't have pushed him off a cliff!"

Harry rubbed his head. "Let's get down the facts on her hubby's accident. His ski binding broke and he tumbled. His head rammed into a tree at the edge of the trail." Harry looked up from his notes. "Carol would certainly know what to *tell* someone else to do. Or she could have damaged the bindings at home before he left on his trip. She had to have known all about the equipment, to be a medalist."

Sharon's sigh came from her toes. She never won a point with Harry when he was in his dig-to-China-if-you-have-to mood. She shrugged and went back to the chart. Antagonizing him would just draw out the process.

"What was Carol doing at the time of her husband's death?"

Harry consulted the Ewald record. "She was with Ms. Rey in Santa Fe, looking for Native American rugs." He looked up. "So they obviously *did* know each other before their husbands died."

Sharon stayed studiously focused on her notes. Anything she said at this point would just add fuel to his fire.

Harry turned a page. "Put Benning Craig next. Our other 'cliff diver.'" He scanned the long article. "Benning Craig owned a successful dot-com company. They sold replicas of antique cast-iron toys and mechanical banks online. He also patented several video games. Erin inherited a purported eight-million-dollar fortune at his death." Harry waited for Sharon to catch up.

"Oh, looky here! Died *alone*, the morning after a night on the town. Police said his climbing harness came loose and he fell. No evidence of foul play." Harry flipped to the second page. "Surmised that he'd been careless in his hungover state—documented by the residual alcohol level. Erin, his second wife, was out of town, visiting her ill mother." He winked at Sharon. "At least it doesn't say she was buying rugs with Mora and Carol."

Harry ducked as Sharon threw an eraser at him.

But Sharon was seriously getting miffed. Was Harry *really* going to look at every woman they'd met as a killer?

"The Craigs had no children," Harry continued, "a fact publicly lamented by the toymaker. 'I can't wait to sit on the floor and play trains with a son,' he said in a *Today Show* interview."

Harry looked up from the article. "I don't know much about wilderness ventures, but it *does* seem foolish for a person to go climbing while sauced."

"Does it say anything else about Erin?" Sharon poised the marker over the comments field.

"She put those millions to work. Erin Craig is the owner of a women-only construction company."

"Someone told me that at the marathon, said they worked for her."

Harry held up a clipping. "Here's a story about child adoption and her. She wanted to adopt and her husband said no; he wanted only natural children. So she volunteers to help battered children and their mothers in the BWEF."

Sharon rubbed her chin. "Can we find *any* connection among all the deaths?" She put her marker down and went to look over her partner's shoulder.

"Nothing obvious," said Harry. "Pryor fell off a boat. Ewald and Rey died on the ski slopes."

Harry patted his stomach. "Let's sign out for lunch and come back and look at some more newspapers. See if we have any department files on the deaths. I'm becoming convinced there *is* something here." At Sharon's annoyed look, he continued, "All I'm saying is that you haven't convinced me that this is all unsubstantiated musings."

Sharon marched towards the elevator.

Harry scurried to catch up with her, stuffing his notebook in his pocket. "Look, even *you* have to admit this all seems like a pretty heavy coincidence!"

Chapter 142

SHARON SPOTTED LEIGH cutting flowers as she drove into the driveway of the Pryor mansion. She parked and walked up to the absorbed woman. "Got a minute?"

Leigh started and dropped the basket she held, spilling cut roses over the lawn.

"Sorry. I thought you heard me pull in." Sharon stooped to help retrieve the flowers.

Leigh straightened and held out the flower basket for Sharon's bunch. Today she wore shorts and a tank top. Yellowing bruises were still visible under her tan, but obviously fading.

Sharon pointed to a large blemish on Leigh's arm. "I came to talk to you about *those*. Let's get honest here: *Did* Quentin ever hit you?"

Leigh led Sharon around to the patio and sank into a white wicker chair. She set the basket on a table next to a stack of magazines.

The dancer sat motionless, biting her lip. Then she raised her head proudly. "I've always denied it, calling it my due. But I admit, at times he *did,* when I annoyed him." She stood and walked to the edge of the garden. "It was something private between us and shouldn't concern you." She picked up the basket. "Now, if you'll excuse me a moment, I want to give these to Cook to arrange. They need water."

Sharon was shocked by what she'd just heard. Not only in her sorrow for the dancer, but by its implications in the case.

Sharon idly picked up a dance magazine from the table and flipped through it. She paused at some writing scribbled in the margin of the contents page:

Gym 7:20
Leave for bank 9:02

Trip to Sacramento

25th sail to Catalina from Redondo Beach Marina

Whose handwriting was this? If it was Quentin's, why was he reading a dance magazine? Could Leigh have been spying on her husband—and making notes about his schedule where she was sure he wouldn't find them? If so, why?

The twenty-fifth was the day Quentin died…

Harry would find the worst in these notes. Sharon was somewhat inclined to also.

She looked up to see Leigh returning. She couldn't filch the magazine without breaching protocol, so she held it up and pasted on a smile. "May I take this to show my daughter?" Sharon asked. "She got interested in dancing through her cheerleading."

Leigh smiled back at her. "Of course, Sharon. And keep it. I've gotten my full use out of it."

Chapter 143

SHARON COLLINS WRESTLED with her thoughts as she paced her apartment, her steps quiet, so as not to wake her kids. Should they let the past remain unchallenged? Or…was Harry right in saying there was *too* much coincidence to do that? Every one of those Outreach Committee women was a widow—except Mrs. Whitmore, and her husband was gone a lot. Every *one* of their husbands had died in an accident.

Sharon sat at the kitchen table, nibbling the crumbs at the bottom of a bag of chocolate-chip cookies. But widows, especially those with money, had more time to devote to good works. So maybe this was a case of *correlation,* rather than *causation.* She refilled her coffee cup and returned to her notes.

Harry doesn't understand; he's a man. No matter how caring he is, he'd never understand what it's like to survive abuse. Women understand and know. They carry always the memory of pain, tears, and insecurity. Sharon's thoughts continued their whirlwind. *And the Outreach Committee definitely does good things.*

The widows talked about how helpful committee members were after their husbands died. Why didn't at least one of them mention working with the committee before they were widowed? Leigh Pryor did join two months before her husband drowned, after he was made finance chairman.

Sharon jumped as the phone's ring pierced the silence. "Hello?" she whispered. "Hi, Harry. No, you didn't wake me. I'm whispering 'cause the kids are asleep." Cradling the phone, she listened while she reached for her shoe under the table. "What was found?" She twisted the phone cord around her finger and let the cord unwind. "I'll leave as soon as I get my neighbor to stay with the kids."

Harry slapped a file folder in the center of Sharon's desk. "Your Outreach Committee friends are in big trouble now."

"My friends? Hardly…" She picked up the folder. "What is this supposed to tell me?"

"One: Leigh Pryor was admitted recently to that private clinic in Rolling Hills, with head injuries from a 'fall' at her home. She was released three weeks ago. Apparently she'll make a full recovery."

Sharon had planned to fill in Harry on her conversation with Leigh—she'd been stalling, truth be told—but this definitely wasn't the time. "I can tell from that look in your eyes, you have more to shock me with."

"The analysis of the blood on Quentin Pryor's boat wasn't all his own A-positive. Someone with O-negative bled there too."

Chapter 144

Mora's danger radar was flashing. The sheriffs had been asking too many questions: more than in any of the other post-dispatch situations. She called an emergency OC meeting—maybe their last.

"Leigh, where have you been? We've been waiting." Mora didn't have time for sitting around—or niceties.

Leigh looked the most flustered Mora had ever seen her. "I was waylaid by a call from Sharon Collins. She said they wanted to get my DNA, to rule me out."

Mora felt a knot form in her stomach. "Rule you out? From what?" Her radar kicked up to high alert.

"She said there was DNA in Quentin's boat that wasn't his. And they wanted to rule me out."

Erin gasped. Mora looked at her sharply.

"I suppose it won't do any harm to comply," Leigh continued. "Though I wonder why would there be DNA different from Quentin's?"

"Damn! Shit! I know why," mumbled Erin. The others stared at her, wide-eyed. "When he head-butted my nose trying to get away, I bled all over my hand. I grabbed the boat to steady myself."

Leigh let out a cry.

"I'm sorry." Erin looked down at her hands. "This is all my fault."

"Ladies, there's no time for recriminations." Mora stood up. "We're launching Operation Courage *now*. You know the drill."

Chapter 145

SHARON'S TORMENT DID NOT END with her reluctant agreement that she and Harry should detain the members of the Outreach Committee—and insist on obtaining DNA samples.

Those women simply *couldn't* have done what her partner suspected them of. They were on the committee to save lives, not take them.

Sharon was silent on the way to the first home on their list—except to give Harry directions from the route she'd mapped before they left.

"Still mad at me, partner?" Harry didn't look happy either, but she couldn't help that. They'd agreed when they started working together that they wouldn't hold back what they thought during an investigation. That they'd work together even when they disagreed.

"Not mad, just think you're insensitive. Accusing battered women; making their lives hell again."

"If you can't be objective, just say so."

Sharon sank down in her seat. "I'll be objective if you will."

"*I* will."

A bright-pink *Azalea Construction* sign stood in the middle of Leigh Pryor's front yard. Cook answered the door. "I'm sorry you missed her," she told them. "Just this morning, Ms. Leigh went off on an adventure. It's about time she took a vacation."

Harry's face reddened. "When do you expect her back?"

Cook shook her head. "She said she was going to play it by ear."

Sharon pointed to the yard sign. "Is Leigh remodeling the house?"

Cook nodded. "Before she left, she called Ms. Erin and talked about plans for turning this big house into a shelter for abused women." Cook slapped her hand over her mouth. "Oh, I shouldn't say that. Miss Leigh said to keep it a secret. Those poor ladies that will come to this shelter are hiding from the men who beat them up."

Sharon glowed with the information that Leigh was creating a shelter. She patted the distraught woman's arm. "It's okay. Sheriffs have to know where all the shelters are so we can take women there."

"Whatcha doing with Mrs. Pryor's furniture and stuff?" Harry looked like he was about to burst.

"Oh, I'm to have a sale and give the money to the BWEF. I'll put an ad in the newspapers." Cook waved her hand towards the formal living room. "This furniture was all here when we came. Only the antiques in the study are Miss Leigh's. She gave those to me. I'll take them with me when the construction starts."

"Sounds like she'll be gone some time." Harry's tight voice almost croaked.

"I don't know, sir. I just know she wants to be rid of this house where she wasn't happy."

Sharon led the way to the steps, hoping her partner would follow.

As they pulled into the drive at the Rey home, Harry had to maneuver around a carpet-cleaning van, a window washer's truck, and the house cleaner's car. He took out his identification and rang the doorbell. When it was not answered, he knocked on the door with his nightstick. "Probably can't hear the bell over the vacuums."

An overall-clad man wielding a squeegee answered. "May I help you, sir?"

"We're here to see Mora," said Sharon brightly.

"I'm sorry; Ms. Rey is not available."

"When do you expect her?" Harry's words were cordial but spoken through clenched teeth.

"I've been instructed to help prepare the home to be closed indefinitely."

Damn. Sharon bit her lip and shook her head. It *couldn't* be true. The women were running! Her heart thumped and sweat streamed between her breasts. She'd been wrong—big time!

"She's to let me know her plans later." The foreman wiped his hands on his overalls. "Is there anything *I* can help you with?"

"Just one more question," Harry said sourly. "When did Ms. Rey leave?"

"I'm not sure, sir. I wasn't here. I'm head of her maintenance company." Sharon could see the lie in his eyes. "Is there anything else you require, sir?"

Harry took out his notebook. "What car does she drive?"

"A Toyota Prius—when she doesn't use the chauffer service."

"You don't happen to know the license number?"

"No, sir, but you can find it on the car. It's in the garage."

Harry's face was now purple. Sharon was afraid he'd explode.

"How is Ms. Rey to contact you?"

Poor Harry was still trying to save his investigation. Sharon almost felt sorry for him.

"I don't know what you're asking, Officer."

"Will she be using her cell phone? Write you a letter? Send a telegram?" Harry took two steps toward the worker and stood inches from him.

The man moved back before answering. "She didn't specify, sir."

Harry turned and ran down the stairs to their car. Sharon trotted after him, her head hanging.

In the car, Harry picked up the microphone.

Sharon put a hand on his arm. "What are you doing?"

"I'm issuing an APB on these women. Agreed?" Harry's eyes were kind. He understood the turmoil in her head.

Sharon nodded. "But shouldn't we check the others first? Then we'll know exactly who we're looking for."

Harry racked the mic. "Okay. Who's next?" Harry's face turned an angry red again.

"Carol Ewald lives a few blocks away."

A big *For Sale* sign greeted the deputies at Carol's house.

"Ms. Ewald said she was going to Europe to live," the realtor told the deputies. "I've been instructed to sell her house furnished and deposit the money according to her instructions when she calls."

"When do you expect to hear from her?" Harry was making a concerted effort to be polite, but Sharon saw the twitch in his cheek and the red in his ears.

"She didn't say. Tell you the truth, I don't think she knew herself."

"Did she take a lot of luggage?" Sharon thought she should participate in the questioning—to show Harry she was being cooperative in spite of her earlier qualms.

"Just one medium suitcase and her cosmetic case. And her wheelchair, of course."

Sharon handed the assistant her card. "Would you please have her call me when she returns?"

Harry ran to the car. "Next is Wilderness Outfitters. We *should* find someone to talk to there." He looked at his watch. "It's eleven a.m. now, so they should be open for business."

Whitmore's Wilderness Outfitters was closed.

A sign on the door announced a temporary closure pending Mrs. Whitmore's return from her vacation. It apologized for any inconvenience.

"Horse cocky!" The look on Harry's face was not pretty. "I'm sure Craig is gone too."

At Azalea Construction, the secretary told them Erin had left that morning on her annual vacation—hiking in the wilderness. She didn't expect to hear from her for at least a week, maybe longer. She assured the deputies that the business was proceeding without the boss. They had jobs that would keep them busy for quite a while.

Harry looked as though he could cry when he climbed in the car. "Time to check *all* the travel agents; see where these women *really* went."

Harry was persistent; Sharon had to say that for him. And how was *she* feeling about all this? She needed to be honest with herself. Deep down she gloried in Harry's frustration. The women so far had outwitted his determination to formally accuse them.

At the mention of a travel agent, Sharon bit her lip. "We don't have to do that."

"What do you mean?"

She hated to squeal, but this was her job. "At the BWEF meeting I attended, I asked to join the Outreach Committee." She frowned. "They said invitation-only and no openings."

"You told me about that." He shook his head. "But what does that have to with researching travel agents?"

"They assigned me to the Community Liaison committee."

"Come on, Sharon! What the hell are you trying to say?"

"Alyson Zender of A to Z Travel is on that committee. She seemed to be a good friend of Mora Rey's."

Harry surveyed PCH as he pulled off his seat belt. "Don't start the car. A to Z's half a block away."

Chapter 146

"Yes, sir, ma'am. Welcome to A to Z Travel." The young man bounced up as Sharon and Harry entered. "Planning a getaway?"

Harry pointed to his badge. "No trip. We're here to find out where Mora Rey is 'vacationing.' We need to contact her."

"Be glad to help. I'm new here, so it may take a while. He motioned to chairs next to the second desk. Please have a seat." He continued to chatter as he pulled out a file drawer. "My boss, Alyson, would have been the one to schedule her. You two are my first customers—well, not really a customer, but you know what I mean."

Harry tapped his foot impatiently but didn't interrupt the eager newcomer.

The agent looked up. "Was that R-A-Y or R-E-Y?"

Sharon looked at Harry. "R-E," she replied softly.

"Thanks. Know when she left?"

Harry squirmed in his chair. "Yesterday or this morning." He cleared his throat. "We're kinda in a hurry."

The young man pulled out a file drawer. "Sure, man. Like I said, I'm new here." He closed one drawer and opened another. "Here it is! Ms. Mora Rey and her four friends are scheduled to fly out this afternoon on Delta through to Haiti, with a stop in Miami." He flipped through the pages. "The rest of the file is missing."

The deputies raced from the shop.

Rushing to the car, Sharon admonished herself again. She'd tripped up majorly. She'd let personal feelings, this time admiration, cloud her thinking—and, yes, stand in the way of her job. Not for the first time she wondered if she was right for detective work. She

459

dropped into the driver's seat and started the car. She said nothing as Harry clicked his seat belt.

After a big sigh, he finally spoke. "I'll call TSA at the International Terminal while you drive." He checked his gun. "Turn on the flashers."

Sharon was thankful he said nothing more. As she drove through rush-hour traffic, her mind flashed back to the events preceding her own life-changing flight—the night she'd left her abusive husband.

"You bitch!" Sharon heard as clearly as if her husband were there. *"This dinner tastes like garbage."* Sharon's lips quivered as she remembered the sound of the plate breaking against the kitchen wall. She flexed the still-misshapen fingers Sean had broken that night. She remembered the paralyzing fear: Fear of making it on her own if she left him; fear of more beatings if she stayed; fear for the kids; and the mind-exploding fear of dying.

These women had taken care of an ugly problem in a way that saved society from doing it. *The way I would've done it,* she realized, *if I'd had the gumption to—and the means.* Sharon bit her lip. Unfortunately, she had to do her job.

Harry interrupted her thoughts. "Sure enough, Delta confirms a group of five women booked to Miami and through to Haiti—and then on to Brazil. One way."

Sharon parked at the curb, and the two dashed into the International Terminal. The traffic on the 405 freeway had seriously delayed them. They waited while the checkpoint guard called her supervisor over to check their weapons.

"We're detaining five women on flight 908 to Miami. What gate?"

"Gate 35. The flight leaves at 1:28." It was now one o'clock. "I'll call ahead for you."

"Thanks, we can't wait." Sharon ran with Harry down the concourse. If they stopped to radio for backup, they'd miss the plane. At Gate 29, Sharon and Harry were mobbed by a group of French-speaking tourists. When they reached Gate 35, the hostess was making the final boarding announcement. Harry flashed his badge at the nearest TSA guard. "We're looking for five fugitives and have every reason to believe they're on this flight."

"I'll call for a spot-check delay." She motioned to the gate agent and the two walked to the side to confer, out of earshot of the last of the boarding passengers.

As the agent disappeared down the gangway, Sharon looked around to make sure the five women were not in the waiting area.

"You may board," the returning agent told them, "but make it brief. It's a full flight, and we have an on-time record to maintain."

Harry nodded to Sharon to precede him. Dread so strong it felt like a blow struck her. How could she live with herself if they arrested the women they sought? Who would run the BWEF with them in jail?

The two deputies walked slowly down the center aisle. Sharon looked to the right, Harry to the left. In the middle of the plane, they stopped and looked at each other. In row twenty-two were five empty seats. The pair said nothing as they continued to the rear of the tourist cabin. Sharon checked the restrooms and they returned to the front door.

"Thank you for your patience," said Harry to the flight attendant as they exited.

Her emotions swinging from disappointment to elation at the women's escape, Sharon made her way to the exit, dancing in step to Harry's angry march.

Chapter 147

Mora, Carol, Taylor, Erin, and Leigh rushed down the International Terminal concourse toward their departure gate. Recognizing the Wagner opera's ringtone of Mora's emergency cell phone, they all froze. What now?

Mora struggled to understand all that the travel agent was telling her. "Thanks for the warning." She turned to the others. "The cops know our itinerary." She snapped the phone closed. "Damn!"

Taylor looked over her shoulder. "Th-Th-They could be here now!"

Mora nodded towards a women's restroom. "Operation Courage just became Operation *Calamity*. You know what to do." Each of the women disappeared into a stall, hauling her carry-on bag with her.

Mora emerged wearing a scarf around her head and a long heavy coat buttoned to her chin. She plodded to the restroom entrance and waited just outside for the others to pass her.

Leigh changed her high heels for ballet slippers and unfolded a cane. After patting Mora on the back, she limped slowly to the ground transportation exit.

Taylor removed her contact lenses and propped horn-rimmed glasses on her nose. She clutched a book on guided tours in Los Angeles as she excused herself for bumping into Mora and headed toward the escalator marked baggage claim.

Carol threw a maroon blanket over her legs and pulled on a gray wig with a red hat and orange hoop earrings attached. She rolled out of the stall, nodded at Mora, and waited for Erin who had changed into a nurse's uniform. They took the elevator to the ground floor.

With her friends accounted for, Mora walked briskly to the taxi stand.

Chapter 148

MORA HEAVED A SIGH when she spotted Taylor arriving at Torrance Airport. The five women were to reconvene at this rendezvous point for the new mission. Soon they'd be safely in the air.

When the two women greeted Clayton Anderson, the aging owner of Anderson Aviation, Mora felt amazingly calm. These steps were irreversible, but they were the right ones—for all concerned. "What about our three passengers?"

"They're on board. My new helper, Adam, helped them with the wheelchair. Then he stowed your luggage in the hold—with the other boxes you had delivered." He motioned to the plane. "You ladies must be going on a mercy mission with all those medical supplies we loaded."

Mora backed to the stairs, easing away from the talkative man.

"We put the food in the galley," the owner continued. He turned to Taylor. "As soon as you complete your walk-around and clear with the tower, you can take off."

"How much fuel do we have on board?" Taylor asked, consulting her pilot's manual on the aircraft.

"Enough to get you to Vancouver, with an hour's safety margin. You can refuel in Oregon, if you like."

"Would it be too much t-t-trouble to top it off?" Taylor asked. "We're traveling l-light and may be able to go further east into Canada without st-st-stopping."

"Not at all. The truck's close by on the north side of the plane. I'll have Adam bring it over."

A few minutes later, the old man called to them up the steps. "Sorry, ma'am, for the delay. Adam must have taken a break. I'll just get the gas truck around here. Won't be long."

463

"Th-Thanks. Weather report's g-good, but you never know." Taylor's seeming calm subdued Mora's concerns. She didn't *appear* to be second-guessing their trip in any way.

Taylor scurried up the stairs and turned left into the cockpit, where she slid into the pilot's seat. Mora pulled up the stairs and followed Taylor, taking the copilot's chair. She waved a thumbs up to Leigh and Erin, who had helped Carol into a soft bench near the side door and stowed her wheelchair beside her. When they were done, they wasted no time belting themselves in across the aisle.

Her passengers secured, Mora turned back to the cockpit and followed the internal checklist as Taylor completed the sequence. The plane was not pressurized, so they'd be flying at a lower altitude.

As Taylor guided the plane into the air, her passengers and copilot cheered and clapped. Mora took a long slow breath and let it out. She could breathe normally now. Stress rolled off her like water bubbling over a waterfall.

As they passed over the Pacific Ocean and turned north, Mora watched the shoreline recede below. She'd enjoyed her life down there, but moving on wasn't such a bad idea. Change brought its own joys.

Chapter 149

WHEN THE PLANE had leveled off at cruising altitude, Mora unbuckled her seat belt and went to the galley to make the coffee and serve the sandwiches she'd ordered. The others appeared relaxed. They enjoyed the blue and green water, pointing out freighters and sailboats. They'd all been so tense for the last three days. Pride in her friends filled her. They made a good team.

After serving the sandwiches, Mora went back to sit with Taylor.

"Help!" Erin's scream came from the back of the plane, near the restroom. Mora turned and saw her wrestling with a bearded man.

Mora held up her hand to motion Taylor to stay in the cockpit. "Keep us flying. I'll handle it."

Leigh jumped up to help her struggling friend. "Erin, be careful. He's got a knife!"

The intruder prodded Erin to a spot near the door. "Open it!" he sneered. "I finally remembered you, camper lady: Miss *Eve*. You're going outside for a little freefall. Longer drop than you sent me on." His laugh echoed in the still cabin. "I don't think you'll survive with just amnesia and a crushed face, though."

"Stay back, Mora," Erin said through clenched lips. "It's that shithead, Marshall." The knife point scraped her chin but drew no blood. Mora sidled to the rear of the plane. Maybe she could get him from behind.

Erin twisted in Marshall's hold and dodged under his arm. He grabbed her jacket and pulled her to him, nailing her with a strong arm to his chest.

"Let's see if you can do something right after all, Eve—or is it Erin? Just couldn't figure out how to get me over the falls at the right spot to kill me," Marshall taunted. He pushed Erin in front of him toward the door.

Taylor entered from the cockpit and stared at the intruder. "Who are y-y-you? You s-sound like my husband, b-but your face is different." She shook her head. "But you *can't* be Marshall. Marshall's dead."

Marshall turned accusingly to his wife, releasing his hold on Erin. "I *thought* you looked familiar, but I couldn't place you. Now, how pathetic is that?"

Her eyes wide with terror, Taylor sank her teeth into her bottom lip.

"So you tried to take me out, did you?" He laughed softly. "God dammit! I always *thought* that pacifist, antiviolence-champion act you put on was fake."

Taylor advanced toward him, her fists clenched. "You beat me, you abused me...and then you stole the core of my life, my business. You *destroyed* me when you did that."

Marshall licked the sweat from his lips. "Ahhhh...so *that's* the horrible thing I did that I didn't want to remember." He swallowed, apparently lost in thought. Finally, he looked back up at Taylor. "I honestly *can't* remember what I did to you, but I suppose if I did what you say, I *am* sorry for it." He looked around at the women in the cabin, who all remained frozen.

As Marshall continued to compose himself, Mora sidled back toward the cockpit and retrieved the gun she'd seen there while going through the final preflight check.

She returned to the galley, pointing the gun straight at Marshall. "Get the duct tape." She motioned to Erin. "Let's tape him to the seat while we discuss our next steps." Marshall's head shot up, his eyes smoldering. Mora felt his anger, pain, and fear. "Your life is saved; but we want to insure that we're safe, too. When we're all calm, we can discuss your future."

Carol had sat pole-straight and still throughout the brief interplay. Now, she let out her breath with a loud whoosh.

So this is what being involved in a face-to-face killing feels like, thought Mora. *The Mount Everest of highs and the Grand Canyon of lows.* She'd thought she would push Marshall out of the plane once Erin was safe. But she realized she couldn't do it. Even if he *hadn't* apologized to Taylor.

Mora breathed deeply. Knowing what she knew now about herself, she doubted she could have carried on with the Outreach Committee. Taylor was right: killing was wrong, no matter how justified.

Marshall firmly affixed to his seat, Mora rejoined Taylor in the cockpit. She corrected the heading and turned to Taylor.

Taylor dissolved into sobs on Mora's shoulder. "I *knew* he was violent. Knew I needed to escape him. But I could only bring myself to kill him after he stole my store from me. *Then* I joined the Outreach Committee. It seemed so easy to have someone else take care of him so I wouldn't have to. It wasn't until Erin came back from Arizona that I realized what I'd done."

The plane hit some turbulence and Mora disengaged the autopilot and took control.

When the plane had stabilized, Mora returned to the passenger cabin. Erin sat on the floor, hugging herself. Mora reached for her hand and pulled her up onto the couch next to Carol.

"Anything you want to say?"

"I worried that I liked killing too much. But I'm actually *relieved* I didn't succeed with Marshall." She looked at Leigh. "I'll still have Quentin on my conscience for the rest of my time here on earth."

And I'll have Reginald on mine, thought Mora. *And ALL of them.* Mora's eyes locked with Carol's, and she saw relief there too—relief that they could finally be honest with themselves.

Chapter 150

SHARON WAVED AT CLAYTON ANDERSON as she and Harry got out of their car at the hangar. "Thanks for calling," she said. "Understand you have a lead for us." *At last!* Real progress.

Anderson pointed to the million-dollar Cessna Citation sitting on the asphalt tarmac. "Don't care about no lead. I got my plane back."

"Are the women here?" Sharon looked around the hangar. "Where are they? We need to talk to them."

"Didn't say *that*. My old helper, Adam Marsh, flew it in." Anderson rubbed his finger and thumb together. "Paid enough cash to cover the rent for the whole time they had the plane—and more."

"Where'd he fly in from?" asked Harry.

"Said he left Mora Rey and the other ladies at the airport in Rio. He didn't know where they were going from there." Clayton paused. "Adam said Mora told him they weren't planning on coming back to the States—ever."

Sharon and Harry exchanged a look. Sharon inhaled deeply and then let it out. "We can find out more when we talk to him," she said.

"That would be hard to do. He came in here, picked up his belongings, and dashed for a cab. Said he was going on a round-the-world tour."

"No kidding?" said Sharon.

"No kidding," said Anderson. "Mora Rey set it up for him."

"It's not fair," Sharon said as she and Harry walked to their black-and-white.

Harry nodded. "I know. I can't believe it either. After *everything*, those gals get off scot-free! But we both know, justice isn't always fair."

"That's not what I mean." Sharon stopped walking. "This means that the Outreach Committee is gone forever—disbanded."

Harry looked at her quizzically. "And that's bad because…?"

"Because I have skills they could have used."

Author's Notes

THE OUTREACH COMMITTEE was written to bring attention to the plague of spousal abuse in the world. One in three women, regardless of economic level, will be abused in her lifetime.

One of the constants in spousal abuse is its tendency to surprise and escalate. The popular man a woman marries doesn't turn murderer overnight. It takes time for him to build up to the furor that eventually causes him to batter, and even kill, his wife or partner. Or perhaps injure her so badly, she is certain to be dependent on him for the rest of her life. Because of this tendency to build, it is hard to spot the abuser before you commit to him.

I compare an abuser to a river. Initially we admire its easy flow, and enjoy swimming in the chilly water and fishing from its banks. Then, when we boat on it, we discover the river's rough flow over treacherous rocks, forming dangerous rapids. Still, we steer around the rapids and continue our journey.

Our river constantly pressures the dam that forms the swimming hole. We see a few drops come through on the other side. Soon the water forms a bigger hole. It may take some time, but the water's demand for control destroys the leaking dam and buries the homes below it.

How do we avoid the treacherous rivers in our lives?

- ∞ We go out cautiously with the man who demands we spend all our time with him.

- ∞ We say goodbye to the man who commands us to forsake our family and other friends for him.

∞ We think hard before dating a man who controls every conversation.

∞ We look closely at a man who insists that his plans for the evening are the only ones worth following.

∞ We listen to a man's words carefully, when, after sulking the entire evening at a family event, he ridicules our family members for months afterward.

∞ We think hard about the personality of the man who is always seeking adoration from the people around him, ignoring us in a crowd while he does so.

∞ We dump the man who makes a date with us and then goes, instead, to play basketball with his buddies, blaming us when we express our anger over it.

It's not easy, avoiding a man who is initially charming and appears to single you out from the crowd. But many other men don't display the tendencies outlined above. They want to be your partner, not control your life. Look for one of them.

Others have compared an abusive relationship to a crack in the windshield that grows in length over time. How would you describe it?

If you recognized an abuser in time and swam to the bank of the river to break free from him, what caused you to do so? What made your attempt a success?

My readers and I would like to know. Please email me at clw@clwoodhams.com

For more thoughts and ideas about domestic abuse, visit my blog at womenbreakfreefromabuse.wordpress.com.

23877090R00267

Made in the USA
Middletown, DE
06 September 2015